THE BOOK OF NIGHT WITH MOON

◆

THE
BOOK
OF
NIGHT
WITH
MOON

Diane Duane

ASPECT®

WARNER BOOKS

A Time Warner Company

Aspect® name and logo are registered trademarks of Warner Books, Inc.

Warner Books, Inc., 1271 Avenue of the Americas, New York, NY 10020

Visit our Web site at
http://warnerbooks.com

 A Time Warner Company

Printed in the United States of America
First Printing: December 1997
10 9 8 7 6 5 4 3 2 1

LIBRARY OF CONGRESS CATALOGING-IN-PUBLICATION DATA
Duane, Diane.
The book of night with moon / Diane Duane.
p.   cm.
ISBN: 0-446-67302-1
1. Cats—Fiction. I. Title.
PS3554.U233B6   1997   97-14214
813'.54—dc21   CIP

Book design and text composition by Kathryn Parise
Cover design by Don Puckey
Cover illustration by Robert Goldstrom

For Keith De Candido

A Note
on Feline
Linguistics

Ailurin is not a spoken language, or not *simply* spoken. Like all the human languages, it has a physical component, the cat version of "body language," and a surprising amount of information is passed through the physical component before a need for vocalized words arises.

Even people who haven't studied cats closely will recognize certain "words" in Ailurin: the rub against a friendly leg, the arched back and fluffed fur of a frightened cat, the crouch and stare of the hunter. All of these have strictly physical antecedents and uses, but they are also used by cats for straightforward communication of mood or intent. Many subtler signs can be seen by even a human student: the sideways flirt of the tail that says "I don't care" or "I wonder if I can get away with this . . ." the elaborate yawn in another cat's face, the stiff-legged, arch-backed bounce, which is the cat equivalent of making a face and jumping out at someone, shouting "Boo!" But where gestures run out, words are used—more involved than the growl of threat or purr of contentment, which are all most humans hear of intercat communication.

"Meowing" is not counted here, since cats rarely seem to meow at each other. That type of vocalization is usually a "pidgin" language used for getting humans' attention: the cat equivalent of "Just talk to them clearly and loudly and they'll get what you mean sooner or later." Between each other, cats subvocalize using the same mechanism that operates what some authorities call "the purr box," a physiological mechanism that is not well understood but seems to have something to do with the combined vibration of air in the feline larynx and blood in the veins and arteries of the throat. To someone with a powerful microphone, a cat speaking Ailurin seems to be making very soft meowing and purring sounds ranging up and down several octaves, all at a volume normally inaudible to humans.

This vocalized part of Ailurin is a "pitched" language, like Mandarin Chinese, more sung than spoken. It is mostly vowel-based—no surprise in a species that cannot pronounce most human-style consonants. Very few noncats have ever mastered it: not only does any human trying to speak it sound to a cat as if he were shouting every word, but the delicate intonations are filled with traps for the unwary or unpracticed. Auo *hwaai hhioehhu uaeiiiaou,* for example, may look straightforward: "I would like a drink of milk" is the Cat-Human Phrasebook definition. But the people writing the phrasebook for the human ear are laboring under a terrible handicap, trying to transliterate from a thirty-seven-vowel system to an alphabet with only five. A human misplacing or mispronouncing only one of the vowels in this phrase will find cats smiling gently at him and asking him why he wants to feed the litter-box to the taxicab? . . . this being only one of numerous nonsenses that can be made of the above example.

So communication from our side of things tends to fall back on body language (stroking, or throwing things, both of which cats understand perfectly well) and a certain amount of monologue—which human-partnered cats, with some resignation, accept as part of the deal. For their communications with most human beings, the cats, like so many of us, tend to fall back on shouting. For this book's purposes, though, all cat-to-human speech, whether physical or vocal, is rendered as normal dialogue: that's the way it seems to the cats, after all.*

One other note: two human-language terms, "queen" and "tom," are routinely used to translate the Ailurin words *sh'heih* and *sth'heih.* "Female" and "male" don't properly translate these words, being much too sexually neutral—which cats, in their dealings with one another, emphatically are not. The Ailurin word *ffeih* is used for both neutered males and spayed females.　　　　　—DD

---

* Cat thoughts and silent communications are rendered in italics.

I am the Cat who took up His stance
by the Persea Tree, on the night we
destroyed the enemies of God. . . .

Pert em hru, c. 2800 B.C., tr. Budge

Bite: bite hard, and find the tenth life.

The Gaze of Rhoua's Eye
(feline recension of
The Book of Night with Moon): lxiii, 18

One

◆

They never turn the lights off in Grand Central; and they may lock the doors between 1 and 5:30 A.M., but the place never quite becomes still. If you stand outside those brass-and-glass doors on Forty-second Street and peer in, down the ramp leading into the Grand Concourse, you can see the station's quiet nightlife—a couple of transit police officers strolling past, easygoing but alert; someone from the night cleaning crew heading toward the information island in the center of the floor with a bucket and a lot of polishing cloths for all that century-old brass. Faintly, the sound of rumblings under the ground will come to you—the Metro-North trains being moved through the upper- and lower-level loops, repositioned for their starts in the morning, or tucked over by the far-side tracks to be checked by the night maintenance crews. On the hour, the massive deep gong of the giant Accurist clock facing Forty-second strikes, and the echoes chase themselves around under the great blue sky-vault and slowly fade.

By five o'clock the previous day's dust will have been laid, the locks checked, the glass on the stores in the Graybar and Hyatt passageways all cleaned: everything done, until it's time to open again. The transit policemen, still in a pair because after all this is New York and you just can't tell, will stroll past, heading up the stairs on the Vanderbilt Avenue side to sit down in the ticketed passenger waiting

1

area and have their lunch break before the day officially starts. Anyone looking in through the still-locked Forty-second Street doors will see nothing but stillness, the shine of slick stone and bright brass.

But there are those for whom locked doors are no barrier. Were you one of them, this morning, you would slip sideways and through, padding gently down the incline toward the terrazzo flooring of the concourse. The place would smell green, the peculiar too-strong wintergreen smell of a commercial sweeping compound. Your nose would wrinkle as you passed a spot on the left, against the cream-colored wall, where blood was spilled yesterday—a disagreement, a knife and a gun pulled, everything finished in a matter of seconds: one life wounded, one life fled, the bodies taken away. But the disinfectants and the sweeping compound can't hide the truth from you and the stone.

You would walk on, pause in the center of the room, and look upward, as many times before, at the starry, painted vault of the heavens—its dusk-blue rather faded, and half the bulbs in the Zodiac's constellations burnt out. The Zodiac is backward. They'll be renovating the ceiling this spring, but you doubt they'll fix *that* problem. It doesn't matter, anyway: after all, "backward" depends on which direction you're looking from. . . .

You would walk on again then, guided by senses other than the purely physical ones, and stroll silently over to the right of the motionless up-escalators, toward the gate to Track 25. Once through its archway, everything changes. The ambiance of the terminal—light, air, openness—abruptly shifts: the ceiling lowers, the darkness closes in. Lighting comes in the form of long lines of fluorescent fixtures, only one out of every three of them lit, this time of day. They shine down in bright dashed lines on the seven platforms to your right, the nine to your left, and straight ahead, on the gray concrete of the platform that serves Tracks 25 and 26. Behind you, a pool of warm light lies under the windows of the glass-walled room that is the Trainmaster's Office. Little light, though, makes it past the platform's edge to the tracks themselves. They are long trenches of shadow between pale gray plateaus of concrete that stretch, tapering, into the middle distance, vanishing into more darkness. The rails themselves gleam faintly only close to where you stand: they too reach off into the dark, converging, and swiftly disappear. Red and green track guidelights shine dully there. A few shine brighter: the track crew members are down there, walking the rails to check for obstructions and wiping the lights off as they come.

You walk quietly down the center platform, letting your eyes get used to the reduced light, until you come to where the platform ends, almost a quarter-mile from the arches of the gates.

You jump down from the tapered end of the platform, into shadow, and walk out of reach of the last fluorescent lights. The red and green lights marking the track switches are your only illumination now, and all you need. Seventy-five feet ahead of you, Tracks 25 and 26 converge. Just off to your right is the walkway to a low concrete building, Tower A, the master signaling center for the terminal. You are careful not to look directly at it: the bright lights inside it, the blinking of switch indicators and computer telltales, would ruin your night-sight. You pad softly on past, under its windows, past the little phone-exchange box at the tower's end, on into the darkness. The still, close air smells of iron, rust, garbage, mildew, cinders, electricity—and something else.

Here you pause, warned by the senses that drew you here, and you wait. Trembling on your skin, and against your eyes, is a feeling like the tremor of air in the subway when, well down the tunnel, a train is coming. But what's coming isn't a train. Everything around is silent, even the subway tunnel three levels below you. Two levels above you now is the block between Forty-ninth and Fiftieth Streets: from there, no sound comes, either. Watching, you wait.

No eyes but yours, acclimated and looking in the right place, would see what slowly becomes visible. The air itself, somehow more dark than the air in front of it, is bending, showing contour, like a plate-glass window bowing outward in a hurricane wind—or inward, toward you. Yet the contour that you half-see, half-sense, is wrong. It bulges like a blown bubble—but a bubble blown *backward,* drawn in rather than pushed out. You half-expect to hear breath sucked inward to match what you almost-see.

The bubble gets bigger and bigger, spanning the tracks. The darkness in the air streaks, pulled past its tolerances. Not-light shows through the thin places; wincing, you glance away. The faintest possible shrilling sound fills your twitching ears, the sound of spacetime yielding to intolerable pressure, under protest: it scales up and up, piercing you like pins—

—and stops, as the bubble breaks, letting through whatever has been leaning on it from the other side. You look at it, blinking. Silence again: darkness. *A false alarm—*

Until, as you shake your head again at the shrilling, you realize that you shouldn't still be hearing it. And out of the blackness in front of you, pattering, rustling, they come. First, just a few. Then ten of them, a hundred of them, more. Hurrying, scuttering, humpily running, their little wicked eyes gleaming dull red in the light from far behind you, they flow at you like darkness come alive, darkness with teeth, darkness shrilling with hunger: the rats.

There is more than hunger in those voices, though, more than just malice in those eyes. Their screams have terror in them. They will destroy anything that gets between them and their flight from what comes behind them, driving them; they'll strip the flesh from your bones and never even stop to enjoy it. Backing away, hissing, you see the huge dark shape that comes behind them—walking two-legged, claws like knives lashing out in amusement at the shrieking rats, the long lashing tail balancing out behind: high above, the blunt and massive head, jaws working compulsively, huge razory fangs gleaming even in this dim light: and gazing down at you through the darkness, the eyes—the small, gemlike, cruelly smiling eyes, with your death in them: *everything's* death.

Seeing this, you do the only thing you can. You *run*.

But it's not enough. . . .

She was sound asleep when the voice breathed in her ear. There was nothing unusual about that: They always took the method of least resistance.

Oh, fwau, *why right this minute?*

Rhiow refused to hurry about opening her eyes, but rolled over and stretched first, a good long stretch, and yawned hard. Opening her eyes at last, she saw the main room was still dark: her *ehhif* hadn't come out to open the window-coverings yet. No surprise there, for the noisemaker by the bed hadn't gone off yet, either. Rhiow rolled over and stretched one more time, for the call hadn't been desperately urgent, though urgent enough. *Please don't let it be the north-side gate again. Not after all the hours we spent on the miserable thing yesterday. Au, it's going to take forever to get things going this morning. . . .*

She stood up, stretched fore and aft, then sat down on the patterned carpet in the middle of the room and started washing, making a face as she began; her fur still tasted a little like the room smelled, of cheese and mouth-smoke and other people from the eating party last night. Rhiow's mouth watered a little at the memory of the cheese, to which she was most partial. She had managed to wheedle a fair amount of it out of the guests. Normally this would have left her with a somewhat abated appetite in the morning, but getting a call always sharpened her stomach, and more so if she was asleep when the call came: it was as if the urgency transmitted straight to her gut and there turned into hunger.

Probably some kind of sublimation, Rhiow thought, scrubbing her ears. *And a* vhai'*d nuisance, in any case.* She leaned back, bracing herself on one paw, and started washing the inside right rear leg.

Well, at least the timing isn't too abysmal. The others will be up shortly, or else they won't have gone to bed at all: just fine either way.

Rhiow finished up, putting her tail in order, and then stood and trotted through the landscape of disordered furniture, noting drinking-vessels left under chairs, a couple of them knocked over and spilled, and she paused to pick up half a dropped cracker with some of that pink fish stuff on it. *Salmon paté,* she thought as she munched. *Not bad, even a night old.* She gulped the last bit down, licked a couple of errant specks of it off her whiskers, and looked around. *I wonder if they left the container out on the counter, like those others?*

But there wasn't time for that: she was on call. The bedroom door was shut. Rhiow started to rear up and scratch on it, then sat back down, having second thoughts: if she wanted both breakfast and an early start, it was smarter not to annoy them. She looked thoughtfully at the doorknob, squinting slightly.

It took only a second or so to clearly perceive the mechanism: friction-dependent, as she knew from previous experience, but not engaged. The door was merely pushed shut and was sticking a little tighter at the top than the bottom, that being all that held it in place.

Rhiow gazed at that spot for a moment, closed her eyes a bit further, and presently came to see the two patches of dim sparkle that represented the material forces at work in the two adjoining surfaces of the stuck spot. Under her breath she said the word that temporarily reduced the coefficient of friction in that spot, then stood on her hind legs and leaned against the door.

It fell open. Rhiow trotted in, feeling the normal forces reassert themselves behind her. One jump took her onto the bed, which sloshed up and down as she padded up the length of it, to a spot beside Iaehh's head. He was facedown in the pillow, a position she had come to recognize over time as meaning he didn't want to get up any time soon. Rhiow blinked, sympathetic if nothing else, and walked over his back to get to Hhuha.

She was on her back, snoring gently. Rhiow put her head down by Hhuha's ear and purred.

No response.

It would have been nice to do this the easy way, Rhiow thought reluctantly, *but . . .* She bumped Hhu's head with her own, purring harder.

"Rrrrgh," said Hhuha, and rolled over, and squinted her eyes tighter shut, and after a moment looked at Rhiow out of them with some disbelief.

She sat up groggily in the bed and looked at the door. "Now how the heck did you get in here? I know he shut that last night."

"Yes, I know, *I* opened it, never mind," Rhiow said, "come on, will you? I have to get an early start. Business, unfortunately." She rubbed against Hhuha's side and purred some more.

"Wow, you're noisy this morning, aren't you? What on earth do you want? Not breakfast already, you pig! You had two whole slices of pizza just a few hours ago."

Don't remind me, Rhiow thought, for her stomach was growling so hard, she was amazed Hhuha couldn't hear it. "Look, it would really help if you would just get *up* and give me my morning feed so I can get on with things—"

"Mike? Mike, get up. I think the kitty wants her breakfast."

"Nnnggghhhh," said Iaehh, and didn't move.

"Oh, will you come *on* already?" Rhiow said, desperately hoping Hhuha didn't notice that her purr was becoming a little forced. "And as for pigs, who ate half a salami last night? And never gave *me* any? Even when I asked. Now *please* get up before it gets so late that I have to leave!"

"Gosh, you really must be hungry. I guess cats digest faster than people or something," Hhuha said, her voice going soft, and she reached out to scratch Rhiow's eyebrows. The tone of voice was one Rhiow had heard before: she got a sense that her *ehhif* liked being "talked to," even when they couldn't hear half of what was being said, and, even if they could, would have no idea what the words meant anyway. This tendency made them either great idiots or very fond of her indeed, and either conjecture only made Rhiow twitchier under the present circumstances. She stomped her forefeet alternately on the coverlet, as much from impatience as from pleasure at having her head scratched.

"Come on, then," said Hhuha. She got out of bed, threw a housepelt around her, and headed toward the kitchen. Rhiow went after her, not in a hurry: this was no time to trip Hhuha halfway there and have to deal with an *ehhif* temper tantrum that might take half an hour to resolve. By the time Rhiow got to the kitchen, Hhuha was cranking a can open.

"Mmm," Hhuha said, "nice tuna. You'll like this."

"I *hate* the tuna," Rhiow said, sitting down and curling her tail around her forefeet. "It's not made from any part of the fish that *you'd* ever eat. You should read more of the label than just the part about the dolphins."

"Yum, yum," Hhuha said, putting the plate down on the floor. "Here you go, puss. Lovely tuna."

Rhiow looked at the gelid stuff with resignation. *Oh, well,* she thought, *it's food, and I need* something *before I go out. And anyway—manners* . . . She reared up and gave Hhuha a good rub around the shins before starting to eat.

"You're a good kitty," Hhuha said, and turned, yawning, to take something out of the refrigerator.

Rhiow purred with amusement and satisfaction as she ate. The compliment was true enough, but also true was that, while she had been rearing up to rub against Hhuha's leg, she had seen where the container of salmon paté had been pushed back behind some drinking containers on the counter beside the *ffrihh*.

"God, I'm glad it's Sunday," Hhuha said, and shut the refrigerator again, heading for the bedroom. "I couldn't bear the thought of work after last night."

Rhiow sighed as she finished one last bite and turned away from the dish, reluctant: eating too much now would make her want a nap, and she had no time for that. "Must be nice to have weekends off," Rhiow muttered, sitting down to wash. "I wish *I* did."

The rest of her personal hygiene took only a few minutes more: her *ehhif* had put a *hiouh*-box out on their small terrace for her, where it was under cover from rain. While using it, Rhiow went off into unfocused mode briefly and could hear them talking as Hhuha opened the window-coverings and the window.

"Mmngnggh . . ." Iaehh's voice. "Did she eat?"

"Uh huh." A pause. "She's out now. . . . I don't know . . . I'm still not sure it's a great idea to have her box out there."

"Oh, come on, Sue. Better there than in the bathroom. *You're* the one who was always muttering about walking in the kitty litter in the morning. Anyway, she's not going to fall or anything."

"I don't mean that. It's encouraging her to get down on that lower roof that worries me."

"Why? It's not like she can get to anywhere else from there. She can roam around and get some fresh air . . . and she's been doing it for months now without any trouble. She would have gone missing a long time back if she could have."

"Well, I still worry."

"*Su*sannnnn . . . She's not stupid. It's not like she's going to try to go twenty stories straight down."

Rhiow put her whiskers forward in a slight smile as she finished tidying the box, then got out and shook her feet fastidiously. Bits of litter scattered in various directions, skittering off the terrace. *They can make water run uphill and fly off to the Moon when they like,* she thought, resigned, *but they can't make* hiouh-*litter that won't stick to your paws. A serious misplacement of priorities . . .*

Rhiow went to the edge of the railed terrace, looked down. Her *ehhif's* apartment was near the corner of the building. Its wall fell sheer to the next terrace, thirty feet down, but she had no interest in that. Off to the left was an easy jump, about three feet, to the concrete parapet of a lower roof of a building diagonally behind theirs, but Rhiow wasn't going that way either. Her intended path lay sideways, along the brick wall itself. Some fanciful builder had built into it a pattern of slightly protruding bricks, a stairstep pattern repeating above and below. The part of it Rhiow used led rightward down the wall to the building's other near corner, about fifty feet away; and six feet below that, in the direction of the street, was the raised parapet of yet another roof, the top of the next building along.

Rhiow slipped through the railings, stepped carefully up onto the first brick, and made her way downward along the wall, foot before foot, no hurry. This segment of her road, the first used each day setting out and the last to manage before getting home, was also the trickiest: no more than two inches' width of brick to put her feet on as she went, nothing to catch her should she fall. Once she almost had, and afterward had spent nearly half an hour washing and regaining her composure, horrified at what might have happened, or worse, who might have seen her. *Wasted time,* she thought now, amused at her younger self. *But we all learn. . . .*

At the corner of the building Rhiow paused, looked around. Soft city-noise drifted up to her: the hoot of horns over on Third, someone's car alarm wailing disconsolately to itself four or five blocks north, the rattle of trays being unloaded at the bakery eastward and around the corner. All around her, the sheer walls of other apartment and office buildings turned blind walls and windows to the sight of a small black cat perched on a two-inch-wide brick, ninety feet above the sidewalk of Seventieth Street. No one saw her. But that was life in iAh'hah, after all: no one looked up or paid attention to any but their own affairs.

Except for a small group of public servants, of whom she was one. But Rhiow spent no more time thinking about that than was necessary, especially not here, where she stuck out like an eye on a week-old fish head. Her business was not to be noticed, and by now, she was good at it.

She measured the jump down to the parapet. No matter that she had done it a thousand times before: it was the thousandth jump and one, misjudged, that would cheat you out of a spare life you had been saving for later. Rhiow crouched, tensed, jumped; then came down on the cracked foot-wide concrete top of the parapet, exactly where she liked to. She made the smaller jump down onto the surface of the roof, looked around again, her tail twitching.

No one there. Rhiow stepped across the coarse cracked gravel as quickly as she could: she disliked the stuff, which hurt her feet. She passed wire vent grilles and fan housings making a low moaning roar, blasting hot air up and out of the air-conditioning systems below; summer was coming on, and the unseasonably hot weather this last week had turned the city-roar abruptly louder. The smells had changed, too, as a result. The air up here reeked of the disinfectant that the biggest *ehhif*-houses put in their ventilating systems these days and also stank of lubricating oil, dust settled since last winter, sucked-out food scents, mouth-smoke, garbage stored in the cellars until pickup day . . .

After that, the fumes and steams coming up from the city street seemed fresh by comparison. Rhiow jumped up on the streetside parapet, looking down. Seventieth reached east to the river, west to where her view was blocked past Third by scaffolding for a new building and digging in the street itself, something to do with the utility tunnels. The street was an asphalt-stitched pattern of paved and repaved blacktop, pierced by the occasional gently steaming tunnel-cover, lined with the inevitable two long lines of parked cars, punctuated by the *ehhif* walking calmly here and there. Some of them had *houiff* on the leash: Rhiow's nose wrinkled, for even up here she could smell what the *houiff* left in the street, no matter how their *ehhif* cleaned up after them.

No matter, she thought. *It's just the way the city is. And better get on with it, if you want it to stay that way.*

Rhiow sat down, curled her tail around her forefeet, and composed herself. Amusing, to be making the world safe for *houiff* to foul the sidewalks in, but that was part of what she did.

Her eyes drooped shut, almost closed, so that she could more clearly see, and be seen by, the less physical side of things. *I will meet the cruel and the cowardly today,* she thought, *liars and the envious, the uncaring and unknowing: they will be all around. But their numbers and their carelessness do not mean I have to be like them. For my own part, I know my job; my commission comes from Those Who Are. My paw raised is Their paw on the neck of the Serpent, now and always. . . .*

There was more to the formal version of the meditation, but Rhiow was far enough along in her work now, after these six years, to (as one of her *ehhif* associates put it) depart from the Catechism a little. The idea was to put yourself in order for the day's work, reminding yourself of the priorities—not your own species-bound concerns, but the welfare of all life on the planet: not your personal grudges and doubts, but the fears, however idiotic they seemed, of all the others you met. There was always the danger that the words would become routine, just something you rattled off at the start of the workday and then forgot in the field. Rhiow did her best to be conscientious about the meditation and her other setup work, giving it more than just speech-service . . . but at the same time, the urge to get going and do the work itself drove her hard. She presumed They understood.

Rhiow got up again, stretched, and trotted off down the roof's parapet to its back corner, which looked inward toward the center of the block between Seventieth and Sixty-ninth. She had egress routes all around the top of the building, but this was the least exposed; this time of day, when even an *ehhif* could see clearly, there was no point in being careless.

At the back corner Rhiow paused, glanced downward into the dusty warm darkness of the alley between the two buildings. Nothing was there but a rat, stirring far down among the garbage bags behind the locked steel door that led to the street. The far windows in the nearest building were all blinded with shades or curtains, no *ehhif* face showing. *Well enough,* she thought, and said under her breath the word that reminds the ephemeral of how it once was solid.

Rhiow stepped out, felt the step under her feet, there as always, and went on down: another step, another, through the apparently empty air, Rhiow trotting down it like a stairway. This imagery struck Rhiow as easier (and more dignified) than the tree-climbing paradigm often used by cats who lived out, and the air seemed amenable enough to the image made real: an empty stairway reaching twenty stories down into the alley's dimness, the stairsteps outlined and defined only by the faintest radiance of woven string structure. The strings held the wizardry in. Inside it, air was briefly stone again, as solid to walk on as it would have been a billion years back, before ancient eruption and the warming sun on Earth's crust let the atmosphere's future components out. Shortly, when Rhiow was down, it would be free as air again. But like all the other elements—in fact, like all matter, when you came down to it, sentient or not—air was nostalgic, and enjoyed being lured into being as it had been once before, long ago, when things were simpler.

Eight feet above the ground, where the surrounding walls were all blind, Rhiow paused. *I could jump on that rat,* she thought. Once again she saw the rustle and flicker of motion, heard the nasty yummy squeak-squeal from inside one of the black plastic garbage bags. Involuntarily, Rhiow's jaw spasmed, chattering slightly—the spasm that would break the neck of the prey clenched in it. Her mouth watered. Not that she would eat a rat, indeed not: *filthy flearidden things,* Rhiow thought, *and besides, who knows what they've been eating. Poison, half the time.* But cornering one, hitting it, feeling the body bruise under your paw and hearing the squeal of pain: that was sweet. Daring the rat's jump at your face, and the yellowed teeth snapping at you—and then, when it was over, playing with the corpse, tossing it in the air, celebrating again in your own person the old victory against the thing that gnaws at the root of the Tree—

No time this morning, she thought, *and you're wasting energy standing here. Let the air get on with doing what it has to. Carrying smog around, mostly . . .*

She went down the last few almost-invisible steps, jumping over the final ones to the dusty brick-paved surface of the alley. The noise inside the garbage bag abruptly stopped.

Rhiow smiled. She said the word that released the air from solidity: upward and behind her, the strings faded back into the general fabric of things from which they had briefly been plucked, and the air dispersed with a sigh. Rhiow walked by the garbage bag toward the streetward wall and the gate in it, still smiling. She knew where *this* one was. *Later,* she thought. Rats were smart, but not smart enough to leave garbage alone. It was two days yet until collection. The rat would be back, and so would she.

But right now, she had business. Rhiow put her head out under the bottom of the iron door, looked around. The sidewalk was empty of pedestrians for half a block; most important, there were no *houiff* in sight. Not that Rhiow was in the slightest afraid of *houiff,* but they could be a nuisance if you ran into them without warning— the ridiculous barking and the notice they drew to you were both undesirable.

A quiet morning, thank Iau. She slipped under and out, onto the sidewalk, and trotted along at a good rate. There was no time to idle, and besides, one of the first lessons a city cat learns is that it's always wise to look like you're going somewhere definite, and like you know your surroundings. A cat that idles along staring at the scenery is asking for trouble, from *houiff* or worse.

She passed the dry cleaner's, still closed so early, and the bookshop, and the coffee-and-sandwich shop—open and making extremely tantalizing smells of bacon: Rhiow muttered under her breath and kept going. Past the stores were five or six brownstones in a row, and as she passed the third one, a gravelly voice said, "Rhiow!"

She paused by the lowest step, looking up at the top of the graceful granite baluster. Yafh was sitting there with a bored look, scrubbing his big blunt face: not that scrubbing it ever made much difference to his looks. The spot was a perfect one for beginning the day's bout of *hauissh,* the position-game that cats everywhere played with each other for territorial power, or pleasure, or both. In *hauissh,* early placement was everything. Now any cat who might appear on the street and try to settle down in the area that Yafh was temporarily claiming as "territory" would have deal with Yafh first—by either confronting him head-on, moving completely out of sight, or taking a neutral stance . . . which would translate as appeasement or surrender, and lose the newcomer points.

Rhiow, since she was just passing through, was not playing. Business certainly gave her an excuse not to pause, but she rarely felt so antisocial. She went up the stairs, jumped onto the baluster, and paced down toward Yafh to breathe breaths with him. "Hunt's luck, Yafh—"

His mouth a little open, Yafh made an appreciative "tasting" face at the scent of her cat food. "If I *had* been really hunting, I could have used some luck," he said. "One of those little naked *houiff,* say . . . or even a pigeon. Even a squirrel. But there's nothing round here except roaches and rats."

Rhiow knew: she had smelled them on his breath, and she kept her own taste-face as polite as she could. "Don't they feed you in there, Yafh? If it weren't for you, your *ehhif* would have those things in their stairwells, if not their beds. You should leave them and go find someone who appreciates your talents."

Yafh made a most self-deprecating silent laugh and tucked himself down into half-crouch again, folding his paws in. After a moment Rhiow joined in the laugh, without the irony. Of the many cats in these few square blocks, Yafh was the one Rhiow knew and was known by best, and some would have found that an odd choice of friends, for one with Rhiow's advantages. Yafh was a big cat for one who had been untommed very young, but unless you took a close look at his hind end, you would never have suspected his *ffeih* status from the way his front end looked. Yafh would fight anything that moved, and had done so for years: he had enough scar tissue to make a new cat from, and was as ugly as a *houff*—broken-nosed, ragged-eared, one eye gone white-blind from some old injury. Where there were no scars, Yafh's coat was white; but his fondness for dust-bathing and for hunting in the piled-up rubbish behind his *ehhif's* building kept him a more or less constant dingy gray. His manner was generally as blunt and bluff as his looks, but he had few illusions and no pretensions, and his good humor hardly ever failed, whether he was using it on others or on himself.

"Listen," Yafh said, "what's food, in the long run? Once you're full, you sleep, whether it's caviar you were eating, or rat. These *ehhif* let me out on my own business, at least: that's more than a lot of us hereabouts can say. And they may be careless about mealtimes, but they don't send me off to have my claws pulled out, either, the way they did with poor Ailh down the road. Did you hear about that?"

"You'll have to tell me later," Rhiow said, and shook herself all over to hide the shudder. Such horror stories had long ago convinced her to leave her *ehhif*'s furniture strictly alone, no matter how tempted she might be to groom her claws on its lovely seductive textures. "Yafh, I hate to wash and run, but it's business this morning."

"They work you too hard," he said, eyeing her sidewise. "As if the People were ever made to work in the first place! The whole thing's some *ehhif* plot, that's what it is."

Rhiow laughed as she jumped down from the baluster. Others might retreat into unease at her job, or envy of it: Yafh simply saw Rhiow's errantry as some kind of obscure scam perpetrated on her proper allotment of leisure time. It was one of the things she best liked about him. "'Luck, Yafh," she said, starting down the sidewalk again. "See you later."

"Hunt's luck to you too," he said, "you poor *rioh*." It was a naughty punning nickname he had given her some time back—the Ailurin word for someone's beast of burden.

Rhiow went on her way, past the empty doorsteps, smiling crookedly to herself. At the corner she paused, looking down the length of Third. The light Sunday morning traffic was making her life a little easier, anyway: there was no need to wait. She trotted across Third, dashed down along the wall of the apartment building on the corner there, and ducked under the gate of the driveway behind it, making for the maze of little narrow alleys and walls on the inside of the block between Third and Lexington.

This was probably the most boring part of Rhiow's day: the commute down to the Terminal. She could have long-jumped it, of course. Considering her specialty, that kind of rapid transit was simple. But long-jumping took a lot of energy—too much to waste first thing in the morning, when she was just getting started, and when having enough energy to last out the day's work could mean the difference between being successful or being a total failure. So instead, Rhiow routinely went the long way: across to Lexington as quickly as she could manage, and then downtown, mostly by connecting walls and rooftops. The route was circuitous and constantly changing. Construction work might remove a long section of useful wall-walk or suddenly top the wall with sharp pieces of glass; streets might become easier to use because they were being dug up, or alternately because digging had stopped; scaffolding might provide new temporary routes; demolition work might mean a half-block's worth of barriers had suddenly, if temporarily, disappeared—at least, until construction work began. Typically, though, Rhiow would have at least a few weeks on any one route—long enough for it to become second nature, and for her to run it in about three-quarters of an hour, without having to think much about her path until she got down near Grand Central and met up with the others.

This morning, she spent most of the commute thinking about Ailh-down-the-road, the poor thing. Ailh was a nice enough person: well-bred, a little diffident—a handsome, close-coated little mauve-beige creature, with brown points and big lustrous green eyes. Not, Rhiow had to admit, the kind of cat one usually meets on the streets in the city; which made her unusual, memorable in her way. But apparently Ailh also couldn't control herself well enough to keep her scratching outside, though she had access to the few well-grown trees in their street. It was a shame. A shame, too, that *ehhif* were so peculiarly territorial about the things they kept in their dens. Being territorial about the den itself, that any cat could understand; but not about *things*. It was one of the great causes of friction between two species that had enough trouble understanding one another as it was. Rhiow wished heartily that *ehhif* could somehow come by enough sense to see that *things* simply didn't matter, but that was unlikely at best. *Not in this life,* she thought, *and not in the next couple either, I'll bet.*

Just west of Third on Fifty-sixth, Rhiow paused, looking down from an iron-spiked connecting wall between two brownstones, and caught a familiar glimpse of a blotched brown shape, skulking wide-eyed in the shadows of the driveway-tunnel leading into the parking garage near the corner. This was one of the more convenient parts of

Rhiow's morning run: a handy meeting place fairly close to the Terminal, where the *ehhif* knew her and her team, and didn't mind them. Not for the first time, Rhiow considered Saash's luck in getting herself adopted by the *ehhif* who worked there. *Luck, though,* she thought, *almost certainly has nothing to do with it, in* our *line of work. . . .*

She jumped down from the wall, ran under a parked car, looked both ways from underneath it, and hurried across the street. Saash, now crouched down against the wall of the garage, saw her coming, got up, and stretched fore and aft.

She was a long-limbed, delicate-featured, skinny little thing. Rhiow wondered one more time whatever could be the matter with her that she didn't seem able to put on weight: Saash was hardly there. Her coloring supported the illusion. In coat she was a *hlah'feihre,* what *ehhif* called a tortoiseshell—but not one of the bold, splashy ones. Saash's coat was patched softly in many shades and shapes of brown, gray, and beige, all running into one another: in some lights, and most especially in shadow, you could look straight at her and hardly see her. It was probably something to do with her kittenhood, which she rarely discussed—but hiding had been a large part of it, and you got the feeling Saash wouldn't be done with that aspect of her life for a long time, if ever. She had never quite grown into her ears, and the size of them gave her a look of eternal kittenishness—while the restless way they swiveled made her look eternally wary and uneasy, despite the ironic humor in her big gold eyes.

"'Luck,'" Rhiow said, and Saash immediately turned her back, sat down, put her left back leg over her left shoulder, and began to wash furiously. Rhiow sat down, too, and sighed. Another cat would probably have sniffed and walked off at the rudeness, but Rhiow had been working long enough with Saash to know it wasn't intentional.

"Is it bad this morning?" Rhiow said.

Saash kept washing. "Not like last week," she muttered. "Abha'h put that white stuff on me again, the powder." There was another second's satisfied pause. "I took a few strips off him while he was putting it on, anyway. Whether the junk *does* help or not, it still smells disgusting. And the taste—!"

Rhiow gazed off in the direction of the street, waiting for Saash to finish washing, and making faces at the flea powder, and scratching, and shaking herself. Rhiow privately doubted that the problem was fleas. Saash simply seemed to be allergic to her own skin, and itched all the time, no matter what anyone did: she couldn't make more than a move or two before stopping to put her fur back in order, even when it was perfectly smooth. When they had started working together, Rhiow had thought the constant grooming was vanity, and blows had been exchanged over it. Now she knew better.

Saash shook her coat out and sat down again properly. "There," she said. "I'm sorry, Rhi. 'Luck to you too."

"You heard?"

"They called me," Saash said in her little breathy voice, "right in the middle of breakfast. Typical."

"I was sleeping myself. Any sign of Urruah yet?"

Saash looked disdainful. "He's probably snoring at the bottom of that Dumpster he was describing in such ecstatic detail yesterday." She made an ironic breath-smelling face, one suggestive of a cat whiffing something better suited for a *houff* to roll in than for any kind of meal.

"Saash," Rhiow said, "for pity's sake, don't start in on him this morning: I can't cope. —Were They more specific with you than They were with me? I got a sense that something was wrong with the north-side gate again, but that was all."

Saash looked over her shoulder and washed briefly down her back. "*Au,* it's the north one, all right," she said, straightening up again. "It looks like someone did an out-of-hours access and forgot that the north gate's diurnicity timings change when it's accessed. So it's sitting there still patent."

"And after we just got the *hihhhh* thing fixed . . . !" Rhiow lashed her tail in irritation.

"My thought exactly."

"But who in the worlds would be accessing it out-hours without checking the rates first? That's pretty basic stuff. Even *ehhif* know enough to check the di-timings before they transit, and they can't even see the strings."

"Well, whoever came through didn't bother," Saash said. "Until we close it down again, the gate won't be able to slide back where it belongs for the day shift. And to get it shut, we'll have to reweave the whole *vhaï*d portal substrate until the egress stringing matches the access web again."

Rhiow sighed. "After we spent all of yesterday doing just that. Urruah's going to love this."

"Whenever he wakes up," Saash said dryly, sitting down to scratch again; but whatever else she might have said was lost as her *ehhif* came bustling up from down the ramp.

"Oh, poor kitty, you still scratchin', I gotta do you again!" Abad cried as he came toward them, feeling around for something in the deep pockets of his stained blue coverall. Abad was a living example of the old saying that an *ehhif* either looks like its cat to begin with or gets that way after a while—a tall, thin tom, fine-boned, brown-complected, with what looked like an eternal expression of concern. As Abad finally came up with the canister of flea powder, Saash took one wide-eyed look, said "*Oh* no!" and took off around the corner of the garage door and down the sidewalk toward Lexington. By the time he got into the open doorway and started looking for her, Saash had already done a quick sidle. Rhiow got up and strolled out onto the sidewalk after them. Abad stood there looking first one way, then the other, seeing nothing. But Rhiow, as she came up beside him, saw Saash slow down by the corner of the apartment building and look over her shoulder at Abad, then sit down again and start washing behind one ear.

"Aah, she hidin' now," Abad said sadly, and bent down to scratch Rhiow, whom he at least could still see. "Hey, nice to see you, Miss Black Cat, but my little friend, she gone now, I don' know where. You come back later and she be back then, she play with you then, eh?"

"Sure," Rhiow said, and purred at the *ehhif* for kindness' sake; "sure, I'll come back later." She stood up on her hind legs and rubbed hard against Abad's leg as he stroked her. Then she went after Saash, who glanced up at her a little guiltily as she stood again.

"You do that to him often?" Rhiow said. "I'd be ashamed."

"We all sidle when we have to," Saash said. "And if your fur tasted like mine does right now, so would *you*. Come on, you may as well . . . we're close, and enough people are out now that they'll slow us down if we're seen."

Rhiow sighed. "I suppose. It's getting late, isn't it?"

Saash squinted in the general direction of the sun. "I make it ten of six, *ehhif*-time."

Rhiow frowned. "That first train from North White Plains is due at twenty-three after, and we can't let it run through a patent gate. Which Dumpster did he say it was?"

"Fifty-third and Lex," Saash said. "By that new office building that's going up. There's a MhHonalh's right next to it, and the workmen keep throwing their uneaten food in there."

At the thought, Rhiow grimaced slightly, and looked over her shoulder to see what Abad was doing. He was still gazing straight toward them, looking for Saash: seeing nothing but Rhiow, he sighed, put the flea powder away, and went back into the garage.

Rhiow stood up and sidled, feeling the familiar slight fizz at ear-tips, whisker-tips, and claws as she stepped sideways into the subset of concrete reality where visible light would no longer bounce off her. Then she and Saash headed south on Lex toward Fifty-third, taking due care and not hurrying. The main problem with being invisible was that other pedestrians, *ehhif* and *houiff* particularly, had a tendency to run into or over you; and since they and other concrete things were still fully in the world of visible light, in daytime they hurt to look at. In the "sidled" state, though, you were already well into the realm of strings and other nonconcrete structures, and so your view was littered with them too. The world became a confusing tableau of glaringly bright *ehhif* and buildings, all tangled about with the more subdued light-strings of matter substrates, weft lines, and the other indicators of forces and structures that held the normally unseen world together. It was not a condition that one stayed in for long if one could help it— certainly not in bright daylight. At night it was easier, but then so was everything else: that was when the People had been made, after all.

Rhiow and Saash trotted hurriedly down Lexington, being narrowly missed by *ehhif* pedestrians, other *ehhif* making early deliveries from trucks and vans, *houiff* out being walked, and (when crossing streets) by cabs and cars driving at idiotic speed even at this time of morning. There was simply no hour, even on a Sunday, when these streets were completely empty; solitude was something for which you had to go elsewhere. One had to weave and dodge, or hug the walls, trying not to fall through gratings or be walked into by *ehhif* coming unexpectedly around corners.

They made fairly good time, only once having to pause when an under-sidewalk freight elevator started clanging away while Saash was walking directly over its metal doors. She jumped nearly out of her skin at the sudden sound and the lurch of the opening doors, and skittered curbward—straight into a *houff* on the leash. There was no danger: the *houff* was one of those tiny ones, a bundle of silky golden fur and yap and not much else. Saash, however, still panicked by the dreadful clanging of the elevator alarm and the racket of the rising machinery, hauled off and smacked the *houff* hard in the face, as much from embarrassment as from fright at jostling into it, and galloped off down the street, bristling all over. The *houff,* having been hit claws-out and hard by something invisible, plunged off down the sidewalk in a panic, half-choking on its collar and shrieking about murder and ghosts, while its bewildered *ehhif* was towed along behind.

Rhiow was half-choked herself, holding in her merriment. She went after Saash as fast as she could, and didn't catch up with her until she ran out of steam just before the corner of Fifty-fourth. There Saash sat down close to the corner of the building and began furiously washing her fluffed-up back fur. Rhiow knew better than to say anything, for this was not Saash's eternal itch: this was *he'ihh,* composure-grooming, and except under extraordinary circumstances, one didn't comment on it. Rhiow sat down back to back, keeping watch in the other direction, and waited.

To Saash's credit, she cut the *he'ihh* short, then breathed out one annoyed breath and got up. "I really hate them," she said as they went together to the curb, "those little ones. Their voices—"

"I know," Rhiow said. They waited for the light to change, then trotted across, weaving to avoid a pair of *ehhif* mothers with strollers. "They grate on my nerves, too. But would you rather have had one of the big ones?"

"Don't tease," Saash muttered as they trotted on toward the next corner. "I feel foolish now for hitting the poor thing like that. It wasn't its fault. And I was sidled too. Those little ones aren't always very resilient thinkers; if I've unhinged it somehow . . ."

"I doubt that." But Rhiow smiled. "All the same, you should have seen the look on its face. It—"

She stopped, ears pricked. From nearby, sounds of barking and snarling and yowling were rising over the muted early-morning traffic noise, becoming louder and louder. The two of them paused and looked at each other, eyes widening—for one of the two lifted voices, they knew.

"Sweet Queen around us," Saash said, *"what's he doing?!"*

They took off at a run, dodging among *ehhif* going in and out of the early-opening bakery at the end of the block, and tore around the corner. A dusty car with one tire flat and another booted was parked on their side of Fifty-third: Rhiow jumped up on its trunk and then leaped to its roof to get a better view. Saash came after, skidding a little on the roof and staring down the street. At the second impact, the car's alarm went off. Rhiow and Saash ignored it, knowing everyone else would, too.

Fifty-third was a mess of construction in this block: several beat-up yellow Dumpsters were lined up head to tail on the north side, and scaffolding towered several stories above them, against the front of two brownstones being renovated. Near the middle Dumpster, which sat with its lid open, a group of men in T-shirts and hard hats, and two others in security guards' uniforms, stood staring in astonishment at something between them and the Dumpster. At the sound of the car alarm, the men gave one glance toward the end of the street, saw nothing, and turned their attention back to what they had been watching.

The barks and growls scaled up into a yipping howl of sheer terror, and the men scattered, some toward the scaffolding, some toward the street. From among them burst a huge German shepherd, tawny and black. Its ears were plastered against its skull, its tail was clamped between its hind legs, and it leapt four-footed into the air and came down howling, and spun in circles, and shook itself all over. But it could do nothing to dislodge the gray-striped shape that clung to its neck, yowling at the top of his voice . . . not in fear or pain, either. Urruah was having a good time.

"Oh, not *today*," Rhiow muttered. "Come on, Saash, we've got to do something, that gate won't wait—!"

"Tell *him*," Saash said, dry-voiced, as the unfortunate *houff* and its rider came plunging toward them. Urruah's eyes were wide, his mouth was wide as he yowled, and he had both front pawfuls of claws anchored in the *houff*'s collar, or maybe in its upper neck behind its ears; his back claws kicked and scrabbled as if he thought he'd caught a rabbit, and was trying to remove its insides in the traditional manner. The dog continued to howl, jump, and turn in circles, and still couldn't rid himself of his tormentor: the howls were more of pain than fear, now. Urruah grinned like an idiot, yowling some wordless nonsense for sheer effect.

Rhiow saw one of the security guards pull out his gun. *He wouldn't be so stupid—!* she thought. But some *ehhif were* profoundly stupid by feline standards, and one might take what he thought was a safe shot at the cat tormenting his guard dog, even if he stood an even chance of hitting the dog instead.

She glanced at the scaffolding above the group of *ehhif*. "Saash," Rhiow said. "That bucket."

Saash followed her glance. "I see it. In front of the Dumpster?"

"That's the spot." Rhiow turned her attention to Urruah and the *houff*.

An almighty crash came from just in front of the second Dumpster. The bucket full of wet cement-sand had come down directly in front of the security guard with the gun. He jumped back, yelling with surprise and fear at being splattered, as the other *ehhif* did; then spun, looking upward for the source of the trouble. There was no one there, of course. Several of the men, including the second security guard, disappeared into the construction site; the man with the gun stood staring upward.

Rhiow, meantime, waited until the *houff* was within clear hearing range—she didn't want to have to shout. As it lurched closer to the car where she and Saash sat, Rhiow chose her moment . . . then said the six syllables of the *ahou'ffriw*. It was not a word she spoke often, though part of the general knowledge of a feline in her line of work. Sidled as she was, Rhiow could see the word take flight like one of the hunting birds that worked the high city, arrowing at the *houff*. The word of command struck straight through the creature, as it had been designed to do when the *houiff* themselves were designed; struck all its muscles stiff, froze the thoughts in its brain and the intended movements in its nerves. The *houff* crashed to the concrete and lay there on its side, its tongue hanging out, its eyes glazed. Urruah went down with it, and after a moment extricated himself and got up, looking confused.

"I don't know about you," Rhiow said softly—and Urruah's head jerked up at the sound—"but *we're* on callout this morning. You had some different business, maybe? The Powers That Be suggested you take the morning off to beat up defenseless *houiff?*"

Urruah squinted to see her better. "Oh, 'luck, Rhiow."

"'Luck is what none of us are going to have if you don't pull yourself together," Rhiow said. "Come on. We've got ten blocks to make before twenty-three after."

"Long-jump it," Urruah said, stepping down off the *houff.*

"*No,*" Rhiow said. "No point in throwing away power like that, when we may have something major to do in a few minutes. Get sidled and come on." She jumped down from the car: Saash followed.

They crossed the street and went on down Lexington again: Urruah first, sidled now, and taking it easy for the moment; then Saash. Rhiow paused just for a moment to look over her shoulder at the *houff*. He was staggering to his feet again, looking groggy but relieved.

Good, Rhiow thought. She went after the others and caught up with Saash first. "That was slick," she said, "with the bucket."

"It was in a bad position to start with. Pull a string or so, change the bucket's moment of inertia—" Saash shrugged one ear back and forward, casual, but she smiled.

Rhiow did, too, then trotted forward to catch up with Urruah. "Now," she said, more affably, "you tell me what all that was about."

He strolled along for a moment without answering. Rhiow was tempted to clout him, but it would be a waste of energy, and it really was difficult being annoyed for long at so good-looking a young tom, at least when he was behaving himself. Urruah was only two and a half, having passed his Ordeal and started active practice a year ago. He was good at what he did, and was pleased with himself, on both professional and physical counts: a big, burly, sturdy tabby, silver and black, with silver-gray eyes, a voice all purr, some very ornamental scars, and a set of the biggest, sharpest, whitest teeth that Rhiow could remember seeing on one of the People in several lives. She occasionally wondered, when Urruah pulled dumb stunts like this, whether those teeth went straight up into his skull and filled most of it, leaving less room for sense.

"That *houff*," Urruah said, as they crossed Fifty-second, "took my mouse."

"Wait a minute," Saash said. "You're trying to tell us that you actually *caught a mouse,* when there was all that perfectly good Mh-Honalh's food in the Dumpster?"

Urruah gave Saash a scathing look. Saash simply blinked at him, refusing to accept delivery on the scorn, and kept on walking. "It was a terrific mouse," Urruah said. "It was one of those bold ones: it kept jumping and trying to bite me in the face. I was going to let it go after a while: you have to respect that kind of defiance! And then that miserable *ehhif* shows up at shift-change and lets his *houff* off the chain where they keep the thing all night, and it comes running out of there, jumps into the street practically on top of me, and *eats my mouse!* Must have a lot of wolf in it or something. But what would *you* have done?"

"Not ride it down the street and nearly get myself shot," Rhiow said dryly. "Or the poor *houff*. A good slapping around would have been plenty. And do you really expect a *houff* to mind People's manners? It didn't know any better. But that *ehhif's* reckless with the *houff*. And it must have been awfully hungry. I wonder what can be done about your poor mouse-eater. . . ."

"Not our problem," Urruah said as they crossed Fifty-first.

"*Everything* in this city is our problem," Rhiow said, "as you know very well. I'd say you owe that *houff* a favor, now; you overreacted. Better arrange a meeting with one of our people on the *houff* side and see what can be done about him. I'll expect a report tomorrow."

Urruah growled under his breath, but Rhiow put her ears back at him. "Business, Urruah," she said. "There's work waiting for us. Put yourself aside and get ready to do what you were made to."

He sighed, and after a half a block his whiskers went forward again. "Tell me it's the northside gate again."

Rhiow grimaced. "Of course it is."

"Somebody did an out-of-hours access," Saash said, "and left it misaligned."

"The substrates still hinged?"

"Hard to tell from just the notification, but I hope so. If we go in prepared to do a subjunctive restring—"

And they were off, several sentences deep into gate-management jargon before the three of them crossed Fiftieth. Rhiow sighed. Saash and Urruah might have frictions, but the technical details of their work fascinated them both, and while they had a problem to solve they usually managed to avoid taking their claws to one another. It was before work, and after, that difficulties set in; fortunately, the team's relationship was strictly a professional one, and no rule said they had to be best friends. For her own part, Rhiow mostly concentrated on balancing Saash and Urruah off against one another so that the team got its work done without claws-out transactions or murder.

Just south of the southwest corner of Fiftieth and Lex was their way down into Grand Central. Outside the delicatessen on the corner, a street grating that covered the west-side ventilation shaft was damaged, leaving room enough to squeeze through without mussing one's fur. They slipped down through it, Urruah first, then Saash and Rhiow, and followed the downward incline of the concrete shaft for a few yards until they were out of sight of the street. All of them paused to let their eyes settle, now blessedly relieved of the bright sunlight. The dimness around them began to be more clearly stitched and striated with the thin radiance of strings, properly separate now, and their colors distinct rather than blindingly run together.

"Smells awful down here today," Saash said, wrinkling her nose.

"Just your delicate sensibilities," Urruah said, grinning. "Or the flea powder."

Saash lifted a paw to cuff him, but Rhiow shouldered between them. "Not now. Your eyes better? Then let's go on."

The concrete-walled shaft was four feet wide and no more than two feet high, low enough to make you keep your tail down as you went. It stretched for about thirty feet ahead before turning off westward at a right angle, where it stopped. Under the end of the shaft was a concrete ledge, much eroded from waste water dripping down it, and below that, a drop of some ten feet to the "back yard," the northeastern bank of sidings where locomotives and loose cars were kept when the East Yard was congested with trains being moved.

One after another they jumped down, avoiding the eternal puddle of water that lay stagnant under the shaft-opening in all but the driest weather. In the darkness the clutter and tangle of strings was more visible than ever, and many of them were pulled curving over to a spot between Tracks 25 and 26, blossoming outward from it in all directions like a diagram of a black hole's event horizon. That particular nodal symmetry meant an open worldgate, and was the signature of Rhiow's business and her team's. With worldgates in place and working properly, wizards out on errands didn't have to spend their own precious energy on rapid transit to get where the Powers That Be assigned them. Without working gates, solutions to crises were slowed down, lives were hurt or untimely ended, and the heat-death of the Universe progressed unchecked or sometimes sped up. That was what all those in the team's line of work were sworn to stop; and moments like this, as Rhiow stood and eyed the incredible mess and tangle of malfunctioning strings, made her wonder why they all kept trying when things kept going this spectacularly wrong.

The strings curving in to the nodal junction shivered with light and with the faintest possible sound, as if all being plucked at once. And the curvature wasn't symmetrical: there should have been a matching "outward" curvature to complement the "inward" one. Taken together, the signs meant an unstable gate, which might shift phase, mode, or location without warning. "Time?" Rhiow said.

"Twenty after," Saash said.

They sprinted through the darkness, across the tracks. Though even a cat's eyes take time to adjust to sudden darkness, they had the advantage of knowing their ground; they were down here three times a week, sometimes more, slipping so skillfully among the tracks and buildings that they were seldom seen. Urruah went charging ahead, delighted as always by a challenge and a chance to show off; Rhiow was astonished to see him suddenly stumble as he came down from a jump over track. Something squealed as he fell on it.

"Irh's balls," he yowled, "it's rats! Rats!"

More squeals went up. Rhiow spat with disgust, for the rats were all over the place, like a loathsome carpet: she'd been so intent on the gate that they hadn't even registered until she ran right into them. Some rats now panicked and ran off shrieking down the tunnels, but for every three that ran, one stayed to try to slash your leg or ear.

Rhiow prided herself on having a fast and heavy paw when she needed it, and she needed it now. She disliked using the killing bite until she was sure the thing being bitten couldn't bite her back in the lip or the eye: the only way to be sure was to crush skulls and break backs first, so she got busy doing that, hitting wildly around her. Up ahead of her, Urruah was yowling delight and rage, and rats flew from every stroke. *But Saash,* Rhiow thought in sudden concern. *She's no fighter. What if—*

She looked over to the left. Saash was crouched down, her eyes gone so wide that they were just black pools with a glint of rim; a rat nearly her own size was crouched in front of her, preparing to jump. Saash opened her mouth and hissed at it.

The rat blew up.

And here I was worrying, Rhiow thought, both revolted and impressed. "Saash," she shouted over the squeals and the cracking of bones, heading after Urruah, "can you extend the range on that spell? We don't have time for this!"

Saash shook herself to get the worst of the former rat off her, hissed, and spat. "Yes," she said. "Believe me, I'd have had it ready for numbers if I'd known! Give me a moment—"

She crouched again, looking intent, and Rhiow concentrated on defending her. The rats were coming faster now, as if they knew something bad was about to happen. Rhiow felt the bite in her tail, another in her leg, and struck out all around her in a momentary fury that she knew she couldn't maintain for long. "Urruah," she yelled, "for the Dam's sake get your mangy butt back here and lend us a paw!"

The answer was a yowl that was actually cheerful in a horrible way. A moment later Rhiow could see him working back toward them by virtue of an empty space around him that moved as he moved. Rats would rush into it, but they wouldn't rush out: they went down, skulls smashed or backs broken. Once Rhiow saw Urruah reach down with that idiot grin, grab a rat perfectly in the killing-bite spot at the base of the skull, and whip around him with the thing's whole body, bludgeoning away the other rodents coming at him. It was disgusting, and splendid.

Urruah jumped right over Rhiow, turned in midair, and came down tail-to-tail with her. Together they struck at the writhing squealing forms all around, while between them Saash scowled at the dirty gravelly ground, with her eyes half-shut. "Nervous breakdown?" Urruah yelled between blows.

Rhiow was too busy to hit him. Saash ignored him completely. A moment later, she lifted her head, slit-eyed, and hissed.

Rhiow went flat-eared and slack-jawed at the piercing sound, more like a train's air-brakes than anything from a tiny cat's throat. Urruah fell over sideways as the force of it struck him. From all around them came many versions of a loathsome popping sound, like a car running over a sealed plastic bag full of liver. Everyone got sprayed with foul-smelling muck.

Silence fell. Saash got up and ran toward the track onto which the gate had slid down. Rhiow went after, followed by Urruah when he struggled to his feet. The fur rose on Rhiow's back as they went, not just from the itch of closeness to the patent gate. From back in the upper-level tunnel came a rumbling, and the tracks ticked in sympathy: the single white eye of the 6:23's headlight was sliding toward them.

Urruah saw it, too. "I could give it a power failure," he gasped as they ran. "No one would suspect a thing."

"It wouldn't stop the train before it ran through the gate."

"I could stop it—"

"You've swapped brains with your smallest flea," Rhiow hissed. The dreadful mass and kinetic energy bound up in a whole train were well beyond even Urruah's exaggerated idea of his ability to handle.

"It'll derail, and Iau only knows how many of those poor *ehhif* will get hurt or killed. Come on—!"

They ran after Saash. She stood in front of the gate, tail lashing violently as she looked the tangle of strings up and down, eyes half-closed to see them better. As Rhiow and Urruah came up with her, she turned.

"It's still viable," she said. "Much better than I feared. The configuration that we left it in yesterday afternoon is still saved in the strings—see that knot? And that one."

Rhiow peered at them. "Can you get them to retie?"

"Should be able to. We can reweave later: no time for it now. This'll at least shut the thing. Urruah?"

"Ready," he said. He was panting, but eager as always. "Where do you want it?"

"Just general at first. Then the substrate. Rhiow?"

"Ready," she said.

First Saash, then Urruah, and at last Rhiow, reared up and hooked claws through the bright web of strings, and began to pull. Saash leaned in deep, set her teeth into another knotted set of burning string-fire, closed her eyes and started work. The fizz and itch in the air started to get worse, while Saash's power and intention ran down the strings through the gate substrate, and the strings obediently writhed and began reweaving themselves over the gaping portal. Through the physical gate itself, not the orderly circle or sphere Rhiow was used to but just a jagged rent in the dark air, nothing could be seen: not the train, not anything else. The gate had been left open on some void or empty place. Cold dark wind breathed from it, mixing peculiarly with the hot metallic breath of the train trundling along through the dimness toward them. *Oh, hurry up!* Rhiow thought desperately, for she couldn't get rid of the image of the train plunging into that jagged darkness and being lost—where? No way of telling. After a catastrophic incursion by such a huge mass, certainly the gate would derange, maybe irreparably. And what would happen to the train and its passengers, irretrievably lost into some hole in existence?

Rhiow pulled forcibly away from such thoughts: they wouldn't help the work. Saash was deep in it, drowned in the concentration that made her so good at this work—claws snagged deep in the substrate as she drew strings out with paws and mind, knitted them together, released them to pull in others. Urruah, his face a mask of strained but joyous snarl like the one he had worn while killing rats, fed her power, a blast of sheer intention as irresistible as the stream from a fire hose, so that the strings blazed, kindling to Saash's requirements and knitting faster every moment. This was what made Urruah the second heart of the team, despite all his bragging and bad temper: the blatant energy of a young tom in his prime, harnessed however briefly and worth any amount of skill.

Rhiow fed her energy down the weave, too, but mostly concentrated on watching the overall progress of the reweave. *There,* she said down the strings to the others, *watch that patch there—* Saash was on it, digging her forelegs into the tangle practically to the shoulders. A moment while she fished around deep inside the weave, as if feeling for a mouse inside a hole in a wall: then she snagged the string she wanted and pulled it into place, and the part of the weave that had threatened to come undone suddenly went seamless, a patch of light rather than a webwork. The tear in the darkness was healing itself. Peering around its right edge, Rhiow saw the train coming, very close now, certainly no more than a hundred yards down the track. *It's going to be all right,* she thought, *it'll be all right, oh, come on, Saash, come on, Urruah—!*

The gate substrate looked less like a bottomless hole now, and more like a flapping, flattening tapestry woven of light on a weft of blackness. The gap was narrowing to a tear, the tear to a fissure of black above the tracks. The roaring train was fifty yards away. Still Saash stood reared up against the glowing weave of substrate, pulling some last few burning strings into order. *Rhi,* she thought, *hold this last bit—*

Half deafened, Rhiow reached in and bit the indicated strings to hold them in place while Saash worked in a final furious flurry of haste, pulling threads in and out, interweaving them. Not for the first time, Rhiow wondered what human had once upon a time seen a gate-technician of the People about her business, and later had named a human children's game with string "cat's-cradle"—

Done! Saash shouted into the weave. It snapped completely flat, a dazzling tapestry along which many-colored fires rolled outward to the borders, bounced, rippled in again. The dark crack in the air slammed shut. Behind it, the blind white eye of the 6:23's locomotive slid ponderously at them in a roar of diesel thunder. Rhiow and Urruah threw themselves to the right of the track, under the platform; Saash leapt to the left. The loco roared straight through the rewoven and now-harmless gate substrate, stirring it not in the slightest, and brakes screeched as the train gradually slid down to the end of its platform and gently stopped.

The train sat there ticking and hissing gently to itself, the huge wheels of one car not two inches from Rhiow's and Urruah's noses. "A little close," Urruah said from where he crouched, wide-eyed, a few feet away.

"A little," Saash said, from the far side. "Rhiow? I want to do some low-level diagnosis on this gate before we leave. The other three I can check from here; but I want to look into this one's log weave and see who left it in this state."

"Absolutely," Rhiow said. "Wait till they move this thing."

It usually took fifteen or twenty minutes for the train to empty out and for the crew to finish checking it. Urruah rose after getting his breath back. "I need to stretch," he said, and walked off to the end of the platform. Rhiow went after him.

Down the track they met Saash, who had had the same idea. At the sight of her, Urruah made a face, his nose twitching. "Aaurh up a tree, look at you! And you *stink!*"

Saash made a matching face, for once unwilling to sit down and wash. But then she grinned. "Your delicate sensibilities?" Saash said sweetly.

Urruah had the grace to look sheepish. He wandered away through the carnage. "Not a trick you'd want to use every day. But effective . . . !"

"It saved us," Rhiow said softly. "And them. Nice work, Saash."

Saash looked wry. "I know what I'm good for. Fighting isn't it."

"Technical expertise, though . . ." Rhiow said.

"Rats," said Saash, "make a specific shape in space. There's a way they affect strings in their area, one that no other species duplicates. There's a way to exploit that." She shrugged her tail; but she smiled.

"Keep that spell loaded," Rhiow said, heartfelt. "We may need it again."

From down the track came a rumble and groan of wheels as the train started backing out into the tunnel where all the upper-level tracks merged. Rhiow and the team moved a couple of tracks eastward to avoid it, Urruah wandering ahead. "So what will we do after this?" he said.

"Get cleaned up," Rhiow said, with longing.

"I mean after that. . . . We could go down to the Oyster Bar and romance the window lady."

Rhiow flicked an ear in mild exasperation, wondering how Urruah could think of any food, even oysters, when surrounded by a smell like this. But they were a passion of his. Occasionally Rhiow had secretly followed Urruah down to the restaurant's pedestrian-service window after finishing work, and had seen him stand there in line with the other commuters—provoking much amused comment—and then wheedle bluepoints out of one of the window staff, a big broad blond lady, by force of purr alone. For her own part, Rhiow would not normally have done something so high-profile in the Terminal itself. But Urruah had no shame, and Rhiow had long since given up trying to teach him any.

"Window's not open on Sunday," Saash said. "Do you ever think about anything but your stomach?"

"I sure do. Just the night before last there was this little ginger number, with these big green eyes, and she—"

Saash sat down in a clean spot behind a signal and started having herself a good scratch, yawning the while. "Urruah, you've obviously mistaken me for someone who's even slightly interested in your nightly exploits."

"*Au,* it's not your fault," Urruah said magnanimously. "You can't help not taking an interest, poor thing: you're *ffeih,* after all."

Rhiow smiled slightly: she had given up trying to teach Urruah tact, too. But there was no arguing the statement, on either Saash's part or her own. Before her wizardry, while still very young with her *ehhif,* Hhuha had taken Rhiow to the vet's and unqueened her. Saash had had this happen, too, so long ago that she couldn't even remember it. Being *ffeih* did free you from certain inconvenient urges; sometimes Rhiow wondered how still-queened wizards managed when heat and an assignment coincided. "Still," Rhiow said, "Saash has a point. Till tomorrow, it's MhHonalh's or nothing for you, my kit."

"Worth waiting for," Urruah said, unconcerned, still ambling along. He paused, peering down. "Here, you missed one, Saash. Iau's sweet name, but these things are getting big this year—"

He broke off. "Rhiow? This isn't a rat."

The alarm in his voice made Rhiow's heart jump. She hurried over and stood with him to stare down unhappily at the small sodden heap of fur and limbs lying on the rail. Sometimes you ran into them down here, People who were sick or careless, and ran afoul of the trains: there was nothing much you could do but send their bodies on and wish them well in their next life. *So young,* she thought sadly: this catling could hardly have been out of his 'tweens, still kittenish and not yet old enough to worry about sex.

"Poor kit," Saash said. "I wonder—"

He moved. A gasp, a heave of his chest, a kick of one leg. Another heave of breath.

"I don't believe it," Rhiow said. She bent down and gave his head a lick. He tasted foul, of cinder and train fumes as well as rat blood. She breathed breaths with him: the scent/taste was hurt and sick, yes, but not dead yet.

And someone said in her head, *Rhiow? Are you free?*

It was a voice she knew, and one she had expected to hear from, but not right this minute. The others heard it, too, from their expressions.

Urruah made a wry face. "The Area Advisory," he said. "I guess we should be honored."

"We got *that* shut," Saash said, flicking an ear at the gate. "We're honored. —You go on, Rhi. We'll see to this one . . . and I'll start those deep diagnostics. I've checked all four gates' logs now. The other three are answering properly: no effect on them from this event. One thing, though. The log weave on *this* one is blank. No transits or accesses showing since the midnight archive-and-purge of the log."

Rhiow blinked at that and started to demand explanations, but Saash turned away to the catling. "Ask me later."

Rhiow jumped up onto the platform. "Next train's at seven oh four," she said, looking over her shoulder at them.

Urruah gave her a tolerant look. "It's clear over on Track Thirty-two," he said. "We'll be fine."

Rhiow sighed. She was a mess, a layer of dust and track cinders kicked up by the North White Plains local now stuck to the rat detritus that had sprayed her, but there was no time to do much about it. She shook herself hard, scrubbed at her face enough to become slightly decent—then trotted on up the platform, out through the gate, and into the main concourse.

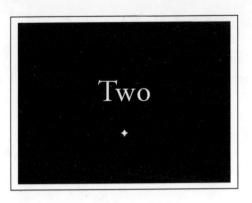

Two

♦

Here Rhiow stayed by the wall with some care, for the place was slowly becoming busy. Great beams of dusty sunlight slanted down into the concourse from the tall east windows; the big Accurist clock's deep-throated bell began tolling seven.

Rhiow gazed around, seeing very little stillness in the place. It was all *ehhif* moving, going, heading somewhere; except up the steps on the Vanderbilt Avenue side, where the ticketed waiting area was, and the coffee bar next to it. In the coffee bar, with the Sunday *Times* piled up on the glass table in front of him, and a cup of something hot to one side, sat a tall dark-haired *ehhif* in jeans and running shoes and a beige polo shirt. As Rhiow looked at him, the *ehhif* glanced up from the section he was reading, and then looked right down at her and raised his eyebrows: a good trick, since she was invisible.

Rhiow trotted across the concourse and up the stairs, pausing only a moment near the bottom of the staircase to enjoy the residual scent of fish floating up from the Oyster Bar downstairs. At the top of the steps, she wove and dodged to miss a couple of transit cops coming out of the Metro-North police offices off to the left, and slid among the tables, to where Carl Romeo sat.

He was handsome, as *ehhif* went, broad-shouldered and narrow-waisted, with high cheekbones, clear gray eyes, and a face that looked friendly to her—though of course it was always dangerous to

felidomorphize. How he had turned up so fast, even with a malfunctioning gate, wasn't hard to imagine: an Area Advisory was not limited
to public transit in the performance of his duties.

"*Dai stihó,* Har'lh," she said, tucking herself up comfortably under
the table. She did not speak Ailurin to him. To one of another species
but in her own line of work, she could use the Speech, and preferred
to: its detailed professional vocabulary made errors of understanding
less likely.

"*Dai,*" Carl said, using the paper to cover his attention to her.
"Rhiow, what was all this about?"

"The integration we did yesterday came undone," Rhiow said.
"Saash is working on the technical details for me; we'll know more in
a while. But we were able to reinstate before the North White Plains
local came in."

Carl rustled his *Times* aside and reached for his cappucino. "You
and your team don't usually need to do things twice," Carl said. "Is
there something I should know about?"

"Nothing regarding team function," Rhiow said. "But I'm disturbed
about the condition we found the gate in, Har'lh. The symptoms were
of someone using it without due care. However, the logs show *no*
transit, not even any accesses . . . which is odd. Either the gate was
not used, and this malfunction had some other cause"—and she shuddered: that was a nest of mice Rhiow was unwilling to start ripping
open—"or someone out on errantry *did* access it, and then wiped the
logs on purpose. Not very ethical."

Carl smiled, a thin humorless look. "That's putting it mildly." For a
few moments he said nothing, and Rhiow wished she could guess all
of what was going on in the mind behind that face. *Ehhif* could be in-
scrutable even after you'd learned to understand their expressions;
one of the Area Advisories, the two people ultimately responsible for
all the wizards working in the greater metropolitan area, could be expected to know things and have concerns Rhiow could only guess at.
About some of those concerns, though, Rhiow felt she could safely
speculate.

She wondered if Carl was thinking what she was: that, though all
wizards were supposed to be in service to the Powers That Be, some-

times . . . just sometimes . . . one or another of them will shift allegiances. There was, after all, one of those Powers that had had a profound disagreement with all the Others, very early on in the Universe. It had lost some of Its strength, as a result, but not all: and It was still around. Dealing with the Lone Power could seem very attractive to some, Rhiow knew; but she considered such dealings unacceptably hazardous. This was, after all, the same Power that had invented death and turned it loose on the worlds . . . a final nasty offhand gesture before turning Its back on the establishment that It felt had spurned It. The Lone One was as likely to turn on Its tools as on Its enemies.

Carl looked at her. "You're thinking of rogues," he said.

"I'd think you would be, too, Har'lh," Rhiow said, "the evidence being what it is at the moment."

He folded the first section of the paper, put it aside. "It's circumstantial at best. Can you think of any way a gate's logs might wipe accidentally on access or transit?"

"Not at first lick," Rhiow said, "since gates are supposedly built not to be able to function that way. But I'll take it up with Saash. If anyone can find a way to make a gate fail that way, she can. Meanwhile, I'll go Downside myself later on and check the top-level spell emplacement, just to make sure one of the other gate structures isn't interfering with the malfunctioning one."

"If you like . . . but I'm not requiring it of you."

"I know. I'd just like to be sure the trouble isn't some kind of structural problem."

"All right. But watch yourself down there."

"I will, Advisory."

"Anything else I need to know about this?"

Rhiow sneezed, a residual effect from the foul rodent-smell down on the tracks, not to mention the way she smelled herself. "A lot of rats down there, Har'lh. A *lot*."

Carl raised his eyebrows. "The early spring," he said, "combined with this hot weather? That's what the paper says. Some kind of screwup in the normal breeding season—"

Rhiow laid her whiskers back, a "no" gesture. "A lot of rats *since yesterday*. In fact, to judge from the quality of the smell, since this morning. —That's the other thing: we found a hurt youngster back there."

"Feline? Human?"

"Feline. About the same age for us as a human child of nine. I think he ran into those rats: he's all bitten up. Urruah and Saash are seeing to him. He should be all right, after some care."

"Very well." Carl picked up the magazine section. "The other gates are behaving themselves?"

"No signs of trouble."

"You don't think I need to declare them off-limits till you can look into this in detail?"

Rhiow thought. There were three other worldgates associated with the Terminal. Taking them offline would throw the whole weight of the area's extraspatial transit on the Penn Station gates. Penn was underequipped to handle such a load—its two gates normally handled only onplanet work, and one of them would have to be extensively restrung at very short notice if the Grand Central gates went down. Jath, Hwaa, and Fhi'ss, the technical team handling Penn, would not thank her at all.

But it wasn't a question of their feelings: what mattered was safety. Still, the nodes and string structures around the other two track-level gates, seen at a distance, looked fine; and she had Saash's report. . . .

"I'll double-check them shortly," Rhiow said. "But Saash says the gates at Thirty-two and One-sixteen, and the Lexington Avenue local gate, are patent and functional, and their logs and access-transit structures answered properly when interrogated. Her snap assessment is likely to be as accurate as my more leisurely one. If I find anything when I go Downside, I'll advise you. But on present data, I would advise you to leave the gates as they are."

Carl nodded. "I'll take One-sixteen home and check it," he said.

"Don't be seen," Rhiow said. "Nothing runs on the lower levels on Sunday."

Carl smiled slightly. "There are more ways to be invisible than to sidle," he said. "Let's talk tomorrow morning, then." He sipped at his cappucino, then squinted briefly at her. "Rhi, what *is* that all over you? You look awful."

She smiled slightly at him. "Occupational hazard. I told you the rats were thick down there . . . about an eighth of an inch thick, at the moment. —You on call all alone this weekend?"

Carl nodded. "Tom's in Geneva at the Continental-regionals meeting; he'll be back Wednesday. I'm handling the whole East Coast, just now."

"Not much fun for you," Rhiow said, "having no one to split shifts with."

Carl waved the cappucino at her. "I drink a lot of this. I get jangled, but I survive."

Rhiow got up and shook herself again, not that it helped. "Well, give T'hom my best when you hear from him," she said. "Go well, Advisory . . . and watch out for that caffeine."

"*Dai stihó,* Rhiow," Carl said. "Stay in touch. And mind the rats."

"You got *that* in one," she said, and headed down the stairs.

When Rhiow got back down to the tracks, she found that Saash and Urruah had moved over to the far side, near the wall. Between them lay the kitling, now curled into a tight ball. He was cleaner: Saash was washing him, and looked up from that now as Rhiow came over.

"How is he?" Rhiow said.

"He woke for a moment," Saash said, "but went right out again—understandable. No bones broken, no internal injuries. He's just bitten up and shocked to exhaustion. Sleep's best for him, and a wizardry to kill the filth in the bites. But not here."

"No, indeed not," Rhiow said, glancing around. No *ehhif* terminal staff were out on the tracks as yet, but it wouldn't do for any to come along and find this kitling. The *ehhif*'s relations with terminal cats had become somewhat difficult over the last few years. Every now and then the place was "swept," and sick or indigent cats found there were taken away, along with sick or indigent *ehhif* who had also taken refuge in the tunnels for shelter rather than food. "Well, he's got to have somewhere to rest. But I can't help: the outside places near my den are too dangerous for a kit."

"I live in a Dumpster," Urruah said, with execrable pride. "There would be room . . . but I don't think it's the place for him if he's sick."

"No," Rhiow said, "but it's good of you to offer." She didn't say what she was thinking: that attempting to keep a young tom barely out of kittenhood in close company with a tom of siring age was a recipe for disaster, whether the tom lived in a Dumpster or a palace, and whether he was a wizard or not. Mature toms couldn't help their attitude toward kittens in general, and male ones in particular, no matter how they tried.

"I think I can put him up," Saash said. "There are a lot of places way down and back in the garage where the *ehhif* never go. One big high ledge that I use sometimes will serve: it's four levels down. None of the *ehhif* go down there except to fetch cars out, and not often—it's long-term storage space. This kitling won't be heard, even if he cries, and if I have to, I can lay a barrier to hold either him or the sound in till he's well enough to go."

"You'll have to spend some time there to be sure he's settled," Rhiow said, "and if he catches you, Abha'h will powder you again—"

Saash hissed softly, but the sound was resigned. "I suppose it's in a good cause," she said. "And I have to eat sometime; he'd catch me then anyway. Will you two lend a hand with the jump? I don't propose to carry him all the way home in my mouth."

"No problem. Urruah?"

"As long as she does the circle," Urruah said, emitting a cavernous yawn. The morning's exertions were beginning to catch up with him.

Rhiow yawned, too, then laughed. "Quick," she said, "before we all fall asleep where we stand . . ."

Saash glanced around her, eyeing the area, and with a quick practiced flick of her tail laid out the boundaries of the spell, sweeping the area clean of random string influences and defining the area where she wanted the new ones to anchor. When the anchors were in place, looking like a cage of vertical bright lines around the edges of the circle, Saash added the only ingredient needed: the words. She said one word in the Speech, and the anchors leaned inward above them, knotting into the tip of a cone. Then three more words—the medium-precision versions of Saash's and Rhiow's and Urruah's names, and a fourth generic medium-precision term for their "passenger," with only the physical characteristics of his size and color added in, since they didn't know his name or anything about his personality. With the details completed, the dirt and cinders under their feet went webbed with still more bright lines, the anchors that would hold the four of them inside the spell. "Location's coming," Saash said to Urruah. "Ready?"

He turned and snagged one of the anchor strands in his teeth, ready to feed power down it. "Go."

Saash recited a string of coordinates in the Speech, and then said the last word that knotted the spell closed and turned it loose. Urruah bit hard on the string, feeding power down it. The whole structure blazed: the "cone" of strings collapsed down on them, pushed them down and out through its bottom. A moment when the world was a tangle of lines of fire—

Then dimness reasserted itself. The four of them stood and sat and lay on a concrete shelf four feet wide and ten feet long, high up at the far end of a room much longer than it was wide. The shelf's edge was a sheer drop of twenty feet to a floor painted with white lines and covered with blocky machinery, in which *ehhif*'s cars were stacked three high.

The string structure snapped away to nothing. "*Au,* I'm glad there are gates," Saash said, and flopped down on her side. "Who'd want to do that every time you wanted to go any distance? It's bad enough for ten blocks."

"That's why Iau gave us feet," Rhiow said. "Urruah? You okay?"

He sat down, blinking. "I will be after I eat something."

He's fine, Rhiow thought, amused. "Now let's see about this one—" She peered at the kitling. Under the grime, most of which Saash had gotten off, he was white with irregular black patches on back and flanks and face: one splotch sat on his upper lip, creating an effect like Carl's mustache. Ear-tips, tail-tips, and feet were black. *Hu-rhiw* was the Ailurin name for this kind of pattern: day-and-night. He lay there breathing hard, ears back, eyes squeezed shut.

Conscious, Rhiow thought, *but unwilling to accept what's been happening to him. And why wouldn't he be?* For not all People believed in wizards. Many who did believe were suspicious of them, thinking they somehow desired to dominate other People, or else they mocked wizards as unnecessary or ineffective, saying that they'd never seen a wizard do anything useful. *Well, that's the whole point,* Rhiow thought, *to do as much good as possible, as quietly as possible. What the Lone One doesn't have brought to Its attention, It can't ruin.* But the generally dismissive attitude of other People was something you got used to and learned to work around. After all, the situation could have been much worse . . . like that of the *ehhif* wizards. Rhiow often wondered how they got anything done, since hardly any of their kind knew they existed or believed in them at all, and preserving that status quo was part of their mandate.

That little body still lay curled tense; Rhiow caught a flicker of eyelid. *Conscious, all right. We'll have some explaining to do, but it can wait.* "Saash," she said, "would you feel inclined to give him a bit more of a wash? He'll wake."

"Certainly." Saash too had seen that betraying flicker. She curled closer to the youngster and began enthusiastically washing inside one ear. Only the most unconscious cat could resist that for long.

The youngster's eyes flew open, and he sneezed: possibly from the washing, or the smell that still lingered about him. He tried to get up, but Saash put a paw firmly over his midsection and held him down.

"Lemme go!"

"You've had a bad morning, kit," Rhiow said mildly. "I'd lie still awhile."

"Don't call me kit," he said in a yowl meant to be threatening. "I'm a tom!"

Urruah gave him an amused glance. "Oh. Then we can fight now, can we?"

"Uhh . . ." The kit looked up at Urruah—taking in the size of him, the brawny shoulders and huge paws, and, where the tips of the forefangs stuck out so undemurely, the massive teeth. "Uh, maybe I don't feel well enough."

"Well, then," Urruah said, "at your convenience." He sat down and began to wash. Rhiow ducked her head briefly to hide a smile. It was, of course, an excuse that the rituals of tom-combat permitted: most of those rituals were about allowing the other party to escape a fight and still save face.

"You have reason not to feel well," Saash said, pausing in her washing. "About fifty rats took bites out of you. You lie still, and we'll work on that."

"Why should you care?" the kit said bitterly.

"We have our reasons," Rhiow said. "What's your name, youngster?"

His eyes narrowed, a suspicious look, but after a moment he said, "Arhu."

"Where's your dam?" Saash said.

"I don't know." This by itself was nothing unusual. City-living cats might routinely live in-pride, even toms sometimes staying with their mother and littermates; or they might go their own way at adolescence to run with different prides, or stay completely unaligned.

"Are you in *hhau'fih?*" Saash used the word that meant any group relationship in general, rather than *rrai'fih,* a pride-relationship implying possible blood ties.

"No. I walk alone."

Rhiow and Saash exchanged glances. He was very young to be nonaligned, but that happened in the city, too, by accident or design.

"There'll be time for those details later," Rhiow said. "Arhu, how did you come to be down there where we found you, in the tunnel?"

"Someone said I should go there. They laughed at me. They said, *I dare you . . .*" Arhu yawned, both weariness and bravado. "You have to take dares. . . ."

"What was the dare?"

"She said, *Walk down here, and take the adventure that comes to you—*"

Rhiow's eyes went wide. "'She.' What did she say to you first?"

"When?"

"Before that."

A sudden coolness in Arhu's voice, in his eyes. "Nothing."

"*Fwau,*" Rhiow said; a bit roughly, for her, but she thought it necessary. "Something else has to have been said first." She thought she knew what, but she didn't dare lead him. . . .

Arhu stared at her. Rhiow thought she had never seen such a cold and suspicious look from a kit so young. Pity rose up in her; she wanted to cry, *Who hurt you so badly that you've lost your kittenhood entire? What's been done to you?* But Rhiow held her peace. She thought Arhu was going to give her no answer at all: he laid his head down sideways on the concrete again. But he did not close his eyes, staring out instead into the dimness of the garage.

Come on, Rhiow thought. *Tell me.*

"I was in the alley," Arhu said. "The food's good there: they throw stuff out of that grocery store on the other side of it, the Gristede's. But the pride there, Hrau and Eiff and Ihwin and them, they caught me and beat me up again. They said they'd kill me, next time; and I couldn't move afterward, so I just lay where they left me. No one else came for a good while. . . . Then she must have come along while I was hurting. I couldn't see her: I didn't look, it hurt to move. She said, *You could be powerful. The day could come when you could do all kinds of good things, when you could do anything, almost, with the strength I can give you . . . if you lived through the . . . test, the . . . hard time . . ."* Arhu made an uncertain face, as if not sure how to render what had been said to him. "She said, *If you take what I give you, and live through the trouble that follows—and it* will *follow—then you'll be strong forever. Strong for all your lives."* His voice was going matter-of-fact now, like someone repeating a milk-story heard long ago against his dam's belly. "I wanted that. To be strong. I said, *What could happen to me that would be worse than what's already happened? Do it. Give it to me.* She said, *Are you sure? Really sure?* I said, *Yes, hurry up, I want it now.* She said, *Then listen to what I'm going to say to you now, and if you believe in it, then say it yourself, out loud.* And I said it, though some of it was pretty stupid. And it was quiet then."

"Hmm. Where was this alley, exactly?" said Urruah.

"'Ru, shut up. You can check the Gristede's later. Arhu," Rhiow said, "say what she told you to."

A little silence, and then he began to speak, and a shiver went down Rhiow from nose to tail: for the voice was his, but the tone, the meaning and knowledge held in it, was another's. "In Life's name, and for Life's sake, I assert that I will employ the Art that is Its gift in Life's service alone. I will guard growth and ease pain. I will fight to preserve what grows and lives well in its own way: nor will I change any creature unless its growth and life, or that of the system of which it is part, are threatened. To these ends, in the practice of my Art, I will ever put aside fear for courage, and death for life, when it is fit to do so—looking always toward the Heart of Time, where all our sundered times are one, and all our myriad worlds lie whole, in That from Which they proceeded. . . ."

No hesitation, no uncertainty; as if it had been burned into his bones. Rhiow and Urruah and Saash all looked at one another.

"Then what happened?"

He stirred. "After a while, I felt better, and I saw I could get away—none of *them* were there. I walked out into the street. It was quiet. It was late, just the steam coming up out of the street, you know how it does. I walked a long time until I saw inside there, inside those doors. It was all bright and warm, but the doors were shut. I thought, *It's no use, there's no way to get in.* But then—" Now he sounded dreamily mystified, though at a remove. "Then someone— then I heard *how* to get in, if I wanted to. I knew more than I knew a minute before: a way to move, and words to say. And she said, *Do that, and then go in and see what happens. I dare you.* So I did. I said the words, and I walked in through the doors . . . *through* them! . . . and then on under the sky-roof, and on down through those littler doors, down into the dark . . ."

Arhu trailed off, and shivered. "I'm tired," he said, and closed his eyes.

Saash, lying beside him, looked at Rhiow thoughtfully, then started to wash the top of Arhu's head.

Rhiow sat down and let out a breath. *Well,* she said silently to the others, in the form of the Speech that goes privately from mind to mind, *it would appear that the Powers That Be have sent us a brand-new wizard.*

Not a wizard yet, Urruah said, his eyes narrowing. *An overgrown kitten on Ordeal. And since when do the Powers dump a probationer on already-established wizards? The whole point of Ordeal is that you have to survive it alone.*

None of us, Saash said, *ever does it* completely *alone. There's al-*

ways advice, at first: from Them, or other wizards. That's most likely why he's been sent to us. Who else has he got?

That's the problem, Rhiow said. *You* know *there are no accidents in our line of work. This kit was sent to us. He's going to have to stay with us, at least until he's started to take this seriously.*

No way! Urruah hissed.

Rhiow stared at him. *You heard him,* she said. *"I said it, though some of it was pretty stupid." He's not clear yet about the meaning of the Oath he's taken. If he hadn't met us, that would be his problem, and the Powers': he'd live or die according to the conditions of his Ordeal and his use of the wizardry bestowed on him. But we found him—you found him!—and under the conditions of our own Oaths, we can't let him go until he understands what he's brought on himself. After he does, he's the Powers' business: he and They will decide whether he lives and becomes a wizard, or dies. But for the time being, we're a pride in the nurturing sense as well as the professional one . . . and that's how it will be. You have any problems with that?*

She stared until Urruah dropped his eyes, though he growled in his throat as he did it. Rhiow cared not a dropped whisker for his noise. Urruah was still young in his wizardry but also profoundly committed to it, and though he could be lazy, tempery, and self-indulgent, he wouldn't attempt to deny responsibilities he knew were incumbent on him.

"So," Rhiow said aloud. "Saash, you seem to have become queen for the day. . . ."

Saash made a small ironic smile, suggestive of someone enjoying a job more than she had expected. "It's all right, I can manage him. He'll sleep sound for a while. . . . I made one of the small healing wizardries to start the wounds cleaning themselves out."

"Make sure you sleep, too. I'll make rounds in the Terminal in a while; Har'lh wanted the gates double-checked. Urruah, it would help if you held yourself ready while Saash is awake, in case she needs anything."

"All right," he said, and he brightened. "It'll be *ehhif* lunchtime soon, and they'll be throwing lots of nice leftovers in that Dumpster around the corner. Then there's this alley with the Gristede's. Thirty-eighth, you think, Saash? . . ."

Rhiow's whiskers went forward in amusement as she turned to jump down. For the moment, she wasn't sure which was motivating Urruah more: the desire for food or the prospect of a good scrap with a tough pride. "Eat hearty," she said, "and keep your ears unshredded. Call if you need anything: you'll know where to find me."

"Working," Urruah said, in a voice of good-natured pity.

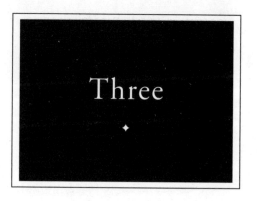

Three

An hour later Rhiow strolled across the concourse again, under a "sky" glowing blue with reflection from brilliant sunshine glancing blindingly from the polished acreage of floor. She had checked the main tunnel gates first, and finished with the Lexington Avenue local gate, near the left-hand end of the platform. All their logs were reporting as they should have, including the malfunctioning gate's log, which now showed eight accesses since its repair. Things were back to normal.

For the time being, Rhiow thought, as she headed one last time toward the upper-level track gates. The problem with worldgates was that they were inherently unstable. Space didn't like to be broached, however briefly: it strove to reseal itself by any means. Standing worldgates needed constant adjustment and maintenance to compensate for changes in local string structure caused by everything from seasonal changes in the Earth's orbit to anomalies in local conditions—solar wind, sunspots, shifts in the ionosphere or the planet's magnetic field. After a while you learned to anticipate the gates' quirks, and you routinely prepared for trouble before the full and new of the Moon, at the solstices, during close cometary passes. And every now and then, like today, the gates would find a new and totally unexpected way to make your life interesting.

Part of Rhiow's mind kept worrying at the problem of the malfunctioning gate's lost logs while she made her way over to the gate that was best for long-range accesses, the one near Track 32. Besides that, though, she was thinking about Arhu and about all those rats. There'd been no reason for so many of them to be down there. What had attracted them? Where had they gotten in from? . . . Probably some passageway to the outside needed to be blocked up. Somewhere under these streets, in the tangle of tunnels and conduits too complex for even one of the People to know, the rats must have found entirely too suitable a breeding-place. As she passed through the door to the platform, Rhiow's mouth quirked with distaste at the taint of dead rat that still lingered in the tunnel air. To her, rats were a symbol of the entropy that wizards spent their lives slowing: a persistent, hungry force, implacable, that might be fought to a standstill, but rarely more, and which would quickly grow past control if ignored. . . .

Halfway down the platform, a slender blond-haired she-*ehhif* in dark skirt and jacket stood waiting, a briefcase under one arm. Rhiow smiled at the sight of her, knowing immediately that she was not waiting for the train—though she would claim to be, should anyone question her. The odds of her being noticed at all in so busy a place were minimal. If she *were* noticed, her manner of leaving wouldn't surprise anyone. She would simply be there one moment, and gone the next, and anyone watching would assume that they'd simply somehow missed seeing her walk away. Even if someone looked at that wizard right at the moment she passed the gate, the nature of wizardry itself would protect her. Almost no nonwizardly creature is willing to see the "impossible," even right under its nose, and shortly it finds all kinds of explanations for the strange thing it saw. This useful tendency meant that many short-duration wizardries didn't have to be concealed at all. Other kinds were simply invisible to most species, like the glowing, shimmering webwork of the gate where it hung face-on to the platform, the surface of the web slowly beginning to pucker inward in the beginning of patency.

Rhiow strolled on down to the she-*ehhif*. At the flicker of motion, seen out the corner of an eye, the woman turned and saw Rhiow coming, and raised her eyebrows. *"Dai stihó,"* the woman said. "Was this one down this morning?"

"For a change, no," Rhiow said. "This will come in phase in about thirty seconds. Got far to go?"

"Not too far, but Penn's a mess right now, and I'm on deadline," the woman said. "Vancouver, and then Kamchatka."

"Oh, the oil spill."

"If we can get authorization from the Powers That Be for the time-slide," the woman said, and smiled slyly, "it'll be, '*What* oil spill?' But we won't know until we check with the A.A. in Vancouver."

"Well, *dai*," Rhiow said, as the woman turned toward the gate, "and good luck with the Advisory. And with Them . . ."

"Thanks. You go well, too," the woman said, stepping forward as the center of the gate's string structure puckered fully inward into metaextension. A human wizard couldn't see the strings without help, but she certainly could see the metaextension's sudden result. Hanging in the air before them was a round (or actually, spherical) window into deep gray shadow with the beginnings of dawn outside it, a sky paling above close-planted pine trees. A park, perhaps, or someone's backyard, there was no telling—a given wizard set the coordinates to suit his mission's needs. Had Rhiow been curious about the location, she could check the gate's log later. For the moment, she watched the young woman step into the predawn dimness, and heard her speak the word that completed the wizardry, releasing the hyperextended strings to pop back out of phase.

The gate-weft persisted in metaextension just a second or so—a safety feature—and then the curvature snapped back flat as if woven of rubber bands, light rippling up and down the resonating strings as the structure collapsed into a configuration with lower energy levels. The spherical intersection with otherwhere vanished: the tapestry of light lay flat against the air again, waiting.

That's working all right, at least, Rhiow thought. Last week, as the wizard had mentioned, *this* had been the gate that had needed adjustment. Three mornings out of five, its web had refused to extend properly, making it impossible to use without constant monitoring.

Saash had had to stand here sidled all during rush hour, running the gate on manual and being jostled by insensible commuters. Her comments later had left Rhiow's ears burning: that soft breathy little voice sounded unusually shocking when it swore.

Rhiow smiled at the memory, and said silently, *Saash?*

A pause, and then, *Here.*

I'm over by your favorite gate. I'm going Downside to make sure none of the others is fouling it.

A slight shudder at the other end. *Better you than me,* Saash said.

How's our foundling?

Sleeping still. Go ahead, Rhi; Urruah's around if anything's needed.

Dai, then.

You too. And be careful . . .

Rhiow let the link between them lapse, and watched the gate, letting its weft steady and the colors pale from their use-excited state. Then she reached into the weave with a paw and plucked at one specific string, a control structure. The whole weave of the gate resonated with light and power as it ran a brief diagnostic on its own fabric. Then it displayed a smaller glowing pattern, a "tree" structure—many-branched at the top, narrowing to a single "trunk" at the bottom.

With a single claw, Rhiow snagged the trunk line. The string blazed, querying her identity: the access for which Rhiow was asking was restricted.

Rhiow hung on to the string. The power blazing in it ran up through claw and paw and sizzled along her nerves, hunting for her access "authorization" from the Powers That Be. It found that, along with Rhiow's memory of her own acceptance of the Oath, woven together into the tapestry of life-fire and thought-fire that was how the wizardry perceived her brain. Satisfied, the wizardry rebounded, ran burning out of her body and down the weft of the gate. The tapestry rippled with light; the string structure puckered inward. The sphere in the air snapped open.

Warm green shadow shading down to a rich brown, slanting golden light leaning through the dimness in shafts . . . And that smell. Rhiow did not linger but leapt through, and waved the gate closed behind her with a flirt of her tail.

She landed in loam, silent, springy, deep. Rhiow came down soundlessly but hard, as always forgetting the change until it actually came upon her—and then, within a breath's time, she was wondering how she'd ever borne the way she'd been until a second ago, bound into the body of one of the People, not even a very big body as the People reckoned such things. Rhiow lifted the paw that had plucked the gate-string out, found it ten times bigger, the claw an inch-long talon; looked down at the print that paw had left in the soft loam, and found it as wide across as an *ehhif*'s hand was long. The usual unbelieving look over her shoulder reassured her about her color: she was still glossy black. She would have found it difficult to handle if that had changed as well.

Rhiow stood surrounded by many brown pillar-trunks of shaggy-barked trees, limbless this far down: their first branches began far above her head, holding out thin-needled bunches of fronds like an *ehhif*'s hands with fingers spread. No sky could be seen through the overlapping ceiling of them, though here and there, ahead and to the sides, some gap of growth let the sun come slanting through to pool, tawny-golden, on the needle-carpeted floor. Rhiow padded along toward where more light came slipping among trunks more sparsely set, a bluer, cooler radiance.

A few minutes later she stepped out from among the trees onto a mossy stone ledge lifted up above the world; she looked downward and outward, breathing deep. The breeze stirring among those trees and rustling their tops behind her had nothing to do with New York air: it was a wind from the morning of the world, bearing nothing but the faint clean smell of salt. In a sky of cloudless, burning blue, the sun swung low to her right, passing toward evening from afternoon; westward, low over the endless green hills, its light burnished everything gold.

It was summer here. It was always summer here. The sun lay warm on her pelt, a lovely basking heat. The wind was warm and always bore that salt tang from the glimmering golden-bronze expanse of ocean just to the east. The whole view, excepting the occasional cliff-face or ledge like the one on which Rhiow stood, was covered with the lush green of subtropical forest. Here was the world as it had been before magnetic fields and poles and climates had shifted. Whether it was actually the same world, the direct ancestor-in-time-line of Rhiow's own, or an alternate universe more centrally placed in the scheme of things, Rhiow wasn't sure—and she didn't think anyone else was, either. It didn't seem to make much difference. What mattered was that her own world was grounded in this one, based on it. This was a world more single and simple, the lands not yet fragmented: everything one warm, green blanket of mingled forest and grassland, from sea to sea. The wind breathed softly in the trees, and there was no other sound until from a great distance came a low coughing roar: one of her Kindred, the great cats of the ancient world, speaking his name, or the name of his prey, to the wind.

At the sound, Rhiow shivered briefly, and then smiled at herself. The People were descended from the dire-cats and sabertooths who roamed these forests—or *had* descended from them, willingly, giving up size and power for other gifts. Either way, when one of the People returned to this place, the size of the cat's body once again matched the size of its soul, reflecting the stature and power both had held in the ancient days. Reflex might make Rhiow worry at the thought of meeting one of those great ones, but for the moment, she was at least as great.

Rhiow gazed down from that high place. Perhaps half a mile below and a mile eastward, the River plunged down in a torrent that she thought must haunt the dreams of the lesser streams of her day, trickles like the Mississippi and the Yangtze. In her own time and world, this would become the Hudson, old, wide, and tame. But now it leapt in a roaring half-mile-wide wall of water from the deep-cut edge of what would someday be the Continental Shelf, falling a mile and a half sheer to smash deafening into its first shattered cauldron-pools, and then tumbled, a lakeful every second, on down the crags and shelves of its growing canyon, into the clouded sea. The spray of the water's impact at such velocity, spread so wide, made a permanent rainbow as wide as Manhattan Island would be someday.

And the island— Rhiow looked behind her, northward: looked up. Lands would change in times to come. Continents would drift apart or be torn asunder. Countries would be raised up, thrown down, drowned, or buried. But through the geological ages, one mountain of this coastland would persist. The indomitable foundation of it, a solid block of basalt some ten miles square, would be fragmented by earthquakes, half-sunk with the settling of what would become North America; the land around it would be raised hundreds of feet by glacier-dumped silt and stone, and the water of the massive, melted icecaps would nearly submerge what remained, coming right up to what endured of its ancient, battered, flattened peak. But that had not happened yet. And even when it did, New Yorkers would remember—not knowing the memory's source—and call the place the Rock.

Rhiow looked up. Far higher than she could see, standing so close to its base, the Mountain reared up to high heaven. There was no judging its height. Its slopes, towering above and to either side like a wall built against the northern sky, were clothed in forest. The trees were mighty pale-barked pillars, primeval seed-parents of the darker, younger trees among which the gate had left her, some of the parent-trees now hundreds of feet in circumference. In rank after rank they speared upward, diminishing, finally becoming hidden among their own branches, merely a green cloud against the farthest heights. Amid the cloud, though, where the great peak began (even from this aspect) to narrow, one slender arrowy shape, distinct even at this distance, speared higher than all the others: one tree, *the* Tree—the most ancient of them, and, legend said, the first.

Rhiow gazed at it, mute with awe. Maybe someday she would have leisure to climb the Mountain and look up into those branches, to sit in the shadow of the Tree and listen to the voices that spoke, so legend said, from that immense green silence. Not now: perhaps not in this life: perhaps not until after the ninth one, if luck and her fate led her that far. It was dangerous enough for her just to be here—as dangerous as it was for any being to remain, for a prolonged period, out of its own time or space.

Meantime, though, she might briefly enjoy the sight of the true and ancient Manhattan, the living reality of which the steel- and concrete-clad island was a shadowy and mechanistic restatement. *Ehhif* built "skyscrapers" half in ambition, half in longing—uncertain why the ambition never satisfied them no matter how they achieved it, and not remembering what they longed for. They had been latecomers, the *ehhif:* they had not been here very long before the world changed, and this warm, still wilderness went chill and cruel. It was the Lone One's fault, of course. That fact the *ehhif* dimly remembered in their own legends, just as they vaguely remembered the Tree, and an ancient choice ill-made, and the sorrow of something irrevocably lost.

Rhiow sighed, and turned her back on the lulling vista of the Old World, padding back among the trees. Better get on with what she had come here to do, before being here too long did her harm.

Rhiow made her way silently through the dimness beneath the trees toward the great cliff-outcroppings on this side of the Mountain's foot. Thinking of the Lone One brought Arhu to mind again. *No question who he heard speaking to him,* Rhiow thought, *the first time, at least.* She knew well enough the voice that had awakened her this morning, and which spoke to all feline wizards on behalf of the Powers That Be: the wisdom that first whispered in your ear to offer you the Art and the promise of your Ordeal, and then, assuming you survived, taught you the details of wizardry from day to day and passed on your assignments. Tradition said the one Who actually spoke was Iau's daughter, Hrau'f the Silent, Whose task was to order creation, making rules and setting them in place. The tradition seemed likely enough to Rhiow: the voice you "heard" had a she-ish sense about it and a tinge of humor that agreed with the old stories' accounts of Hrau'f's quiet delight in bringing order from chaos.

But the question remained: whose voice had spoken second? For Queen Iau had other daughters. There was another "she" involved with wizardry, one whose methods were subtle, whose intentions were ambivalent—and rarely good for the wizard. . . .

Rhiow came to the bottom of the scree-slope that ran up to the base of the cliff-face. Here the trees bore the scars of old stonefalls: boulders lay among the pine needles, and the brown soft carpet grew thinner toward the sheer bare cliff. At the top of the scree-slope, jagged, silent, and dark, yawned the entrance to the caves.

She padded up the stones, paused on the flat rubble-strewn slab that served for a threshold, and gazed in. It was not totally dark inside, not this near to the opening—and not where the master anchor-structures for the New York gates all hung, a blazing complex of shifting, rippling webs and wefts, burning in the still, cool air of the outer cave.

Rhiow sat down and just looked at them, as she always did when she made this trip. Learning the way these patterns looked had been one of her first tasks as a young wizard. Her Ordeal had revealed that she had an aptitude for this kind of work, and afterward the Powers had assigned Rhiow to old Ffairh to develop her talent. She remembered sitting here with him for the first time, her haunches shifting with impatience, both with delight at her splendidly big new body, and with the desire to get up and do something about the patterns that hung before her, singing and streaming with power. Or rather, to do something *with* them.

Ffairh had stared at her, eyes gleaming, and Rhiow had stopped her fidgeting and sat very still under his regard. Ffairh had been nothing much to look at in their homeworld—a scruffy black-and-white tom without even the rough distinction of scars, crooked in the hind leg and tail from where the cab hit him. Here, though, where the soul ruled the body, Ffairh stood nearly five feet high at the shaggy, brindled shoulder, and the sabers of his fangs were nearly as long as Rhiow's whole body back home. The weight and majesty of his presence was immense, and the amused annoyance in those amber eyes, which down by Track 116 had seemed merely funny, now took on a more dangerous quality.

"Don't be so quick to want to tamper," Ffairh had said. "No one exploring this world has been able to find a time when these wizardries *weren't* here . . . and exocausal spell-workings like that always mean the Powers are involved. No one knows for sure which One wove them. Aaurh herself, maybe: they're strong enough for it. They're old and strong enough to be a little alive. They have to be, to take care of themselves and protect themselves from misuse: for wizards can't watch them all the time. *Most* of the time, though . . . and you'll find that's what you'll spend these next few lives doing, unless They retire you, or you slip up. . . ."

He had been right about that, as about most things. Ffairh was two years gone now: where, Rhiow had no idea. He had let his sixth life go peacefully, in extreme old age, and if he'd since come back, Rhiow had yet to meet him. But he had refused to go before completely training his replacement. Now, as she sat and examined the gate-wefts for abnormalities, Rhiow smiled at the memory of her head ringing from yet another of the old curmudgeon's ferocious cuffs and Ffairh's often-repeated shout, "Will you hurry up and learn this stuff so I can *die?!*"

She had learned. She came here more often than need strictly required, though not so often for repeated exposure to endanger her: about that issue, Rhiow was most scrupulous. She was just as scrupulous, though, about knowing the gates well, and knowing this part of them—the root of the installation—best of all. The wizardries that manifested as the string structures of the four Grand Central gates were only extensions: branches, as it were, of the Tree. The "trunk" of the spells, the master control structure for each of them, was here, in the Old World—the upper levels of the true Downside, of which Grand Central's and Penn's "downsides" were mere sketchy restatements. The "roots" of the spell structure, of course, went farther down . . . much farther, into the endless, tangled caverns, down to the roots of the Mountain, the heart of this world. But that wasn't somewhere Rhiow would go unless the Powers That Be specifically ordered it. They never had, during her management of these gates, and Rhiow hoped they never would. Ffairh had gone once and had described that intervention to her, in a quiet, dry fifteen-minute monologue that had given her nightmares for weeks.

But there was no need to consider any action so radical at the moment. Rhiow spent a good while looking over the interrelationships of the Grand Central gates with the Penn complex, making sure there were no accidental overlaps or frayings of the master patterns, which needed to remain discrete. It happened sometimes that some shift in natural forces—a meteor strike, a solar microflare—would so disrupt "normal" space that the spell patterns in it would be disrupted, too, jumping loose from the structures that held them. Then the abnormally released forces would "backlash" down the connection to the master structures here in the Old World, causing a string to pop loose and foul some other pattern. There was no sign of that, though. The four Grand Central patterns and the smaller, more tightly arrayed Penn wefts were showing good separation.

Rhiow got up and padded to the shifting, shimmering weft of the third of the Grand Central gates, the north-sider at Track 26. A long while she scrutinized it, watching the interplay of forces, the colors shimmering in and out. Everything looked fine.

Truth was more than looks, though. Rhiow took a few moments to prepare herself, then reached out a paw, as she had done in Grand Central, extended a claw, and hooked it into the wizardry's interrogation weave.

The question, as always, was who was interrogating whom. How you put life into a wizardry, a bodiless thing made of words and intent, Rhiow wasn't sure, but if Aaurh had indeed set the gates here, that was explanation enough. She had not invented life, but she was the Power that had implemented it, and the stories said that, one way or another, life got into most of what she did. The *gate* certainly thought it was alive. While Rhiow quested down its structure, assessing it from inside as she might have assessed her own body for hurt or trouble, the gate felt it had the right to do the same with her. It was unnerving, to feel something unfeline, and older than your world, come sliding down your nerves and through your brain, rummaging through your memories and testing your reflexes. Quite cool, it was, quite matter-of-fact, but disturbed.

Disturbed. So was Rhiow when the gate was finished with her, and she unhooked her claw from the blazing, softly humming weft. Panting and blinking, she stood there a moment with streaked and blurring afterimages burning in her eyes: the all-pervasive tangle of strings and energies that was the way the gate perceived the world all the time. To the gate, proper visual images of concrete physical structures were alien. Therefore there was no image or picture of whoever had come and—interfered with it—

Rhiow started to get normal vision back again. Still troubled by both her contact with the gate and by what it had perceived, she sat down and began to wash her face, trying to sort out the gate's perceptions and make sense of them.

Something had interfered. Some*one*. The gate did not deal in names and had no pictures: there was merely a sense of some presence, a personality, interposing itself between one group of words of control and another, breaking a pattern. Associated with that impression was a sense that the interposition was no accident: it was *meant*. But for what purpose, by whom, there was no indication.

And when that break in the pattern was made, something else had thrust through. The gate held no record of what that thing or force might have been: the energy-strands holding the gate's logs had been unraveled and restrung. They now lay bright and straight in the weave, completely devoid of data. The initial break was sealed over by the intervention Rhiow and the team had done this morning. But the gate, in its way, was as distraught as anyone might be to wake up and find himself missing a day of his life.

Rhiow was upset, too. *What came through . . . ?* she thought, gazing at the gate-weft. She thought of the dry chill flowing from the jagged, empty tear in the air they'd found waiting for them that morning. *A void place . . .* There were enough of those, away in the outer fringes of being, worlds where life had never "taken." Other forces moving among the worlds liked such places. They used them to hide while preparing attacks against what they hated: the worlds full of light and life, closer to the Heart of things . . .

Rhiow shuddered. She needed advice. Specifically, she needed to talk to Carl, and to her local Senior, Ehef, when she had rested and sorted her thoughts out. But rest would have to come first.

Rhiow stood up and once more slipped a paw into the gate-weft, watching the light ripple away from where she felt around for its control structures. *You're all right now,* she said to the gate. *Don't worry; we'll find out what happened.*

From the gate came a sense of uncertainty, but also of willingness to be convinced. Rhiow smiled, then looked wistfully at the huge, glossy, taloned paw thrust into the webwork. It would be delightful to stay here longer—to slip down into those ancient forests and hunt real game, something nobler and more satisfying to the soul than mice: to run free in the glades and endless grasslands of a place where the word "concrete" had no meaning, to hold your head up and snuff air that tasted new-made because it *was* . . .

Her claw found the string that managed the gate's custom access routines. The gate's identification query sizzled down her nerves.

Rhiow held still and let it complete the identification, and when it was done, paused. *Just for a while . . . it wouldn't hurt . . .*

Rhiow sighed, plucked the string toward her, softly recited in the Speech the spatial and temporal coordinates she wanted, and let the string loose.

The whole weft-structure sang and blazed. Before her, the sphere of intersection with her own world snapped into being. A circular-seeming window into gray stone, gray concrete, a long view over jagged pallid towers to a sky smoggy gray below and smoggy blue above, and the sun struggling to shine through it: steam smells, chemical smells, *houff*-droppings, car exhaust . . .

Rhiow looked over her shoulder, out of the cave, into the green light with its promise of gold beyond . . . then leapt into the circle and through, down onto the gravel of the rooftop next to her building. Behind her, with a clap of sound that any *ehhif* would mistake for a car backfiring, the gate snapped shut. Rhiow came down lightly, so lightly she almost felt herself not to be there at all. She glanced at her forepaw again. It seemed unreal for it to be so small. But *this* was reality.

Such as it was . . .

When she got back up to the apartment's terrace again, the glass terrace doors were open, and Hhuha and Iaehh were having breakfast at the little table near it. The whole place smelled deliciously of bacon. "Well, look who's here!" Iaehh said. "Just in time for brunch."

"She's been out enjoying this pretty day," Hhuha said, stroking Rhiow as she came past her chair. "It's so nice and sunny out. Mike, you should feel her, she's so warm. . . ."

Rhiow smiled wryly. Iaehh chuckled. "No accidents: this cat's timing is perfect. I know what *she* wants."

"Sleep, mostly," Rhiow said, sitting down wearily and watching him fish around on his plate for something to give her. "And if you'd had the morning I had, you'd want some, too. These four-hour shifts, they're deadly."

"All right, all right, be patient," Iaehh said, and reached Rhiow down a piece of bacon. "Here."

Rhiow took it gladly enough; she just wished she wasn't falling asleep on her feet. "You spoil that cat," Hhuha said, getting up and going over to the *ffrihh*. "*I* know what she wants. She wants more of that tuna. You should have seen her dive into it this morning! We've got to get some more of that."

"Oh Queen Iau," Rhiow muttered around the mouthful, "give me strength." She cocked an eye up at Iaehh. "And some more of that before I go have a nap . . ."

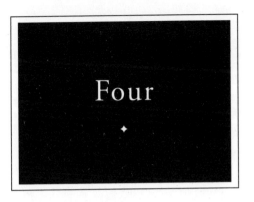

Four

◆

"The hour's main news stories, from National Public Radio: I'm Bob Edwards. . . . The South Kamchatka oil spill has begun to disperse after Tropical Storm Bertram shifted course northeastward in the early morning hours, Pacific time, causing near-record swells between the Bay of Kronockji and Shumshu Island at the southern end of Russia's Kamchatka Peninsula. The spill from the crippled Japanese tanker *Amaterasu Maru* threatened the economically important fishing grounds off the disputed Kurile Islands, and had significantly increased tensions between Russia and Japan at a time when the disposition of the Kuriles, claimed by Japan but occupied by the Soviet Union since the end of World War Two, had been thought by diplomatic sources to be nearing resolution. —President Yeltsin's special envoy Anatoly Krischov has returned to Moscow from Teheran after talks aimed at resolving the escalating border crisis in the Atrek valley between Iran and Turkmenistan, where rebel tribesmen have clashed with both Iranian and Russian government forces for the fourth day in . . ."

Rhiow rolled over on her back, stretched all her legs in the air, and yawned, blinking in the late afternoon light. The sound of the *ra'hio* being turned on had awakened her. *A long day,* she thought. *I don't usually oversleep like this . . .*

She twisted her head around so that she was looking at the living room upside down. A soft rustling of papers had told Rhiow even before her eyes were open that Hhuha had just sat back down at the other end of the couch. Iaehh was nowhere to be seen; Rhiow's ears told her that he was not in the sleeping room, or the room where he and Hhuha bathed and did their *hiouh.* So he was out running, and could be gone for as little as a few minutes or as long as several hours.

Rhiow knew in a general way that Iaehh was doing this to stay healthy, but sometimes she thought he overdid it, and Hhuha thought so, too; depending on her mood, she either teased or scolded him about it. "You're really increasing your chances of getting hit by a truck one of these days," she would say, either laughing or frowning, and Iaehh would retort, "Better that than increasing my chances of getting hit by a massive cardiac, like Dad, and Uncle Robbie, and . . ." Then they would box each other's ears verbally for a while, and end up stroking each other for a while after that. Really, they were very much like People sometimes.

Rhiow yawned again, looking upside down at Hhuha. Hhuha glanced over at her and said, "You slept a long time, puss." She reached over and stroked her.

Rhiow grabbed Hhuha's hand, gave it a quick lick, then let it go and started washing before going for her breakfast. *So,* Rhiow thought while the news headlines finished, *there's still an oil spill.* This by itself didn't surprise her. Timeslides, like any wizardry meant to alter the natural flow and unfolding of time, were rarely sanctioned when other options were available. Probably the Area Advisory for the Pacific Region had noticed the availability of a handy alternative instrumentality: natural, "transparent" in terms of being unlikely to arouse *ehhif* suspicions, and fairly easily influenced—of all the languages that humans use, only the wizardly Speech has no equivalent idiom for "everyone talks about the weather, but no one does anything about it."

Oh well, Rhiow thought. *One less thing to worry about.* She spent a couple more minutes putting her back fur and tail in order, then got down off the couch, stretched fore and aft, and strolled over to the food dish. Halfway across the room, her nose told her it was that tuna stuff again, but she was too hungry to argue the point.

Wouldn't I just love to walk over to you, she thought about halfway down the bowl, looking over her shoulder at Hhuha, *and say to you, loud and clear, "I'd think that last raise would let you spend at least sixty cents a can." But rules are rules . . .*

Rhiow had a long drink, then strolled back to jump up on the couch and have a proper wash this time. She had finished with her head and ears when Hhuha got up, went to the dining room, and came back with still more papers. Rhiow looked at them with distaste.

As Hhuha sighed and put the new load down on the couch, Rhiow got up, stretched again, and carefully sat herself down on the papers; then she put her left rear leg up past her left ear and began to wash her back end. It was body language that even humans seemed sometimes to understand.

Rhiow was pretty sure that Hhuha understood it, but right now she just breathed out wearily. She picked Rhiow up off the pile and put her on the couch next to it, saying, "Oh, come on, you, why do you always have to sit on my paperwork?"

"I'm sitting on it because you hate it," Rhiow said. She sat down on it again, then hunkered down and began kneading her claws into the paperwork, punching holes in the top sheet and wrinkling it and all the others under it.

"Hey, don't do that, I need those!"

"No, you don't. They make you crazy. You shouldn't do this stuff on the weekend: it's bad enough that they make you do it all day during the week." Rhiow rolled over off the paper-pile, grabbing some of the papers as she went, and throwing them in the air.

"Oh, kitty, don't!" Hhuha began picking the papers up. "Not that I wouldn't like to myself," she added under her breath.

"See? And why you should pay attention to that stuff when *I'm* here, I can't understand," Rhiow muttered, as Hhuha picked her up and put her in her lap. "See, isn't that better? You don't need this junk. You need a cat."

"Talk talk, chatter chatter," Hhuha said under her breath, straightening the paperwork out. "Probably you're trying to tell me I shouldn't bring my work home. Or more likely it's something about cat food."

"Yes, now that you mention—" Rhiow made a last swipe at one piece of the paperwork as it went past her nose in Hhuha's hand. "Hey, watch those claws," Hhuha said.

"I would never scratch you, you know that," Rhiow said, settling. "Unless you got slow. Put that stuff *down.* . . ."

Hhuha started rubbing behind Rhiow's ears, and Rhiow went unfocused for a little while, purring. There were People, she knew, who saw the whole business of "having" an *ehhif* as being, at best, old-fashioned—at worst, very politically incorrect. The two species really had no common ground, some People said. They claimed that there could be no real relationships between carnivores and omnivores, predators and hunter-gatherers: only cohabitation of a crude and finally unsatisfactory kind. Cats who held this opinion usually would go on at great length about the imprisonment of People against their will, and the necessity to free them from their captivity if at all possible—or, at the very least, to raise their consciousness about it so that, no matter how pleasant the environment, no matter how tasty the food and how "kind" the treatment, they would never forget that they were prisoners, and never forget their own identity as a People presently oppressed, but who someday would be free.

When all ehhif *civilization falls, maybe,* Rhiow thought, with a dry look. *Make every* ehhif *in the city vanish, right this second, and turn every cat in Manhattan loose: how many of them will be alive in three weeks? Cry "freedom!"—and then try to find something to eat when all you know about is Friskies Buffet.*

She made a small face, then, at her own irony. Maybe it would be better if all cats lived free in the wild, out of buildings, out of *ehhif* influence; maybe it would be better if that influence had never come about in the first place. But the world was the way that it was, and such things weren't going to be happening any time soon. The truth remained that *ehhif* kept People and that a lot of People liked it . . . and she was one.

That's the problem, of course, she thought. *We're embarrassed to admit enjoying interdependence. Too many of us have bought into the idea that we're somehow "independent" in our environment to start with. As if we can stop eating or breathing any time we want . . .*

She sighed and stretched again while Hhuha paused in her scratching and started going through her papers once more. *Anyway, what's the point,* Rhiow thought, *in making sure People are so very aware that they're oppressed, when for most of them there's nothing they can* do *about it? And in many cases, when they truly don't want to do anything, the awareness does nothing but make them feel guilty . . . thus making them more like* ehhif *than anything else that could have been done to them. That outwardly imposed awareness satisfies no one but the "activist" People who impose it. "I suffer, therefore you should too . . ."*

Granted, Rhiow's own position was a privileged one and made holding such a viewpoint easy. All languages are subsets of the Speech, and a wizard, by definition at least conversant with the Speech if not fluent in it, is able to understand anything that can speak (and many things that can't). Rhiow's life with her *ehhif* was certainly made simpler by the fact that she could clearly understand what they were saying. Unfortunately, most cats couldn't do the same, which tended to create a fair amount of friction.

Not that matters were perfect for her either. Rhiow found, to her annoyance, that she had slowly started becoming bilingual in Human and Ailurin. She kept finding herself thinking in slang-*ehhif* terms like *ra'hio* and *o'hra:* poor usage at best. Her dam, who had always been so carefully spoken, would have been shocked.

Rhi? said Saash inside her.

I'm awake, Rhiow said silently.

Took you long enough, Saash said. *Believe me, when this is over, I've got a lot of sleep to make up.*

Oh? Rhiow said.

Our youngster, Saash said dryly, *has been awake and lively for a good while now. It's been exciting trying to keep him in here, and I don't think I'll be able to do it much longer. I had to teach him to sidle to distract him even this long—*

You mean you had to try *to teach him to sidle,* Rhiow said.

I mean he's been sidling for the last two hours, said Saash.

Rhiow blinked at that. Nearly all wizardly cats had an aptitude for sidling, but most took at least a week to learn it; many took months.

Sweet Queen about us, Rhiow thought, *what* have *the Powers sent us? Besides trouble . . .*

All right, Rhiow said to Saash. *I'll be along in half an hour or so. Where's Urruah?*

He's having a break, Saash said. *I sent him off early. . . . I thought maybe there was going to be a murder.*

Oh joy, Rhiow thought. To Saash, she said, *Did he go off to the park? He mentioned the other day that some big tom thing would be going on over there.*

He mentioned it to me too, Saash said. *Not that I understood one word in five of what he was saying: it got technical. He left in a hurry, anyway, and I didn't want to try to keep him.*

I just bet, Rhiow thought. When Urruah was in one of those moods, it was more than your ears were worth to try to slow him down. *All right. Hold the den; I'll be along.*

Somewhat regretfully—for quiet times like this seemed to be getting rarer and rarer these days—Rhiow got down out of Hhuha's lap, sat down on the floor and finished her wash, then went out to the terrace to use the *hiouh*-box.

Afterward, she made her way down from the terrace to the top of the nearby building and did her meditation—not facing east for once, but westward. The smog had been bad today; Rhiow was glad she had been inside with the air-conditioning. But now that the day was cooling, a slight offshore breeze had sprung up, and the ozone level was dropping, so that you could at least breathe without your chest feeling tight. And—probably the only positive aspect to such a day— the Sun was going down in a blaze of unaccustomed splendor, its disk bloated to half again its proper size and blunted to a beaten-copper radiance by the thick warm air. Down the westward-reaching street, windows flashed the orange-gold light back in fragments; to either side of Rhiow, and behind her, skyscraper-glass glowed and in the heat-haze almost seemed to run, glazed red or gold or molten smoky amber by the westering light.

Rhiow tucked herself down and considered the disk of fire as it sank toward the Palisades, gilding the waters of the Hudson. As a wizard, she knew quite well that what she saw was Earth's nearest star, a glimpse of the fusion that was stepchild to the power that started this universe running. *Rhoua* was what People called it. The word was a metonymy: Rhoua was a name of Queen Iau, of the One, in Her aspect as beginner and ender of physical life. Once cats had understood the Sun only in the abstract, as life's kindler. It had taken a while for them to grasp the concept of the Sun as just one more star among many, but when they did, they still kept the old nickname.

The older name for the Sun had been *Rhoua'i'th,* Rhoua's Eye: the only one of Her eyes that the world saw, or would see, at least for a good while yet. That one open Eye saw thoughts, saw hearts, knew the realities beneath external seemings. The other Eye saw those and everything else as well; but no one saw *it.* It would not open until matter was needed no more, and in its opening, all solid things would fade like sleep from an opening eye. A blink or two, and everything that still existed would be revealed in true form, perhaps final form— though that was uncertain, for the gathered knowledge of matters wizardly, which cat-wizards called *The Gaze of Rhoua's Eye,* said little about time after the Last Time or about how existence would go after Existence, in terms of matter, passed its sell-by date. But there was little need to worry about it just yet while Rhoua still winked. The day the wink turned to a two-eyed gaze . . . *then* would be the time to be concerned.

. . . *For my own part,* Rhiow told the fading day, *I know my job; my commission comes from Those Who* Are. *Some I will meet today who think that day is blind and that night lies with its eyes closed; that the Gaze doesn't see them, or doesn't care. Their certainty of blindness, though, need not mean anything to me. My paw raised is Their paw on the neck of the Serpent, now and always . . .*

Rhiow finished her meditation and stood, stretching herself thoroughly and giving one last look to that great burning disk as the apartment buildings of the western Hudson shore began to rear black against it. Having, like many other wizards, done her share of off-planet work, Rhiow found it difficult to think of Rhoua's Eye as anything less than the fiery heart of the solar system. It still amused her, sometimes, that when the People had found out about this, they had had a lot of trouble explaining the concept to the *ehhif.* Some of the earlier paintings in the Metropolitan Museum of Art were potentially rather embarrassing, or at best amusing, in this regard—images of big eyes and sun-disks teetering precariously on top of cat-headed people, all hilariously eloquent of *ehhif* confusion, even in those days when *ehhif* language was much closer to Hauhai, and understanding should have been at least possible if not easy.

Rhiow made her way down to the street, sidled before she passed the iron door between her and the sidewalk, and then slipped under, heading west for Central Park.

She was surprised to meet Urruah halfway, making his way along East Sixty-eighth Street through the softly falling twilight, with a slightly dejected air. He slipped into the doorway of a brownstone and sat down, looking absently across the street at the open kitchen door of a Chinese restaurant. Clouds of fluorescent-lit steam and good smells were coming out of it, along with the sounds of a lot of shouting and the frantic stirring of woks.

"I would have thought you'd still be in the park," Rhiow said, sitting down beside him.

"The rehearsal's been put off until tomorrow," Urruah said. "One of the toms is off his song."

Rhiow made an oh-really expression. Urruah, like most toms, had a more or less constant fascination with song. She had originally been completely unable to understand why a tom should be interested in the mating noises that another species made: still less when the other species was not making these noises as part of mating, but because it was *thinking* about mating, *in the abstract*. But Urruah had gone on to explain that this particular kind of *ehhif* singing, called *o'hra*, was not simply about sex, but was also some kind of storytelling. That had made Rhiow feel somewhat better about it all, for storytelling was another matter. Dams sang stories to their kits, grown People purred them to one another—gossip and myth, history and legend: no one simply *spoke* the past. It was rude. The thought that *ehhif* did the same in song made Rhiow feel oddly closer to them, and made her feel less like Urruah was doing something culturally, if not morally, perverse.

"So," Rhiow said, "what will they do now?"

"They'll keep building that big structure down at the end of the Great Lawn; that wasn't going to be finished until tonight anyway. To-morrow they'll do the sound tests and the rest of the rehearsal. The other two toms are fine, so there shouldn't be any more delays."

Rhiow washed an ear briefly. "All right," she said. "We're going to have to take Arhu out and show him our beat . . . not that I particularly care to be doing that so soon, but he already knows how to sidle—"

"Whose good idea was *that?*" Urruah said, narrowing his eyes in annoyance.

"Mine," Rhiow said, "since you ask. Come on, Urruah! He would have had to learn eventually anyway . . . and it turns out he's a quick study. That may save his life, or, if he dies on Ordeal, who knows, it may make the difference between him getting his job done and not getting it done. Which is what counts, isn't it?"

"Humf," Urruah said, and looked across the street again at the restaurant. "Chicken . . ."

"Never mind the chicken. I want you on-site with him for this first evening at least, and as many of the next few evenings as possible. He needs a good male role model so that we can start getting him in shape for whatever's going to happen to him." She gave him an ap-proving look. "I just want you to know that I think you're handling all this very well."

"I *am* a professional," Urruah said, "even if he does make my teeth itch. . . . But something else is on my mind, not just o'hra, as you doubtless believe. That oil spill intervention you mentioned? I heard that they got the authorization for the timeslide they wanted."

Rhiow blinked at that. "Really? Then why is the spill still on the news? That whole timeline should have 'healed over' by now . . . excised it-self. We're well past the 'uncertainty period' for such a small change."

"Something went wrong with it."

Rhiow put her whiskers back in concern. Timeslides were expen-sive wizardries, but also fairly simple and straightforward ones: hear-ing that something had "gone wrong" with a timeslide was like hearing that something had gone wrong with gravity. "Where did you hear about that?"

"Rahiw told me; he heard it from Ehef—he saw him this morning."

The source was certainly reliable. "Well, the situation's not a total loss anyway," Rhiow said. "That tropical storm sure 'changed course.' You could tell *that* was an intervention with your whiskers cut off."

"Well, of course. But it wasn't the intended one. And a failed time-slide . . ." Urruah's tail lashed. "Pretty weird, if you ask me."

"Probably some local problem," Rhiow said. "Sunspots, for all I know: we're near the eleven-year maximum. If I talk to Har'lh again this week, I'll ask him about it."

"Sunspots," Urruah said, as if not at all convinced. But he got up, stretched, and the two of them headed back down East Sixty-eighth together.

They wove their way along the sidewalk, taking care to avoid the hurrying pedestrians. As they paused at the corner of Sixty-eighth and Lex, Urruah said, "There he is."

"Where?"

"The billboard."

Rhiow tucked herself well in from the corner, right against the wall of the dry cleaner's there, to look at the billboard on the building across the street. There was a *picture* on it—one of those flat representations that *ehhif* used—and some words. Rhiow looked at those first, deciphering them; though the Speech gave her understanding of the words, sometimes the letterings that *ehhif* used could slow you down. "'The—three—' What's a 'tenor'?"

"It's a kind of voice. *Fvais,* we would say; a little on the high side, but not the highest."

Rhiow turned her attention to the *picture* and squinted at it for a good while; there was a trick to seeing these flat representations that *ehhif* used—you had to look at them just right. When she finally thought she had grasped the meaning of what she saw, she said to Urruah, "So after they sing, are they going to fight?" The word she used was *sth'hruiss,* suggesting the kind of physical altercation that often broke out when territory or multiple females were at issue.

"No, it's just *hrui't:* voices only, no claws. They do it everywhere they go."

That made Rhiow stare, and then shake her head till her ears rattled. "Are they a pride? A pride of *males?* What a weird idea."

Urruah shook his head. "I don't know if I understand it myself," he said. "I think *ehhif* manage that kind of thing differently . . . but don't ask me for details."

Rhiow was determined not to. "Which one's your fellow, then? The one who went off voice."

"The one in the middle."

"He's awfully big for an *ehhif,* isn't he?"

"Very," Urruah had said with satisfaction and (Rhiow thought) a touch of envy. "He must have won hundreds of fights. Probably a *tremendous* success with the shes."

Rhiow thought that it didn't look like the kind of "big" that won fights. She had seen pictures of the *ehhif*-toms who fought for audiences over at Madison Square Garden, and they seemed to carry a lot less weight than this *ehhif.* However, she supposed you couldn't always judge by sight. This one might be better with the claws and teeth than he looked.

"So all these *ehhif* are coming to listen to him in, what is it, three nights from now? Is he that good?"

"He is *magnificently* loud," said Urruah, his voice nearly reverent. "You can hear him for miles on a still night, even without artificial aids."

Rhiow put her whiskers forward, impressed almost against her will. "If I'm free tomorrow," she said, "maybe I'll go with you to have a look at this rehearsal."

"Oh, Rhiow, you'll love it!" They crossed the street and walked back toward the garage where Saash stayed, and Urruah started telling Rhiow all about *ah'rias* and *ssoh'phra-ohs* and endless other specialized terms and details, and Dam knew what all else, until Rhiow simply began saying "Yes," and "Isn't that interesting," and anything else she could think of, so as not to let on how wildly boring all this was. *For me, anyway,* she thought. Occasionally, thinking he'd been invited to, or that someone nearby was in the slightest bit interested, Urruah went off on one of these tangents. If you didn't want to hurt his feelings—and mostly his partners didn't, knowing how it felt to have a personal passion used as a scratching-post by the uncaring—there was nothing much you could do but nod and listen as politely as you could for as long as you could, then escape: the suddenly discovered need to do *houih* was usually a good excuse. Rhiow couldn't do that just now, but once more she found herself thinking that Urruah was a wonderful example of one of a wizard's most useful traits: the ability to carry around large amounts of potentially useless information for prolonged periods. *That,* she thought, *he's got in abundance.*

"Oh, I forgot," she said at last, almost grateful to have something else to talk about. "Did you talk to the canine Senior about that *houff?*"

"Yes," Urruah said. "Rraah's going to arrange some kind of accident for him—have him 'accidentally' cut loose from the building site, late one night. Apparently he's got a home waiting for him already."

"Good," Rhiow said. They turned the corner into Fifty-sixth, and down the street Rhiow saw Saash sitting outside the garage, a little to one side of the door, through which light poured out into the evening. She wasn't even sidled, and her fur looked somewhat ruffled, as if she was too annoyed to put it in order. Cars were going in and out at the usual rate, and Saash was ignoring them, which was unusual; she was normally very traffic-shy, but right now she just sat there and glared.

Saash looked at Rhiow and Urruah as they came up to her, and as the saying goes, if looks were claws, their ears would have been in rags. "What kept you?" she said.

"Where's the wonder child?" Urruah said.

"He's inside," Saash said, "playing hide-and-seek with the staff. Abha'h's going out of his mind; he can't understand why one minute he can see the new kitten and the next minute he can't. Fortunately he thinks it's funny, and he just assumes that Arhu is hiding under one car or another. However, he's also decided that the new kitten should have flea powder put on him, and needless to say, that's the moment Arhu chooses to disappear and *not* come visible again, which means *I* got the flea powder instead of him—"

Urruah began to laugh. Saash gave him a sour look and said, "Oh yes, it's just hilarious. You should have heard the little *sswiass* laughing. I hope I get to hear him laugh at *you* like that."

Rhiow suppressed her smile. "Who knows, you may get your chance. Did you get some sleep, finally?"

"Some. How about you?"

"I've slept better," Rhiow said. "I had odd dreams. . . ."

"After having been in the real Downside," Saash said, relaxing enough to scratch, "that's hardly a surprise. Just think of the last time . . ."

"I know." Rhiow preferred not to. "But I'm not sure I noticed everything I should have there: I want to go talk to Ehef this evening."

"About the gate?"

"Not entirely." Rhiow twitched an ear back toward the depths of the garage. "The circumstances, our involvement with him . . . the situation isn't strictly unusual, but it's always good to get a second opinion."

Saash flicked her tail in somewhat sardonic agreement. "Should be interesting. Come on," she said, "let's go see if Abha'h's caught him yet."

They waited for a break in the traffic, then slipped in through the door and made their way down into the garage and among the racks of parked cars. They passed Abad, who was looking under some of the cars racked up front in a resigned sort of way; he was holding a can of flea powder. Saash gave it a dirty look as they passed.

They found Arhu crouching under a car near the back of the garage, snickering to himself as he watched Abad's feet going back and forth under the racks. He looked up as they came, with an expression that was much less alarmed than any Rhiow had seen on him yet, but the edge of hostility on his amusement was one that she didn't care for much. "Well, hunt's luck to you, Arhu," she said, politely enough, "though it looks like you're doing all right in that department . . . if you consider this a hunt and not mere mouse-play." She and the others hunkered down by him.

"Might as well be," Arhu said after a moment. He watched Abad go off. "They're real easy to fool, *ehhif*."

"If you couldn't sidle, you'd be singing another song," said Urruah.

"But I can. I'm a wizard!"

Rhiow smiled a slight, tart smile. "*We* are wizards," she said. "*You* are still only a probationer-wizard, on Ordeal."

"But I can do stuff already!" Arhu said. "I went through the doors last night! And I'm sidling!" He got up and did it while they watched, strolling to and fro under the metal ramp-framework, and weaving in and out among the strings: there one moment and gone the next, and then briefly occluded in stripes of visibility and nonvisibility, as if strutting behind a set of invisible, vertical venetian blinds. He looked ineffably smug, as only a new wizard can when he first feels the power sizzling under his skin.

"Not a bad start," Saash said.

Urruah snorted. "You kidding? That's one of the most basic wizardries there is. Even some cats who *aren't* wizards can do it. Don't flatter him, Saash. He'll think he really might amount to something." His slow smile began. "Then again, go ahead, *let* him think that. He'll just try some dumb stunt and get killed sooner. One less thing to worry about."

Rhiow turned and clouted Urruah on the top of his head, with her claws out, though not hard enough to really addle him. He crouched down a very little, eyeing her, his ears a bit flat. *When I want your assessment of his talents,* she said silently, *I'll ask you for it, Mister Couldn't-keep-a-dog-from-eating-his-mouse-earlier.* Aloud she said, "You know as well as I do that the Oath requires the protection of *all* life, including life that annoys you. So just stuff your tail in it."

Urruah glared at her, turned his head away. Rhiow looked back at Arhu. "Tell me something to start with. What *do* you know about wizards? I don't mean what Saash has been telling you, though it's plain she hasn't been able to get much through your thick little skull. I want to hear what you know from before we met you."

He squirmed a little, scowling. "Wizards can do stuff."

"What stuff? How?"

"Good stuff, I guess. I never saw any. But People talk about them."

"And what do they say?" Urruah said.

Arhu glared back at him. "That they're stuck up, that they think they're important because they can do things."

Urruah started slowly to stand up. Rhiow glanced at him; he set-

tled back again. "And probably," Rhiow said just a touch wearily to
Arhu, "you've heard People say that wizards are using their power
somehow to help *ehhif* control People. Or that they're just trying to
make all the other People around be their servants somehow. And
somebody has to have told you that it's not real wizardry at all, just
some kind of trick used to get power or advantage, some kind of
hauissh or power game."

Arhu looked at her. "Yeah," he said. "All that."

"Well." Rhiow sat down. "'Just tricks'; do you think that? After you
went through the doors?"

She watched him struggle a little, inwardly, before speaking. He
desperately did not want to admit that he didn't understand something, or (on the other side) admit to feeling more than cool and blasé
about anything . . . especially not in front of Urruah. Yet at the same
time, he *liked* the feel of what he'd done the night before: Rhiow recognized the reaction immediately . . . knowing it very well herself.
And she knew the thought that there might be *more* of that was tantalizing him. It was the Queen's greatest recruitment tool, the one that
was the most effective, and the most unfair, for any living being—but
especially for cats: curiosity. *You are unscrupulous,* she said privately
to the Powers That Be. *But then You can't afford to be otherwise. . . .*

"That happened," Arhu said finally. He looked, not at Rhiow, but
at Urruah, as if for confirmation: Urruah simply closed his eyes . . . as-
sent, though low-key. "I felt it. It was real."

"Urruah's right, you know," Rhiow said. "Even nonwizardly cats
can sometimes walk through things . . . though usually only in moments of crisis: if you're not a wizard, the act can't be performed at
will. *You'll* be able to, though . . . if you live through what follows."

"Whatever it is, I can take it," Arhu said fiercely. "I'm a survivor."

Saash shook herself all over, then sat down and scratched. "That's
nice," she said, very soft-voiced. "We get a lot of 'survivors' in wizardry. Mostly they die."

Rhiow tucked herself down in the compact position that Hhuha
sometimes called "half-meatloaf," the better to look eye-to-eye with
the kit. "You said you heard a voice that said 'I dare you,'" she said.
"We've all heard that voice. She speaks to every potential wizard,

sooner or later, and offers each one the Ordeal. It's a test to see if you have what it takes. If you don't, you'll die. If you do, you'll be a wizard when the test is over."

"How long does it take?"

"Might be hours," Urruah said. "Might be months. You'll know when it's over. You'll either have a lot of power that you didn't have a moment before . . . or you'll find yourself with just enough time for a quick wash between lives."

"What's the power *for,* though?" Arhu said, eager. "Can you use it for anything you want?"

"Within limits," Saash said. "Walk in other elements and other worlds, talk to other creatures, even not-live things sometimes—go places no other People not wizards have ever been or seen—"

"Other creatures?" Arhu said. "Wow! *Any* other creatures?"

"Well, mostly—"

"Even *ehhif?* Cool! Let's go talk to that cop and freak him out!" He started toward the garage door.

Rhiow grabbed him by the scruff and pushed him down with one paw. "*No.* You may *not* use the Speech to communicate with members of other species unless they're wizards, or unless you're on errantry and the job specifically requires it."

"But that's *dumb!*"

"Listen, kitling," Urruah said, leaning over Arhu with a thoughtful expression. "If you start routinely talking to *ehhif* so they can understand, there's a chance that eventually one of them's going to *believe* that you're talking. And before you know it they've thrown you in a scientific institute somewhere and started drilling holes in your skull, or else they're taking you apart in some other interesting way. More to the point, if you do that, they'll start doing it to *other* People too. A lot of them. I wouldn't want to cause something like that, not ever, because sooner or later you're going to find yourself between lives, and the explanations that would be demanded of you by the Powers That Be—" He shook his head slowly. "If I started seriously thinking that you might actually pull a stunt like that, I'd just grab you and kick your guts out right now, Ordeal or no Ordeal. So take notice."

"Then this wizardry isn't any use," Arhu muttered, scowling. "You say you can do all this stuff, and then you say you're not *allowed* to do it! What's the point?"

Rhiow felt herself starting to fluff up. Urruah, though, said mildly, "It's not quite like that. Are you *allowed* to fight with me, kitling?"

Arhu glared at Urruah, then he too began to bristle. Finally he burst out: "Yes, I am! But if I did, you'd *shred* me!"

"Then you understand the principle," Urruah said. "We're *allowed* to do all kinds of things. But we don't do them, because the result in the long term would be unfortunate." He smiled at Arhu. "For us or someone else. Till you come to know better, just assume that the results would be unfortunate for *you*. And in either the long term or the short . . . they would be."

Rhiow noticed that his claws were showing more than usual. *Wonderful,* she thought, remembering the saying: *Old tom, young tom, trouble coming!* "You'll find in the next few days," Rhiow said, "that there are a fair number of things you can do . . . and they'll be useful enough. You'll like them, too. Keep your ears open: when you hear the whisper . . . listen. She doesn't repeat herself much, the One Who Whispers."

Arhu looked up at that. "We're not working *for* anyone, are we?" he said, suspicious. "The People are *free.*"

Rhiow wanted to roll her eyes but didn't quite dare: Arhu was a little too sensitive to such things. "She'll suggest something you might do," Rhiow said, "but whether you do it or not is your choice."

"That's not exactly an answer."

Urruah stood up. "He makes my head hurt," Urruah said. "Give him the power to change the world and he complains about it. But then, if he's not willing to cooperate with the Powers Who're the source of the power, why should he learn anything more about it? Not that he *will.*" He looked amused.

"All right, all right," Arhu said hastily, "so I want to learn. So when do I start?"

They looked at one another. "Right away," Rhiow said. "We have to go inspect the place we take care of, make sure things are going right there. You should come with us and see what we do."

Arhu looked at them a little suspiciously. "You mean your den? You're a pride?"

"Not the way you mean it. But yes, we are. The place we take care of—you remember it: the place where we found you. *Ehhif* living here use it as a beginning and ending to their journeys. So do *ehhif* wizards, and other wizards too, though the journeys are to stranger places than the trains go. . . ."

"There are *ehhif* wizards?" Arhu laughed out loud at the idea. "No way! They're too dumb!"

"Now who's being 'stuck up'?" Urruah said. "There are plenty of *ehhif* wizards. Very nice people. And from other species too, just on this planet. Wizards who're other primates, who're whales . . . even wizards who're *houiff.*"

Arhu snickered even harder. "I wouldn't pay any attention to them. *Houiff* don't impress *me.*"

"You may yet meet Rraah-yarh," said Urruah, looking slightly amused, "who's Senior among the *houiff* here: and if you're wise, you'll pay attention to her. *I* wouldn't cross her . . . and not because she's a *houff,* either. She may look like half an ad for some brand of *ehhif* Scotch, but she's got more power in one dewclaw than you've got in your whole body, and she could skin you with a glance and wear you for a doggie-jacket on cold days."

Rhiow kept quiet and tried to keep her face straight over the thought that *everything* toms discussed seemed to come down to physical violence sooner or later. Saash, though, leaned close to Arhu and said, "You are now on the brink of joining a great community of people from many sentient species . . . a kinship reaching from here to the stars, and farther. Some of your fellow-wizards are so strange or awful to look at that your first sight of them could nearly turn your wits right around in your head. But they've all taken the same Oath you have. They've sworn to slow down the heat-death of the Universe, to keep the worlds going as best they can, for as long as they can . . . so that the rest of Life can get on with its job. You want great adventure? It's here. Scary things, amazing things? You'll never run out of them . . . there are any nine lives' worth, and more. But if you don't pass your Ordeal, *this* life, none of it's ever going to happen."

"You willing to find out how hot you *really* are?" Urruah said. "That's why the Whisperer has spoken to you. Take her up on her offer . . . and the Universe gets very busy trying to kill you. Live through it, though . . . and there'll be good reason for the queens to listen to you when you sing."

Once more Rhiow kept her smile under control, for this kind of precisely applied power play was exactly what she had needed Ur-ruah for. Tom-wizards tended to equate management of their power with management of their maleness: no surprise, since for toms in general *all* of life was about power and procreation. But it was language Arhu would understand until he grew old enough to understand wizardry, and life in general, in terms of *hauissh,* the power-and-placement game that ran through all feline culture. Rhiow almost smiled at the memory of Har'lh once equating *hauissh* with an old human strategy-game and referring to it as "cat chess," but the metaphor was close enough. All cat life was intrinsically *ha'hauis-sheh,* or "political" as Har'lh had translated it; and as the saying went, those who did not play *hauissh* had *hauissh* played on them, usually to their detriment. As a team manager, Rhiow had long since made her peace with this aspect of the job, and always made sure her own placement in the game was very secure, then directed her attention to placing her team members where they would do the most good, and felt guilty about the manipulation only later, if ever.

"So," Rhiow said. "Let's get on with it, young wizard. We usually walk, and you'll need to learn the various routes before we teach you the faster ways to go." She stood up. "First route, then: the hardest one, but the one that exposes us least to notice. Can you climb?"

Arhu positively hissed with indignation. Rhiow turned away, for fear the smile would slip right out, and as she passed, Saash lowered her head so that (without seeming to do so on purpose) it bumped against Rhiow's in passing, their whiskers brushing through one another's and trembling with shared and secretive hilarity. *Oh, Rhi,* Saash said silently, *were we ever this unbearable?*

I was, Rhiow said, *and you would have been if you'd had the nerve. Let's dull his claws a little, shall we? . . .*

✦

The run to Grand Central along the High Road, which normally would have taken the three of them perhaps twenty minutes, took nearly an hour and a half; and the dulling of Arhu's claws, which Rhiow had intended in strictly the metaphorical sense, happened for real—so that when they finally sat down on the copper-flashed upper cornice of the great peaked roof, looking down at Forty-second, Arhu was bedraggled, shaking, and furious, and Rhiow was heartily sorry she had ever asked him whether he could climb.

He *couldn't*. He was one of those cats who seem to have been asleep in the sun somewhere when Queen Iau was giving out the skill, grace, and dexterity: he couldn't seem to put a paw right. He fell off walls, missed jumps that he should have been able to make with his eyes closed, and clutched and clung to angled walks that he should have been confident to run straight up and down without trouble. It was a good thing he was so talented at sidling, since (if this performance was anything to judge by) he was the cat Rhiow would choose as most likely to spend the rest of his life using surface streets to get around: a horrible fate. *It may change,* she thought. *This could be something he'll grow out of. Dear gods, I hope so . . .* Finally she'd said to the others, out loud, "I could use a few minutes to get my breath back," and she'd sat down on the crest of the terminal roof. It was not *her* breath Rhiow was concerned about, while Arhu sat there gasping and glaring at the traffic below.

Why is *he so clumsy?* Urruah said silently as they sat there, letting Arhu calm himself down again. *There's nothing wrong with him physically, nothing wrong with his nerves . . . they're the right "age" for the way his body is developing.* He was the one of them best talented at feeling the insides of others' bodies, so Rhiow was inclined to trust his judgment in this regard.

It's like he can't see the jump ahead of him, Saash said. *There's nothing wrong with his eyes, is there?*

No. Urruah washed one paw idly. *Might just be shock left over from last night, and the healing, and everything else that's happening.*

He didn't look shocky to me in the garage, Rhiow said.

Believe me, Saash said, *especially before you got there, shock was the last thing he was exhibiting. This is something of a revelation.*

After a few moments, Rhiow got up and walked along the rounded copper plaques of the roof's peak to where Arhu sat staring down at the traffic. "That last part of the climb," she said as conversationally as she could, "can be a little on the rough side. Thanks for letting me rest."

He gave her a sidelong look, then stared down again at the traffic and the *ehhif* going about their business on the far side of Forty-second Street, walking through the glare of orange sodium-vapor light. "How far down is it?" he said softly.

It was the first thing Rhiow had heard him say that hadn't sounded either angry or overly bold. "About fifty lengths, I'd say. Not a fall you'd want . . ." She looked across the street, watching the cabs on Vanderbilt being released by the change of lights to flow through the intersection into Forty-second. A thought struck her. "Arhu," she said, "you don't have trouble with heights, do you?"

He flicked his tail sideways in negation, not taking his eyes off the traffic below. "Only with getting to them," he said, again so quietly as to be almost inaudible.

"I think the sooner we teach you to walk on air, the better," Rhiow said. "We'll start you on that tomorrow."

He stared at her. "Can you do that? I mean, can I—"

"Yes."

She sat still a moment, looking down. After a few breaths Saash came up behind, stepping delicately and effortlessly as usual, and looked over Rhiow's shoulder at the traffic and at the dark, graceful, sculpted silhouettes that came between them and the orange glow from beneath. "A closer view than you get from the street," she said to Arhu. "Though you do miss some of the fine detail from this angle."

"What are they?"

" 'Who,' actually," Saash said. "*Ehhif* gods."

"What's a god?"

Rhiow and Urruah and Saash all looked at one another. *My,* Urruah said silently, *we are going to have to start from scratch with this one, aren't we? . . . Hope he doesn't survive to breed. I wouldn't hold out much hope for the next generation.*

"Very powerful beings," said Saash, giving Urruah a look. "Cousins to the Whisperer: they're all littermates under the One, or so we think. Each species has its own, even *ehhif.*"

Arhu sniffed at the idea and squinted at the carved figures. "One of them looks like he's falling asleep."

"She," Rhiow said.

"How do you tell?"

Urruah opened his mouth, but Rhiow said, "Some other time. That one's a queen, Arhu: the other two're toms."

"What's that one got on his head?"

"It's something *ehhif* wear," Saash said; "it's called a *hha't.* But don't ask me why it's got wings on it."

"Symbolic of something," Rhiow said. "All these carvings are. That middle one is a messenger-god, I believe. The 'sleepy' one, she's got a book; that's a way *ehhif* communicate. The other one, he's probably something to do with the trains. See the wheel?"

"There has to be more to it than just that, though," Urruah said. "Someone involved in the construction has to have known what this was going to be, besides just a place where the trains come and go. It can't just be coincidence that the Lord of Birds is shown there at the center of it all; they've always been the symbols of speed in getting around, especially of nonphysical travel. And then that one there, the queen, has the Manual, and the one in the middle has the stick with the Wise Ones wound around it: the emblem of what's below, in the Downside, under the roots of the worldgates. There have to have been wizards on the building's design team."

"I'll leave it to you to conduct some research on the subject," Rhiow said. "But there was wizardry enough about the place's building, even at the merely physical level: it never shut down, even when the construction was heaviest. Eight hundred trains came and went each day, and some of them may have been late, but they never stopped . . . and neither did other kinds of transit. Speaking of which, let's get on with our own business. We're running late."

She walked on down the roof-cornice, taking her time. "All very scenic," she said casually to Urruah, "but tomorrow we'll take the Low Road, all right?"

"The Queen's voice purrs from your throat, oh most senior of us all," Urruah said, following her at a respectable distance. She didn't look at him, but she twitched one ear back and thought, *I'm going to take this out of your hide eventually, O smart-mouthed one. Don't give him ideas. And don't make fun of his ignorance. It's not his fault he has no education, and it's our job to see that he gets one.*

I would say, Urruah said with a silent wrinkling of his whiskers, *that we have our job cut out for us.*

Rhiow kept walking toward the end of the roof. "There's an opening down here," she said to Arhu as they went. "It's a little tricky to get through, but once in, everything else is easy. How much other experience have you had with buildings?"

He shrugged. "Today."

She nodded. He was young and inexperienced enough not even to have the usual cat-reference, which likened buildings to dens, or in the case of the taller ones, to trees hollowed out inside. Rhiow had always been a little amused by this, knowing what trees the city buildings were echoes of. She'd occasionally heard humans refer to the city as a jungle: that made her laugh, too, for she knew the real "jungle," ancient and perilous, of which the shadowy streets were only a reflection.

"Well, you're going to start picking up more experience fast," she said. "This is one of the biggest buildings in this city, though not the tallest. If you laid the almost-tallest building on the island—see that one, the great spike with the colored lights around the top?—yes, *that* one—laid it down on its side and half-buried it as the Terminal's buried, then this would *still* be larger than that. There are a hundred thousand dens in it, from the roof to the deepest-dug den under the streets, at the lower track levels. But we'll start at the top, tonight. The path we'll take leads under this roof-crest where we're walking, to the substructure over the building's inner roof. You said you came through the main concourse . . . did you look up and see blue, a blue like the sky, high up?"

Arhu stopped well clear of the edge of the roof, which they were nearing, and thought a moment. "Yes. There were lights in it. They were backwards. . . ."

His eyes looked oddly unfocused. *The height bothers him,* Rhiow thought, *no matter what he says . . .* And then she changed her mind, for his eyes snapped back to what seemed normalcy. *Well, never mind. A trick of the light . . .*

"Backwards," though. "Saw that, did you?" she said, which was another slight cause for surprise. "Very perceptive of you. Well, we'll be walking above that: it's all a built thing, and you'll see the bones of it. Come here to the edge now and look down. See the hole?"

He saw it: she saw his tongue go in and out, touching his nose in fright, and heard him swallow.

"Right. That's what I thought the first time. It's easier than it looks. There's just a tiny step under it, where the brick juts out. Stretch down, put your right forepaw down on that, turn around hard, and put yourself straight in through the hole. Urruah?"

"Like this," Urruah said, slipping between them, and poured himself straight over the edge into the dark. Arhu watched him find the foothold, twist, and vanish into the little square hole among the bricks.

"Do that," Rhiow said. "I'll spot for you. You won't fall: I promise."

Arhu stared at her. "How can you be sure?"

Rhiow didn't answer him, just gazed back. Sooner or later there was always a test of trust among team-working wizards—the sooner, the better. Demonstrations that the trust was well-founded never helped at this stage: start giving such proofs and you would soon find yourself handicapped by the need to provide them all the time.

She kept her silence and spoke inwardly to the air under the little "step" of outward-jutting brick, naming the square footage of air that she needed to be solid for this little while—just in case. Arhu looked away, after a moment, and gingerly, foot by foot, started draping himself over the edge of the cornice, stretching and feeling with his forefeet for the step.

He found it, fumbled, staggered— Rhiow caught her breath and got ready to say the word that would harden the air below. But somehow Arhu managed to recover himself, and turned and writhed or fell through the hole. A scrabbling noise followed, and a thump.

Rhiow and Saash looked at each other, waiting, but mercifully there was no sound of laughter from Urruah. They went down after Arhu.

Inside the hole, they found Arhu sitting on the rough plank flooring that ran to the roof's edge underneath the peak, and washing his face in a very sincere bout of composure-grooming. A line of narrow horizontal windows, faintly orange-yellow with upward-reflected light from the street, ran down both sides of the roof, about six feet below its peak, and northward toward Lexington. From below those windows, thick metal supporting beams ran up to the peak and across the width of the room, and a long plank-floored gallery ran along one side, made for *ehhif* to walk on.

Cats needed no such conveniences. Urruah was already strolling away down the long supporting beam at just below window-level, the golden light turning his silver-gray markings to an unaccustomed marmalade shade.

Arhu finished his *he'ihh* and looked down the length of the huge attic. "See the planks under the beams and joists there?" Rhiow said. "On the other side of them is the sky-painting that the *ehhif* artist did all those years ago, to look like the summer sky above a sea a long way from here. The painting's trapped, though: when they renovated the station some years back, they glued another surface all over the original painting, bored new holes for the stars, and did the whole thing over again."

Arhu looked at Rhiow oddly. "But they had one there already!"

"It faded," Saash said, shrugging her tail. "Seems like that bothered them, even though the real sky fades every day. *Ehhif* . . . go figure them."

"Come on," Rhiow said. They walked along the planks, ducking under the metal joists and beams every now and then, and Arhu looked with interest at the corded wires and cables reaching across the inside of the roof. "For the lightbulbs," Saash said. "The walking-gallery is so that, when one of the brighter stars burns out, the *ehhif* can come up here and replace it."

Arhu flirted his tail in amusement and went on. "Here's our way down," Rhiow said as they came to the far side of the floor. "It's all easy from here."

A small doorway stood before them, let into the bare bricks of the wall: the door was shut. Urruah had leaped down beside it and was leaning against it, head to one side as if listening.

"Locked?" Rhiow said.

"Not this time, for a change. I think the new office staff are finally learning." He looked thoughtfully at the doorknob.

The doorknob turned: the door clicked and swung open, inward. Beyond it was a curtain: Urruah peered through it. "Clear," he said a moment later, and slipped through.

Rhiow and Saash went after him, Arhu followed them. The little office had several desks in it, very standard-issue, banged-up gray metal desks, all littered with paperwork and manuals and computer terminals and piles of computer-printed documentation. More golden light came in from larger windows set at the same height as those out in the roof space.

"Some *ehhif* who help run the station work here during the 'weekdays,'" Rhiow said to Arhu as they headed for the office's outer door, "but this is a 'weekend,' so there's no fear we'll run into them now. We're seven 'stories,' or *ehhif*-levels, over the main concourse; there's a stepping-tree, a 'stairway' they call it, down to that level. That's where we're headed."

Urruah reared up to touch the outer door with one paw, spoke in a low yowl to the workings in its lock: the door obligingly clicked open with a soft squeal of hinges, letting them out into the top of a narrow cylindrical stairwell lit from above by a single bare bulb set in the white-painted ceiling. The staircase before them was a spiral one, of openwork cast iron, and the spiral was tight. While Saash pushed the door shut again and spoke it locked, Urruah ran on down the stairs two or three at a time, as he usually did, and Rhiow found herself half-hoping (for Arhu's benefit) that he would take at least one spill down the stairs, as he also usually did. But the Tom was apparently watching over Urruah this evening. Urruah vanished into the dimness below them without incident, leaving Rhiow and Saash pacing behind at a more sedate speed, while behind them came Arhu, cautiously picking his way.

Faint street sounds came to them through the walls as they went, but slowly another complex of sounds became more assertive: rushing, echoing sounds, and soft rumbles more felt than genuinely heard. At one point near the bottom of the stairs, Rhiow paused to look over her shoulder and saw Arhu standing still about half a turn of the stairs above her, his ears twitching; his tail lashed once, hard, an unsettled gesture.

"It's like roaring," he said quietly. "A long way down . . ."

He's nervous about getting so close to where he almost came to grief, Rhiow thought. *Well, if he's going to be working with us, he's just going to have to get used to it. . . .* "It does sound that way at first," she said, "but you'd be surprised how fast you get used to it. And at how many things there are to distract you. Come on. . . ."

He looked down at her, then experimentally jumped a couple of steps down, Urruah-style, caught up with her, and passed her by, bouncing downward from step to step with what looked like a little more confidence.

She followed him. In the dimness below them, she could see a wedge of light spilling across the floor: Urruah had already cracked open the bottom door. Through it, the echoes of the footfalls and voices of *ehhif* came more strongly.

"Now get sidled," Saash was saying, "and keep your wits about you: this isn't like running around under the cars in the garage. *Ehhif* can move pretty fast, especially when they're late for a train, and you haven't lived until you've tripped someone and had them drop a few loaded Bloomie's bags on you."

Arhu merely looked amused. He had sidled himself between one breath and the next. "I don't see why *we* should hide," he said. "If you take care of this place, like you say, then we have as much right to be here as all of them do."

"The right, yes," Rhiow said. "In our law. But not in *theirs*. And in wizardry, where one species is more vulnerable than the other to having its effectiveness damaged by the conflict of their two cultures, the more powerful or advanced culture gives way graciously. That's us."

"That's not the way People should do it," Arhu growled as they stepped cautiously out into the Graybar passage, one of the two hallways leading from Lexington Avenue to the concourse. "I don't know a lot about *hauissh* yet, but I do know you have to fight to get a good position, or take it, and keep it."

"Sometimes," Urruah said. "In the cruder forms of the game . . . yes.

But when you start playing *hauissh* for real someday, you'll learn that some of the greatest players win by doing least. I know one master who dominates a whole square block in the West Eighties and never so much as shows himself through a window: the other People there know his strength so well, they resign every day at the start of play."

"What kind of *hauissh* is that?" Arhu said, disgusted. "No blood, no glory—"

"No scars," Urruah said, with a broad smile, looking hard at Arhu.

Arhu looked away, his ears down.

"Last time they counted his descendants," Urruah added, "there were two hundred prides of them scattered all over the Upper West Side. Don't take subdued or elegant play as a sign that someone can't attract the queens."

They came out into the concourse and paused by the east gallery, looking across the great echoing space glinting with polished beige marble and limestone, and golden with the brass of rails and light fixtures and the great round information desk and clock in the middle. The sound of *ehhif* footsteps was muted at the moment; there were perhaps only a hundred of them in the Terminal at any given moment now, coming and going from the Sunday evening trains at a leisurely rate. Then even the footstep-clatter was briefly lost in the massive bass note of the Accurist clock.

Arhu looked up and around nervously. "Just a time-message," Saash said. "Nine hours past high-Eye."

"Oh. All right. What are all those metal tubes stuck all over everything? And why are all the walls covered with that cloth stuff?"

"They're renovating," said Saash. "Putting back old parts of the building that were built over, years ago . . . getting rid of things that weren't in the original plans. It should look lovely when they're done. Right now it just means that the place is going to be noisier than usual for the next couple of years. . . ."

"The worldgates have occasionally gotten misaligned due to the construction work," Rhiow said. "It means we've had to keep an extra close eye on them. Sometimes we have to move a gate's 'opening' end, its portal locus, closer to one platform or away from another. It was the gate by Track Thirty-two, last time: they were installing some kind of air-conditioning equipment on Thirty-two, and we had to move the locus far enough away to keep the *ehhif* workmen from seeing wizards passing through it, but not so close to any of the other gates' loci to interfere with them. . . ."

"What would happen if they *did* interfere?" Arhu said, with just a little too much interest for Rhiow's liking.

Urruah sped up his pace just enough for Arhu to suddenly look right next to him and see a tom two and a half times his size, and maybe three times his weight. "What would happen if I pushed those big ears of yours down their earholes, and then put my claws far enough down your throat to pull them out that way?" Urruah said in a conversational tone. "I mean, what would be your opinion of that?"

They all kept walking, and when Arhu finally spoke again, it was in a very small voice. "That would be bad," he said.

"Yes. That would be *very* bad. Just like coincident portal loci would be bad. If you were anywhere nearby when such a thing happened, it would feel similar. But it would be your whole body . . . and it would be *forever*. So wouldn't you agree that these are both events that, as responsible wizards, we should do all we can to forestall?"

"Yeah. Uh, yes."

"Track Thirty, team," said Rhiow. "Right this way, and we'll check that the Thirty-two gate is where it belongs. Saash, you want to go down first and check the gate's logs?"

"My pleasure, Rhi."

They strolled down the platform, empty now under its long line of fluorescent lights. No trains were expected on 30 until the 10:30 from Dover Plains and Brewster North; off to one side, on 25, a Metro-North "push-pull" locomotive sat up against the end-of-track barrier, thundering idly to itself while waiting for the cars for the 11:10 to Stamford and Rye to be pushed down to it and coupled on. Arhu stopped and gave it a long look.

"Loud," Urruah said, shouting a little.

Arhu flicked his tail "no." "It's not that—"

"What is it, exactly?" Rhiow said.

"It roars."

"Yes. As I said, you get used to the roaring."

"That's not what I mean." He sat down, right where he was, and kept staring at the loco. "It—it *knows* it's roaring." He turned to Urruah, almost pleading. "It can't—it can't be *alive?*"

"You'd be surprised," Urruah said.

"A lot of wizards can 'hear' what we normally consider inanimate things," Rhiow said. "It's not an uncommon talent. Talking to things and getting them to respond, the way you saw Urruah talk to the door upstairs, that takes more practice. You'll find out quickly enough if you have the knack."

Arhu got up as suddenly as he had sat down, and shook himself all over: it took a moment for Rhiow to realize that he was hiding a shudder. "This is all so strange. . . ."

"The Downside is a strange place," Urruah said, beginning again to stroll toward the end of the platform, where Saash had disappeared over the edge and down to track level. "Always has been. There are all kinds of odd stories about these tunnels, and the 'underworld' in this area. Lost colonies of web-footed mutant *ehhif* . . . alligators in the sewers . . ."

"And are there?"

"Alligators? No," Urruah said. "*Dragons,* though . . ." He smiled.

Arhu stopped again, looked at him oddly. "Dragons . . ." He turned to Rhiow. "He's making it up. Isn't he?"

Arhu desperately wanted to think so, that was for sure. "About the dragons?" Rhiow said. "No, that's true enough . . . though not the way you might think. The presence of the worldgates can make odd things happen, things that even wizardry can't fully explain. These tunnels sometimes reach into places that have little to do with this city. They aren't a place to wander unless you know them well. Sometimes not even then . . ."

"But the *ehhif*—I heard about them. Lots of them live down here, everybody says, and they're always hungry, and they eat . . . rats, and, and . . ."

"People? No, not these *ehhif,* anyway," Urruah said. "And while some *ehhif* do indeed live down in the tunnels and dens under the streets, it's not as many as their stories, or ours, would make you think. Not as many People, either."

"Problem is, *ehhif* don't see well in the dark," Saash said, leaping up out of it and walking down the platform toward them. "Either for real, or in their minds. When they try to tell stories about what they think they've seen down here, they tend to get confused about detail. Even for People, it's never that easy to be accurate about this darkness. It reaches down too deep, to things that are too old. A story that seemed plain when you started, soon starts drawing darkness about itself even while you think you have it pinned down broken-backed in the daylight. . . ."

Arhu was looking unusually thoughtful. "How's the gate?" Rhiow said.

"Answering interrogations normally," Saash said. "No resonances from our wayward friend at the end of Twenty-six: it's sitting over there and behaving itself as if nothing had ever gone wrong."

"Its logs are all right?"

"They're recording usage normally again, yes."

"That's so strange," Urruah said. "How are you going to explain it all to Har'lh when he asks for that report?"

"I'm going to tell him the truth, as usual," Rhiow said, "and in this case, that means we don't have the slightest idea what went wrong. Come on, Arhu, we'll show you how a gate looks when it's working right."

They walked on down to the end of the platform and jumped off. Arhu came last: he was slow about it.

"Before we go on," Rhiow said. "Arhu, if any of this starts to frighten you, say so. You had a bad day, and we know it. But we work down here all the time, and if you're going to be with us, you're going to need to get used to it. If you think you need time to do that, or if you can't stay here long, say so."

Arhu's tongue came out and licked his nose nervously, twice in a row, before he finally said, "Let's see what's so hot down here."

"One thing, anyway," Urruah said, his voice full of approval. He headed off into the darkness.

The glitter and sheen of the hyperstrings of the gate was visible even before they were out of the glare of the fluorescents. The locus, a broad oval hanging some twenty yards along from the end of Track

30, was relaxed but ready for use: its characteristic weave, which to Rhiow always looked a little like the pattern of the Chinese silk rug her *ehhif* had on the dining-room floor at home, radiated in shimmering patterns of orange, red, and infrared. Arhu stared at it.

"It *is* alive," he said.

"Could be," Rhiow said. "With some kinds of wizardry, especially the older and more powerful ones, it's hard to tell. . . ."

"Why is it here?"

"For wizards to use for travel, as I said."

"No, wait, I don't mean why. *How* did they get here? This one, and all the others I can feel—"

"I see what he means," Saash said. "To have so many gates in one place *is* a little unusual. It may have to do with population pressure. All these millions of minds packed close together, pressing against the structure of reality, trying to get their world to do what they want . . . and hundreds of years of that kind of pressure, started by people who came here over great distances to found a city where they could live the way they wanted to, have things their way— Sooner or later, even the structure of physical reality will start to bend under such pressure. Or maybe not 'bend.' 'Wear thin,' so that other realities start showing through. They say that this is the city where you can get anything: in a way, it's become true. . . . If there's no gate in so populous and hard-driven a place, the theory says, one will eventually appear. If there was already a naturally occurring gate, it'll spawn others."

"But there's always been at least one gate here," Urruah said, "since long before the city: the one leading to the true Downside, the Old Downside."

"Oh, yes. If I had to pick one, I'd bet on the gate over by One-sixteen, myself: it just feels stabler than the others, somehow. But all the gates' signatures have become so alike, after all this time, that you'd be hard put to *prove* which was eldest. Not my problem, fortunately . . ."

Rhiow sat down, looking the gate over. "It does seem to be behaving. You want to run it through the standard patency sequence? We should check that this week's bout of construction hasn't affected it."

"Right." Saash sat up on her hindquarters, settling herself and reaching up to the glowing weft, spreading her claws out to catch selected strings in them and pull—

She froze, then reached in and through the webbing of the gate once more, feeling for something—

"Rhi," she said, "we've got a problem."

Rhiow stared as Saash grasped for the strings again—and once more couldn't get a grip on them. In the midst of this bizarre turn of affairs, the last thing Rhiow would have expected to hear was purring, except she did hear it, then turned in surprise and saw Arhu standing there rigid, looking not at Saash or the gate, but out into the darkness beyond them. The purr was not pleasure or contentment: it was that awful edgy purr that comes with terror or pain, and the sound of it made Rhiow's hackles rise.

"Arhu—"

He paid no attention to her; just stood there, trembling violently, his eyes wide and dark, his throat rough with the purr of fear.

"Something's coming," he said.

They all listened for the telltale tick of rails, for the sound of an unscheduled loco down in the main tunnel past Tower U, where forty tracks narrowed to four. But no such sound could be heard. Neither could what Rhiow half-expected—the squeak of rats—though just the thought made her bristle.

Flashback, Urruah said silently. *We've brought him down too soon.*

"Arhu," Rhiow said, "maybe you and Urruah should go back out to the concourse."

"It won't make any difference," Arhu said, his voice oddly dry and drained-sounding. "It's coming all the same. It came before. Once, to see. Once, to taste. Once, to devour—"

"Get him back out there," Rhiow said to Urruah.

Urruah reached over past her, grabbed Arhu by the scruff of the neck as if he were a much smaller kitten than he was, leapt up onto the platform with him, and hurried off down it, half-dragging Arhu like a lion with a gazelle. Fortunately the youngster was still sidled: allowing any watching station staff to view the spectacle of him being dragged down the platform by something that wasn't there, Rhiow thought, would have produced some choice remarks from Har'lh later.

Rhiow turned her attention back to Saash, who was hissing softly with consternation and anger. "What's the matter?"

"*I don't know.* I interrogated it not five minutes ago and it was fine! Here—" She pulled her paws out of the gate-weave, then carefully put out a single claw and hooked it behind the three-string bundle that led into the interrogation routines. Saash pulled, and the lines of light stretched outward and away from the weft structure, came alive with flickers of dark red fire that ran down the threads like water.

"See? That's fine. But the gate won't hyperextend, Rhi! The control functions aren't answering. It's simply refusing to open."

"That can't happen. It *can't.*"

"I'd have thought a gate couldn't have its logs erased, either," Saash hissed, "but this seems to be our week for surprises. *Now* what do we do? There is simply no way I can do this"—she pushed her forepaws through the strings again, leaned back, and pulled, and her paws simply came out again, without a pause—"without getting a response. It's like dropping something and having it not fall down. In fact, gravity would be *easier* to repeal than hyperstring function! What in Iau's name is going *on?"*

"I wish I knew," Rhiow said, and heartily she did, for life was now much more complicated than she wanted it to be. "We need advice, and a lot of it, and fast." She looked over at the gate. "If it's not functional, you'd better shut it down. I'll notify Har'lh."

"Rhi," Saash said with exaggerated patience, "what I'm trying to tell you is that I can*not* shut it down. Though the gate diagnoses correctly, none of the command structures are palpable. It's going to have to hang here just like this until it starts answering properly, and we'd better pray to the Queen that the thing doesn't come alive again without warning, with some train full of coffee-swigging commuters halfway through it."

Rhiow swallowed. "Go check the others," she said. "I want to make sure they're not doing the same thing. Then get yourself right out of here."

Saash loped off into the darkness. Rhiow sat and looked at the recalcitrant gate. *I really need this right now,* she thought.

The gate hung there and did nothing but glow and ripple subtly, splendid to look at, and about as useful for interspatial transit as that silk rug back in her *ehhif*'s den.

Miserable vhai'*d thing,* Rhiow thought, and looked out into the darkness, trying to calm herself down: there was no time to indulge her annoyance. No trains were coming as yet, but something needed to be done so that the commuters would *not* meet this gate before it was functioning correctly again.

Rhiow trotted hurriedly westward down the track, toward Tower A. Directly opposite the tower was a portion of switched track, used to shunt trains into Tracks 23, 24, and 25, and crossing more shunting track for Tracks 30 through 34. She found the spot where the two "joints" of track interleaved in a shape like an *ehhif* letter X, or like an N or V, depending in which direction the interleave was set.

Rhiow glanced up hurriedly at the windows of the tower. There were a couple of the station *ehhif* sitting there, watching the board behind them, its colored lights indicating the presence of trains farther up the line. She could read those lights well enough, after some years of practice, to know that no moving train was anywhere near her, and the *ehhif* weren't likely to turn and see her before she did what needed doing.

She stood on the little black box set down in the gravel beside the switch and looked at it with her eyes half-shut, seeing into it, watching how the current flowed. Not a complicated mechanism, fortunately: it simply moved the track one way or the other, depending on what the tower told it.

Rhiow closed her eyes all the way, put herself down into the flow of electricity in the switch, and told the switch that she was the tower, and it should move the track *this* way.

It did. *Clunk, clunk,* went the track, and it locked in position: the position that would shunt an incoming train away from Tracks 23, 24, and 25.

Rhiow glanced up at the tower. One of the men inside at the desk was looking over his shoulder at a control board, having heard something: an alarm, or maybe just a confirming click inside the tower that the switch was moving. *Right,* Rhiow thought, and leapt over to the switched track itself. The switch had been the hard part. This would be easier.

She put her paws on the cool metal of the track and spoke to it in the Speech. *Why do you want to lie there with your atoms moving so slowly? Why so sluggish? Let them speed up a bit: here's some energy to do it with. . . . A bit more. Go on, keep it up. Don't stop till I tell you.*

Then she got her paws off it in a hurry because the metal was taking her seriously. The segment of track went from cool to a neutral temperature she couldn't feel, to warm, to hot, to *really* hot, in a matter of seconds. She loped away quickly while it was still shading up from a dull apple-red to cherry-red, to a beautiful glowing canary-yellow. A few seconds more to the buttercup-yellow stage, and the steel of the two pieces of track had fused together. *All right, that's fine, you can stop now, thank you!* she yowled silently to the metal, jumped up onto the platform, and skittered back toward the concourse.

A few moments later the Terminal annunciator came alive and started asking the trainmaster to report to Tower A immediately. Rhiow, panting a little but pleased with herself, came out into the concourse and found Saash, Urruah, and Arhu waiting for her: Saash looking flustered and annoyed, Urruah looking very put-upon, and Arhu deep in composure-grooming again, with one ear momentarily inside out from the scrubbing he was giving it.

"I welded the switching track by Tower A," she said to Saash. "Nothing's going onto Tracks Twenty-three through Twenty-five that isn't picked up and carried there, at least not until they replace that track. Might take them a couple of days."

"Well, don't expect me to know what's wrong with that gate by then," Saash said. "I haven't got a clue. We need advice."

"I agree. What about you?" Rhiow said to Arhu. "Are you all right?"

He glanced at her, then went back to washing. Urruah looked over his head and said to Rhiow, "He was a little rocky for a few moments when I brought him out. Then he just blinked and looked dozy."

"Arhu?"

He looked up this time. "I'm all right," he said. "I just remembered . . . *you* know."

I wish I did know, Rhiow thought, for she still had no satisfactory explanation for what this kitling had been doing down there the other day, or for exactly what had caused what happened.

"Come on," she said, "let's walk. This place is going to be crawling with station people in a few minutes."

They headed for the Graybar passage again. Rhiow spared herself a few seconds more to revel, just briefly, in the relative quiet of the terminal this time of day, this time of week. The soft rush of sound, echoing from the ceiling 120 feet above, was soothing rather than frantic: an easygoing bustle. People down for a Sunday in the city, heading home again; people who lived here, returning after a day out of town; or subway riders emerging to pick up a sandwich or a late newspaper, or a coffee. That bizarre, dark smell . . . Rhiow wondered what Arhu thought of it, for it had taken so long for her to get used to it as anything but a stink. Now she was so accustomed to the scent of coffee in the Terminal that she couldn't imagine the place without it, any more than without the faint aromas of cinders and steel and ozone. "Arhu," she said—

But he wasn't there. And Rhiow smelled something in the air *besides* coffee, and suddenly everything became plain.

All our worries about his education, she thought. *Did any of us think about getting him something to* eat??

The smell of roasting meat, and cold meat, and meat as yet uncooked, was extremely noticeable, and it was coming from right in front of them—from the Italian deli that had a branch here, one of a big chain. Also in front of them, and now much closer to the meat, was Arhu. "Oh, wow," he shouted as he tore toward the open glass-fronted deli counter, mercifully inaudible over yet another noisy announcement-request, for the stationmaster this time, "what *is* that, I want some!"

They ran after him. Rhiow's fur stood right up all over her in fear. *Oh, Gods, look at him, he's come visible—*

Arhu had already dodged around the side of the deli counter and was now behind it, standing on his hind legs, reaching and pawing for the meat that the white-aproned *ehhif* there was slicing. *Pastrami,* Rhiow thought, her mouth starting to water as she ran, *oh, what I wouldn't give for some pastrami at the moment . . . !* But Arhu couldn't reach, and succeeded only in snagging the *ehhif*'s apron. Arhu crouched down, ready to jump up onto the deli counter—

He fell over backward in an utterly comical manner . . . or so it looked to the big swarthy *ehhif,* who glanced down to see what had caught in his apron. But the cause was Urruah, who (still sidled) had simply reared up on his hind legs again, grabbed Arhu once more by the scruff of the neck, and thrown himself over backward, so that the two of them fell down in a heap.

The *ehhif* stared. Arhu struggled, his legs waving around wildly, until he realized that he wasn't going anywhere, and that (to judge by the soft but very heartfelt growling noises coming from just behind him) he would be truncating his present life by trying to. The *ehhif* laughed out loud . . . as well he might have at the sight of a young and apparently very uncoordinated cat, lying on his back and kicking like a crab.

"Arhu!" Rhiow hissed at him. "Get out of there!"

Urruah let Arhu go, looking blackest murder at him. Arhu righted himself, shook himself all over, looked with desperate longing at the meat, and then at Urruah, and slunk back around the deli counter.

Urruah came close behind him. Rhiow thought for a moment, then came unsidled, and sat down against the wall as Urruah shouldered Arhu out into the concourse again, out of the *ehhif*'s direct view. He craned his neck to try to see where Arhu had gone, and couldn't; then went back to his work, chuckling.

Urruah sat down between Arhu and the deli counter, and glanced over at Rhiow. *I'm going to kill him. You know that.*

I think you won't. Besides, you'd have to wait your turn, at the moment. "So," Rhiow said to Arhu, who was on the point of turning around and trying to find another way around the counter. "What was *that* supposed to be?"

"I'm hungry! Look at all that stuff up there! They're *caching!*"

He tried to get around Urruah again. Urruah hunched up his shoulders and narrowed his eyes in a way that suggested Arhu could do this only if he was willing to leave his skin behind.

"*Ehhif* save food," Rhiow said. "It's weird, I know, but they do it. Let it pass for the moment. You're starting to look like one of those people who has to be taken everywhere twice: the second time, it's always to apologize. Arhu, *stop* it and sit down for a moment!!"

"But I *want* it."

"So do I, and we'll have some shortly, but anybody with more than used *hiouh*-litter between their ears would know not to dance around the way you did! Like a *houff,* I swear. Anybody would think you're a stray." She used *auuh,* the worst of the numerous words for the concept.

"I *am* a stray," Arhu said sullenly.

"Not anymore, you're not. You can be a ragged-eared, scarred-up, shameless, unwashed, thieving, bullying reprobate later in life if you want, or else you can be respectably nonaligned. Just as you please. But right now you're in-pride, and you'll behave yourself respectably, or I'll know why."

"Oh, yeah?" he spat. "Why?"

Rhiow hit him upside the head, hard, with her claws just barely in, and knocked Arhu flat. The thump was audible some feet away: one or two *ehhif* passing by glanced over at it.

"*That's* why," she said, as Arhu started to get up, then crouched down to avoid another blow, and glared up at Rhiow, wincing and flat-eared. She held the paw ready, watching him with eyes narrowed. "And don't flatter yourself to think you can make so much trouble for me that I'll let you run away from your beatings, either. The Powers sent you to us, and by Iau we'll keep you and feed you and teach you to know better until you're past your Ordeal, or of age, or this-life dead: you won't get away from us any sooner than that." She glanced around at the others. "Isn't that so?"

Saash blinked and looked off vaguely in another direction. Urruah yawned, exhibiting every one of his teeth, long, white, and sharp; then he looked lazily at Arhu, and said, "I like the dead part."

Oh, thank you so much for your help, Rhiow said silently to them both, growling softly. *Saash, didn't you think to get him something to eat, all today?*

I was about to, when he started his little stunt with Abad. And then you showed up, and we went straight out, and I assumed you would stop for something, but no, we had to come straight here, by the High Road, no less, and by the time we got near food he was ravenous, and why do you expect him to have behaved otherwise?

Rhiow bristled . . . and then took a breath and let it out. *Well, you know,* she said, after a moment, *you may have something there. So box my ears and call me a squirrel.*

Saash looked at her with annoyed affection. *Not today. I'm saving up all your beatings to give them to you all at once. Probably kill you.*

"What's a life or two between friends?" Rhiow muttered. "I'm sorry. Now, Arhu, listen to me, because you've got to get this through your head. We do *not* go out of our way to attract attention. A wizard's business is *not to be noticed.* And it's not *ehhif* attention we're working to avoid! We've been doing strange things around them all through their history, and they still haven't worked out what's going on. There are much worse things to worry about. Though we work for the Powers That Be, not all the Powers are friendly . . . and if you carelessly raise your profile high enough to get noticed by one of them in particular, She'll squash you flatter than road pizza, eat all your nine lives, spit them up like a hairball, and leave you nothing but a voice to howl in the dark with! She is no friend to wizards, or life, or any of the other things you took your Oath to defend. And even if you don't take your Oath seriously yet, *She* does . . . and *will,* if She catches you."

He stared at her, ears down, still wide-eyed: not the usual insolent look. *Maybe it got through,* she thought. *I hope so.* "So behave yourself," Rhiow said, "because I'm personally going to see to it that your ears ring from moonrise to sunset until you do. —Meanwhile, we're not going to linger here; we've been visible too long already. But for the Dam's sweet sake if you *have* to come out in public and beg, at least do it with some dignity. Watch this."

She slipped around the counter and strolled through the door over to the open space just beside the big glass counter laden with all the meat and cheese: then she sat down demurely and put her tail about her feet. There she waited.

The big man behind the counter had gone back to the business of making a pastrami and Swiss on rye. Rhiow gazed at him steadily, and when he felt the pressure of her look, she opened her mouth and trilled. It was practically a shout for a cat, but Rhiow knew that *ehhif* heard this sound as a small conversational half-purr, not grating or intrusive, but inquisitive and polite. When he looked over at her, Rhiow did it again, stretching her mouth a bit out of shape to approximate the human smile, far more pronounced than a cat's.

The man looked at her thoughtfully for a moment. Then he shrugged. He glanced from side to side to see whether anyone was watching, then reached down to the pile of pastrami he had already cut, and threw a big slice in Rhiow's direction.

She was ready for this. In an instant she was up on her hind legs and had caught it in her paws. Then she dropped it, picked it up in her teeth, and trotted around the counter and out with it: not hurried, but businesslike, with her tail up and confident.

Off to one side, Rhiow dropped it for the others to share. The sound of the *ehhif*'s laughter was still loud behind the counter. "The outside's got pepper on it: it's an acquired taste," Rhiow said to Arhu. "Better just eat the middle. —Now did you see how that went? I picked up that technique from my *ehhif:* don't ask me why, but they think it's hilarious. If I go back, that man will give me more to see me do it again."

"It's a waste of time," Arhu muttered around his mouthful. "You could have just sidled and took it."

"No, I couldn't. You can't take anything but yourself with you when you sidle. If you steal, you do it visibly . . . and that's just as it should be."

"Then you might as well have just taken it anyway. You could have gotten in and out of that glass thing before he knew what had happened."

"No," Rhiow said. "For one thing, you'd never be able to come back here and get more: they'd chase you on sight. But more importantly, it's rude to them."

"Who cares? They don't care about us. Why should we care about them?"

The pastrami was gone. "Come on," Urruah said, glancing around: "let's get ourselves sidled before the transit cops show up and get on our case."

They slipped around a corner from the deli and sidled, then started to walk back out toward the concourse. "They do care, some of them," Saash said.

Arhu hissed softly in scorn. "Yeah? What about all the others? They'll kick you or kill you for fun. And you can't tell which kind they are until it's too late."

Rhiow and the others exchanged glances over Arhu's head as they walked. "It's not their fault," Urruah said. "They generally don't know any better. Most *ehhif* aren't very well equipped for moral behavior as we understand it."

"Then they're just dumb animals," Arhu said, "and we should take what they've got whenever we like."

"Oh, stop it," said Rhiow. "Just because we were made before they were doesn't mean we get to act superior to them."

"Even if we *are?*"

She gave him a sidelong look. "Queen Iau made them," Rhiow said, "even if we're not sure for what. Ten lives on, maybe we'll all be told. Meanwhile, we work with them as we find them. . . ." Arhu opened his mouth, and Rhiow said, "No. Later. We have to get moving if we're going to catch Ehef during his business hours."

"Who's Ehef?" Arhu said.

"Our local Senior wizard," Urruah said. "He's five lives on, now. This life alone, he must be, oh, how old, Rhi?"

"A hundred and sixty–odd moons-round," Rhiow said, "thirteen or so if you do it by suns-round, *ehhif*-style. Oldish for this life."

"A hundred and sixty *moons?*" Arhu goggled. "He's *ancient!* Can he walk?"

Urruah burst out laughing. "Oh, please, gods," he said between laughs, "let him ask Ehef that. Oh please."

"Come on," Rhiow said.

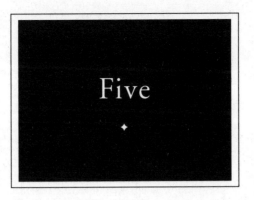

Five

✦

The walk down to Fifth and Forty-second is never an easy one, even on weekends: too many windowshoppers in from out of town, too many tourists, and even a sidled cat has to watch where it walks on Fifth Avenue on Sunday. But by nine-thirty on a Sunday night, almost everything is closed, even the electronics shops that litter the middle reaches of Fifth, festooned with signs declaring CLOSING-OUT SALE! EVERYTHING MUST GO! and attracting the unsuspecting passersby who haven't yet worked out that, come next week, nothing will be gone but their money. As a result, a pedestrian, whether on two feet or four, can stand for a moment and gaze across at the splendid Beaux-Arts façade of the New York Public Library's Forty-second Street building—especially in the evening, when it glows golden with its landmark lighting—and enjoy the look of the place without being trampled by man, machine, or beast.

The four of them crossed with care in the lull between red lights, and Arhu stood looking up the big flight of steps, and from one side to the other, at the massive shapes of the two lions carved out of the pale pink Tennessee marble. Feral Arhu might have been, but no cat with brains enough to think could have failed to recognize the two huge, silent figures as images of relatives.

"Who are they?" Arhu said.

"Gods," Urruah said pointedly. "Some of *ours.*"

Rhiow smiled. "They're Sef and Hhu'au," she said, "the lion-Powers of Yesterday and Today."

Arhu stared. "Are they real?"

Saash smiled slightly. "If you mean, do they exist? Yes. If you mean, do they walk around looking like that? No," Saash said. "But they're *like* that. Big, and powerful . . . and predatory, each in his or her own way. They stand for the barriers between what was, which we can't affect, and what will be—which we can, but only by what we do in the present moment."

"Except if you get access to a timeslide," Urruah said, "when you can go back in time and—"

"Urruah," Rhiow said, glaring at him, "go eat something, or do something *useful* with that mouth, all right?" To Arhu she said, "We do *not* tamper with time without authorization from *Them,* from the Powers That Be. And even They don't do it lightly. You can destroy a whole world if you're not careful or else you can wipe yourself out of existence, which tends to have the same effect at the personal level even if you're lucky enough not to have caused everyone else not to have existed as well. So don't even *think* about it. And you'll find," she added, as the smug we'll-see-about-that expression settled itself over Arhu's face, "when you ask the One Who Whispers for details on time travel anyway, that you won't be given that information, no matter how you wheedle. If you press Her on the subject, your ears will ring for days. But don't take *my* word for it. Go ahead and ask."

Arhu's face went a little less smug as he looked from Saash to Urruah and saw their knowing grins: especially Urruah's, which had a little too much anticipation in it. Rhiow looked sidewise at Saash. *This "heavy-pawed dam" role isn't one I ever imagined myself in,* Rhiow said silently. *And I'm not sure I like it. . . .*

Saash glanced at her, a little amused. *You're betraying a natural talent, though. . . .*

Thanks loads.

"If they're Yesterday and Today," Arhu said, "then where's Tomorrow?"

"Invisible," Urruah said. "Hard to make an image of something that hasn't happened yet. But he's there, Reh-t is, whether you see him or not. Like all the best predators, you never see him till it's much too late. Walk right through him, feel the chill: he's there."

Arhu stared at the empty space between the two statues, and shivered. It was a little odd. Rhiow looked at him in mild concern for a moment.

They went in, trotting up the stairs and weaving to avoid the *ehhif*. Arhu kept well over to the right side, skirting the pedestal of Sef's statue. *You scared the child,* Rhiow said to Urruah.

It's good for him, Urruah said, untroubled. *He can use some scaring, if you ask me.*

They came up to the top of the steps, and Rhiow took a moment to coach Arhu in how to handle the revolving door. Inside the polished brass doors, they stood for a moment, looking up at the great entrance hall, all resplendent with its white marble staircases. Then Rhiow said, "Come on, this way . . ." and led them off to the left, under the staircase and the second-floor gallery, and past the green travertine marble doorway that opened into the writers' room; then right, around the corner to a door adorned with a sign reading STAFF ONLY, and an arrow pointing down with the word CAFETERIA.

Arhu sniffed the air appreciatively. "Don't get any ideas," Urruah growled, "that's today's lunch you're smelling, and it's long eaten."

Rhiow heard his stomach growl, and carefully didn't chuckle out loud. She reared up and pushed the door open: outside of opening hours, it wasn't locked. It leaned inward with the usual squeak, and they trotted in and up the stairs to the central level of the stacks.

When they were out of the stairwell, Arhu loped over to the edge of the inner stack corridor and looked down through the railings. "Wow," he said, "what *is* all this stuff?"

"Knowledge," Rhiow said, stepping up beside him and looking up at the skylights and four stories of books, and down at three stories more: four and a half miles of shelving, here and in the tunneled-out space under Bryant Park, pierced here and there by the several staircases that allowed access between levels, and the selective retrieval system that moved between levels, its vertical conveyor arms picking up books that had been called for and dropping off books to be returned. It was the genius of this building, its arrangement in such a way as to hide this great mass of shelf space—so that even when you knew it was here, it was always a shock to see it, as much cubic space as would be in a good-sized apartment building, and not an inch of it wasted.

In the center of it all, on the level at which they had entered, was a large pitlike area filled with desks and carrels, with a wide wooden-arched opening off to one side. Right now this opening, where *ehhif* would come from the main reading room on the side to pick up books, was shuttered and locked, in case thieves should somehow get in through the great reading room windows by night and try to steal books for collectors. The rarest books were all now up in little wood-paneled, iron-grilled jails in the Special Collections, second-floor front, isolated from the main reference stacks by thick concrete walls and alarm systems. Ehef had told Rhiow once that you could hear the books whispering to each other in the dark through the trefoil-pierced gratings, in a tiny rustling of page chafing against page, prisoners waiting for release. Rhiow had come away wondering whether he had been teasing her. Wizards do not lie: words are their tool and currency, which they dare not devalue. But even wizardry, in which a word can shape a world, has room for humor, and there had been an whimsical glint in Ehef's eyes that night. . . .

She smiled slightly. "This way," Rhiow said, and led the way over to the central core of carrels, where the computers sat two to a desk, or sometimes three. Several of the monitors were turned on, casting a soft blue-white glow over the desks; and on one desk, sprawled comfortably with one paw on the keyboard, and looking thoughtfully at the screen in front of him, lay Ehef.

He looked over at them with only mild interest as they came, though when his eyes came to rest on Arhu, the expression became more awake. Ehef's coloration was what People called *vefessh,* and *ehhif* called "blue"; his eyes, wide and round in a big round platter of a face, were a vivid green that set off the plush blue fur splendidly. Those eyes reflected the shifting images on the screen, pages scrolling by. "Useless," he said softly. "Not even wizardry can do anything about the overcrowding on these lines. Phone company's gotta do something. —Good evening, Rhiow, and hunt's luck to you."

"Hunt's luck, Senior," she said, sitting down.

"Wondered when you were going to get down to see me. Urruah? How they squealin'?"

"Loudly," Urruah said, and grinned.

"That's what I like to hear. Saash? Life treating you well?"

She sat down, threw a look at Arhu, and immediately began to scratch. "No complaints, Ehef," she said.

"So I see." He looked at Arhu again, got up, stretched fore and aft, and jumped down off the desk, crossing to them. "And I smell new wizardry. What's your name, youngster?"

"Arhu."

Ehef leaned close to breathe breaths with him: Arhu held still for it, just. "Huh. Pastrami," said Ehef. "Well, hunt's luck to you too, Arhu. You still hungry? Care for a mouse?"

"There are *mice* here?"

"Are there mice here, he asks." Ehef looked at the others as if asking for patience in the face of idiocy. "As if there's any building in this city that *doesn't* have either mice, rats, or cockroaches. Mice! There are hundreds of mice! Thousands! . . . Well, all right, *some."*

"I want to catch some! Where are they?"

Ehef gave Rhiow a look. "He's new at this, I take it."

Arhu was about to shoot off past Rhiow when he suddenly found Urruah standing in front of him, with an attentive and entirely too interested expression. "When you're on someone else's hunting ground," Urruah said, "it's manners to ask permission first."

"If there are thousands, why should I? I wanna—"

"You should ask permission, young fastmouth," said Ehef, his voice scaling up into a hiss as he leaned in past Urruah's shoulder with a paw raised, "because if you don't, I personally will rip the fur off your tail and stuff it all right down your greedy face, are we clear about that? Young people these days, I ask you."

Arhu crouched down a little, wide-eyed, and Rhiow kept her face scrupulously straight. Ehef might look superficially well-fed and well-to-do, but to anyone who had spent much time in this city, the glint in his eyes and the muscles under his pelt spoke of a kittenhood spent on the West Side docks among the smugglers and the drug dealers, with rats the size of dogs, dogs the size of ponies, and *ehhif* who (unlike the tunnel-*ehhif*) counted one of the People good eating if they could catch one.

"Please don't rip him up, Ehef," Rhiow said mildly. "He's a little short on the social graces. We're working on it."

"Huh," Ehef said. "He better work fast, otherwise somebody with less patience is going to tear his ears off for him. Right, Mr. Wise-mouth?" He moved so fast that even Rhiow, who was half-expecting it, only caught sight of Ehef's paw as it was just missing Arhu's right ear; the ear went flat, which was just as well, for Ehef's claws were out, and Arhu crouched farther down.

"Right," said Ehef. "Well, because Rhiow suggests it, I'll cut you a little slack. You can't help it if you were raised in a sewer, a lot of us were. So what you say is, 'Of your courtesy, may I hunt on your ground?' And then I say, 'Hunt, but not to the last life, for even prey have Gods.' So come on, let's hear it."

Only a little sullenly—for there was a faint, tantalizing rustling and squeaking to be heard down at the bottom of the stacks—Arhu said, "Of your courtesy, may I hunt on your ground."

"Was that a question? Who were you asking, the floor? One more time."

Arhu started to make a face, then controlled it as one of Ehef's paws twitched. "Of your courtesy, may I hunt on your ground?"

"Sure, go on, you, catch yourself some mice, there's a steady sup-ply, I make sure of that. But don't eat them all or I'll skin you before anybody's gods get a chance. Go on, what are you waiting for, don't you hear them messing around down there? Screwing each other, that's what that noise is, mouse sex, disgusting."

Hurriedly, Arhu got up and scurried off. Rhiow and the others looked after him, then sat down with Ehef.

"Thanks, Ehef," Rhiow said. "I'm sorry he's so rude."

"Aah, don't worry about it, we all need a little knocking around in this life before we're fit to wash each other's ears. I was like that once. He'll learn better; or get dead trying."

"That's what we're hoping to avoid. . . ."

Saash blinked, one ear swiveling backward to follow the rustling-going on above. "'I make sure there's a steady supply'? I wouldn't think that's a very professional attitude for a mouser."

"I got more than one profession, you know that. But the day I eat every mouse in the place, that's the day they decide they don't need a cat anymore."

"And, besides," Saash said dryly, "'even prey have gods.'"

"Sure they do." Ehef settled himself, stretched out a paw. "But ethics aside, look, it's not like the old times anymore, no more 'jobs for life.' With the budget cuts, if these people want to give me cat food, they have to pay for it themselves. Bad situation, nothing I can do about it. So I make sure they think I'm useful, and I make sure I don't have to go out of my way to do it. Why should I go hunting out when I can eat in? I bring the librarians dead mice every day, they bring me cat food, everybody's happy. Leaves me free for other work. Such as consultation, which reminds me, why didn't you call to make sure I was available first?"

Rhiow smiled. "You're always available."

"The disrespect of youth."

"When have I ever been disrespectful to you? But it's true, you know it is. And I usually do call first, but I had a problem."

Ehef's ears swiveled as he heard the scampering downstairs. "So I see. Not the one I thought, though." His whiskers went forward in a dry smile. "Thought you finally figured out what to do with that spell."

"What? Oh, that." Rhiow laughed. "No, I'm still doing analysis on it, when I have the time. Not much, lately. The gates seem to take up most of it . . . and that's the problem now."

"All right." He blinked and looked vague for a moment, then said, "I keep a sound-damper spell emplaced around the desks: it's active now, he won't hear. Tell me your troubles."

She told him about their earlier failure with the gate. Ehef settled down into a pose that Rhiow had become very familiar with over the years: paws tucked in and folded together at the wrists, eyes half-closed as he listened. Only once or twice did he speak, to ask a technical question about the structure of the gate. Finally he opened one eye, then the second, and looked up.

So did Rhiow. It was very quiet downstairs.

"He couldn't get out of here, could he?" she said.

"Not without help. Or not without turning himself into a mouse," said Ehef, "which fortunately he can't do yet, though I bet that won't last long. But never mind. Pretty unsettling, Rhi, but you have to see where this line of reasoning is going to take you."

"I wasn't sure," she said. "I thought a second opinion—"

"You hoped I would get you off the hook somehow," Ehef said with that slightly cockeyed grin that showed off the broken upper canine. "You've already talked this through with Saash, I know—otherwise you wouldn't waste my time—and she couldn't suggest anything at our level of reality that could cause such a malfunction." He glanced up at Saash: she lashed her tail "no." "So the problem has to be farther in, at a more central, more senior level. Somewhere in the Old Downside."

This agreed with Rhiow's opinion, and it was not at all reassuring. Wizards most frequently tend to rank universes in terms of their distance to or from the most central reality known—the one that all universes mirror, to greater degree or lesser, and about which all worlds and dimensions are arranged. That most senior reality had many names, across existence. Wizards of the People called it *Auhw-t,* the Hearth: *ehhif* wizards called it Timeheart. It was the core-reality of the universes: some said it was the *seed*-reality, parent of all others. Whether this was the case or not, worlds situated closer to the Hearth had an increased power to affect worlds farther out in life's structure. The Old Downside was certainly much more central than the universe in which Earth moved, so that what happened there was bound to happen here, sooner or later. And a failure in the effect of the laws of wizardry in a universe so central to the scheme of things had bad implications for the effectiveness of wizardry here and now, on Earth, in the long term.

"You mean," Rhiow said, "that something is changing the way the Downside gating structures behave?"

Ehef shrugged his tail. "Possible."

"Or else something's changing the locks on the gates," Saash said suddenly, with a peculiar and disturbed look on her face.

"That would probably be the lesser of the two evils," Ehef said, "but neither one's any good. Worldgating's one of the things that keeps this planet running . . . not that the world at large notices, or ought to. If wizards in high-population areas like this have to start diverting energy from specialized wizardries just to handle 'rapid transit,' they're not going to be able to do their jobs at peak effectiveness . . . and the results are going to start to show in a hurry. Someone's going to have to find out what's going wrong, and fast." Ehef looked up at Rhiow. "And you found the problem . . . so you know what that means. *You* get to fix it."

Rhiow hissed very softly. "Which means a trip Downside. *Hiouh.* Well, you can tell the Powers from me that they're going to have to find someone else to mind the baby while we do what we're doing. He's on Ordeal, but he doesn't understand the ramifications of the Oath as yet, and we're not going to have time to teach him *and* do this at the same time. Nor can we take the chance that he might sabotage something we're doing in a moment of high spirits—"

"Sorry, Rhi," Ehef said. "You're stuck with him. The 'you found the problem, you fix it' rule applies to Arhu as well. Your team must have something to offer him that no other wizards now working have; otherwise he wouldn't be here with you."

"Maybe they do," Rhiow said, starting to get angry, "but what *about* my team, then? How're they supposed to cope, having to do their jobs— and particularly nasty ones, now—while playing milk-dam to a half-feral kitten? He's an unknown quantity, Ehef: he sounds *odd* sometimes. And I have no idea what he's going to do from one moment to the next, even when he's *not* sounding odd. Why should my team be endangered, having to look out for *him?* They're past their own Ordeals, trained, experienced, and necessary—who's looking out for *their* needs?"

"The same Ones who look after them usually," Ehef said. "No wizard is sent a problem that is inappropriate to him or to his needs. Problems sent to a team are always appropriate to the *whole* team . . . whether it looks that way, at this end of causality, or not.

Right now, you can question that appropriateness . . . what wizard doesn't, occasionally? But afterward, things always look different."

"They'll look a *lot* more different if we're dead," Urruah said softly.

"Yeah, well, we all take that chance, don't we? But even crossing the street's not safe around here, you know that. At least if you die on errantry, you know it was for a purpose. More assurance than most People get. Or most other sentient beings of whatever kind." He glanced up at the stairway to the next level of the stacks, where scampering sounds could be heard again. "As for him, he's almost certainly part of the solution to this problem. Look at him: almost *too* young to be doing this kind of thing . . . and all the more powerful for it. You know how it is with the youngest wizards: they don't know what's impossible, so they have less trouble doing it. And just as well. We learn our limits too soon as it is. . . ."

"If we survive to find them," Saash said, dry-voiced.

"Yeah, well. I didn't hold out much hope for *you* when we first met," Ehef said. "You'd jump at the sight of your own shadow." Saash glanced away. "And look at you now. Nice work, that, yesterday: you kept cool. So keep cool now. That might be what this youngster's been sent to you for. But there's no way to tell which of you will make the difference for him." He glanced at Urruah, somewhat ironically.

Urruah closed his eyes, a you-must-be-joking expression, and turned his head away.

Rhiow opened her mouth, then closed it again, seeing Ehef's expression—annoyed, but also very concerned. "Rhiow," he said, "you know the Powers don't waste energy: that's what all this is about. If you found the problem, *you're meant to solve it*. You're going to have to go down there, and I'm glad it's not me, that's all I can say."

Rhiow made a face not much different from Arhu's earlier one. "I was hoping you could suggest something else."

"Of course you were. If I were in your place, I would too! But it's my job to advise you correctly, and you know as well as I do that that's the correct advice. Prepare an intervention, and get your tails down there. Look around. See what's the matter . . . then come home and report."

Down below, the soft sound of squeaking began again. Ehef wrinkled his nose. "I wish they could do that more quietly," he muttered.

"Oh?" Rhiow said, breathing out in annoyance. "Like toms do?"

"Heh. Rhi, I'll help every way I can. But my going along wouldn't be useful in an intervention like this. Adding someone else on wouldn't help . . . might hurt."

"And him?" Urruah flicked an ear at the stacks above them. "*He* sure got added on."

"Not by me. By *Them*. You gonna argue with the hard-to-see type standing out there between those two big guys out front? Or with the Queen? I don't think so. She has Her reasons."

"What possible *good* can he be?"

"What do I look like, Hrau'f the Silent? How would *I* know? Go down there and find out. But go prepared."

They thought about that for a while. Then Ehef said to Urruah, "Toms. That reminds me. You going to that rehearsal tomorrow morning? I heard tonight's was canceled."

"Uh, yes, I'm going."

"You know Rahiw?"

"Yeah, I saw him earlier."

"Fine. You see him there, you tell him I have the answer to that problem he left with me. Tell him to get his tail back up here when it's convenient."

"All right. You're not going, though?"

"Aah, that kind of thing, *ehhif* stuff, I know multicultural is good, but I got no taste for it, my time of life. You youngsters, you get out there, have a good time, listen to the music, maybe make a little of your own, huh?"

Urruah squeezed his eyes shut, a tolerant expression, eloquent of a tom dealing with someone who'd been *ffeih* for so long that he couldn't remember the good things in life. Ehef grinned back and cuffed Urruah in front of one ear, a lazy gesture with the claws out, but not enough force or speed to do any harm. "You just lick that look out of your whiskers, sonny boy," he said. "I knew you when you didn't know where your balls were yet, let alone how many of them to expect. I've got other things to do with my spare time lately." He threw an annoyed glance at the computer.

Rhiow smiled, for this was hardly news, although getting Ehef to talk about this new hobby had been difficult at first. She had known what was going on, though, for some years—since the library installed its first computer system and announced that it was calling it CATNYP.

"I wouldn't have thought you were the techie type," Saash murmured.

"Yeah, well, it grows on you," Ehef said. "Horrifying. But we have an *ehhif* colleague working with the less, shall we say, 'visible' aspects of the CATNYP system. She's been busy porting in the software for putting *The Book of Night with Moon* online."

Rhiow blinked at that. *The Book of Night with Moon* was probably the oldest of the human names for what cat-wizards called *The Gaze of Rhoua's Eye*, the entire assembled body of spells and wizardly reference material, out of which Hrau'f whispered you excerpts when you needed them. Humans had a lot of other regional names for the *Book*, many of them translating into "the Knowledge" or a similar variant. *Ehhif* wizards who got their information from the Powers That Be in a concrete written or printed form, rather than as words whispered in their ears or their minds, often carried parts of the *Book* as small volumes that were usually referred to casually as "the Manual," and used for daily reference. "Wouldn't have thought it was possible," Rhiow said. "The complexity . . . and the sheer volume of information that would have to be there . . ."

"It works, though," Ehef said, jumping up onto one of the nearby desks with a computer terminal on it. "Or at least it's starting to . . . the beta-test teams have been working on it for some years now. There was some delay—I think the archetypal 'hard copy' of the *Book* was missing for a while—but a team out on errantry found it again and brought it back. Since then the work's been going ahead steadily on versions tailored to several different platforms, mostly portable computers and organizers. This is the first mainframe implementation, though. We're trying to give it a more intuitive interface than previously, a little less structured: more like the input you get from the Whisperer when you ask advice."

Rhiow jumped up after him, followed a moment later by Urruah and Saash. "I've seen the *ehhif* Manuals," Saash said, sitting down and tucking her tail around her as she looked with interest at the computer.

"They change in size—the information comes and goes as the wizard needs it. How does a computer version of the *Gaze* handle that?"

"You're asking *me?*" Ehef said, looking at the computer's screen, which at the moment was showing a screen-saver image of flowing stars . . . but the stars looked unnervingly more real than the ones on Rhiow's *ehhif*'s computer screen. "Not my specialty area. Dawn says the software has 'metaextensions into other continua,' whatever *that* means." He put out a paw, touched the screen: the stars went away, replaced by the white page and lion logo for the library.

"Touch-sensitive," Rhiow said. "Nice."

"Gives the keyboards a little relief. Or they can use these." He put a paw on the nearby mouse, waggled it around.

Urruah looked at it. "I always wondered why they called these things 'mice.'"

"Has a tail. Makes little clicky squeaky noises. Breaks if you use it hard enough to have any real fun with it. Would have thought that was obvious."

"But to *ehhif?*"

Ehef shrugged his tail. "Anyway, this is convenient enough for wizards who use a text-based version of the *Book*'s information and need to stop into the research libraries to check some piece of fine detail. Later, when we work the bugs out, we'll allow access from outside. Maybe let it loose on the Internet, or whatever that turns into next."

"You mean whatever *you* turn it into," Rhiow said, with a slight smile.

"Come on, Rhi, it doesn't show *that* much," Ehef said mildly. "Anyway, *someone* has to help manage something so big. And *ehhif* are so anarchic. . . . *Au,* what do I need *this* for right now?" Ehef muttered, and reached out for the mouse, moved it a little on the table.

"What?" Rhiow said. She peered at the screen. A little symbol, a stroke with a dot under it, had appeared down in the right-hand corner: what *ehhif* called an "exclamation point." Ehef had clicked on it, and another little window had popped up on the screen: this now flickered and filled with words.

"It's the usual thing," he growled: "I'm between systems here, and half the time She Whispers, and half the time She sends me E-mail, and sometimes she does *both,* and I never know which to— All right, *now* what is it?"

Rhiow turned away politely, as the others did, but privately she was wondering about Ehef's relationship with one of the Powers That Be, and how he could take such a tone with Hrau'f herself. "Huh," Ehef said finally, finishing his reading. "Well. Not that serious. Rhi, there's something in the Met you're supposed to have a look at. They've been bringing out some archival material that was in storage in Egyptian. Written stuff, in old *ehhif.* She says, check the palimpsest cases."

"For what?" Rhiow flicked her ears forward but could hear nothing from the Whisperer herself.

"She says you'll know it when you see it."

Rhiow put her whiskers forward good-humoredly at that: it often seemed that Hrau'f was not above making you do a little extra work for your own good. "Strange," she said, "getting news from her written down like that."

"*Ffff,*" Ehef said, a disgusted noise, "you don't know *how* strange it looked until we got the Hauhai font designed. *Technology.*" He pronounced it as a curse word, and spat softly. "If I ever find out which of us suggested to the *ehhif* that the wheel should be round instead of square, I'm going to dig up her last grave and shred her ears. —Oh, *there* you are, finally. You leave me some?"

Arhu was standing by the desk, looking considerably thicker around the middle than he had just a little while ago. Rhiow was briefly shocked at how thin Arhu was, when a full meal produced a whopping gut-bulge like the one he presently sported.

"Thank you," Arhu said, and burped.

"Well, may Iau send you good of it, you young slob," Ehef said, ironic, but still amused.

"Yeah, that reminds me," Arhu said, and burped again, "who *is* this Iau you're all yowling about all the time?"

Rhiow opened her mouth, then shut it again and looked away in embarrassment.

To her surprise, though, Ehef merely produced a very crooked smile. "Kitling, we got a saying in this business. 'Stupidity can be accidental. Ignorance is on purpose.' Ignorance gets your ears shredded. The only thing that saved *you* is, you asked the question. *Always* ask. You may get your ears shredded anyway, but afterward you'll still be alive to wear them. Maybe." He gave Rhiow a dry look. "Maybe you should take him up to the Met with you. He keeps going on like this, he's likely to run into the Queen in the street one day and get his features rearranged. She's patient, but I don't know if She's *this* patient."

"It won't be tonight, I don't think," Rhiow said.

He looked at her narrow-eyed for a moment. "You think it's wise to put this off?"

"I'm only feline, Ehef," Rhiow said, and yawned; there was no point in hiding it. "Give me a break. It's been a lively couple of days, and it's going to get worse. We'll get it taken care of . . . but my team and I need some sleep first, and I need a good long talk with the Whisperer tonight before we go Downside. I want to make sure I have the right spells ready to protect us. You know why."

"Yes," Ehef said. "Look, I'll ask the Penn team to keep an eye on your open gate. But that's going to have to be your main concern when you've had a little rest. You did a nice interim solution, but you know it won't last. They'll be cutting that piece of bad track out even as we speak. Tomorrow night—morning after next, tops—they'll replace it, and if that gate's not behaving right, *then* where are we? Go home, get your sleep. Meanwhile, we'll get some help to watch the top side of the gate for you, act as liaison if you need anything from Above when you're ready to get working down there."

"Thanks, Ehef," Rhiow said. "I'll appreciate that."

Arhu yawned, too, and looked somewhat surprised as he did so. "I'm tired," he said. "Can we go back to that little den now?"

"Not a bad idea," Saash said. "Rhi, when should we meet tomorrow?"

"A little after noon, I guess," she said. "Sound all right? Urruah?"

"I'll be up earlier," he said. "That rehearsal. I'll walk you three home first, though."

"The Tom's own chivalry. Senior . . . thanks again for the help."

"We're all in this together," Ehef said, settling down on the desk again. "Go well on the errand, wizards."

They purred their thanks, all but Arhu, and headed out. As they made their way toward the door to the main front hall, Arhu whispered, none too quietly, "What do you want more spells for? Are we going to have a fight? Is something going to happen?"

"You'll find out soon enough," Saash said, "when your Ordeal really gets started."

"This looks pretty much like an ordeal already," Arhu muttered, glancing from Rhiow to Saash. He did not look at Urruah.

Urruah smiled, and they went out.

As it turned out, they got slightly sidetracked on the way home. Rhiow wanted Arhu to know the way to her own neighborhood, so they went there first. There was no rush to get anywhere, so Rhiow and the others strolled down Seventy-first at their ease: Rhiow, in particular, with the intense pleasure of someone who is off shift for the moment and has the luxury of enough time to stop and smell the roses. Or, more accurately, time to smell and appreciate, each in its proper way, the trees, air, cars, gutters, weeds, flowers, garbage cans, and other endemic wildlife of the city: the squirrels, sparrows, starlings, passing *ehhif* and *houiff,* the rustlings above and below ground, the echoes and the whispers; steam hissing, tires and footsteps on concrete, voices indoors and outdoors: and above and around it all, the soft rush of water, the breeze pouring past the buildings—now that there was enough temperature differential for there to *be* a breeze—and very occasionally, from high up, the cry of one of the Princes of the Air about his business, which in this part of the world mostly amounted to killing and eating pigeons. Her Oath aside, Rhiow's personal opinion was that the city was oversupplied with pigeons, and as part of their position in the natural order of things, the Princes were welcome to as many of them as they could eat. They reminded her too much of rats, with the unwelcome and unnecessary addition of wings.

There were no pigeons in the street at the moment, though, because *hauissh* was in progress . . . and any pigeon careless or foolish enough to drop itself into the middle of a bout of *hauissh* rapidly became an aspect of play, and shortly thereafter an object of digestion.

Cars, *ehhif,* and *houiff* did pass through, and took part in play, without knowing they did.

Indeed there was nothing overt that would have led any *ehhif* to suspect that a game as old as felinity was going on up and down the length of the block of Seventy-first between First and Second; reputations were on the line, and from many windows eyes watched, hindered from gameplay, perhaps, but not from intelligent and passionate interest.

Rhiow sidled through it all with her tail up, as did the rest of the team. So close to home, it wouldn't have done to be visible on the street: if one of the neighbors should mention her presence there to Iaehh or Hhuha, there would be endless trouble. As it was, she needed to be sidled anyway, to avoid the many *ehhif* who were on the street this time of the evening.

"Hey, *ffeih*-wizard!" came a comment from one of the streetside terraces above. "Had a good roll on your back lately?"

Rhiow put her whiskers forward and strolled on by, not even bothering to look up, though Arhu did. Urruah and Saash wore expressions suggesting calm tolerance of idiocy. ". . . If she's so terrific and powerful and all," said the predictable second voice, "why can't she make the kittening part grow back, and do something *really* useful with herself?"

Rhiow kept walking, showing no reaction to the others and schooling herself to be slightly amused. There were People in her neighborhood, as in every neighborhood where a feline wizard worked, who knew about her and found her either funny or repugnant; and who found the concept of wizardry laughable or even hateful. These People in particular—the two extremely spoiled and opinionated pedigreed Himalayans six stories up, in one of the penthouse apartments of the new building near the corner—were sure that Rhiow was living evidence of some kind of convoluted plot against their well-being: a parasite, possibly a traitor, and certainly not proper breeding material. Rhiow, for her own part, was sure that they were pitifully bored and ignorant, had nothing to do with their days but culture their spite, and had almost certainly never done a useful thing since their eyes came open. ". . . can't really be much of a Person," one of them said spitefully, meaning to be heard, "if you haven't even made kittens *once . . .*"

"Not much point in making them if you're not going to be able to tell what they *are,* my dear."

"Ooh, me*ow,*" Rhiow muttered, and kept walking.

"They need a nice little plague of fleas to take their minds off their 'troubles,'" Urruah said under his breath, coming up alongside her.

"Please. That would be so unethical."

"But satisfying. Just think of them scratching . . ."

". . . and give them the satisfaction of thinking the universe really *is* after them? Please." *All the same . . .*

The team paused about a third of the way down the street; Rhiow ducked into the entranceway of an apartment building and sat for a moment, peering down the sidewalk. There was a row of five brownstones across the street, their front steps still largely identical despite the renovations of the past few decades; they faced across to a large modern apartment building and two other brownstones, one on each side of it. On the first floor, far left windowsill of the left-hand brownstone, a small milk-chocolate-colored cat sat hunched up, roundbacked, golden eyes half-shut, as if looking at nothing. Across the street, sitting upright, was a large, dirty white tom; he was looking intently at the top of a wall between the two brownstones directly across from him. Shadows fell across that wall, cast by a thick raggy carpet of some kind of climbing vine that scaled up the nearest wall of the adjoining building.

Rhiow stood for a moment and waited to see if any other players would reveal themselves to so cursory an analysis, but after a few seconds she gave it up. "Come on," she said, and walked with the others over to where the white cat sat; he glanced at them as they came. It was Yafh, of course, dominating the block's gameplay as usual. It was a good thing he was so genial about it; life with him could have become extremely annoying otherwise.

She went up the stairs toward the other two, pausing briefly beside Yafh as she came up even with him. Protocol dictated that a nonplayer await permission from players before passing or approaching their chosen stances too closely; to obstruct or intervene in a player's field of view while another player was moving could damage not only that player's score, but others' scores as well.

Yafh had been sitting with eyes half-closed, watching the brown cat across the street without seeming to watch her. Now he stood, stretched fore and aft, and turned his back on the proceedings: a gesture readable to all players as indicating the intention to temporarily abandon play without loss of stance.

"Hey there, Rhiow," he said, and stalked off to one side of his stance. "Haven't seen you for a while."

"Business," she said, and they breathed breaths companionably before she sat down. "Goodness, who gave you the fish?"

"Restaurant round the corner," Yafh said. "Perfectly lovely fish heads, why they don't keep them I can't imagine. *Ehhif* have no taste. Urruah? How's the hunting?"

"Not bad, not bad."

"Saash . . . don't often see you down this way. 'Luck to you. And who's this youngster?"

"Arhu."

"'Luck to you, son. Come to see how the professionals do it?"

"Nowhere better," Urruah said, before Arhu could open his mouth. "How's the bout going?"

"Third sequence, twenty-eighth passage," Yafh said. "The balances have shifted."

"You mean you're *not* winning as usual?"

"'Winning.' What an *ehhif* word. We'll see how the situation looks by next week."

"You want to understand the Game," Urruah said to Arhu, "this is the Person you come to."

"I don't understand it very well," Arhu said, in a small voice.

Rhiow glanced at him, wondering briefly where this sudden and becoming modesty had come from. Or maybe he was simply impressed by all of Yafh's scars. "Well, that's no surprise," Rhiow said. "Years now I've been following *hauissh,* and I'm not sure *I* understand anything but the basics yet. Yafh is a master, though; what he doesn't know about it isn't worth knowing."

"All you need to know, young tom," Yafh said, "is that *hauissh* is the Fight—or the best version of it we've got left. Everything else is commentary."

"But . . . *She* says *life* is the Fight," Arhu said.

"'She'?" Yafh said. "Oh, the One Who you wizards say Whispers to you? Well, probably she's right. But one thing's for sure, life is *hauissh*."

"There speaks the enthusiast," Saash said dryly. "Arhu, don't let him fool you. Yafh eats, drinks, washes, and sleeps *hauissh*. If it didn't exist, he would have to invent it."

"Don't talk naughty," Yafh said, settling himself down in a way that suggested he had less concern about the elegance of his position than his comfort. "Takes a god to invent something this complex, something with this kind of elegance, this subtlety. You tell me now, young tom: who do you think's holding down the most important stance at the moment?"

Arhu looked around him in bemusement. "Her," he said, flirting his tail sideways to indicate the handsome chocolate-brown cat who crouched, immobile as a statue, on one of the nearby walls between two buildings.

"And you'd wouldn't be too far off. Trust Hmahilh' to hog a good spot at the earliest opportunity. But *why?*"

Arhu looked up and down the street. "Because she can see everybody else," he said, "and not everybody else can see her."

"Right. That's part of it, but not all. So try this. We have six players out there: seven, counting me, as of a moment ago. I don't officially count right now, but for this analysis, you can keep my stance in. Look at the pattern, see what you see about it. Not the People: the relationships. Take your time, don't look too hard."

Yafh sat washing his face, ineffectively as usual: the grime never did seem to come off, but at least he was always seen to be making the effort. Arhu looked out at the street for a few moments, and then said, "There's— Is there an empty place they're all pointed at, in the street? Between the cab parked there and the big car?"

"A natural talent," Yafh said, looking around at Rhiow and Urruah with approval. "Boy's got the Eye. That's the spot," he said to Arhu.

"That's where the Tree is: with the Serpent wound around it, gnawing at the root. . . ."

"There's no Tree there! That's the middle of the street!"

"It's there in spirit," Yafh said. "All *hauissh* is anchored at the Tree. It's all the original Fight, really; but since we can't chuck lightning-bolts at the Old Snake the way Aaurh and Urrua did, we use move-ment and stealth as a weapon, and seeing as the bolt we strike with, and position as influence. Anyone who sees anyone else *could* strike them with a lightningbolt if they had one. And the Tree is always the center."

Arhu sat down, looking puzzled for a moment. "Maybe I do see. . . ."

Yafh scrubbed behind one ear. "Hmahilh' there is in one of the classic positions just now, the *fouarhweh*. Thousands of hours of commentary have been made about it, just in the last century; it would take you a fair amount of study to understand even a few of the major implications for play as it might progress over the next sev-eral hours or days. But she's holding down a variant of the position the Great Tom would have held—"

"—before he dies," Arhu said, looking at the empty spot, the life slowly starting to drain out of his voice. "For the Old Serpent rises against him and strikes him with its venom, and the Great Cat falls with a great cry, and striveth to rise but cannot; and breath and warmth swiftly go from him so that his Enemy rises over his poisoned body and leaps upon Aaurh the Mighty. Great and terrible is their struggle, so that seas leap from their beds and the earth is riven, and the torn sky rains fire—"

Yafh looked at Rhiow with mild surprise. Urruah was watching Arhu uneasily, but Arhu paid no attention at all, his whole regard be-ing bent on the spot in the street, through which an *ehhif* with a *houff* on the leash was walking. The *houff*, at the sight of them sitting on the steps, started to bark, but for Arhu, it might not have been there at all. "—Yet even so Aaurh at last is lapped in the Serpent's coils, and crushed in them, and she falls, and her power fails out of the world. Then Iau sees that the light has gone from the Moon, and the Sun is blackened with fair Aaurh's dying; and She rises in Her majesty and says, *What has become of My children? Where is Aaurh the warrior, and sa'Rráhh the Tearer, wayward but dear to Me? And what has become of My Consort and the light of his eye, without which My own is dark?* —Then Iau draws Her power about Her, and goes forth in grief and rage; and all things hear Her cry: *Old Serpent, turn You and face Us, for the fight is not done—!*"

"He's been well educated, I'll give you that," Yafh said to Rhiow, blinking a little.

"All the best teachers," Urruah said, sounding dry, but still unsettled.

"That's right, young tom," Yafh said to Arhu, as Arhu abruptly sat up a little straighter, blinking himself. "That's the whole pattern of the gameplay of *hauissh,* right there in the old words. There are endless variations on the theme, as you might well think. But the Queen raises up Her dead, though not forever, as we know; and then the Fight starts up again . . . and so it goes."

"*Yafh,*" came a deafening and strangely pitched shout from across the street, "*let's get on with this! Are you in stance, or out?*"

Everyone winced at the noise. Rhiow smiled, a little crookedly. The source was Hmahilh'. Delicate, graceful little creature though she was, with her demure semi-*ehhif* smile, she was also profoundly deaf: when she spoke, the noise was so alarming that Rhiow was often amazed that bricks didn't shatter. Rhiow had tried several times, as any wizard might, to treat the deafness, but there was something about the nerve damage that resisted treatment. Rhiow half-suspected that the trouble was not the nerves, but the less educable "limbic" areas of Hmahilh's brain, which had gotten so used to being deaf that they couldn't understand there were other options, and so ignored or stubbornly undid any repair to the cranial nerves involved. As a result, a conversation with Hmahilh', while enjoyable enough for her cultured and humorous qualities, otherwise tended to resemble an interview with a fire siren.

"Here, young tom," Yafh said, "you watch this now. She's always worth watching. All right, all right," he yowled back at Hmahilh', "I'm in, already."

"What??"

With a sigh, he turned to face her, a signal she would recognize. Arhu sat watching this, seemingly fascinated, and Rhiow took the opportunity to gesture the others over to a neighboring doorstep where they could watch without being anywhere near another player's stance.

As they went, Rhiow said to Saash, "Are you feeling all right? It's been a busy day . . . but you look tireder than usual."

"Yes, well. There were some more mice in the garage this morning. I was trying to catch them . . ."

"And?"

Saash flicked her ears backward and forward, a hopeless gesture. "Nothing. As usual. I'm so glad I live in the city, and have access to an *ehhif* with a can opener. If I were a country Person, I'd be dead of starvation by now."

Rhiow gave Saash a sympathetic look. She had never been a hunter: it was as if there were something missing in her makeup, perhaps the essential sense of timing that told you when to jump. Either way, the situation had always struck Rhiow as a little unfortunate, or strange, in someone whose technical expertise and timing in other matters were so perfect.

"So what did you do about it, finally?"

"This morning? Nothing. I mean, I could have blown the mice up, but besides being overkill, what good would that have been? The garage *ehhif* would just have thought a car ran them over or something. When Arhu's done here, I'll ask him to see what he can do. Have to keep the *ehhif* impressed with our usefulness, after all: otherwise we might have to find somewhere else to stay . . ."

"Oh, surely not. Abha'h likes you, he wouldn't try to get rid of you!"

"True. But he's not the boss in the garage. I'll be making sure Zhorzh sees whatever we catch."

Rhiow sighed. "You let me know if you need any help," she said.

They sat on the doorstep two doors down from Yafh's stance. "Our boy is spending more and more time in weird-vision land," Urruah said, looking with some concern at Arhu.

"Just as well," Rhiow said. "It's his wizardry . . . He seems to *see* things . . . and then try to *avoid* seeing them. I'm getting concerned about the avoidance."

"Can you blame him? I'm not sure *I'd* want to be sitting on a doorstep one moment and looking at the original Battle at the Dawn of Time the next!"

Saash sat straight and scratched for a moment or so, then started washing. "I think the problem might be that he hasn't really done much wizardry yet. Spells, I mean."

"Yes," Rhiow said. "Everything has sort of been done *to* him, hasn't it?" Rhiow cocked her ears, then; for the statement, once made, created a sort of silence around itself. When you were a wizard, you learned to pay attention to those silences: they were often diagnostic. Sometimes the Whisperer whispered very quietly indeed. "And you're right: I haven't really seen him *do* a spell. Initiate one, I mean. Well, he walked through a door or so, and in the air. And the sidling . . ."

"As regards the physical stuff, he's pretty good," Saash said. "It's the nonphysical I'm more worried about. Nine-tenths of our work is nonphysical. . . ."

"There are a lot of different styles of wizardry," Urruah said. "I think we should try to cut him a little slack, here. Not everyone jumps straight in and starts doing fifty spells a day."

"*You* did," Saash and Rhiow said, practically in unison.

"Well, we can't all be me."

Rhiow and Saash looked at each other and gave silent praise to Iau the Queen of Everything that this was so. "But it's not like there's a quota," Urruah said. "Or some kind of template for Ordeals. Everybody knows you get the occasional 'sleeper' Ordeal that takes months or years. Or 'second' Ordeals, if you don't finish your first one."

"The universe doesn't usually have that much time to spare for the first kind," Rhiow said, "as you know; and the second kind is as rare as working balls on a *ffeih'*d tom, as you also know. His passivity just worries me a little, that's all."

"He's a tom," Urruah said, with a wink. "He'll grow out of it."

This time Rhiow did not bother looking physically at Saash, and didn't have to: she could inwardly hear the small, stifled groan. "You are in, how shall I put it, unusually *male* mode tonight," Rhiow said. "Got another bout of *o'hra* coming on?"

"Night after next. It's the big night, the concert. I'm going to need the time off, Rhi."

"Take it, for Aaurh's sake," she said, waving her tail. "Get the hormones out of your system. If that's possible."

Urruah smirked briefly, but then folded himself down, and after a few seconds, looked a touch more serious. "Maybe the problem is that he just hasn't noticed how much *fun* wizardry is," Urruah said. "How good it feels."

"I would suspect not," Saash said, with a little more tooth in her voice than usual, "since his first experience of it came immediately before being almost torn to shreds by rats. . . ."

"'Ruah," Rhiow said, "I have to admit that Saash has a point. And pushing Arhu won't help. Till he comes to understand that satisfaction claws-on, there's no point in describing it. If he has what it takes to make a good wizard, he'll know it when he feels it . . . no matter how he may rationalize it to himself and others as time goes on."

". . . Well, I hope he *has* that time. Otherwise the crunch-part of his Ordeal may come upon him and he won't have anything useful prepared. In which case . . ." Urruah chattered his teeth briefly, the way a cat will when seeing a rat or a bird, anticipating the jaw spasm that will snap its neck.

"We'll see how he does," Rhiow said, and yawned. "You going to see him home, Saash?"

"Yes. The mice . . ."

"That's right. All right, then . . . you call me in the morning when you're ready, and I'll take him down on patrol again: show him the differences between the gates, get him familiar with the track layout on the upper level." She yawned once more. "Sweet Iau, but I have *got* to get off days. . . . I am just not a day person. Urruah, you take tomorrow evening off, though I wouldn't mind having you on call during the early daylight hours, at least till I get up."

"No problem. This is going to be going on for a while, and Yafh's right about one thing: watching Hmahilh' is always educational. She's some strategist."

"Right. I'll have a walk around the block, then turn in. 'Luck, you two."

"'Luck, Rhi . . ."

She went down the steps, looked up at Yafh and Arhu as she passed. "Hunt's luck, gentlemen . . . I'm done for today."

"Don't want to stay and see the epic struggle?" Yafh said. "You're working too hard, Rhiow."

"Smile when you say that, Yafh. 'Luck, Arhu . . . see you in the morning."

"All right," he said, but he was still gazing at that empty spot . . . with less of an estranged look, this time. The expression was thoughtful, and Rhiow was not entirely sure what to make of it . . . but then, that was becoming the story of her life, where Arhu was concerned.

She saluted them both with a flirt of her tail and walked on down the block. From above, a voice said, "Oh, look, she's going to go out and try to get some after all."

"It won't matter. . . . Even if she knew what to do with a tom, she couldn't find any really *select* blood."

Rhiow had had about enough for one night. She laughed out loud. "What, like *yours?*" she said, intending her voice to carry as well as theirs had. "Hairballs at one end, fur-mats at the other, and twenty pounds of flab apiece in the middle? This is considered 'select'? Things must be pretty bad in the Himalayas."

Feline laughter came from all up and down the street. There was a flustered silence from above, followed by annoyed hisses and growling. Rhiow turned the corner to finish her circuit of the block, then headed for home, walking up the air to her own rooftop and smiling slightly.

When Rhiow got home, she found that Hhuha had gone to bed already. Iaehh was sitting up late, in the big leather chair by the empty fireplace, reading. As Rhiow's small door clicked, he looked up in slight surprise, rubbing his eyes. "Well, there you are. I was wondering if I was going to see you today."

Rhiow sighed. "Yes, well," she said, "we all have long workdays sometimes." She went to her dish for a long drink of water.

Iaehh put his book down, got up, and took the dish right out from under her nose.

"Hey!"

"You can't drink that," Iaehh said, "it's got cat food in it." He started to refill it from the sink.

"As if I care at the moment!" Rhiow said. "Do you know how salty that pastrami can be? Put it back!"

"Here," Iaehh said, "here's some fresh."

"Well, thanks," Rhiow said, and sighed again, and started to drink once more.

"Your 'mom,'" Iaehh said softly, sitting down with his book again, "is terrible about giving you fresh water."

"My 'mom,'" Rhiow said under her breath as she drank. She smiled slightly. There was no question that Iaehh had noticed over time that Rhiow was, to use the annoying *ehhif* phrase, more "her" cat than his: he teased them both about it, Hhuha directly and Rhiow in the usual one-sided dialogue.

Well, it wasn't Iaehh's fault, Rhiow supposed. He simply had no gift for making a lap the way Hhuha did. He somehow seemed to have more than the usual number of bones. Nor (when he did make a lap) did he seem capable of sitting still for more than thirty seconds. Always running in all directions was Iaehh: running to work, running home, running out to the store, just plain running. She liked him well enough: he was thoughtful. He just wasn't soft or still the way Hhuha was; and when he held her, no matter how affectionately, there was never that sense that Rhiow had with Hhuha that there was a purr inside the *ehhif* too, and their two purrs were in synch. *Just a personality thing. But he does mean well. . . .*

She finished with the water and came over to him to thank him: jumped up in his lap and began to knead his knee and purr. "Ow," he said, "ow ow OW ow—"

"Sorry," Rhiow said, and curled around and settled herself, still purring. "Here now, you just sit still and relax—"

He stroked her while propping the book off to one side, on the other knee, under the lamp. For a little while they sat that way, Rhiow closing her eyes and beginning to feel blessedly calmer after the day she'd had. Saash had reported in briefly that after they'd left the bout of *hauissh,* she'd bedded Arhu down without trouble; he'd be out until at least dawn and maybe longer, from the looks of him. Urruah had been very good, better than she'd expected. So had Saash.

How long they'd be that way, as tomorrow progressed, was a good question. For once it had become plain that they would all have to go Downside, she had felt Urruah's and Saash's fear at once. There was no hiding it from team members, not when the three of them had worked together so closely, for as long as they had. . . .

Iaehh sighed and put the book down. "Oh, come on," Rhiow said under her breath, "couldn't you have made it a record? Thirty seconds or so?" But no: he lifted her, got up, and carefully put her down on the seat where he had been.

"I'm bushed," he said. "This way when I get in bed and your mom says, 'Did she come in?' I can say, 'Yes,' and be allowed to go to sleep. 'Night, plumptious cat."

She breathed out in resignation and watched him make the rounds of the apartment, checking the locks, turning out the lights, finally slipping through the bedroom door and closing it softly behind him.

Rhiow lay there, looking around the room in the faint yellow light that came up in stripes through the narrow venetian blinds: reflection from the streetlights down the alley outside.

"Plumptious," she thought. *Is that a real* ehhif *word? I must look that up.*

Oh, well . . . I have other things to do first.

Rhiow started washing, beginning as she did so to make a mental list of the spells she thought they would need for their journey. She felt like stuffing her head full of everything she could coax out of the Whisperer, and all the other spells she routinely carried with her, useful-seeming or not, from the air hardener right down to the "research" spell that had come with her Ordeal. But normally, the Whisperer would let you carry only so much; Her preference, apparently, was for you to call on Her as you needed new material. She would then provide it for you, whole, in your mind. There was a certain extra security, though, in having the spell ready to go, all spoken in your mind except for the final syllable. . . .

But still.

Downside . . .

In the darkness, now that there was no one to see, Rhiow shuddered. Bad enough that time had done nothing whatever to mellow her memories of the team's last trip. But now there was an added problem: Arhu's voice, dry and strange, crying: *It doesn't matter. It's coming anyway.*

And what had the *rest* of that meant? *It came before. Once to see. Once to taste. Once to devour—*

She tried washing a little to get her composure back, but it didn't help. Finally she stopped and, instead of flinching away from the issue, "turned" in mind to face it.

Their intervention Downside had been bad the last time: *bad.* She had not been able to eat for days afterward: the mere feeling of food in her mouth made her retch and choke, so that her *ehhif* took her to the vet, where she endured indignities she couldn't prevent for the sake of explanations she couldn't make. Finally they had brought her home again, defeated by finding nothing physically wrong, and Rhiow had eventually found her appetite once more. But it had taken her a good while to gain back the lost weight, and all that time her food had tasted like dust, no matter what choice delicacies Iaehh and Hhuha had tempted her with.

She had seen the Ones Below, the Old Ones, the Wise Ones, the Children of the Serpent . . . and what they were doing to each other.

They were intelligent: that had been the worst of it. They had been the lords of the world, once. But something had gone very wrong.

. . . Like any wizard of every species from here to the galaxy's rim, Rhiow knew the generalities. The Powers That Be had made the worlds, under the One's instruction. Each Power had gone Its way, making the things that seemed to It most likely to forward the business of Creation as a whole. Abruptly, then, matters changed as one of the Powers, without warning, brought forth something that none of the others had expected or desired. It invented entropy: it created death.

War broke out in heaven. When the conflict died down, that one Power, furious with the others for the rejection of Its gift, was cast out into the darkness. But there was no getting rid of It so simply: the Lone Power (as various species called it) had been part of creation from the first, and It was part of it still.

There was relative quiet for a while after the battle as worlds formed, seas cooled, atmospheres condensed. Slowly life awakened in the worlds, ascended through each environment's necessary stages of physical complexity, and became intelligent. The Powers relaxed, at first: it now seemed as if Creation was going well.

But each species that became intelligent found itself being offered a chance, a Choice, by an often beautiful form that appeared to its first members early in its history. The Choice, after other issues were stripped away, was usually fairly simple. Take the path that the Powers seemed to have put before it—or turn aside into a path destined to make the species that trod it wiser, more powerful and blessed . . . more like gods.

The Choice took countless forms, each cunningly tailored to the species to which it was offered. But under its many guises, no matter how fair, it always spelled Death. The Lone Power went from sentient race to race, intent on tricking them into it: offering, again and again, the poisoned apple, the casket that must not be opened. Many species believed the fair promises and accepted the gift, condemning themselves to entropy and death forever after. Some species accepted it only partially, came to understand their error, and rejected it with greater or lesser levels of success, often involving terrible sacrifices that resonated back to earlier battles and sacrifices deep in time. Some species, by wisdom, or luck, or the unwinding of complex circumstance, never accepted the poisoned Gift at all . . . with results that various other creatures find hard to accept: but even on Earth, there are species that are never seen to die.

Rhiow shifted uncomfortably on the chair. The People had been offered the Choice just as everyone else had: like so many other species on Earth, they had not done well. They had been lucky, though, compared to the Wise Ones. Once upon a time, that had been a mighty people, coming to their dominance of the planet long before the primates or other mammals. Offered the Choice—and the Lone Power's gift, disguised as the assurance that their dominion would never fail while the sun shone—the reptilian forefathers of the Wise Ones chose what the great dark-scaled shape offered them. For a while, Its words were true: the great lizards strode the world and devoured what they would. But it was little more than an eye-blink in terms of geological time before, without warning, the hammerblow fell from the sky. The skies darkened with the massive amounts of dust thrown up by the initial meteoric impact and the earthquakes and volcanic eruptions that followed. The sun no longer shone. The winds rose and stripped the lands bare: the great lizards, almost all of them, starved and died, lamenting the ill-made Choice . . . and hearing, in the howl of the bitter wind and the endless storms of dust and snow, the cruel laughter of the One who had tricked them.

Not *all* of them had died, of course. Some had found refuge in other worlds, places more central. One of those worlds was the one where the Old Downside lay. Down under the roots of the Mountain, the descendants of the survivors of the Wise Ones had found their last refuge. There they nursed their slow cold anger at the changes that had come over the world they ruled. They were no friends toward mammals, which they considered upstarts—degenerate inheritors of their own lost greatness. And to a mammal, the alien reptilian mindset that (at the beginning of things) had made the great lizards the exponents of an oblique and unusual wisdom now merely made them almost impossible to understand—treacherous, dangerous. Even some of the older *ehhif* stories had apparently come to reflect a few shattered fragments of the truth: tales of a tree, of a serpent that spoke, of an ancient enmity between mammals and serpents.

The enmity certainly remained. It hardly seemed to Rhiow as long as a year ago when she and Urruah and Saash had gone down into the caves under the Mountain for the first time, in search of the cause of a recurrent malfunction plaguing the gate that normally resided over by the platform for the Lexington Avenue line. They had inspected the "mirror" gates up at the top of the caves and had found that intervention there would not be sufficient. Slowly they had made their way down into the caverns—a night and a day it had taken them to reach the place; they had even had to sleep there, uneasy nightmare-ridden sleep that it had been. Finally they had found the secondary, "catenary" gate matrix, the place where the immaterial power "conduits" of the upper gates came up through the living stone.

They had also found the Wise Ones, waiting for them just before the cavern where the catenary matrix lay.

There had been a battle. Its outcome had not been a foregone conclusion, even though the three of them were wizards. Rhiow and her team, driven to it, much regretting it (except possibly for Urruah, Rhiow thought), had killed the lizards who'd attacked them, and then began repairs on the gate. It had been clumsily sabotaged, apparently by the lizards interfering with the hyperstrings that led the catenary's energy conduit up through the stone: nonphysical though those "tethers" were, active tunneling under the right circumstances could displace them . . . and the Old Ones, by accident or other means, had gotten it right. Fortunately the damage had not been too serious. Rhiow and her team had rooted the gate-conduit more securely, caused new molten stone to flow in and reinforce its pathway through the stone, and had started to make their retreat.

That was when they found more of the lizards, furtive and hasty, devouring the bodies of those Rhiow and the others had killed. Urruah had charged them, scattering them: and the three of them had made their way hurriedly back to the surface and to the gateway to their own world. But Rhiow had not been able to forget the sight of an intelligent being, tearing the flesh of one of its own kind for food. *What kind of life is that for any creature? Down there in the dark . . . with nothing to eat but . . .*

She shivered again, then started breathing strong and slow to calm herself. *Whisperer,* she said silently, *I have work to do. Tell me what I need to hear.*

What do you have in mind? the answer came after a moment.

Rhiow told her. Shortly what she needed to see had begun laying itself out before her mind: spell diagrams, the complex circles and spheres in which the words and signs of the Speech would be inscribed—either on some actual physical surface, or in her mind. From much practice and a natural aptitude, Rhiow had come to prefer the second method: she had discovered that a spell diagram, once "inscribed" in the right part of her memory, would stay there, complete except for the final stroke, or sigil, that would finish it. For the rest of it—words, equations, descriptions, and instructions—she simply memorized the information. Like other peoples with a lively oral tradition, cats have good memories. And Rhiow knew there was always backup, should a detail slip: the Whisperer was always there, ready to supply the needed information, as reliable as a book laid open would be for an *ehhif*.

You could carry too much, though—burden yourself with useless spells and find yourself without quick access to the one you really needed—so you had to learn to strike a balance, to "pack" cleverly. Rhiow selected several spells that could be used to operate on the "sick" gate—each tailored to a specific symptom it had been showing—and then several others. To the self-defense spells she gave particular thought. One line of reasoning was that the Old Ones, having been so thoroughly routed last time, wouldn't try anything much now. But Rhiow was unwilling to trust that idea—though it would be nice if it turned out that way. She packed several very emphatic destructive spells, designed not to affect a delicate gate halfway through its readjustment: spells designed to work on the molecular structure of tissue rather than with sheer blunt destructive force on any kind of matter, knives rather than sledgehammers. It was like Saash's approach to the rats—nasty but effective.

Finally Rhiow couldn't think of anything else she would need. The knowledge settled itself into her brain, the images and diagrams steadying down where she could get at them quickly. She began to relax a little. There was really nothing more to be done now but sleep. She would make sure she ate well in the morning: going out underfueled on one of these forays was never smart.

Rhiow closed her eyes, "looking" at the spell diagrams littering the workspace in her mind, a glowing word-scattered landscape. Other spells, recently used, lay farther out on the bright plain, less distinct, as if seen through mist: the last few months' worth of work, a foggy, dimly radiant tapestry. Even the spell that Ehef had mentioned was visible way off there, right at the edge of things, the "hobby" spell that she had picked up on her own Ordeal so long ago. *Well, at least that's behind me.*

It's not behind Arhu, though. Poor baby. I hope he makes it.

But so many of us don't. . . .

She sighed, feeling sleep coming, and passed gratefully into dream.

The warmth was all around her but slightly stronger from one side, like the fire her *ehhif* would light in the apartment's old fireplace once in a while, in the winter, when they thought they could get away with it. The Whispering had died away some time ago; now there was only the comforting presence of the Silent One, and the hint of a rumbling, reassuring purr that ran through everything.

Madam, Rhiow said, *I'm frightened.*

So are we all, in the face of That, the answer came. *Or almost all of us are. My sister the Firstborn wasn't. But that was always her style, to go into battle laughing, as if there were no possibility of defeat. Maybe she knows something the rest of us don't. Or that may simply be in her nature as our Dam made it. For the mortal and the semimortal, at least change, the learning of courage, is an option. But for those of us whose natures were set at the beginning of things, we must, I fear, simply be afraid while we keep on doing our jobs. A god that forgets the virtues of specialization, trying to do things It was never designed for, soon becomes no god, but a tyrant.*

Like your other sister, madam . . .

I don't speak of her, the answer came. *We see enough of her as it is.* You *will shortly see more.*

I really don't want to, Rhiow said.

Little enough attention the worlds pay to what any of us want, the answer came. As always, there was a slight edge of humor in the Whisperer's voice, but it was more muted than usual. *Desire, though . . . and intention . . . those are other powers to which even the Powers must answer. Go do your job, daughter. I'll do mine. Perhaps both of them may yet come to something. . . .*

The silence became complete, though, still reassuring, the warmth remained. The dim glow of the spells faded, and Rhiow slept.

Six

Morning came up clear but not at all cool, and Rhiow was awakened early by Hhuha complaining as she got dressed. "Must be eighty out there already," she was saying to Iaehh. "And the damn air conditioner at the office is on the blink again. I swear, a company that makes profits every year that could be mistaken for the GNP of a small country, but they'll let the staff sit there and swelter for two weeks in a row before they get someone in to fix the thing so it doesn't produce heat in August. . . ."

"Sue, you should quit," Iaehh said.

Rhiow got up and stretched and went over to where Hhuha leaned against one of the counters in the kitchen. "Here he goes again," she said under her breath, rubbing against Hhuha's legs, and then went to the food bowl. This argument was one that happened about once a month, these days. Hhuha was a salaried consultant for one of the larger computer companies with offices in the city; but before this job, she had been "freelance"—nonaligned, Rhiow thought this meant—and had worked for whom she pleased. Iaehh—who was presently still wrapped in only his bathrobe and was leaning against the other counter, facing Hhuha—thought Hhuha should be freelance again, even though it meant less certainty about how much they would have to eat each week or (sometimes) whether they would eat at all.

"I wish. Damn contract," Hhuha said, pouring milk in her coffee.

"Some of that down here, please?" Rhiow said loudly.

"So don't sign it the next time."

"Don't tempt me. . . ."

"I *am* tempting you. Don't commit yourself to them again. Go independent and let them pay twice what they're paying now if they want your services. Otherwise, let someone *else* pay twice what they're paying."

Hhuha put the milk away, sighing. "I don't know . . . I've gotten kind of used to the steady paycheck. . . ."

"I know you have."

"Excuse me? *Milk?*" Rhiow said, standing up on her hind legs and patting the bottom of Hhuha's skirt. "Oh, sweet Iau, but I wish just once I could say it so you would understand. Hello? *Hhuha?!*"

Hhuha looked at Rhiow, bent down and stroked her. "More cat food, honey? Sure. I don't know, though, Mike . . . There's so much competition out there . . . and so much uncertainty. In your job, too. You and I can starve. But someone else wouldn't understand if the food ran out. . . ."

She straightened up and started to open another can of cat food. "Don't blame it on *me,*" Rhiow said. "You should do what makes you happy. . . . Oh, gods, not the tuna again! —Look, Hhuha! Saucer! Empty! *Milk!!*"

"Wow, she really likes that stuff," Iaehh said. "Better get some more."

"I'll stop by the store on the way home."

"But, hon, you really should think about it. The hours there are wearing you out. You keep having to bring work home. They're not giving you the support they promised. They can't even keep the air conditioners working, as you say. You're not *happy* there. . . ."

Rhiow sighed, hating to look ungrateful, and went over to the *ffribh,* stood up on her hind legs against it, and patted the handle, looking mournfully at Hhuha.

"What?" Hhuha said.

"You put the milk away without offering her any," Iaehh said.

"Why can't more toms have brains like yours?" Rhiow said, and went straight to him and rubbed his legs, too, while Hhuha opened the *ffrihh* and got the milk out again. "What a clever *ehhif* you are."

"Won't be any left for your coffee," Hhuha said.

"Never mind, give it to her," Iaehh said. "I'm running late as it is. I'll have something at the office."

"You wouldn't *be* running late if you'd gotten up when the alarm clock rang."

And they were off again about another favorite subject: the routine ignoring and silencing of the dreadful little bedside *ra'hio* that spouted news reports at them all hours of the day and night, but especially in the morning, when it began its recitation with a particularly foul and repetitive little buzzer. Rhiow was always glad when they turned it off . . . though this morning she had to admit she had been pleased enough, while it was still on, to hear it fail to mention anything terrible happening in Grand Central overnight. "Oh, thank you," she said, and purred, as Hhuha bent down and poured the milk.

"Hey, don't bump the hand that feeds you, my puss; the milk's going to go all over the floor."

"I'll take care of that, don't you worry," Rhiow said, and drank.

Hhuha and Iaehh went back toward the bedroom, still arguing genially. It was barely argument, really: more like what People called *f'hia-sau,* or "tussle," where any blows struck were affectionate, the claws were carefully kept in, teeth did not break skin, and the disagreement, if it really was one, was replayed more as a pastime than anything else. *They really are so like us, some ways,* Rhiow thought, finishing the milk and sitting up to wash her face. *I wonder if you could teach them Ailurin, given enough time? Repeating one word enough times, in the right context, until they got it . . .*

"Bye, honey," Hhuha said, and as she passed through the living room, "bye, puss, have a nice day . . ."

"From your mouth to the Queen's ear," Rhiow said as the front door closed behind her, and meaning it most fervently.

She was still washing when Iaehh came out of the bedroom in his "formal" sweats, with his office clothes and his briefcase over his shoulder in a backpack. "Byebye, plumptious one," he said, heading for the door. "Don't eat all that food at once, it's got to last you . . ."

Rhiow threw a meaningful look at the bowl full of reeking tuna, but it was lost on Iaehh: he was halfway out the door already. It clicked shut, and one after another came more clicks as he locked the other locks.

"Plumptious" again. Is he trying to say I'm putting on weight? Hmm.

Rhiow sighed, finished her wash, and went out her own door, into the warm, ozony air, heading for the rooftops.

Half an hour later she caught up with Urruah at the Bear Gate to Central Park. There were actually two sets of statues there—one of three bears, one of three deer—but from the predator's point of view, it was naturally the bears that mattered.

"'Luck," Rhiow said, as they breathed one another's breath. "Oh, Urruah, not more MhHonalh's!"

He wrinkled his face a little, an annoyed expression. "I thought I got all the tartar sauce off that fish thing first."

"All this fried food . . . it's going to catch up with you one day."

"*You* should talk. What kind of oil are they packing that tuna cat food in? Smells like it comes out of somebody's crankcase."

Rhiow thought privately that, for all she knew, he was right. . . . They walked into the park, heading southward along the broad paved expanse of its roadway loop, staying well to one side to miss the *ehhif* on Rollerblades and the *ehhif* with strollers. "You sleep well last night?"

"Considering where we're going today?" Urruah said. "What do *you* think? . . . I kept hearing Saash dreaming all night. Her nerves are in shreds."

Rhiow sighed. "I missed that. Guess my little chat with the Whisperer tired me out."

"Well, I had one, too." Urruah sighed. "I'm well enough stocked with spells: right up against the limit, I'd say. My head feels twice its normal size."

Rhiow waved her tail in agreement. "We'll have to spend a little time coordinating before we head down . . . make sure none of us are carrying duplicates."

They made good time down through the park, heading to a level about even with the streets in the upper Sixties. There, a huge stage had been erected at the southern end of the big green space that city People called somewhat ironically *Eiuev,* the Veldt, and which *ehhif* called the Sheep Meadow. It wasn't sheep milling around in it now, though, but what looked like about five hundred *ehhif* dealing with the technical and logistical end of preparing for a meeting of many thousands: cables and conduits being laid and shielded, scaffolding secured, sound systems tested. The squawks and hisses and feed-back-howls of mispositioned speakers and other equipment had been echoing for blocks from the park since fairly early in the morning, making it sound as if a herd of large, clumsy, and very broken-voiced beasts were staggering around the place and banging into things. "They're doing sound checks now, though," Urruah said.

"Sound," Rhiow said, wincing slightly at yet another yowl, "wouldn't seem to be a problem."

"No, that was accidental. It'll be voices they're checking, soon. Come on."

They slipped close, behind one of the larger trees that stood at the bottom border of the meadow, and which was behind the security cordons still being erected, a maze of orange nylon webbing stretched from tree to tree. There were plenty of small openings in it so that Rhiow and Urruah had no trouble stepping through and making their way close to the stage, under one of the big scaffolding towers.

A great crowd of *ehhif,* in T-shirts and shirtsleeves, were already sitting around tuning their instruments, making a scraping and hooting cacophony that made Rhiow shake her head once or twice. "It's the Metropolitan Opera's orchestra, without the first chairs," Urruah said.

Rhiow blinked, since all the chairs seemed to be there. "Smart of them to start early," she said. "They'll miss the heat."

Urruah sighed. "I wish I could," he said. In hot weather, the thickness of his coat often bothered him.

"So do a little wizardry," Rhiow said. "Cool some of this wind down: keep a pocket of it for yourself."

"Naah," Urruah said. "Why waste the energy? . . . Look, it's starting—"

Rhiow craned her neck as the musicians quieted down a little. The *ehhif* who appeared was not the one in the poster, though, but a short, round, curly-haired tom, who came to stand in front of the orchestra with a small stick or wand in his hand. Rhiow peered at that. "He's not one of *us,* is he?"

Urruah stared at him. "The conductor? Not that I know." He cocked his head to one side, briefly listening to the Whisperer, and then said, "No, she says not. —Here he comes!"

On the stage above the musicians, a big burly figure appeared, also in a shortsleeved shirt and dark pants. Rhiow supposed that as *ehhif* went, he was handsome enough; he had a surprising amount of facial fur. He stepped up to the front of the stage, exchanged a few words with the small round *ehhif:* there was some subdued shuffling and tapping of bows on strings among the musicians.

The small round *ehhif* made a suggestion, and the larger *ehhif* nodded, stepped back to find his right position on the stage. For a few moments there was more howling and crackling of the sound system; then quiet. The conductor-*ehhif* raised his wand.

Music started. It sounded strange to Rhiow, but then most *ehhif* music did. Urruah, though, had all his attention fixed on the big *ehhif,* who suddenly began to sing.

The volume was surprising, even without mechanical assistance: Urruah had been right about that, at least. Rhiow listened to about a minute's worth of it, then said to Urruah, low, "So tell me: what's he yowling about?"

"The song's called *'Nessun dorma.'* It means that no one's going to sleep."

"With *that* noise," Rhiow said, "I could understand why not. . . ."

"Oh, come on, Rhi," said Urruah, "give it a chance. Listen to it."

Rhiow sighed, and did. The harmonies were strange to feline ears and didn't seem to want to resolve correctly; she suspected no amount of listening was likely to change that perception soon, for her anyway. But at least her knowledge of the Speech made meaning available to her, if nothing else, as the man stood and sang with passion approaching a tom's of his hope and desire, alone here under the starlight. . . . When the stars' light faded and the dawn rose up, he sang, then he would conquer . . . though at the moment, who or what would be conquered wasn't quite clear: the song itself hadn't yet provided much context. Perhaps some other tom? There did seem to be a she-*ehhif* involved, to whom this tom sang—though there was no sign of her at the moment, she being out of sight in the story, or the reality, or both. That at least was tomlike enough: an empty place, the lonely silent night to fill with song, whether or not there was any chance of fulfillment. *Or perhaps,* Rhiow thought as he sang, *it's the she herself, the one he woos, that he's intending to conquer.* If there was more intended to the conquest than just sex, though, the thought made Rhiow smile a little. Toms who tried domination or other such maneuvers with their mates too soon after the act itself got nothing but ragged ears and aching heads for their trouble.

It was a little odd, actually, to hear such power and passion come from someone standing still on a bare stage, holding, not a she, but only a piece of cloth in one hand, which he kept using to wipe his face. He paused a moment, and behind him the recorded voices of some other *ehhif* sang sweetly but mournfully that he and they might all very well be dead in the morning if he *didn't* conquer. . . . Yet the tom-*ehhif* sang on with assurance and power, answering them fearlessly; his last note, amplified rather beyond need, made Rhiow put her ears down flat for the loudness of it rather than the tone, which was blindingly true, and went on for longer than seemed possible with even such a big chest's breath. Rhiow was almost unwillingly held still by the long, cried note at the end of the conquer-word, *vinceeeeeeer-rro!* as if by teeth in her scruff; alien as the sound was, any cat-tom who had a voice of such power would rightly have had his choice of shes.

The *ehhif* let the note go. The last chords of accompaniment crashed to an end, and the technical staff responded, some of them, with a chorus of good-natured hoots and applause. After that torrent and slam of sound, the hoots of horns and the city's rush seemed a little muted.

The *ehhif* spoke a few words to the short round curly-haired *ehhif* conducting the musicians, then waved the cloth casually at the technical people and retreated to the back of the stage to have a long drink from a bottle of water. The *ehhif* conducting the musicians turned to talk to them now, and Rhiow looked a little sidewise at Urruah, a feline gesture of reluctant agreement. "It reminds me a little," she said, "of the part in the *Argument* when the Old Tom sings. Innocent, though he's all scars: and hopeful, though he knows whose teeth will be in his throat shortly."

Urruah nodded. "That's one connection I've thought of, yes. . . ."

"I can see why they'll need all these fences," Rhiow said as they got up and strolled away. "The she-*ehhif* would be all over him afterward, I'd think. Probably wear him out for any more singing."

"They don't, though. It's not meant personally."

"That's the strangest part of it, for me," Rhiow said. "I don't understand how he can sing like *that* and have it *not* be personal. That was real fighting stuff, that last note. He should have had his claws in someone's guts, or his teeth in someone else's scruff, afterward."

Urruah shook his own head as well. "They're not us. But later on in the story, there's a fight."

"Another tom?"

"No, in the story this tom fights with the queen. She has this problem, see . . ."

Rhiow half-closed her eyes in good-natured exasperation, for he was off and running again. Like most toms, Urruah had trouble grasping how, for queens, the fascination with song in any of its forms was strictly seasonal. When you were in heat, a tom's voice was, admittedly, riveting, and the song it sang spoke directly to your most immediate need. Out of heat, though, the tendency was to try to get away from the noise before you burst out laughing at the desperate, impassioned cacophony of it—a reaction not at all appreciated by the toms near a queen in heat, all deep in the throes of competitive artistic and erotic self-expression.

Most of Urruah's explanation now went over Rhiow's head, as they walked back uptown, but at least he had something to keep his mind off what the rest of the day's work was going to involve. He finished with the tale of the tom fighting with the queen—after which the queen apparently surrendered herself to the tom (*What a crazy fan-*

tasy, Rhiow thought)—and started in on some other story, many times more complicated, that seemed to involve a river, and a piece of some kind of metal. "And when you take this piece of metal and make it into a *hring,* it makes you master of the universe. . . ."

Rhiow had to laugh at that. "*Ehhif?* Run the *universe?* Let alone the world . . . What a dream! They can't even run the parts of it they think they *do* run. Or at least none of them who aren't wizards seem able to. Look at them! Half of the *ehhif* on the planet go to bed with empty stomachs: the other half of them die of eating themselves sick. . . ." She gave Urruah a cockeyed look. "And what about your great *ehhif*-tom there? No way he's that size naturally. What does he mean by smothering a wonderful voice like that with ten fur coats' worth of fat? Whichever *ehhif*-god is in charge of mistreating one's gifts should have a word with him. Probably will, too, if he doesn't get off his great tail and do something about it pretty soon."

Urruah began muttering something vague about the artistic temperament. Rhiow immediately perceived that this was something Urruah had noticed, and it bothered him, too. "Well, look," she said. "Maybe he'll get himself straightened out. Meanwhile, we're almost at the Met. They'll be on the steps, if I know Saash. Anything you need to tell me about today's work before we meet up with them?"

He stopped, looked at her. "Rhi . . ."

She let him find his words.

"How do you cope?" he said finally. "My memory's not clouded about last time. We almost died, all three of us. Now we're going to have to go down there again—and it may even be the same place this time. Am I wrong?"

"No," Rhiow said, "I don't think so. It could well be the same spot: the gate we're servicing this time has its roots in the same catenary."

"It could be an ambush," he said. "Another sabotage, better planned than the last. Certainly the problem's more serious. If someone caused it on purpose, they'd know a service team would have to be down there very quickly. Not like the last time, where there was enough slack in the schedule that we might have come down any time during the space of a week or two. Half the lizards in Downside could be waiting there for us."

"It's a thought I've considered," Rhiow said. "Though the Whisperer didn't seem to indicate it was going to be quite *that* dangerous. She usually gives you a hint . . ."

". . . If she knows," Urruah said.

There was that too. Even the gods were sometimes caught by surprise. . . . "'Ruah," Rhiow said, "I'm as well prepared as I can be. So are you. Saash will be, as well."

"That leaves only Arhu," Urruah muttered. "And what *he* might do, I'll bet the gods don't know, either. Irh's balls, but I wish we could dump him somewhere."

"Don't get any ideas," Rhiow said. "He may save your skin yet."

Urruah laughed. They looked at each other for a moment more, then made their way around to the steps of the Met.

Saash and Arhu were waiting for them in the sunshine, or rather, Saash was sitting scratching herself and putting her fur in order, alternately, and Arhu was tearing back and forth across the steps, sidled, trying to trip the *ehhif* going up and down. Fortunately, he was falling down the steps as often as running successfully along them, so the *ehhif*, by and large, weren't doing more than stumble occasionally. As they walked over to Saash, and Rhiow breathed breaths with her and wished her hunt's luck, Urruah looked over at Arhu, who, seeing Rhiow, was now running toward them. "You sure you want to stop with just the Met?" Urruah said, loudly enough to be heard. "I'd take him across the park, afterward. Natural History. Some skeletons there he ought to see—"

"*No,*" Rhiow said, a touch angrily. "He's going to have to make up his own mind about what we see. Don't prejudice his opinions . . . and whatever it is he's going to be good for, don't make him less effective at it."

Urruah grumbled, but said nothing further. Arhu looked from Urruah to Rhiow, a little puzzled, and said, "What are we supposed to do?"

"Courtesy first," Rhiow said. "Hunt's luck to you, Arhu."

"I had some," he said, very proud. "I caught a mouse."

Rhiow looked at Saash: Saash flicked an ear in agreement. "It got into the garage this morning," she said. "Out of someone's car: I think it had been eating some fast food crumbs or something. He did it right in front of Zhorzh, too. Very clever." She threw him a look that was half-amused, half-annoyed, and Rhiow put her whiskers forward in slight amusement.

"Well, good for you," Rhiow said. "Nicely done. Let's go in, then, and see the gods. We have a busy day ahead of us, and we want to be out of here before lunchtime." *So that you won't be tempted to start stealing sandwiches out of* ehhif *hands . . .*

Sidled, they slipped in through a door that some poor tom-*ehhif* found himself holding open for about seven *ehhif*-queens, one after another. *Ehhif* were gathering at the turnstiles where people made contributions to the museum; Rhiow and her team went around them to one side and went on up the white marble steps to the next floor. Rhiow led them sharply to the right, then right again along the colonnade next to the stairs, then left to pass through the Great Hall, and toward the wide doorway over which a sign said, in *ehhif* English, EGYPTIAN ART.

The light was dimmer, cooler, here. The walls were done in a shade of deep blue-gray; through the skylights above, the sun fell pale, as if coming through a great depth of time. Against the walls, and on pedestals and in glass cases in the middle of the great room, were ancient sculptures and tombs and other things, great and small, belonging to *ehhif* who had lived in a very different time.

Arhu lagged a little behind the others, looking in (for once) undisguised astonishment at the huge solemn figures, which gazed out cooleyed at the *ehhif* strolling among them. Rhiow paused a moment to look back at Arhu, then turned to join him as he looked at the nearest of the sculptures, a massive sarcophagus in polished black basalt, standing on end against a wall. Nearly three feet wide, not counting the carven wig surrounding it, the serene, lordly *ehhif* face gazed at, or past, or through them, with the imperturbability of massive age.

"It's big," Arhu said, almost in a whisper.

Rhiow wondered if what he was really thinking about was size. "And old," she said, "and strange. These *ehhif* used to keep their dead in containers like this; it was to keep their bodies safe."

"Safe *how?*"

"I know," Rhiow said, "after a body dies, the further processes of death tend not to have any trouble finding it. But these *ehhif* did their best to give it difficulty. I'm afraid it was from something we told them, or rather our ancestors did. About our lives—"

They walked along a little. "You get nine," Arhu said, looking around at the everyday things in the glass cases: a glass cup here, rainbowed with age and exposure; a shoe there, the linen upper and leather sole still intact; a little farther on, a crockery pot shaped like a chicken, intended to magically produce more chicken in the afterlife.

"We do," Rhiow said, "but it seems that *ehhif* don't. Or if they do, there's no way to tell, because they don't remember anything from the last life, as we do—none of the useful memories or the highlights, the People you knew or loved . . . anyway, *ehhif* don't think they come back. But when People back then told them how *we* did, and told them about the Living Ones, the *ehhif* got confused, and they thought we meant that *they* were going to do something similar. . . ."

They caught up with Saash and Urruah, who were standing in front of a massive granite sphinx. "What's a 'Living One'?" Arhu said. "Is that another kind of god?"

Rhiow smiled slightly. Should an uninstructed young wizard see such a being going about its business, he could be forgiven for mistaking it for a god. "Not quite so elevated," Urruah said. "But close."

"After your ninth life," Saash said, "well, no one's *really* sure what happens . . . but there's a story. That, if in nine lives you've done more good than evil, then you get a tenth."

"With a mind that won't get tired," Urruah said, "and a body that won't wear out, too fast and tough for even Death to claw at . . . so you can go on to hunting your great desire, right past the boundaries of physical reality, they say, past world's end and in toward the heart of things. . . ."

"If you ever see a Living One, you'll know it," Rhiow said. "They pass through, sometimes, on Iau's business. . . ."

"Have you ever seen one?" Arhu said, skeptical again.

"As it happens, yes."

"What did it look like?"

Rhiow threw an amused glance at the sphinx. "Not like that," she said, remembering the glimpse she had once caught, very early in the morning, of a feline shape walking casually by the East River in the upper Seventies. To the superficial glance, *ehhif*'s or People's, it would have appeared to be just another cat, a dowdy tabby. But the second glance showed how insubstantial, almost paltry, mere concretely physical things looked when seen with it, at the same time. Shortly thereafter the cat-shape had paused, then jumped down onto the East River, and walked off across it, with a slightly distracted air, straight along the glittering path laid along the water by the rising sun and out of sight.

"Well, I sure hope not," Arhu said, somewhat scornfully. "Half the stuff in here is just lion-bodies with *ehhif*-heads on them."

"The *ehhif* did that because they were trying to say that they knew these beings the People were describing to them were intelligent . . . but essentially feline in nature. *Ehhif* can't help being anthropomorphic—as far as they're are concerned, they're the only intelligent species on the planet."

"Oh please!" Arhu said, laughing.

"Yes, well, it does have its humorous aspects . . ." Saash said. "We enjoy them the best we can. Meanwhile, here's their picture of someone who *is* one of our Gods."

They walked on a little to where a long papyrus was spread out upright in a case against the wall. "It all starts with her," Saash said, first indicating the nearest statue. In more of the polished black basalt, a regal figure stood: *ehhif*-bodied, with the nobly sculpted head of one of the People—a long straight nose, wide, slightly slanted eyes, large graceful ears set very straight and alert. Various other carvings here wore one kind or another of the odd Egyptian headwear, but this figure, looking thoughtfully ahead of her, was crowned with the Sun: and on her breast, the single, open Eye.

"Iau," Urruah said. "The Queen, the Creatress and Dam. '. . . In the first evening of the worlds, Iau Hauhai'h walked in the Silences, hearing and seeing, so that what She heard became real, and what She saw was so. She was the Fire at the Heart; and of that Fire She grew quick, and from it She kittened. Those children were four, and grew swiftly to stand with their queen.'"

"It's the oldest song our people know," Saash said to Arhu. "Any of us can hear it: the Whisperer taught it to us first, and the wizards who heard it taught it to everybody else. And everybody else taught it to the *ehhif* . . . though they got mixed up about some of the details—"

"You're good at this, Saash," Rhiow said, "you do the honors. . . . I need to check those palimpsests that Ehef mentioned. Or Herself, rather." Rhiow glanced over at a third statue, farther down the hall.

"You go ahead," Saash said. Rhiow strolled off toward the papyrus cases in the back of the hall as the others went on to pause before another statue, nearly nine feet tall, standing by itself. Rhiow glanced at her in passing, too: she was not easy to go by without taking some kind of notice. Lioness-headed, holding the lightning in her hands, this tall straight figure was crowned again with the Sun, but a horned Sun that looked somehow more aggressive and dangerous; and the Eye she wore glared. Her face was not as kindly as the Queen's. The lips were wrinkled, fierce; teeth showed. But the eyes were relentlessly intelligent: this Power's rages would not be blind ones.

"'Aaurh the Mighty,'" Saash said, "'the Destroyer by Flame, who came first, burning like a star, and armed with the First Fire. She was Her Dam's messenger and warrior, and went where she was sent swift as light, making and ending as Iau taught her. . . .'"

Rhiow went back to the glass cases ranked against the wall, jumped up on the first one she came to, and started walking along the line of them. She visited here as often as she could, liking the reminder of the People/*ehhif* joint heritage, of this time when they had been a little closer, before their languages became so widely parted. As a result of all the visiting, there was little of this material with which Rhiow was not familiar, but every now and then something new came out of storage and was put out for public view.

The palimpsests were such material. They were not true palimpsests—recycled parchment used for writing, the old writing having been scraped off with knives—but an equivalent. Paper made from the papyrus reed was mounted on long linen rolls to make books, and the paper scraped clean of the old soot-based inks when the book was wanted for something else.

Rhiow peered down at the first palimpsest she found in the case she was standing on, turning her head from side to side to get the best angle on it. The *ehhif* of that period had had two different ways of writing: the hieratic writing, all pictograms, and the demotic, a graceful curled and swirled language, as often written vertically as horizontally, which shared some structural attributes with the present written form of the Speech. True to their names, these palimpsests had no visible writing left and were here mostly as examples of how papyrus was recycled (so Rhiow read from the museum's explanatory notes inside the case). But for one of the People, and a wizard, used to seeing the invisible, such paperwork was more revealing. Rhiow squinted a little at the first palimpsest, doing her best to make out the dim remnants of the characters there. *Of barley, eight measures,* she read, *and of water, twenty measures, and of the day's bread-make, a lump of a fist's size: let all be set in the sun for nine days, and when the mixture smelleth fair and the life in it hath quietened, let all be strained and poured into larger vessels so that twenty measures more of water may be added—*

Rhiow snickered. *A beer recipe* . . . The *ehhif* of that time liked their beer, having invented it, and were constantly leaving jars of it out for the gods. That it always vanished afterward struck the *ehhif* of that time as proof of deity's existence; it was evidence of their youth and innocence as a species that they rarely noticed how drunk the neighbors were the next morning.

Rhiow glanced up, looked over her shoulder at the others. They were in front of yet another statue, in a light gray stone this time. This figure was seated, with a roll of papyrus in her lap; again her head was that of one of the People, but wearing a more reflective look than that of Iau the Queen, and a much milder one than her sister. "'Then came Hrau'f the Tamer,'" said Urruah, "'who calmed the fires Aaurh set, and put things in order: the Lady of the Hearth, who burns low, and learns wisdom, and teaches it. In every still, warm place she may be found, in every heart that seeks. She speaks the Silent Knowledge to the ears of those who can hear. . . .'"

Rhiow twitched her tail meditatively and stepped along the top of the glass case to look at the next palimpsest, puzzling over the faintly visible characters. This one had been more thoroughly scraped off than the last, but she could still read the earlier writings. A long column of the demotic script ran down the side of the ordered page full of hieratic characters, stick-figures of birds and upheld hands and feathers and snakes, eyes and chairs and wiggly lines. At the top of the scripture, the hieratic writing was easier to read, though Rhiow still had to squint. — *he performeth this by means of the mighty words of power that proceed from his mouth, and in this region of the Underworld he inflicteth with the knife wounds upon Aapep, whose place is in heaven—*

An odd phrase. Rhiow knew that Aapep was one of the many *ehhif* names for the Lone Power in Its aspect of Old Serpent. She twitched her tail in bemusement, kept reading. — *Ye are the tears of my Eye, and Iau in Her name of Mai-t the Great Queen-Cat and Sekhet the Lioness shall redeem the souls of men; She shall pour flame upon thy darkness, and the River of Flame down into thy depths; from the lake the depths of which are like fire shall the Five arise; atru-sheh-en-nesert-f-em-shet—*

The rhythm changed abruptly, and Rhiow's tail lashed. It was the Speech, written crudely as *ehhif* had done in those days when trying to work the multiple-compound feline vowels into their own orthography: two out of every three vowels were dropped out here. *Part of a spell?* she thought. *Something jotted down by some human wizard of that time?* For it was just a fragment: the circular structure familiar to wizards everywhere was absent.

Rhiow looked up for a moment, and saw Saash and Urruah eyeing each other with a slightly dubious expression, as if to say, *And what about . . . the other one? Do we mention . . . ?*

Saash looked up at the next glass case close to them, instead. "And over here—" she started to say.

But Arhu was staring at the floor. Saash and Urruah glanced down at the spot he was staring at: Rhiow did, too, half-expecting to see a bug there. Arhu, though, said, very slowly, "'. . . Then after her came sa'Rráhh, the Unmastered Fire . . . burning both dark and bright, the Tearer, the Huntress; she who kills unmindfully, in rage, and without warning, and as unreasonably raises up again.'" He swallowed, his tongue going in and out, that nervous gesture again. His voice was dry and remote. "'It is she who is strongest after Aaurh the firstborn, knowing no bounds in her power, yet desiring to find those bounds: the Dreadful, the Lady of stillbirths and the birth that kills the queen, but also of the Tenth Life: the Power who is called Lone, for she would hear no wisdom, and her Dam would not have her, driving her out in her wildness until she might learn better.'" Arhu gulped again, but his voice still kept that remote, narrative quality, as if someone else were speaking through him. "'In every empty place and in all darknesses she may be found, seeking, and angry, for still she knows not what she seeks.'"

He looked up, openly scared now.

"Yes," Saash said. "Well, you plainly know now what the Whisperer's voice sounds like. If she goes out of her way to warn you about her sister . . ."

Rhiow flicked one ear forward and back. *Well, madam, you're taking proper care of him. But what about me? What am I supposed to make of this? It makes no sense whatever—* She moved a little farther down to look at the rest of the scraped-off papyrus. *—semit-her-abt-uaa-s; mhetchet-nebt-Tuatiu ash-hrau khesef-haa-heseq—*

Rhiow stopped, feeling something suddenly shift in the back of her mind. In the darkness there, light moved, reshaped itself, recognizing something that belonged to it.

The words were winged: they flew, fluttered in the darkness inside her, lodged among the other scrawls and curves of light. A moment's shifting, shuffling, as things resettled themselves. Then quiet again . . . but it was an unsettling sort of silence.

In that darkness in the back of her mind, though, there was no dramatic change: absolutely nothing was happening. Rhiow looked up, licking her nose uneasily. The others had moved on again. "Here's what the story's all about," Urruah said. "The first battle . . ."

They went to look at the glass case. Near the head of the long rolled-out papyrus was a picture of a huge Tree, under which stood a slightly disreputable looking tabby-tom, holding a great curved knife or sword in one hand, and using it to chop a large snake into ample chunks, the way someone in a hurry might cut up salami. The furious snake glared at the Cat, the impression being that simply being cut in pieces was not going to slow it down permanently.

Rhiow, her tail still lashing with bemusement, jumped down from the case and went to join them. "The Cat who stood under the Great Tree on the night the enemies of Iau, the agents of evil, were destroyed," said Saash.

"Urrua," Rhiow said. "He who Scars, the Lightning-Clawed—"

Arhu, who had been recovering a little, looked up at Urruah and started to grin. Urruah grimaced. "It was a pun," Urruah said, very annoyed. "My mother loved puns." For in Ailurin, adding the terminal aspirant to the Great Tom's name turned it into *urruah*, "flat-nose," a joke-name for someone who'd acquired so much scar tissue there that he could hardly breathe.

Rhiow smiled slightly, seeing Arhu getting ready to start teasing again. Saash said, "It says, 'There dropped from the Queen one last child, and he Burned dark and tore Her in his passing. And still His children tear Hers as He tore, when queen and tom come together.'" Urruah rolled his eyes slightly, as he tended to when this part of the full litany was recited. "'Murderer of the young is He, sly Trickster, silent-roaming sire of all dangers that abide our people: but sudden Savior also, one-eyed Wanderer in the dark, midnight Lover, lone Singer, He Who Scars and is Scarred: Urrua, Whom the Queen bore last, the Afterthought, Her gift to Herself.'"

At the phrase "murderer of the young," Arhu looked suddenly at Urruah, who at least had the grace not to smile. When Rhiow finished, Arhu sat, looked down the hall and up again at the papyrus, and said, "So when was this big fight?"

"A couple million years ago," Saash said.

"The beginning of time," said Urruah.

"Now," said Rhiow.

Arhu looked from one to another of them, baffled.

"Well," Rhiow said, "all three are true, really. This universe was barely cooling down from the fireball of its birth when the fight started. It's been refought many times since, though some battles stand out. And . . ." she sighed, looked down at Arhu, "we're going out to fight it again, this afternoon. And you're coming with us."

He stared at her . . .

. . . then leapt up and yowled with joy.

People all around the big room stared, didn't see anything, went back to looking at the exhibits. "This is *great!*" Arhu yelled. "We're going to have a fight! This is going to be *terrific!* When can we leave? Let's go now!"

More heads were turning all around. Rhiow looked at Urruah. *Not even you,* she said silently, *could have been this excited about the prospect of going into a fight that could possibly get you killed.*

I don't know, Urruah said, seriously seeming to consider it. *Maybe I was.*

Rhiow sighed again. "Let's get you out of here," she said to Arhu, "before security shows up." She glanced over Arhu's head at the others. "We need to confer and eliminate any duplicate spells you're carrying . . . and then we've got to get down to the Terminal. Our backup will be waiting."

They headed out. As they went, Rhiow threw one last look over her shoulder at the statue of the Queen. *What am I looking for?* she asked herself a moment later. Poor rude rendering of another species' mystery that it was, done by creatures who couldn't ever quite get clear on the concept— But even so, sometimes it was consoling to have a concrete image to look at, however misleading one knew the concreteness to be, or the image of a regard that might actually fix on you.

The stone Queen, however, looked thoughtfully out into the dim blue space of the Egyptian Collection, apparently thinking her own thoughts. It was an expression that suggested to the viewer, *What are you looking at Me for? Go work out your own salvation.*

It was, of course, the only kind of look most People would accept from their Maker. But Rhiow, at this moment, found herself thinking:

Maybe I've been with ehhif *too long. . . .*

She went after the other three.

Did you get what you came for? Saash said.

Rhiow shivered. *I think a little bit more,* she said.

Seven

✦

The lunch rush was just beginning out in the streets, but there wasn't much the team could do about that except hug the building side of the sidewalk, all the way down, and try to keep from being trampled. It was a relief to get into Grand Central, where few people hugged the walls: the crush was in the middle, a river of legs and briefcases and shopping bags, flowing faster in the center of the stream than by the banks.

Rhiow and her team made their way down to Track 30. She was relieved, on passing the Italian deli, to find it so completely thronged with *ehhif* that not even the most reckless kitling could have gotten near it without doing violence to the crowd. Even so, Arhu threw a longing glance at it as they passed, then looked guiltily at Rhiow.

"Maybe later," she said, "if you're good." *And we're all still in one piece* . . .

A train from Rye had just come in, and the last of its passengers were filtering off. Far down the platform, off to one side, stood two *ehhif* watching the others get off the train: a boy and a girl. They were young; Rhiow was no expert on ages, but she thought perhaps the young queen-*ehhif* was fourteenish, the tom a year or so younger. They looked like anyone else who might have come off the train— both wearing shorts and oversized T-shirts and beat-up running shoes, the queen wearing a fanny pack: a couple of suburban kids, apparently fresh in from Westchester for a good day's hanging out. But these two had something none of the other commuters had—the shift and tangle of hyperstrings about them, which meant that they too were sidled.

"Prompt," Saash said, as they walked down the platform toward the two.

"Har'lh's plainly been keeping an eye on things," Rhiow said. *Good. Because if we need help, I'd prefer it to be the kind that an Advisory would send . . .*

As the team came up to them, the two young *ehhif* hunkered down to a level more comfortable for conversation. "We're on errantry," said the young queen, "and we greet you."

"You're well met on the errand," Rhiow said. "We can definitely use some help on this one."

"Yeah, that's what Carl said. I'm Nita; this is Kit."

"Rhiow; and Urruah there, and Saash; and Arhu—"

The young queen-*ehhif* looked at Arhu with interest. "You're new to this, aren't you," she said.

He gave her a look. "So what?"

"Hey, take it easy," she said. "You just reminded me a little of my sister, that's all."

"The day I look like any *ehhif*'s sister—"

Nita smiled, a little crookedly. "Sounds like her, too," she said, under her breath, to her partner.

"She only meant," said the young tom-*ehhif,* "that her sister just passed Ordeal a little while ago."

Arhu blinked at that. Rhiow said to him, "It happens sometimes that you get littermates who're wizards. Not so often as it used to: the tendency is for the trait to skip a couple of generations between occurrences in a family."

"Yeah," Kit said. "My dad says he thinks it's so your parents won't be too scared to have more kids . . . and so that you won't, either."

"I thought *ehhif* wizards usually kept their business secret from nonwizards," Saash said, curious. "Supposedly humans don't believe in wizardry . . . is that right?"

"Mostly they don't. Oh, we keep it private from everybody but family. It's the wizard's choice, in our species. Hide it or spill it, you can get in nearly as much trouble either way. But I guess we're lucky . . . our parents coped pretty well after the initial shock, though we still have a little trouble with them every now and then." Kit looked around him. "It's been pretty noisy down here this morning— they were pulling up a piece of track down there. Had to have jack-hammers used on it: the guys said it had been melted right into the concrete. I take it that means this gate is the busted one."

Rhiow flirted her tail in agreement. "Yes. We'll be using a different one for our access, though: the Lexington Avenue local gate—it's had the least use lately. Har'lh tells me you've worked with it before?"

"Yeah," Nita said, "when its locus was still anchored upstairs. We used it for a rapid-transit jump when it was dislocated, some years ago. It was the usual thing—someone was digging up the potholes on Forty-second and messing with the high-tension power cables during a sunspot maximum. The combined structural and electromagnetic disruptions made the gate's stabilizer strings pop out of the anchor stratum, and the portal locus came loose and jumped sixty stories straight up." She smiled a small, dry smile. "Tom and Carl said that getting it back where it belonged, afterward, was interesting. That was you, was it?"

"Not me," Rhiow said, "my predecessor, Ffairh. He told me about it, though."

"And then after all that, you had to move it over to Lex, didn't you? But they'd moved the deli it was in back of when the construction started here."

"That's right, when they started renovating the Hyatt passageway. Everything's been pretty ripped up lately. . . ." Rhiow looked around her. "Well, your expertise will be welcome . . . we're going a long way down on this run, and keeping the gate anchored and patent is going to be important."

"Shouldn't be a problem," Kit said. "Carl says you took a lot of care last time to fasten the gate down good and tight. We'll make sure it stays stuck open for you while you're down there. There shouldn't be any way a patent gate can be dislocated or interfered with."

Rhiow had her doubts this week. "That's what conventional wisdom would say," she said, "but the gates' behavior lately hasn't been conventional."

Nita shook her head. "We'll do the best we can for you," she said. "If we need help, we'll yell for Carl."

"Right. Let's get started," Saash said, and headed over for the gate.

It was as they had left it the other day: hanging there, the warp and weft of the hyperstrings glowing a slightly duller red than before, token of a lack of extension in the last day. Once more Saash sat up on her haunches, reached in, and plucked at the gate's diagnostic strings: they followed her claw outward, and light sheened down them, violet in the darkness. "Same as yesterday," she said to the two young wizards.

"Looks perfectly normal," Kit said.

"Yes, well, watch." Saash reached in again for the activation strings, pulled, and again came out with a double pawful of nothing.

Nita whistled softly. "Weird."

"Yes. I was kind of hoping it might have corrected itself," Saash said, sounding wry and slightly amused, "but fat chance."

Rhiow looked at her and was silently impressed, not for the first time, at the way Saash could hold such a casual tone when she was shivering inside. But that was her way, at work. Later, after this was done—assuming everything went all right—she would complain neurotically about her terror for days. But at the moment, she sounded like she was going for a nice sleep in the sun, followed by cream. *I wish I could sound that confident. . . .*

Saash let go of the strings, settled back to all fours again, and glanced around. "So here's what we'll do," she said. "I'm going to pull the Lexington Avenue local gate's locus out of its present location and tether it over here temporarily so that you can keep an eye on both the bum gate and the one we've used. Theoretically we should be able to use the broken one to come back after we've fixed it; then the Lex gate can have the temporary tethers broken and it'll just snap back into place."

"Sounds sensible," Nita said. "One of us can stay over by Lex and redirect any wizards who turn up there to use it before the change in the gate's location shows up in their manuals."

"Fine," Saash said, "let's go, then." She trotted off, and the young queen-*ehhif* went after her, looking carefully down-track as she followed.

Arhu looked after the two of them, while the young tom-*ehhif* sat down on the edge of the platform, looking at the gate. "It must be an interesting line of work," Kit said. "I bet you get to travel a lot."

Rhiow laughed softly. "I wish! No, we're here mostly. The New York gates get nearly as much use as the ones at Tower Bridge or Alexandria. Not as much usage as the complex at Tokyo, maybe . . . but those would be the only ones to beat us. As a result, we're always having to fix something that's busted." She put her whiskers forward, slightly amused at a memory. "Last time I was scheduled for a weekend off, I got all the way to the big Crossings worldgating facility on Rirhath B before one of *their* gates broke, and I found myself helping them service it. . . ." She made the extra-large smile that an *ehhif* would understand. "'Wizard's holiday.'"

The young tom chuckled. "Yeah," he said, "I've had a couple of those myself—"

The darkness in front of them suddenly had another gate hanging in it: more oval than the first one, hanging closer to the cinders and concrete of the floor, almost in contact with the rails. It hyperextended as they watched, the bright lines of its curvature pulling inward and apparently away to vanishing-point eternity before disappearing altogether, replaced by the oval image of the end of the Lexington Avenue local platform, and Nita standing there, looking through the aperture with an interested expression. Saash leapt neatly through, and the image vanished in lines of bright fire as the curvature snapped back flat again behind her. Numerous unnaturally bright "tether" lines could be seen stretching from equidistant points around the edges of the gate-weave, up into "empty" air or down into the ground, radiating outward in an array corresponding roughly (as it would have to, in a space with one dimension too few) to the vertices of a tesseract.

"Everything's set," Saash said. "Khi-t, I would strongly recommend that you put a general-warding circle around both of these when we're out of your way and down there working. I don't *know* that anything from that side might try to come through a patent gate, if it should stumble across one; but there are creatures in that part of Downside that, though they're just animals by both our standards, could cause a lot of trouble if they got loose in here."

"I'll take care of it," the young *ehhif*-tom said. He opened the book he was carrying, leafed through it for a moment and ran his finger down one page. "These personal-description parameters look right to you?"

Saash and Rhiow both looked down at the wizard's manual, which obligingly shifted the color of its printing so that they could more easily read the graceful curves of the printed version of the Speech; and Rhiow cocked her head to one side, hearing at the same time the Whisperer's translation of the printed material. "That's fine," she said. "Just one thing—" She put a paw out to the small block of print containing the symbols that, in wizardly shorthand, described Arhu. There were a lot of blank spaces in the equation that summed him up for spelling purposes. "*That* configuration," she said, "is changing rapidly. And in unexpected ways. Keep an eye on it. . . ."

"Will do," Kit said.

"Let's go," said Saash. She reared up, slipped her paws into the weave of the second gate, and pulled the lines of light outward, wove them together—

The gate hyperextended again, this time the lines of its intraspatial contours seeming to be pulled to a much farther-out infinity than last time—impossible, but so it seemed, regardless. The lines stretched and stretched outward, and there was almost a feeling of the watcher being pulled outward as well, drawn thin, almost to nonexistence. *Odd,* Rhiow thought. *Possibly something to do with this locus being so close to one that's malfunctioning—*

—then *snap,* the feeling was gone: and through the gate came the golden light of somewhere else's summer afternoon . . .

Urruah leapt through without apparent hesitation, though Rhiow knew he had gone first so that no one should know how nervous he had been. "Just jump through," Rhiow said to Arhu. "At all costs, stay clear of the edges: even though there are safeties on the locus boundaries, if one of them goes wrong somehow, you could lose a tail, or leg, or something you'd miss more. You'll feel heavy on the other side. Be prepared for it. . . ."

She purposely hadn't told him what else he was going to need to be prepared for, as Ffairh hadn't told her, all that time ago. Better not to create impressions about the desirability of one's state Downside . . . there would be enough temptations later. Arhu swallowed, crouched and tensed, and jumped through, almost as neatly as Urruah had.

There was a thump on the other side, and a yowl . . . but much deeper than a cat's yowl would have been. Kit craned his neck to see through, looking slightly concerned. "He okay?"

Rhiow laughed softly. "That's the question of the week. He's not hurt, anyway."

More yowling, this time tinged with surprise, was coming through the open gate. "Rhi," Saash said, "let's go, shall we, before our wonder child restarts those legends about giant demon cats in the tunnels . . . ?"

Rhiow chuckled. "You've got a point."

"*Dai stihó,*" Kit said, the wizard's casual greeting and goodbye in the Speech to another one: *go well.*

"Thanks," Rhiow said. She jumped through the gate: Saash let go the control strings, took aim, and followed her.

There was the usual moment's worth of disorientation as Rhiow felt her body adjust to its new status; then her vision cleared, and everything was fine again. Rhiow shook herself all over, settling the pelt—it was so close and short, compared to her usual fur, that she always felt slightly naked for the first few seconds. Saash, true to form, was sitting down and having a good scratch, watching Arhu with amusement.

"—Look at me! *Look* at me! I'm *huge!*" Arhu was going around and around in a circle, trying to get a good look at himself, but mostly looking as if he were chasing his tail. It was an amusing sight: the white patch at the tail's end was now nearly as long by itself as the whole tail had been. Rhiow thought privately that, if he survived to come here to hunt later, he was going to have to do it by speed, for camouflage wasn't going to be one of his strong points, not splashed all over with black and white the way he was. *Though, then again,* she thought, *on moonlit nights, in broken country, it might work*. . . . "And look at you!" Arhu said, staring at Saash. She smiled a little crookedly, and Rhiow put her whiskers forward in amusement. Saash was certainly worth looking at: a tortoiseshell lioness, almost a ton of muscle. "And you!" Arhu said to Rhiow. "And, oh wow," he said, seeing Urruah, whose tabby patterning had kept its color but gone much more tigerish, to suit his shape and size; he was nearly a taxicab high at the shoulder.

"What happened? Can we do this at home?"

"No," Urruah said. "Cats' bodies are the same size as their souls, here. Your soul remembers our ancient history, even if your body doesn't. . . ."

"*Look* at all this! Where are we?"

"*IAh'hah.*" Saash used the Ailurin slang that was as close as the average cat could come to pronouncing "New York."

He stared at Saash. "You're crazy!"

"This is New York, all right," Urruah said. "Five hundred thousand years ago, maybe . . . and ten or twenty worlds over."

"But this isn't *our* world," Arhu said, not entirely as a question.

"No," Rhiow said, looking up and around through the golden air. "Ours is related to it . . . but this one is older . . . or it's simply still the way ours was, long ago. Hard to tell: time differs, from world to world."

"And things that happen here . . . happen at home too?"

"Yes. Often in different shapes, ones you might not expect at first. Know how when you look in a puddle, you see yourself? But the image is twisted: the wind touches it, it wrinkles . . ."

"Yeah."

"Like that. Except *this* world would be the real you . . . and our world would be the image in the puddle, the mirror."

Arhu opened his mouth, shut it again. "You mean . . . this is the *real* world? *This* is the way we're supposed to look?"

"I didn't say that." Now it was getting tricky. It had taken Rhiow a good couple of years' study to fully understand the implications of interdimensional relations between worlds. "This world is . . . in some ways . . . realer than ours. Closer to the center of things. But, Arhu, there are other worlds a lot more central than this one . . . and you can go *sshai-sau* trying to define reality merely in terms of centrality. I wouldn't suggest you start working on a definition at this early stage. Let's just say that this is a place where you can be different . . . but you take care not to do it for too long."

"Why not? I like this! It would be great to be this way all the time!"

The paw came down on him, heavy, from behind, and pushed Arhu down flat. Arhu twisted his head around to gaze up into the huge, silver-gray face that loomed over him, narrow-eyed, fangs showing just a little. Though Urruah's markings always went tigerish when he was Downside, he always looked, to Rhiow, more leopard-like. But in this form he was also still the biggest of them: and for all the lions' fearful reputation, leopards are known even by *ehhif* to be the more dangerous and terrible hunters, wily and fearfully powerful.

"You wouldn't like it," Urruah said, "if you didn't have a mind."

Arhu just lay there and looked at him.

"Oh, sure," Urruah said, "hunt big game, conquer a territory miles long, be big, be strong, eat anything you like, have trees fall over at the sound of your roar: sounds great, doesn't it? But there's a price, because none of us are supposed to stay out of our proper worlds for very long. Little by little you start to forget who you are. You forget your other lives if you've had any. You lose your wizardry, assuming you've achieved it. You lose your history. Finally you lose your name. And then it's as if you never existed at all, since when you die and Iau calls your name to issue you with your next life, no one answers. . . ." Urruah shrugged.

Arhu lay there looking rather stunned. "Okay, okay," he said, "I guess I see your point. I like being me."

Urruah stood back and let him up. Arhu shook himself off, sat down, and took a moment's *he'ihh* to correct his slightly rumpled head fur. "But that stuff only happens if you stay here a long time?" he said.

"As far as we know, yes," Rhiow said.

He looked rather sharply at her. "So what happens if you die Downside *before* you forget?"

It was the crucial question, the one that had made it harder than usual for Rhiow to get to sleep last night. "I don't know," she said.

"You mean . . . even if you have more lives . . . you *still* might not come back." He was wide-eyed. "You mean you just die *dead* . . . like a bug or an *ehhif?*"

"Maybe," Rhiow said. The Whisperer was silent about this possibility . . . and the concept that Hrau'f the Silent *herself* had no information on this subject was not one that filled Rhiow with joy. Moreover, she had absolutely no desire to be one of those who would supply the information. . . .

Arhu shook his head until his ears rattled, then craned his neck to look up, gazing at the rank above rank of gigantic trees, vanishing above them into the mist of a passing cloud. "It's a mountain . . ." he said.

"It's *the* Mountain," Saash said. "This is the center of everything."

"What's that tall thing up at the top . . ." His voice trailed off, his ears twitching, as the Whisperer had a word with him.

"Oh," he said then, and sat down with a thump.

"Yes," Rhiow said. "And down among the Tree's roots, into the caverns, is where we're going."

"What, in the dark? I don't want to go down there! I want to go over *there!*" He was staring at the narrow flicker of sunny veldtland showing westward, past the forests. A faint plume of dust hung above it, golden in the late sun: distant herds of game on the move. But then he threw a look over his shoulder at Urruah, who had resolutely turned his back on the vista.

"I just bet you do. Later," Rhiow said. "Business first." She looked around them, caught Urruah's eye, and nodded toward the cave entrance, in which hung the main control matrices for all the Grand Central and Penn gates, all shimmering and alive with the fiery patterns of normal function. Rhiow glanced back at the still-open gate through which they had come, and flirted her tail at Kit, who was standing there watching on the other side. He sketched her a small salute in return.

Can you hear me all right? she said inwardly.

No problems, Kit said, the same way. It was a little odd: his thought to her sounded like one of her own—the way inward speech between her teammates did. But this was Speech-based telepathy rather than thought grounded in Ailurin, and Kit's thought had a pronounced *ehhif* accent. *Am I clear?*

Just fine. "I feel a lot better with them there," Rhiow said, turning away and making her way sideways along the "threshold" stone, to where Saash already had her claws into the weave of the malfunctioning gate.

"Those were *ehhif* wizards?" Arhu said, padding along beside her.

"Yes."

"Very nice people," Urruah said. "Very professional."

"Hmf," Arhu said. "They don't look like much to me."

"That they were here to meet us," Rhiow said, "indicates that Har'lh thinks they're two of the most powerful wizards available in this area. The younger the wizard, the more powerful . . ." She carefully did not say why, in case the Whisperer had not yet mentioned it to Arhu: *because the young don't know what's impossible yet, and do it anyway.* "The only wizards better at being powerful for a long time while young are the ones who're whales. They stay children longest. Our latency period isn't that long, relatively . . . so we have to make up in extreme cleverness and adaptability what we lose early on in sheer power."

She was gazing past the gates' control matrices, toward the back of the cavern, and the darkness. "You don't want to go down here, really, do you . . ." Arhu said.

"No."

"You're nervous. I mean, I heard you being . . . I mean, you didn't say, I just thought . . ."

"You're beginning to be able to 'hear' some of what goes on in people's minds," Rhiow said, wondering how she was going to hide her discomfort at this realization. "Some wizards are better at it than others." She threw him a look. "You want to keep what you hear to yourself, by and large."

"Oh? Why?"

"Because," she said, phrasing it very carefully, "we're likely to start hearing you, too . . . and if you start saying out in the open what you hear other People thinking, they're likely to do the same for *you* . . ."

His eyes widened a little at that, and he stared somewhat guiltily at Urruah. *Good,* Rhiow thought, amused, and turned her attention to Saash.

"How is it?" she said.

Saash was balancing on her haunches again, eyeing the web of the master locus for the malfunctioning gate. She reached out a paw, slipped it into the shining weft, hooked a claw behind a carefully selected bundle of strings, and pulled. They stretched out toward her correctly, but the gate still refused to hyperextend.

"No good," she said to Rhiow. "There's a blockage of some kind between this gate and the power source, the catenary. We're going to have to go down and troubleshoot the linkage from the bottom up."

Her voice was unusually flat and matter-of-fact. Rhiow, though, noticed Arhu watching her, and said, "I'm not wild about this, either. But we're all adequately armed. . . ."

"We thought so last time too," Saash said.

Urruah had already slipped behind the gates and was looking down into the darkness of the caverns, listening hard. As Rhiow came up to him, he turned his head and said, "Quiet today."

"Not 'too quiet'?"

"No," Urruah said, falling silent again, and Rhiow listened and saw what he meant. The water that had tunneled out of these caverns, however many millennia ago, was still doing the same work, and you could usually faintly hear the dripping of it, echoing up from below. The sound was not entirely gone, today, but was somewhat more subdued than Rhiow was used to.

"It might have been a little droughty here, lately," Rhiow said.

"It might not mean anything at all," said Saash, coming up to join them, with Arhu behind her.

Rhiow lashed her tail "maybe," a touch nervously. "Well," she said. "The sooner we catch this rat, the sooner its back'll be broken. Arhu—stay with us. Don't go exploring. There are miles of these caverns: no one knows all their branchings, and some of the smaller ones aren't stable. You could seal yourself in if you meddled with the wrong pile of rocks . . . and we wouldn't be able to get you out."

"But we can go *through* things," Arhu said. "I did it in your big den, the station. A wizard who was stuck could go through the rock—"

Saash and Rhiow exchanged a look. *Too smart, this one* . . . "Yes," Urruah said, "but if you try it so close to the main control structures of the gates, you could have real trouble. You're halfway through a tunnel wall, say, and a nearby gate activates; the power running up to it from the catenary below makes some very minor shifts in the elementary structure of the stone . . . and all of a sudden, the stone you described in your spell, when you started your little walk, isn't the *same* stone anymore. Your spell doesn't work on that changed stone because the initial description's no longer accurate. The spell structure unravels, and you get stuck half in the wall and half out of it. In an argument like that . . . the stone's older than you are: it wins."

Arhu's eyes went so round that Rhiow thought they looked ready to pop out of their sockets. "So keep close," she said. "And Arhu— keep alert. There are creatures who live down in these caves who don't like us."

Urruah sniffed down his nose, an oh-what-an-understatement kind of noise. "Come on," Rhiow said. "Let's get this over with."

She led them down into the dark.

She remembered the way well enough from their last intervention here, though even if she had not, the Whisperer knew the main routes perfectly well—the explorations and interventions of other wizards, like Rhiow's old master Ffairh in his time, would have been preserved in the Whispering for anyone who might later need the information. As it was, it was a shame that the context of where they were going and what they might meet tended to keep them from enjoying this place on its own merits: in their upper regions, at least, the caverns in the Mountain were beautiful enough.

The water had been a long time doing its work. As the main cavern narrowed and began to slope downward, Rhiow picked her way along among the upward-poking spines of pale stone, wondering a little at the lacy structure of some of them: each had its cousin-spike hanging down from the ceiling above. All these were dry now, the areas of active cavern formation having receded farther down into the Mountain. But up here, Rhiow would have welcomed the occasional drip or tinkle of water; it would have distracted her from the image that always struck her, when they were forced to come this way, that they were walking into a particularly fangy set of jaws, backed by a dark and hungry gullet of stone. If you weren't careful, you could imagine the jaws closing—

Cut that out, she thought. The "gullet" narrowed and sloped down before them until it was only a few feet wide, and the light from outside the main cavern opening failed in the darkness beyond it. This was the only place in the Old Downside where Rhiow found herself wishing she had a proper Person's body rather than this ancient and attractive, but oversized, persona. The walls here always brushed against her shoulders as she slipped through, yet there was no corresponding feeling of her whiskers being anywhere near the walls, as there would have been were she in her own body. The resultant sensation was disconcerting, disorienting.

The walls squeezed down closer: the tunnel kinked, kinked again. Rhiow slipped forward absolutely silently, listening hard. When she had nightmares about being attacked here, the nightmares always involved this spot: hemmed in by stone, no room to turn around, something bad behind her, something worse waiting in front. She knew that attack so high up, so close to the light and the day, was wildly unlikely. But still, it was the unlikely things that would kill you—

Sudden relief, as the feeling of stone touching her sides fell away, and the sound changed, even though it was only the nearly inaudible little dry sound that Rhiow's paw-pads made on the stone. She activated one of the spells she had brought with her, saying the last word of it, and well ahead of her a tiny spark of faint green light came into being, floating high up in the air. The color was carefully chosen: the Wise Ones did not see in this frequency.

Behind her, first Saash, then Arhu, and finally Urruah slipped into the larger cavern, looking around. In the faint light a vast array of more stalactites—whole glittering white or cream or rust-banded chandeliers of them—could be seen hanging from the ceiling. There were fewer standing stalagmites here; gaps in the spiky ceiling and the shattered rubble on the floor showed where the occasional groundshake or mere structural weakness had wrought much damage over many years.

"It's pretty," Arhu said, sounding rather befuddled.

"It is," Saash said. "Sometimes I wish we could make a proper light when we come down here. . . ." She shrugged her tail.

Rhiow shrugged back, and said, "Come on. We've got at least an hour's walk ahead of us. . . ." *Assuming we don't run into anything that makes us need to go another way. Oh, please, Queen Iau, just this once, let it be easy for us. . . .*

Rhiow had her doubts, though, as she led them downward through that cavern and into the next one, as to whether this prayer was at all likely to be answered. When you were in the company of a wizard on Ordeal, anything could happen, and probably would. The odds against a quiet intervention were fairly high.

Behind her, as she padded through the wide entry into the next cavern, Arhu was saying to Saash, "Why are you so nervous?"

Saash breathed out. "We were down here before, about a sun's-round ago. Not a good trip."

"What happened?"

"Bad things," Urruah said from behind Arhu, his voice plainly suggesting that one might happen right now if Arhu didn't shut up.

He shut up. They walked a long way: down, always down, through galleries and arcades of stone, mighty halls as big as the concourse in Grand Central, twisting hallways as broad as the Hyatt passage. Sometimes the links between caverns squeezed to tunnels as narrow as the first one, or narrower: once the ceiling of one of these tunnels dropped so low that Rhiow had to get down on her belly and crawl forward, a few inches at a time, pushing herself along with an effort. Behind them she could hear the others doing the same, Urruah last and suffering most because of his size—grunting and swearing very softly under his breath. It was at such times, her own breath sounding intolerably loud to her, the others', behind her, sounding even louder, that Rhiow always got the feeling that the Mountain was listening: that the stone itself was alive—though impassive—and watching them, though without any feeling of interest as a living being would understand it . . . without anything but a sense of weight. Hostility she could have coped with: benign neglect would have been fine. But *this* gave her the creeps, the sense of the stone piled up above her, the Mountain pressing down on her back, on her head. . . .

Cut it out, she told herself, annoyed, and pushed forward. . . .

They went onward, and downward. The sound of water faded away to nothing or grew again, by turns. The little green light bobbed ahead of them into places where water was now actively dripping so that they were rained on under the earth, and Saash muttered and hissed under her breath, having to stop every twenty paces or so to shake water out of her eyes or smooth back into place some patch of fur that she simply could not leave alone any longer. Generally Saash was pretty good about controlling her fur fixation when she was on errantry, but down here she had problems, and Rhiow was in no mood to call her on them: she had problems of her own. *The weight of the stone, the silence of it . . . watching . . .*

She thought of the cool stony regard of the statue of Queen Iau in the Met and broke away from the other imagery with pleasure. The comfortable, dusky blue light of that space: it would be a pleasure to be back up there again, strolling among the ancient things. Rhiow thought of the clay chicken pot there, with a very realistic chicken carved on the upper side of it, and how she had laughed once to see an almost exact duplicate of the thing in the window of a kitchen shop in the upper Eighties, off First Avenue. Down in this darkness, it was all too easy to stop believing in sunlight, and museums, and traffic noise, and taxi horns blaring, and all the rest of normal life in the city. Yet all those things—the buildings, the *ehhif,* the noise, and the hurry—had their roots here, in the roots of the Mountain, in this darkness, this silence. Without this, none of those could exist.

They went onward, and downward. Several times Rhiow stopped, and the others—perhaps looking elsewhere—ran into her from behind, or into each other, so that soft hisses were exchanged, or the occasional cuff. Once Arhu—who had been uncharacteristically silent, catching the others' mood, or perhaps himself unnerved at the way he was starting to hear the waiting, listening stone—crowded too close to Saash. She stopped suddenly, perhaps hearing something: Arhu bumped into her, Urruah bumped into Arhu, and Arhu turned around and actually hit Urruah in the head. Rhiow turned just in time to see the pale green spark of surprise in Urruah's eyes, the flicker of anger, and then the sudden and very welcome return of humor. He said *rrrrrr* under his breath, and Arhu backed into Saash, who promptly smacked him.

Arhu started to say *rrrrr* on his own behalf, but Rhiow shouldered between him and Saash. "All right," she said, "come on. Tension. All our nerves are shredded like the Great Tom's ears at the moment: why try to pretend they're not? We don't have much farther to go. Arhu, how are you holding up?"

"It reminds me of, of—" His tail was lashing. "Never mind. Let's go."

They went on again: still downward. The sound of dripping water had faded away again; there was nothing now to be heard but their own breaths, and the faint sound of their paw-pads on the dry, rough stone—sometimes a *tchk* as one of them kicked or shifted a bit of stone, and the sound fell flat and loud into the surrounding stillness. The little green light was starting to make Rhiow's eyes water, and sometimes her concentration on it faltered, so that it flickered slightly in the dark, like a candle guttering out. *It would be nice,* she thought, *if there were wizardries you could just start and ignore afterwards. . . .* But there were no such things. A wizardry needed attention at regular intervals, redescription of its basic tenets, of the space you intended to affect, and the effect you were trying to have; otherwise it lapsed—

—the light went out—

Rhiow stopped short. *I didn't do that—*

Utter stillness behind her. The others were holding their breaths. Then Arhu whispered, "Is that a light up there?"

Her eyes were relaxing back to handling complete darkness again, or trying to—in night this total, even the keenest-eyed feline was helpless. But there was indeed a faint, faint glow coming from up ahead—

It's the catenary, she thought. *Thank you, Iau.*

But why did my light go out? . . .

"It's the power source," she whispered back to Arhu. "We're almost where we're going. Saash?"

The dim, dim light started to seem brighter with time; as she turned, Rhiow could actually see Saash's face, and her ears working. She had the best hearing of any of them.

"Nothing," she said very softly. "Let's do what we have to, Rhi, and get ourselves out of here again. We've been lucky."

So far, Rhiow heard her add.

Silently Rhiow agreed. "The next chamber is very big," she said to Arhu. "It has to be: the catenary structure is what feeds power up to the gate loci, and its inwoven wizardry very carefully controls a large clear space around it. We'll have to deactivate that wizardry before we start working, and before that we'll be laying down a protective circle. You must stay inside that circle at all costs, no matter what happens to any of us: if you venture outside it while the catenary's control wizardry is down, and accidentally come in direct contact with the energy of the catenary—you'll be dead, that's all. Clear about that?"

"Uh huh," Arhu said, and Rhiow heard him gulp.

"Good. Come on, crew."

She led the way toward the faint glow. The tunnel narrowed and kinked again, then opened out into the next chamber.

Here the stone was more gray than pale. The chamber had numerous openings, and a floor that was flattish and devoid of stalagmites, dropping to a shallow depression in its middle. From that depression, right out of the solid stone of the floor, almost straight up to the ceiling and apparently into and through it, a tightly coiled and interwoven bundle of hyperstrings stretched. Up and down it, in many colors, ran a fierce, bitter light, much more dangerous-looking than the weft of the gates above. The whole structure jittered and sizzled with power, all the while wavering slightly in the air as if it were a plant swaying in some breeze. The effect was actually caused by the hyperstrings' bundled structure being more than usually affected by changes in gravitic stresses and the local magnetic field, and, for all Rhiow knew, by neutrino flow.

"Wow," Arhu said from behind her. "How are you going to fix *this?*"

"By shutting it down and taking it apart," Rhiow said. "Urruah?"

"I'll make the circle," he said, and started pacing out, to one side of the cavern, the protected area from which they would operate. As he paced, looking intently at the floor and occasionally pushing a bit of cracked stone or rubble out of the way, the sigils and symbols of the Speech started to appear glowing on the stone, a long flowing sentence-equation. All their names, and descriptions of them all, were woven into it as well: otherwise the spell would have no way to know who it was protecting. All the rest of the written circle, looking more and more as Urruah worked like a glowing vinework of words in the Speech, was in the most technical of its dialects, mostly involving the control and redirection of energy flows, and based on words that had originally been Ailurin. Of all wizards working on Earth, the People knew most about energy—being able to clearly perceive aspects of it that *ehhif* and other species' wizards couldn't. Even non-wizardly People had an affinity with warmth, a link to fire and the Sun, which other species had noticed: it was traceable back to this native talent for seeing and managing energy flows.

Rhiow glanced at Saash: she was watching the openings into the cave, listening, on guard. Rhiow strolled over to have a look at Urruah's work—it was routine, in a group wizardry, to check your teammates' work, as a failsafe to catch errors. Urruah was making a third pass around the circle, its design growing more and more complex. Again and again the symbol for the word *auw,* "energy," appeared in numerous compound forms. Most of the terms that Urruah was using here were specialist terminologies relating to *auwsshui'f,* the term for the "lower electromagnetic spectrum," which besides describing "sub-matter" relationships such as string and hyperstring function also took in quantum particles, faster-than-light particles, wavicles, and sub-atomics. He was paying less attention, for this spell's purposes, to *efviauw,* the electromagnetic spectrum, or *iofviauw,* the "upper electromagnetic spectrum," involving straightforward plasma functions, fission, fusion, and gravitic force: gating energies were by and large subtler and more dangerous than any of these.

The circle completed, Urruah stopped after a few moments and actually panted a little, looking back at his handiwork.

"You all right?"

"Yes," he said. "It just takes it out of you a little, dumping it all out at once like that."

"I know. Nice job, though." Rhiow paced around the circle, looking at it. "Seems complete. Saash? Come check your parameters. Arhu, look at this—"

The other two came over. Rhiow pointed at one gappy sequence of symbols. "See that?" she said to Arhu. "That's your name—or the version of it we use for spelling. Look at the version of your name that the Whisperer shows you inside your head—check it against this version, make sure this one's right. A spell is nothing but descriptions of things, and people, and something you want to have happen. When you trigger the spell, the description it contains *will change what you've described*. Describe *yourself* wrong, and you'll change . . . whether you like it or not."

He squinted at the glowing network of symbols. "Yeah. Uh, right."

"Take your time over it. Be sure. Saash?"

"It's fine. He knows me well enough by now." She glanced up at Urruah, amused. "Though I'm not sure I scratch *that* much."

"If you don't now," Urruah said, with some amusement, "you will later."

Saash hissed, a sound of affectionate annoyance. Arhu looked up then and said, "I think—" He put a paw out, hesitated. "Can I touch it?"

"Sure," Urruah said, "it's not active yet."

"There's a piece missing here—" He put a paw on one spot where there was a "place-holding" gap with several graceful curves stitched over it, indicating, to a wizard's eye, *To be continued* . . . All their names had such gaps, here and there, but Arhu's had whole chains of them. "She—" he said, and sounded embarrassed. "She says—"

"Go ahead, put it in," Urruah said. "The matrix will pick it up from you. Make a picture of it in your head."

Arhu frowned and thought, while he did so jutting his chin out in a way that made Rhiow smile slightly, thinking of Yafh around the corner from her: he got a similar "concentrating" look while pondering imponderables, endearing because of how witless it made him look. After a second, a pair of symbols appeared in the place-holding area, and the to-be-continued sigil relocated itself farther along in the diagram. Rhiow looked thoughtfully at the new symbols. They looked familiar, but she couldn't place them. . . .

The Whisperer spoke briefly in her ear, just a word or two.

Rhiow froze. *Oh, no,* she thought. *Not really. No . . .*

She straightened hurriedly. "All right," she said, "we're in order. Saash, are you ready? Anything that needs to be done to the catenary before we get inside?"

"Not a thing. Let's start."

"Arhu, jump in," Rhiow said, and did so herself.

Saash followed; Urruah was last in. He planted his paws, claws out, in the "trigger" area of the spell, and said the word that would initiate the circle.

It blazed, the vinework that had been distinguishable part by part and in detail when dimmer now bloomed into a blur of white-golden fire, shimmering and alive. Urruah looked vacant-eyed for a moment, then said to Rhiow, "It's powered up for the next twenty minutes or so."

"Good. Let's go. Saash?"

She was sitting in the circle, scratching. Rhiow said nothing; Urruah glanced at her, his whiskers forward, and looked back down at the circle.

"Do you have a skin problem or something?" Arhu said.

Rhiow hissed at him and cuffed him, not too hard. "If she did, it would still be preferable to your tact problem," she said. "You just be still and watch."

Saash sat up then and looked over at the catenary.

It began, slowly, to drift toward them: a pillar of structured, high-tension fire, like a rainbow pulled out into hair-fine strands and plugged into much too high a current, ready to blow something out: itself or you.

Arhu watched it come, wide-eyed. "Is this safe?" he said.

"Not at all," Rhiow said calmly. "If that power came undone and we weren't in here, we'd be ash. If that. The power bound up in that could melt the whole island of the city into a bowl of slag half a mile deep if it was given enough time. The only thing that's going to control it, when it gets in here with us, is Saash. Got any more comments on the condition of her fur?"

He stared, watched the catenary drift closer. "Nice color," Arhu said, and his tongue went in and out twice, very quickly.

He'll have a sore nose before the day's done, at this rate, Rhiow thought; but at the same time, she was less interested in the catenary than in that symbol in Arhu's name, now lost in the bloom of fire of the activated circle.

The catenary drifted up against the boundary of the circle, touched it. Light flared at the contact, and the catenary bounced away, drifted back again: another flare, a smell of something singeing, not here but somehow somewhere *else*. Rhiow's nostrils flared. It was the scent of the kind of magic they worked with, in combination with the gate-forces, as inimitable and unmistakable a scent as the cinder-iron-ozone reek of the Grand Central tracks. Subatomic-particle annihilations, hyperstring stress, who knew what caused the smell, or whether it was even real? It meant that things were working . . . for the moment.

The burning, twisting column of the catenary pushed against the circle, bowing it inward in one spot. Saash's eyes were fixed on it, rainbowed with its fires as she guided the catenary in by force of will toward the spell that would catch it and hold it still for operation. "It's going to pop through in a second," she said to Urruah, her voice calm enough, but strained a little higher than usual. "Got the pocket ready for it?"

"Ready." He slid his left paw over to another part of the circle, sank his claws into the fire.

The catenary pushed farther into the circle, the stream and sheen of light down its length getting brighter and fiercer, the smell getting stronger. The circle bent inward to accommodate its passage, a curve-bud of light pushing inward around the contour of the column of fire. Abruptly, with a jerk, the catenary broke free of the circle, broke through—

A smaller circle, the completed "bud," now surrounded the base of the column, where it erupted from the stone: another one encircled it higher up. Rhiow saw Arhu's nervous glance upward. "The spell's spherical," she said. "You need to extend at least one extra dimension along when you're working with these things."

Arhu backed away from the catenary as it drifted into the center of the circle, stopped there. "All right," Saash said, pacing around it once and looking it over. "See that bundle there? The one that looks mostly blue. That's the one for the gate that's giving us trouble."

"How do you want to handle this?"

Saash sat down and had another scratch, looking oddly meditative and calm for someone who was nose to nose with a concentration of power in which a small nuclear explosion might be drowned out, if not entirely missed. "I'm going to shut down everything but Penn, and the one Grand Central gate that Khi-t's holding patent," she said. "The Penn power linkages are right over on the other side of the bundle . . . no need to involve them, and it'll give anyone who needs to do a transit somewhere to divert to for a little while."

"Right." *Kit,* Rhiow said inwardly, *we're taking all the Grand Central gates down but yours.*

Right—we'll divert anyone who shows up. Let us know when you're done.

Saash got up, finished with her scratch, then paced once more around the catenary, looking it up and down. One spot she leaned in to look at with great care, a braided cord of blue and blue-white fires as thick as the wrist of her forepaw. With great care and delicacy, she leaned closer, then shut her eyes—and bit it.

Sparks flew, the light grew blinding; the singeing smell got stronger. Arhu stared.

More than half the catenary went dark, or nearly so.

Saash straightened, looked the pillar of fire up and down. "All right," she said. "That's better." The "dark" bundles and strands weren't completely dead, but now shone only as brightly as the weft of one of the gate matrices up at the surface. She sat up on her haunches in her preferred operating position and reached into the dark bundles, pulling out a hefty double clawful of them.

"Here," she said suddenly to Arhu, "come on over here." He did, looking dubious. "Right. Now hold these for me. Don't be scared, they won't hurt you. Much," she added, her whiskers going forward just a little as she shoved the pulled-out strings at him, and Arhu, more from reflex than anything else, grabbed them and hung on. His eyes went wide with shock as he felt the sizzle of the catenary's power in his paws—the ravening fire of it just barely leashed, and as anxious to get at him as a guard dog on a chain.

"Good," Saash said, not even looking at him as she pulled out another of the bundles of hyperstrings and handed them off to Rhiow. Rhiow settled herself on her haunches as well, hanging onto the strings, and Saash looked over the bundle, slipped a careful claw behind three or four of the strings, and slashed them. They leapt free, glowing and hissing softly, and lashing like angry tails. "Don't let those hit you," she said conversationally to Arhu, "they'll sting. Rhi, remember last time, when that whole bundle came loose at once?"

"Please," Rhiow muttered. "I'd rather be attacked by bees. At least they can sting you only once."

Saash was elbow-deep in the catenary now, slowing down a little in her work. "Hmm," she said. "I wonder . . ." She leaned in again, pulled forward one particular minor bundle of strings, glowing a pale gold, and took it behind her front fangs, closed her mouth; then looked unfocused for a moment, an expression like the "tasting" look she made when breathing breaths with someone. After a few seconds, Saash's eyes flicked sideways toward Rhiow. "Aha," she said.

"'Aha,'" said Rhiow, slightly edgy. Her mind was on those openings all around them, but more on Arhu. "Care to give us an explanation of what that means in the technical sense?"

"String fatigue," Saash said.

Rhiow blinked. You came across it, occasionally, but more usually in the gate matrices, higher up. Usually a hyperstring had to be most unusually stressed by some repetitive local phenomenon to degrade to the point where it stopped holding matter and energy together correctly.

"There's a bad strand here," Saash said. "It's not conducting correctly. Tastes 'sick.'"

"What would have caused that?" Urruah said.

Saash shrugged her tail. "Sunspots?"

"Oh please."

"No, seriously. You get more neutrinos at a maximum. Add that to the flare weather we've been having recently—get a good dose of high-energy stuff through a weak area in a hyperstring, it's likely enough to unravel. In any case, it's not passing power up the line to the gate."

"I thought the power conduits were all redundant, though," Urruah said.

"They are. That's the cause of the problem here. The 'sick' strand's energy states have contaminated the redundant backup as well because they're identical and right against each other in the bundle." Saash looked rather critically at the catenary. "Someone may have to come down here and rebraid the whole thing to prevent it happening again."

"*Please* don't say that," Rhiow said. "Can you fix it now?"

"Oh, I can cut out the sick part and patch it with material from another string," said Saash. "They're pretty flexible. I'd just like to know a little more about the conditions that produced this effect."

"Well," Rhiow said, "better get patching. Are the other strings all right?"

"I'm going to finish the diagnostic," Saash said. "Two minutes."

They seemed long to Rhiow, although nothing bad was happening. Her forearms were aching a little with the strain of holding the hyperstrings at just the angle Saash had given them to her; and meanwhile her eyes kept dropping to that symbol, almost lost in the fire of the circle but not quite. It was simple: two curves, a slanted straight line bisecting them—in its way, rather like the symbol that even the *ehhif* had known to carve on the Queen's breast.

The Eye—

She looked up suddenly and found Arhu sitting there with his claws clenched full of hyperstrings and gazing down at it, too, while Saash, oblivious, pulled out several bright strings in her claws and began to knit them together. Arhu's expression was peculiar, in its way as meditative as Saash's look had been earlier.

"They have a word for it, don't they?" he said.

"For what?" Rhiow said. "And who?"

"For this," Arhu said, glancing up again at his paws full of dulled fire. *"Ehhif."*

"Cat's-cradle," she said. "For them it's just play they do with normal string, a kitten's game."

"They must have seen us."

"So I think, sometimes," Rhiow said.

Arhu's glance fell again to the symbol, to the Eye. "So has someone else," he said.

Rhiow licked her nose and swallowed, nervous.

"All right," Saash said after a minute. "That ought to be the main conduit of the bad gate repaired. I'll just do the second here, and we'll be finished."

"Hurry," Rhiow said.

"Can't hurry quality work, Rhi," Saash said, intent on what she was doing. "How's the circle holding up?"

Urruah examined it critically. "Running a little low on charge at the moment. How much longer is this going to take you?"

"Oh . . . five minutes. Ten at the outside."

"I'll give it another jolt." Urruah bent down: the circle dimmed slightly, then brightened.

Arhu looked up from the circle then. Not at the catenary, not at Saash: up into the empty air.

"They're coming," he said.

Rhiow looked at him with alarm. *"Who?"*

But she was afraid she knew perfectly well.

"He didn't lie," Arhu said, looking at Urruah with rather skewed intensity. "They *are* here."

"Uh oh," Urruah said. "You don't mean—"

"The dragons—!"

And then the roaring began. It was not very near yet—but it was entirely too near, echoing down through one of those openings . . . or all of them.

Rhiow rapidly went through the spells she was carrying in her head, looking for the one that would have the most rapid results against the attackers she was expecting. One of them was particularly effective: it ran down the adversary's nerves and rendered them permanently unresponsive to chemical stimulus—the wizardly equivalent of nerve gas, and tailored specifically to the problem at hand. But it wouldn't be able to get out of a protective circle; you would have to drop the circle to use it. And those who were coming were fast. If you miscalculated, if one of them jumped at you and put a big long claw through your brain before you could get the last word out—

"Rhiow? *Rhiow!*"

Her head snapped around. Arhu was still sitting there with his claws full of strings, but now they were trembling because he was. "What's that noise?" he said.

"What you said was coming," she said.

"What I said—" He looked confused.

"This is what he did before, Rhi," Urruah said, looking grim. "Saash?"

"Not right now," Saash said, her voice desperately level. "If I don't finish this other patch, the whole job'll have to be done again. Let them come."

"Oh, sure," Urruah said. "Let them 'tree' us inside the circle, five bodies thick! Then what are we supposed to—"

"No," Arhu said, and the word started as a hiss of protest, scaled up to a yowl. *"No—!"*

The Children of the Serpent burst in.

Rhiow knew that *ehhif* had somewhat rediscovered dinosaurs in recent years. Or rather, rediscovered them *again,* only more visually than usual this time. She had once heard Iaehh and Hhuha idly discussing this tendency for each new generation of their kind to become fascinated with the long names, the huge sizes and terrible shapes. But in Rhiow's opinion, the fascination had to do with the *ehhif* perception that such creatures were a long time ago and far away. And the most recent resurrection of the fascination, in that movie and its sequel, were rooted in a variant on the same perception: that long ago and far away was where and when such creatures *belonged.*

But this too had become one of the places where they belonged. They did not take kindly to intruders. And they certainly would not let any leave alive. . . .

Arhu started to crouch down, trembling, at the sight of them, as if he had forgotten what he was holding. "Saash!" Rhiow hissed, and without missing a beat, Saash let go of the strings she had been working on— they snapped back into place in the catenary—and took hold of the ones Rhiow had held. Rhiow bent down before Arhu could finish collapsing, and snatched the strings out of his paws. He was wide-eyed, crouching right down into a ball of terror: a pitiful and incongruous sight with him in this body, which would have been large and powerful enough to bring down the biggest wildebeest. But the hunt was in the heart, as the saying went: Rhiow couldn't entirely blame him for not having the heart for this one as the Children of the Serpent poured into the cavern and hit the circle, claws out, roaring hunger and rage.

Urruah lifted his head and roared too, but the sound was almost drowned in the wave of shrieks of hate that followed it. Single sickle-claws three feet long scrabbled against the circle, jaws half the size of one of their bodies tried to slash or bite their way in; and everywhere on your body, though nothing touched you physically, you felt the pressure of the little, cold, furious eyes. There was intelligence there, but it was drowned in hatred, and *gladly* drowned. The impression of outraged strength, pebbled and mottled greenish- and bluish-hided bodies throwing themselves again and again at the circle; the impression of raging speed, and the interminable screaming, a storm of sound in this closed-in place: that was what you had to deal with, rather than any single, rational impression of *This is a deinonychus, that is a carnosaur—*

"That's what it was," Arhu was moaning, almost helplessly, like a starving kitten. "That's what it was—"

Rhiow swallowed. "The circle's holding?" she said to Urruah.

"Of course it is. Nothing they can do about it. But how are we going to get out?"

It was a fair question. He had said "five deep"; possibly he had been optimistic. The cavern was now packed so full of saurians that there was no seeing the far wall, except for the part near the roof, above the tallest heads. Rhiow had a sudden ridiculous vision of what Grand Central would look like at rush hour if it were full of saurians, not people: a whole lot like this. *We need shopping bags, though,* she thought, pacing around the circle, forcing herself to look into the terrible little eyes, the jaws snapping futilely but with increasing frustration and violence against the immaterial barrier of the circle: *and Reeboks and briefcases. Or no, maybe the briefcases wouldn't be in the best of taste—*

"Done," Saash said.

"The whole repair?"

"Yes. I'm going to bring up the rest of the Grand Central complex again," Saash said. "Tell our connection to get ready."

Heard that, Kit said. *We're set. Rhiow, if you need help, there's backup waiting.*

Might need it, Rhiow said, *but it's hard to say. Hang on—*

Saash leaned into the catenary again, put out one single claw, inserted it into an insignificant-looking little loop in one string—it looked like a snag in a sweater—and pulled.

The loop straightened, vanished. The catenary came alive again, the full fire of its power bursting up through the strings that had been offline. Saash stood watching it, her head tilted to one side, listening.

"Feels right," she said. "Khi-t?"

We've got the gates back, said another voice: Nita's. *Want us to test the bad one?*

"Please."

The screaming and scrabbling and clawing went on all around them, undiminished. *Okay, it hyperextended all right—*

"I saw that," Saash said. "The catenary's feeding the patched string properly. Shut it again?"

—Closed.

Saash sat down and started to scratch again, looking surprisingly satisfied with herself, under the circumstances. "I deserve some milk."

"So do we," Urruah roared at her, "and we also deserve to get out of here with our pelts intact, which seems increasingly unlikely at the moment! What in Iau's name are we supposed to do *now?*"

Saash looked at the catenary, then back at Rhiow, and slowly her whiskers started to go forward.

"Oh, no, Saash," Rhiow said. "*Oh* no."

"Why not? Have you got anything better?" Saash said. "You want to try the odds of dropping the circle and having time to hit them with the neural inhibitor? I don't *think* so, Rhi! There are so many of them leaning against that spell right now, they'd just squash us to death the second we dropped it, never mind what else they'd do to us. Which they *will*, as you remember from last time."

Rhiow swallowed. Arhu stared at Saash in dumb terror. Urruah said, "Just what are you thinking of?"

Saash started to smile again, a smile entirely in character with a giant prehistoric predator-cat. "I'm going to push the catenary back out there without its 'insulating' spell in place," Saash said.

"Your brain has turned to hairballs!" Rhiow shouted. "What if it degrades the circle on the way through?"

"It won't."

"How sure are you?"

"Very sure. I'll leave the 'insulation' in place until after I've shoved it outside."

"Oh, wonderful, just great! And what about when you take the insulation off, have you thought that it might just degrade the circle *then,* and blast us all to ashes?"

"It shouldn't."

"Shouldn't—!"

"You want to sit here and wait them out?"

Rhiow looked out at the room full of roaring, shrieking saurians. Those at the far side of the room were already settling down to wait.

"It won't work. No matter *how* long we sit here, they'll wait," Saash said. "And sooner or later we're going to need food and sleep, and as soon as the last one of us goes to sleep, and the circle weakens enough to let them in—"

Urruah looked from Rhiow to Saash, then back to Rhiow again. "She's got a point," he said.

Rhiow's tail was lashing. "You think you have a life or so to spare?"

"You want to find out if it matters," Urruah said, more gently than necessary, "down *here?"*

Rhiow licked her nose again, then looked at Saash. "All right," she said. "I concur."

"Right," Saash said.

She looked at the catenary. It drifted toward the edge of the circle; its own protective circles drifted with it.

Some of the saurians nearest the place where it was about to make contact looked at the catenary with the first indications of concern. Its rainbow fire fell into their big dark eyes, turning them into a parody of People's eyes—bright slits, dark irises; they blinked, backed away slightly.

"They're not wild about the light," Urruah said.

Saash nodded. The small circle surrounding the catenary made contact with the larger one: they "budded" together again. As if becoming somewhat uneasy at this, more of the saurians began to back away, and the screaming and roaring started to take on an uncomfortable edge. Some of the saurians nearer the walls stood up again, began to mill around, catching their companions' unease. Saash closed her eyes then and held quite still.

In one swift motion the catenary popped back out through the circle. It was now bereft of the smaller, "child" circles that the main protective circles had generated around it, and saurians jostled away from it as it drifted quickly back to its original position in the center of the cavern.

The saurians parted around it, closing together again nearest the circle, and going back to their raging and scrabbling against its invisible barrier. Saash looked over their heads as best she could, past them, to where the catenary had now settled itself back in place.

"All right?" she said. "Mind your eyes, now."

Rhiow started to close hers but was caught too late. The catenary suddenly stopped being merely a fiercely bright bundle of rainbows and turned into a raging floor-to-ceiling column of pure white fire. Lightning forked out of it in all directions, at least what would have passed for lightning. The whole cavern whited out in a storm of blinding fire that hissed and gnawed at their circle like a live thing. All Rhiow's fur stood on end, and her eyes fizzed in their sockets. Behind her, Arhu cried out in fear. The desperate screams of the saurians were lost in the shrieking roar of the unleashed catenary.

Eventually things got quiet again, and Rhiow scrubbed at her tearing eyes, trying to rub some vision back into them. When she could see again, the catenary was once more sizzling with its normal light. But there was little else left in the cavern that was not reduced to charcoal or ash, and nothing at all left that was alive in the strictest sense . . . though bits and pieces here and there continued to move with lizardly persistence.

Saash stood there, looking around her with grim satisfaction. "Definitely," she said, "not at *all* wild about the light."

Urruah got up and shook himself, making a face at the smell. "I take it I can drop the circle now."

"It's as safe as it's going to get, I think," Rhiow said, "and once it's down, we can use the other spell if we need it." She went over to the crouching Arhu. "Arhu, come on—we have to go."

He looked up and around him, blinking and blinded, but Rhiow somehow got the idea that this blindness had nothing to do with the light. "Yes," he said, and got up. Urruah had hardly collapsed the circle before Arhu was making hurriedly for the cavern-entrance through which they had come. "We have to hurry," he said. "It's coming—"

Urruah looked from Arhu to Rhiow. "*Now* what?"

"What's coming?" Saash said.

"The greater one," he said. "The father. The son. Quick, quick, it's coming!" His voice started to shade upward into a panicky roar. "We've got to get out before it comes!"

Rhiow's tail was lashing with confusion and concern. "I'm willing to take him at his word," she said. "There's no reason to linger—we've done what we came for. Let's get back up to the light."

It took less time than going down had taken. Despite the thought that they might shortly be attacked again, they were all lighter of spirit than they had been—all of them but Arhu. He wouldn't be quiet: the whole way up through the caverns with him was a litany of "It's coming" and "*that's* what it was . . ." and "the greater one," and an odd phrase that Rhiow heard only once: "the sixth claw . . ." Arhu didn't grow silent again until they came up into the last cavern, past the great teeth of stone, to see the red-gold light of that world's sunset, and the green shadows beneath the trees beyond the stony threshold. There he stood for a long time while Saash checked the main matrix for the repaired gate, and he gazed at the declining sun as if he thought he might never see it again.

The thought had certainly been on Rhiow's mind earlier; but now that they were up and out, there were other concerns. She glanced through the patent gate to the darkness beneath Grand Central, from which Kit and Nita were looking through, interested. "Many thanks," she said. "Having you here as backup lent us the confidence to go all out."

Kit made a small, only fractionally mocking bow: Nita grinned. "Our pleasure," she said. "We're all in the same business, after all. Want us to leave this open for you?"

Rhiow looked over at Saash. "No," Saash said, turning away from the matrix she was checking. "I want to check its open-close cycle a couple more times. But nicely done, my wizards. Go well, and let's meet well again."

"Dai," the two said; and the gate snapped from its view of the Grand Central tracks to the usual shining warp/weft pattern.

Rhiow turned to Saash, who said, "The matrix is just fine now. That design flaw in the braiding of the catenary *is* going to have to be looked at, at some point. But not just now . . ."

"No," Rhiow said. "I'll talk to Har'lh about it; I'll have to report to him this evening anyway. But, Saash . . . what a job. And you did wonderfully, too," she said to Urruah. "Not many circles could have taken that punishment."

She went over to where Arhu was standing. He looked at Rhiow with an expression equally composed of embarrassment and fear.

"I screwed up," he said.

She breathed in, breathed out. "No," she said, and gave him a quick lick behind one ear. He stared at her, shocked. "You started your Ordeal. Now at least we have some kind of hint of what your problems are going to be."

He looked at her, and away again, toward the sunset: the sun was gone now, the darkness falling fast.

"Yes," he said, in a voice of complete despair. "So do I."

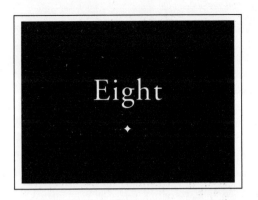

Eight

What with the report for Har'lh, and seeing Saash and Arhu safely back to the garage—for Arhu still seemed very disturbed, though his litany of fear had stopped—it was late before she got home. At the sound of the kitty door going, Hhuha looked up from where she was sitting, reading in the big chair. From inside, in the bedroom, a man's voice was saying, "And now tonight's list of Top Ten Reasons to call the Board of Health—"

"Mike," Hhuha said, "she's back."

Rhiow ran across to her and jumped in her lap, purring, before Hhuha could rise. "Oh, you rotten little thing," Hhuha said, picking her up and nuzzling the side of her face, "I've been worried stiff, where the heck have you been all evening?"

Once again Rhiow wondered, as she had before, which *ehhif* demigod Heck was. "Don't ask," she muttered. "But I'm glad to be back, oh, believe me I am. Mmm, you had pizza again. Any leftovers?"

Hhuha held her away a little, leaving Rhiow's hind legs dangling. "I wish you wouldn't do that," Rhiow added, with a rueful glance down at her legs. "It's hardly dignified."

"I wonder," Hhuha said, "are you getting out somehow?"

From the bedroom, a snort could be clearly heard over the laughter coming from the picturebox. "There's nowhere for her to get out but twenty stories down, Sue," the answer came. "And if she's doing that, how's she getting *back?*"

"I hate it when he's sensible," Hhuha muttered, holding Rhiow close again. "Well, you're okay. I'm so glad. I'll give you some of that nice tuna."

"I'll *eat* it," Rhiow said, "though I must be out of my mind."

But neither of them moved for a few minutes: Hhuha just held Rhiow more or less draped over her shoulder, and Rhiow just let her, and they purred at each other. *Moments like this make it all worthwhile,* Rhiow thought. *Even the almost-getting-eaten-by-dinosaurs part.* For the work she did was as much about keeping Manhattan safe for *ehhif* as for People, and about making it easier for wizards of all kinds to keep the planet going as it should. Wizards had kept various small and large disasters from befalling the city in the past and would do so often again; on the smallest scale, they did it every day. And the purpose, finally, was so that normal life could go on doing what it did—just trying to manage the best it could and finding what joy there was to be found along the way. Entropy was running: the heat was slowly bleeding out of the worlds, and nothing could be done to actually stop the process. But wizards could slow it down, however slightly, and make a little more time for everyone else to purr at each other in. . . .

"You must be hungry," Hhuha said, and didn't move.

"Starving," Rhiow said, and didn't move, either.

She glanced around, her head resting on Hhuha's shoulder. Papers were all over the place again, on the living-room table and in a heap by the chair. "I'm going to shred some of those if I get a chance," Rhiow said lazily, her tail twitching a bit with the pleasant image. "I wish you'd find something else to do with your days; you so dislike what you have to do now."

"Talk talk talk," Hhuha said, having just caught the last few sounds of the sentence as a soft trill. "You *are* hungry, I bet. Come on."

She finally put Rhiow carefully down on the rug and went to open another can of cat food. Rhiow sat, watching it with some resignation, since her nose told her plainly that the leftover pizza was in the microwave, and there was pepperoni on it.

They always leave it there and sneak slices in the middle of the night. Would they ever notice if I just opened it one night, took a slice out, and closed it again? If I timed it right, each of them might think the other one did it. . . .

"How much of that pizza is left?" Iaehh's voice came from the bedroom.

"About half."

"Bring me some?"

"How much?"

"About half."

"Pig."

"Controlling personality."

"Pizza in bed. Disgusting."

"Call it a lifestyle choice."

"You can damn well choose about *half* of about half. I get the rest."

"Forget it," Rhiow said then, with amusement and resignation, as Hhuha filled her bowl again. "It would never work . . . you two talk to each other too much. If this relationship were a little more dysfunctional, I'd eat a lot better, you know that?"

"There you go," Hhuha said, straightening up from the food bowl. "What a good kitty."

Rhiow set about eating the awful tuna at her best possible speed, so that she could get into the bedroom before the pizza was all gone.

Much later, both of them were snoring, and Rhiow lay at the end of the bed, looking at the yellow venetian-blind light and thinking. In particular, she was looking at a chance group of wrinkles in the blanket at the end of the bed: they looked a little like two curves and a slash across them.

The Eye.

We've got a visionary on our hands, Rhiow thought.

Seers turned up occasionally among wizards, just as among non-wizards—though there would always be those who would argue that any seer was probably actually some kind of wizard anyway. The talent was not widespread. Wizards as a class might be more liable, by the nature of their work, to the sudden flash of insight that could be mistaken for genuine future-seeing: and to a lesser extent, they were sensitive to dreams and visions—perhaps the Whisperer, in her most benevolent mode, trying to hint at where danger might lie, since she was not allowed to warn you directly. But some few wizards side-stepped even *her* boundaries and saw clearly what might happen if things kept going the way they were going at present. Some did so with dreadful clarity. They tended not to last long: they were usually claws in the One's paw and (as the myth had it) usually personified the Claw That Breaks, the razor-sharp but brittle weapon that inflicts a fatal wound on the enemy, but itself does not survive the battle. Having a seer in the vicinity meant that the Lone Power would start noticing you back with unusual persistence . . . not a happy scenario. *I had a lot of plans for this life yet,* Rhiow thought. *This is not good.*

"Boy's got the eye," Yafh had said. Rhiow breathed out in rueful amusement, for he had seen it more clearly than any of them.

She thought once more of Arhu's voice crying, *That's what it was. That's what it was—* "'It' what?" she said softly. And she sighed. She was going to have to press him on that point, and it was going to be painful. Rhiow was sure it had something to do with the condition in which they had first found him: she had her suspicions, but she needed confirmation from him, to tie up that particular loose string.

And there were others. One was a very small thing, but it was still bothering her.

Why did my light go out?

Rhiow went back in thought, suddenly, to her first diagnostic on the malfunctioning gate. The gate had as much as told her that it had been interfered with, somehow, during its function.

But nothing should be able to produce such interference except more wizardry.

Another wizard . . .

She shied away from that thought. There *were* rogues, though they weren't much discussed. The common knowledge was that wizardry did not live in the unwilling heart: a wizard uncomfortable with his power, unable to bear the ethical and practical choices it implied, soon lost the power, and any sense of ever having had it. But a wizard who was quite comfortable with the Art, and then started to find ways to use it that weren't quite ethical . . .

Normally such wizards didn't last long. The universe, to which wizardry was integral, had a way of twisting itself into unexpected shapes that would interfere with a rogue's function. Equally, there was no particular safety in assuming that a rogue was willingly cooperating with the Lone One—or with what It stood for. Like many another ill-tempered craftsman, sa'Rráhh the Destroyer was careless with her tools, as likely to throw them away or break them in spite as to reward them for services done. So when rogues appeared, they tended to be a temporary phenomenon.

Yet a personally maintained wizardry, once done and set in motion, shouldn't be able to be interfered with.

Except by the wizard who created it . . .

Rhiow blinked once or twice as that thought intruded.

Did something affect me down there?

She thought hard. The recurring difficulties she had been having with threatening imagery . . .

Surely not.

But when had she ever had anything like that happen before? Certainly she had been scared to the ends of her guard-hairs the last couple of times she'd been Downside. But nothing had gone wrong inside her head.

There were ways, though, to get inside another being's mind against its will. Wizards knew about them . . . but did not use such "back doors" except in emergencies: they were highly unethical.

But if one of my team—

She put the thought aside. It was ridiculous. Saash would never do any such thing: her commitment to the Powers, and to Rhiow personally, was total. She was incorruptible, Rhiow would swear. Urruah was, too: he was just too stubborn and opinionated, once he had his mind made up about which side he was on, to change without signs as readable as an earthquake.

But Arhu . . .

Rhiow found herself thinking, once more, about the weak link, the new link, the new "member" of the team.

That was something she was going to have to deal with, of course, and the sooner the better . . . how much she disliked the idea of having a team member simply thrust on them, even if it *was* by the Powers That Be. Teams of wizards came together willingly, for reasons of work and affinity . . . otherwise they fell apart under the strain of frequent exposures to life-or-death situations. Feline teams, made up of members of the most independent-minded species on the planet, *had* to have close personal relationships and had to be absolutely convinced of each other's reliability.

One came by such certainty only slowly. She and Saash had started working together a while after they met, about a year after Rhiow had passed her Ordeal, maybe two years after Saash's. It had been a casual thing at first—pulling together to do an assigned job, then drifting apart again. But the "apart" periods had become fewer and fewer as they realized they had a specialization in common. This was a commonplace phenomenon among wizards. After the first blaze of power associated with your Ordeal, the power begins to fade somewhat with age: but you soon find something to specialize in, and make up by concentration and narrowing of focus what you lose in sheer brute force, becoming, in a phrase Rhiow had heard Har'lh use once, "a rifle instead of a fire hose." After a while she and Saash started to be "listed" together in the Whispering as "associated talents," the Manual's delicate way of suggesting that they were beginning to become a team. Some time after that, Urruah turned up in their professional life as a "suggested adjunct" for a couple of missions, and simply became part of the team over time.

There were still a lot of things they all didn't know about each other, but wizardry by no means required total disclosure, any more than relationships in the rest of life did. How many lives along you were, what you had gone through in this one . . . how much personal information came out, and when, was all a matter of trust and inclination, and the need for privacy that was inextricably part of feline life and which balanced them both.

Rhiow would swear to the Queen's own face, though, that she knew Urruah and Saash well enough to say that neither of them would ever go rogue or sabotage a wizardry in process. If there *had* been sabotage today, its source was elsewhere.

And as for Arhu . . .

She sighed. She would have to deal with him tomorrow. But not before noontime, anyway. They would all need a good night's sleep tonight, odd as it was to be asleep *now*. Over the next few days, they could all get back to their normal schedules.

Rhiow stretched out on the bed, rolled over so that her feet were in the air in what Hhuha described as the somebody-shot-my-cat position, and let herself drift off to sleep, but not before burping once, gently, as the pepperoni settled itself.

By noon the next day she was at the garage and was surprised to meet Saash by the door, lying sprawled well out of the way of the cars, but there was no sign of Arhu.

"Sleeping," Saash said, washing one paw calmly.

"He could probably use it."

"Don't know, Rhi," Saash said, standing up and arching her back to stretch, then lying down again. "I wonder if he might not be better awake."

"You saw the Eye, then."

"I did. Risky business this, Rhi. He's likely to attract high-profile attention."

"Believe me," Rhiow said, "it's on my mind. How did you sleep?"

"After the jitters went away . . . well enough. But, Rhi, I'm not going down there again for a good long while, not if Iau Dam of Everything walks right in here and offers me Her job."

"Don't see why we should," Rhiow said. "Even Ffairh went only three or four times in his career, and only once down deep."

"May She agree with you," Saash said, and stood up—looked around carefully for any sign of Abad, and then scratched, and afterward sat down and began washing the fur into place again. "Meanwhile, are you going to let him sleep?"

"No," Rhiow said. "And I have an excuse. Where's Urruah this morning?"

"Off again. Something about his *o'hra*."

"Spare me," Rhiow said, putting her whiskers forward. "Look, you get some more sleep if you can. I'll take him off your hands for the day: he can go with me to check the track-level gates out again this afternoon—I want to see if they've replaced that switching track yet. Maybe help them a little if I can, now that the problem with Thirty's solved. If you want me, call."

"Thanks, Rhi," Saash said, and let out a cavernous yawn. "Don't wait for the call, though."

Rhiow sidled herself and made her way up to the ledge where Saash slept. There was Arhu, curled up small and tight, as if trying to pass for a rock. His breathing was so shallow, it could hardly be seen.

She hunkered down near him, and purred in his ear. There was no response.

Right, she thought, and extended a claw, and sank it carefully into the ear closest to the ground.

He whipped upright, eyes wide, and stared at her; then slumped back down again, the eyes relaxing again to a dozy look, with more than a touch of sullenness to it. "What?"

"It's time you were awake," Rhiow said.

"After yesterday? Come on." He put his head down again, closed his eyes.

Rhiow put her claw into the other ear this time, and somewhat more forcefully. Arhu sat up, and hissed. *"What?"*

"Trying *not* to see," Rhiow said, "won't help."

He stared at her.

"That's not what I'm here about," she said, "not mostly, anyway. I promised to teach you to walk on air. The sooner we get this lesson handled, the better . . . since you're going to be going on rounds with us for a while yet, I think, and we can't slow ourselves down all the time by using nonclimbing routes. Get up, have a wash, you'll have your first lesson, and then we'll get you something to eat. Some more of that pastrami, maybe?"

Arhu looked at Rhiow with a little more interest. But the look suddenly went cooler. "I'm not going back down there," he said.

"Good," Rhiow said, a little wearily, "then you and Saash are in complete agreement. It's not high on my list, either. Come on, Arhu, let's get a move on. . . ."

✦

The lesson went quickly: faster than Rhiow would have thought possible. It reinforced a feeling she had been having, that Arhu could learn with blinding speed when he wanted to . . . and right now he wanted to, in order to get rid of Rhiow.

Purposely, therefore, Rhiow spun the lesson out. An hour and a half later, they were standing on the air directly above the roof of Grand Central, maybe thirty stories up, sidled, and fairly close to the windows of the Grand Hyatt. Rhiow had to smile, for many of those windows did not have their curtains pulled, and inside them, one could see (as one almost always could) the occasional pair of *ehhif* doing what Hhuha sometimes facetiously called "the cat-scaring thing." Rhiow could not remember when she had last been scared by it, even by some of the noises Hhuha and Iaehh made in their throes. Arhu, however, had been betrayed by his prurient curiosity, and was watching one pair of *ehhif* with complete and disgusted fascination.

"Don't skywalk where you can easily be seen," Rhiow was saying, while wondering how much of what she told him was sinking in. "If you do it between buildings, make sure the walls are blind . . . or that you're sidled. Which has its dangers, too. Birds won't see you. . . ."

"That could be nice," Arhu said, briefly distracted; he glanced around and licked his chops.

"'Nice'? It could be fatal. There are more kinds of birds in this city than pigeons and sparrows and starlings. If one of the Princes of the Air hits you at eighty miles an hour, you'd better pray you're high enough up for a long-enough fall to reconstruct the wizardry."

"The Princes—"

"And a couple of 'princesses,'" Rhiow said. "There's a falcon-breeding program based on top of a building up near Central Park South. One of the hatchlings, about ten clutches ago, was a wizard: he's been promoted since, to Lord of the Birds of the East—a Senior for his kind. The rest of them are stuck-up as anything, think they're royalty, and kill more pigeons in a given day than they need to. They're a menace. Especially if they hit you with one of those little claw-fists of theirs, at high velocity, while you're invisible. The impact alone might kill you, for all I know. It sure kills the pigeons."

She sighed then as the two *ehhif* fell together, exhausted, at the end of their bout. "Come on," she said. "Enough looking for one day . . ."

Arhu's tail lashed. "If I stop looking at this," he said, almost absently, "I'll just see something else. . . ."

Yes, Rhiow thought, *that's the problem, isn't it.* . . . "Come on," she said, "and we'll go down to the concourse and see about that pastrami. You can't see things while you're eating, I don't think. The chewing is supposed to interfere."

He looked at her with a glitter of hope in his eyes. "All right," he said.

They walked down the air together, Arhu still doing it very slowly and carefully, as if it were a normal stairway; went right down to ground level, nearest the wall, and slipped inside the brass doors. Arhu looked around them as they walked together past the main waiting room toward the concourse.

Suddenly Arhu stopped and stared. "What are *those?*" he whispered.

Rhiow looked over into the waiting room. It had been one of the first areas to have its refurbishment completed, and was now routinely used for art exhibitions and receptions, and sometimes even parties. At the moment, though, the big airy space looked oddly empty, even though there were things in it . . . rather large things. In the center of the room, on a large black pedestal with velvet crowd-control ropes around it, caught in midstride—almost up on its toes, its tail stretched out horizontally and whipping out gracefully behind it— a dinosaur skeleton was mounted. Its huge head, empty-eyed, jaws open, seemed to glare down at the few casual observers who were strolling around it or pausing to read the informational plaque mounted nearby.

Rhiow gazed up at it and smiled sardonically. "Yes," she said, "I guess it doesn't look much like what we were dealing with last night. A lot bigger. These are part of the Museum of Natural History's new exhibition . . . and the *ehhif* are all excited about it because now they think they know, from these new models, how the saurians really held themselves and moved."

Arhu took a few steps toward the biggest of the mounted skeletons . . . cocked his head to one side, and listened. After a moment, he said, "And those are real bones?"

"They dig them up and wire them together," Rhiow said. "It always struck me as a little perverse. But then, they have no way of seeing what we saw last night."

They walked on. "This place looked a lot different, the other night," Arhu said.

"If it's any help, it never looks the same way twice to me," Rhiow said. "I mean, the physical structures are always the same, obviously—well, not always, not with all this renovation and with exhibitions coming and going out in front. But night and day pass, the light changes, the *ehhif* here are never the same ones at any given moment . . . . Though the city still isn't as big as you might think: you'll glimpse the occasional familiar face . . ."

"That's not what I meant," Arhu said, more slowly, with a puzzled expression. "It was bigger, somehow. It echoed."

"It does that more at night than in the daytime," Rhiow said. "Emptier."

"No," Arhu said. "It was full; I saw it full. Or I think I do now." He stopped and stared at the concourse before him: a late lunchtime crowd, the crush easing somewhat. "I heard something . . . a lot of noise. I walked in to find out what it was. Then—" He shook his ears as if they hurt him. "I don't want to think about that," he said.

"You're going to have to, sooner or later. But come on," Rhiow said. "Pastrami first."

Rhiow came unsidled long enough to do her "trick" again for the man in the Italian deli, and he gave her not only pastrami but cheese as well. She shared the pastrami happily enough with Arhu, but never got a chance to do so with the cheese. As soon as he smelled it, he immediately snatched the whole thing and gobbled it, almost choking himself—a topologically interesting sight, like watching a shark eat a mattress. "Oh, this is wonderful," Arhu attempted to say around the mouthful, "what *is* this?"

"Solid milk," Rhiow said, just a little wistfully, watching it vanish. "They have a lot of kinds. This one's called 'mozzarella.'"

"What a terrific invention!"

"So *ehhif* are good for something after all?"

He glanced sidewise at her, and his face shut down again. "Not much besides this."

Rhiow held her peace until he finished the cheese. "Come on, get sidled," she said, "and we'll come back and see him again later: he's a soft-hearted type."

They strolled a little way out into the concourse, sat down by the east wall, out of the way of people's feet, and well to one side of the cash machines. Arhu craned his neck back in the bright noon light and looked up at the ceiling again. "It *is* backward."

"Yes . . . and you saw that before. Seeing is going to be a problem for you now . . . and a gift."

"If it's a gift, they can take it back," he said bitterly. "I can't *stop* seeing things now. Though you were right about the chewing."

"What kinds of things?"

"I don't know what most of them are," Arhu said. "It's like when the Whisperer . . . when she tells you stuff . . . but there's always more than just what she tells you. I see pictures of things behind things behind things, and it all keeps changing. I don't know where to put my feet."

"Images of alternate futures," Rhiow said, wondering if she now was beginning to understand Arhu's clumsiness. Arhu looked at her strangely.

"Anything can change a future," Rhiow said. "Say one thing, do one thing, and it goes one way. Do something else, and it goes another. What would have happened if the Whisperer had offered you the Oath, and you'd said no? What if you'd slipped off the brickwork, the other night? What if the police-*ehhif* had come and caught you trying to steal the pastrami, and they had taken you away to an animal shelter? Each of your futures would have been different. And there are thousands more."

"But which of them is *real?*" Arhu muttered.

Rhiow swished her tail slowly from side to side. "All of them . . . until you make the choice, perform the act. You're only seeing possibilities."

"But it's not just things behind things," Arhu said. "There are other images, things that *stay.*"

"The past," Rhiow said softly. "That at least holds still . . . some ways, anyway. Are you seeing your past lives?"

"No," Arhu said, and then added, very surprised, "I think this is my first one."

"We all have to start somewhere," Rhiow said.

"How many have *you* had?"

She gave him a look. "That's a question you don't usually ask. If the Person you're talking to volunteers the information—"

He scowled, turned away. "That's what Saash said when I asked her what her Ordeal was like."

"And she was right to say so," Rhiow said. "That's personal business, too, as personal among wizards as the issue of lives is among People. Go around asking People questions like that and you're going to get your ears boxed."

Arhu looked scornful. "You guys are sure sensitive. Won't talk about *this.* Can't do *that,* somebody's feelings might get hurt. How do you ever get anything done?"

"If there were *more* People in the world concerned about being sensitive," Rhiow said, rather shortly, "we'd have a lot less work to do. . . . Look, Arhu, you've had a bad time of it so far, I'd say. But we're trying to teach you the rules so that you'll have a better time later. All I can do is warn you how People are going to take the things you say. If you still say them . . ." She shrugged her tail.

They were quiet for a moment. "As to lives," Rhiow said then, "I don't think all that much about my last ones. Most of us don't, I suspect, after the first few, when the novelty of the change wears off. The really persistent memories—big mistakes, great sorrows or joys— they intrude sometimes. I don't go digging. What you stumble across, from day to day, you're usually meant to find for some reason. But caching memories is as sick as caching food, for one of our People. Better to live now, and use the memories, when they come to mind, as a way to keep from making the same mistakes all over again. Use the past as a guide, not a fence."

"The past . . ." He looked out into the golden light of the concourse, toward the sunlight spilling through the south windows. "I don't remember much of mine."

"You don't have to tell me."

"I do," Arhu said, somewhat painfully. "You don't trust me."

There was no answer to that, not right now: and no question but that he was seeing at least some things with surprising clarity. "Arhu," Rhiow said, "it's just that if your gift is seeing . . . and it looks that way . . . you have to try to manage it, *use* it . . . and especially, you have to try to accept what there is to see about yourself, when it comes up for viewing. You *are* the eye through which you see. If the eye is clouded, all the other visions will be, too . . . and at this dangerous time in your life, if you don't do your best to see clearly, you won't survive."

He would not look at her.

He sees something, Rhiow thought. *Something in his own future, I bet. And he thinks that if he doesn't talk about it, it won't happen. . . .*

"For the time being, you just do the best you can," Rhiow said at last. "Though I admit I'd be happier if I knew you were coming to some kind of terms with your Oath."

"I said the words," Arhu said after a little while.

"Yes. But will you hold by them?"

"Why wouldn't I?" The voice was completely flat.

Rhiow swung her tail gently from side to side. "Arhu, do you know what entropy is?"

He paused a moment, listening. "Things run down," he said finally. "Stuff dies. *Everything* dies."

"Yes."

"But it wasn't meant to . . . not at first."

"No," Rhiow said. "Things got complicated. That's the story of the worlds, all in one bowl. All the rest of the history of all the worlds there are, has been about the issue of resolving that complication. It will take until the end of the worlds to do it. Our People have their part to play in that resolution. There will be a lot of fighting . . . so if you like that kind of thing, you're in the right place."

"I wasn't yesterday," he said bitterly. "I couldn't have fought anything. I was fooling myself."

So that much self-vision is in play, whether he thinks so or not, Rhiow thought. "In the strictly physical sense, maybe," Rhiow said. "But nonetheless, you said what you saw. You tried to warn us. You may have given Saash that little impetus she needed to hurry and finish what she had to do before the saurians came in. That's worthwhile, even that little help. You struck your first blow."

"I don't know if I even did it on purpose," Arhu said.

"It doesn't matter," Rhiow said. "The result matters. We got out alive . . . and for a while, there was no way to tell whether we would or not. So, by and large, your presence yesterday made a difference."

She stood up, stretched, let out a big yawn. "Let's get a little more concrete," Rhiow said. "Anyway, I want to have a look at that track."

Together they walked through the concourse, slipping to one side or another to avoid the *ehhif,* and made their way down to the platform for Track 30. A repetitive clanking noise was coming from a little ways down in the darkness, and Rhiow and Arhu paused at the platform's end to watch the workmen, in their fluorescent reflective vests and hard hats, working on something on the ground, which at the moment was completely obscured by all of them standing around it, watching.

Rhiow threw a glance over at the gate, which was visible enough to her and Arhu if not to the workmen; the patterns of color sheening down it said that it was back to normal again. "Good," she said. "And it looks like that track's almost ready to go back into service. Come on," she said, and hopped down off the platform, onto the track bed.

Arhu was slightly uneasy about following her, but after a moment he came along. She led him carefully around the workmen, past the end of Tower A, and then back down in the direction from which they had first come, but this time at an angle, down toward the East Yard, where trains were pulled in for short-term storage during the morning and evening rush hours. She was not headed for the yard itself, but for a fire exit near the north side of Tower C. Its heavy steel door was shut; she glanced over at Arhu. "Down here," she said, and put a paw into the metal.

Arhu hesitated for a moment. "Come on, you did it just fine the other night," Rhiow said.

"Yeah, but I wasn't thinking about it."

"Just remember, it's mostly empty space. *You're* mostly empty space. Just work the solid parts around each other . . ."

Rhiow walked through the door. After a moment Arhu followed, with surprising smoothness. "Nice," Rhiow said, as they went down the stairs together. The light here was dim even by cat standards, and Rhiow didn't hurry—there was always the chance you might run into someone or something you hadn't heard on the way down.

At the bottom of the fire exit, they walked through the door there and came out on the lower track level, on another platform, the longest one to be seen on this level. More fluorescent lights ran right down its length toward a low dark mass of machinery at the platform's end; electric carts and manually powered ones stood waiting here and there. "The tracks on this side are primarily for moving packages and light freight to and from the trains," Rhiow said; "bringing in supplies and equipment for the station, that kind of thing. But mostly that kind of traffic takes place during the evening or late at night. In the daytime, this area doesn't get quite so much official use . . . and so others move in."

Arhu looked alarmed. "What kind of 'others'?"

"You'll see."

They walked northward along the platform to the point where it stopped, across from a sort of concrete-lined bay in the eastern wall. Rhiow jumped down from the platform and crossed the track to the right of it. "This track runs in a big loop," she said, "around the terminal ends of the main tracks and out the other side. Not a place to linger: it's busy night and day. But things are a little quieter up this way."

She ducked into the bay and to the left, pausing to let her eyes adjust—it was much darker down here than out in the cavernous underground of the main lower track area, with all its lines of fluorescents and the occasional light shining out the windows of workshops and locker rooms. Behind her, Arhu stared into the long dark passage. Huge wheels wrapped full of fire hose, and mated to more low, blocky-looking machines, were bolted into the walls, from which also protruded big brass nozzles of the kind to which fire equipment would be fastened. A faint smell of steam came drifting from the end of the corridor, where it could be seen to meet another passage, darker still.

"What is this? And what's that?" Arhu whispered, staring down the dark hallway. For, hunched far down the length of it, against one of the low dark machines, something moved . . . shifted, and looked at them out of eyes that eerily caught the light coming from behind them.

"It's a storage area," Rhiow said. "We're under Forty-eighth Street here; this is where they keep the fire pumps. As for what it is—"

She walked down into the darkness. Very slowly, she could hear Arhu coming up behind, his pads making little noise on the damp concrete. The steam smell got stronger. Finally she paused by the spot from which those strange eyes had looked down the hallway at them. It seemed at first to be a heap of crazily folded cardboard, and under that a pile of old, stained clothing. But then you saw, under another piece of folded cardboard from a liquor store box, the grimy, hairy face, and the eyes, bizarrely blue. From under the cardboard, a hand reached out and stroked Rhiow's head.

"Hunt's luck, Rosie," Rhiow said, and sat down beside him.

"Luck Reeoow you, got no luck today," Rosie said. Except that he didn't say it in *ehhif*. He said, *"Aihhah ueeur Rieeeow hanh ur-t hah hah'iih eeiaie. . . ."*

Arhu, who had slowly come up beside her, stared in complete astonishment. "He speaks our language!"

"Yes," Rhiow said, taking a moment to scrub a bit of fallen soot out of her eye: solid particulates from the train exhausts tended to cling to the ceiling over here because of the steam. "And his accent's pretty fair, if you give him a little credit for the mangled vowels, the way he shortens the aspirants, and the 'shouting.' The syntax needs work, though. Rosie, excuse me for talking about you to your face. This is Arhu."

"Hunt's luck, Arhu," Rosie said, and reached out a grubby hand.

Arhu sat down just out of range, looking even more shocked than he had when the Children of the Serpent burst through into the catenary cavern the night before.

"I don't know if Arhu is much for being petted, Rosie," Rhiow said, and tucked herself down into a comfortable meatloaf shape. "He's new around here. Say hello, Arhu."

"Uh, hunt's luck, Rosie," Arhu said, still staring.

"Luck food not great stomach noise scary," Rosie said sadly, settling back into his nest of cardboard and old clothes. All around him, under the cardboard, were piled plastic shopping bags stuffed full of more clothes, and rags, and empty fast food containers; he nestled among them, arms wrapped around his knees, sitting content, if a little mournful-looking, against the purring warmth of the compressor-pump that would service the fire hose coiled above him.

Arhu couldn't take his eyes off the *ehhif*. "Why is he *down* here?" he whispered.

"Alalal neihuri mejhruieha lahei fenahawaha," Rosie said, in a resigned tone of voice. Arhu looked at Rhiow, stuck about halfway between fear and complete confusion.

"Rosie speaks a lot of languages, sometimes mixed together," Rhiow said, "and I have to confess that some of them don't make any sense even when I listen to them with a wizard's ear, in the Speech; so some of what he says may be nonsense. But not all. Rosie," she said, "I missed that one, would you try it again?"

Rosie spent a moment's concentration, his eyes narrowing with the effort, and then said, "Short den full *hai'hauissh* police clean up."

"Ah," Rhiow said. "There was a big meeting of important people in town, a 'convention,'" she said to Arhu, "and the cops have stuffed all the shelters, the temporary dens, full of homeless people, so they won't make the streets look bad. Rosie must have got to the shelter too late to get a place, huh Rosie?"

"Uh huh."

"'Homeless—'" Arhu said.

"We'd say 'denless.' It's not like 'nonaligned,' though; most *ehhif* don't like to wander, though there are exceptions. Rosie, what have you had to eat since you came down here? Have you had water?"

"Hot cloud *lailihe ruhaith memeze* pan *airindagha.*"

"He's *sshai-sau,*" Arhu said.

"Maybe, but he can speak cat, too," Rhiow said, "which makes him saner than most *ehhif* from the first pounce. You've got a pan down there in the steam tunnel, is that it, Rosie? You're catching the condensation from the pipes?"

"Yeah."

"What about food? Have you eaten today?"

Rosie looked at Rhiow sadly, then shook his head. "*Shhh,*" he said.

"Rats," said Rhiow, and hissed very softly under her breath. "He knows the smell of food would bring them. Rosie, I'm going to bring you some food later. I can't bring much: they'll have to see me, up-stairs, when I take it."

There was a brief pause, and then Rosie said, with profound affec-tion: "Nice kitty."

Arhu turned away. "So this is one of the the People-eating *ehhif* I heard so much about," he said. There was no deciphering his tone. Embarrassment? Loathing?

"He's one of many who come and go through these tunnels," Rhiow said. "Some of them are sick, or can't get food, or don't have anywhere to live, or else they're running away, hiding from someone who hurt them. They come and stay awhile, until the transit police or the Terminal people make them go somewhere else. There are People, too, who drift in and out of here . . . many fewer of them than there used to be. This place isn't very safe for our kind anymore . . . partly because of the Terminal people being a lot tougher about who stays down here. But partly because of the rats. They're bigger than they used to be, and meaner, and a lot smarter. Rosie," Rhiow said, "how much have the rats been bothering you?"

Rosie shook his head, and cardboard rustled all around him. "Nicht nacht night I go up gotta friend rat dog, dog, dog, bit me good, no more, not at night . . ."

"Rats bad at night," Arhu said suddenly.

Rhiow gave him an approving look, but also bent near him and said, too softly for an *ehhif* to hear, "Speak normally to him. You're doing him no kindness by speaking kitten."

"Yes bad, heard them bad, loud, not two nights ago, three," Rosie said, his voice flat, but his face betrayed the alarm he had felt. "Smelled them, smelled the cold things—" There was a sudden, rather alarming sniffing noise from under the cardboard, and Rosie's eyes abruptly vanished under the awning of cardboard, huddled against a sleeve that appeared to have about twenty more sleeves layered underneath it, alternately with layers of ancient newspaper. Rhiow caught a glimpse of a familiar movement under the bottom-most layer that made her itch as if she had suddenly inherited Saash's skin.

The sniffing continued, and Arhu stared at Rosie and actually stepped a little closer, wide-eyed. The cardboard spasmed up and down, and a little sound, *huh, huh, huh,* came from inside it. "Is he sick?" Arhu said.

"Of *course* he's sick," Rhiow muttered. "*Ehhif* aren't supposed to live this way. He's hungry, he's got bugs, he keeps getting diseases. But that's not the problem. He's *sad.* Or maybe afraid. That's 'crying,' that's what they do instead of yowl. Water comes out of their eyes. It makes them ashamed when they do that. Don't ask me why."

She turned away and started to wash, waiting for Rosie to master himself. When the sobbing stopped, Rhiow turned back to him and said, "Did you see them come through here? Did they hurt you? I can't tell by smell, Rosie: it's your clothes."

The cardboard moved from side to side: underneath it, eyes gleamed. "They went by," he said, very softly, after a little while.

"Did you see where they came from?" Rhiow said.

The head shook again.

"Which 'cold things,' Rosie?" Rhiow said.

"They roar . . . in the dark . . ."

Rhiow sighed. This was a familiar theme with Rosie: though he *would* keep coming down here to hide, trains frightened him badly, and he seemed to have a delusion that if they could, they would get off the tracks and come after him. When life occasionally seemed to ratify this belief—as when a train derailed near enough for him to see, on Track 110—Rosie vanished for weeks at a time, and Rhiow worried about him even more than she did usually.

"All right, Rosie," she said. "You stay here a little while. I'll come back with something for you, and I'll have a word with the rats . . . they won't come while you eat. Will you go back to the shelter after the convention's done?"

Rosie muttered a little under his breath, and then said, "*Airaha nuzusesei lazeira.*"

"Once more, please?"

"Try to. No purr not long tired lie down not get up."

Rhiow licked her nose; she caught all too clearly the *ehhif*'s sense of weariness and fear. "We have got to get you some more verbs," she said, "or adjectives, or something. Never mind. I'll be back soon, Rosie."

She turned and hurried away, thinking hard about Rosie's clothes, and putting together a familiar short description of them in her head, in the Speech, and of what she wanted to happen to them, and what was inside them. "Come on, Arhu. You don't want to be too close to him in the next few seconds."

"Why? What's the matter? What's he going to—"

Well down the hallway, Rhiow paused and looked back. In this lighting, it would have taken a cat's eyes to see what she and Arhu could: the revolting little multiple-branched river of body lice making their way in haste out of Rosie's clothes, and pouring themselves very hurriedly out every available opening, out from under the cardboard and out across the floor, where they pitched themselves down a drain and went looking for other prey.

"I wonder if they like rat?" Rhiow said, and smiled, showing her teeth.

She loped back out of the corridor, with Arhu coming close behind her, and together they made their way back to the fire exit.

"But *that,*" she said softly to Arhu, turning to look at him just before she slipped ahead of him through the metal of the door, "was entropy."

Out in the concourse again, the air seemed much fresher than it had a right to in an enclosed space where diesel fumes so often came drifting out of the track areas; and the sunlight pouring through the windows was doubly welcome. Rhiow paced along up the staircase to the Vanderbilt Avenue entrance; sidled again, she and Arhu jumped up on the cream marble colonnade railing and walked along it to where they could perch directly over the big escalators going up into the MetLife building. There Rhiow started a brief wash, a real one this time.

"That was completely disgusting," Arhu said, staring out and down at the shining brass of the information kiosk in the middle of the concourse floor.

"What? The lice? I guess so. But I always do that when I see him. It's a little thing. Can't you imagine how he must have felt?"

"I can imagine it right now," Arhu said with revulsion, sat down, and started scratching as if he too had had Saash's pelt wished on him.

"He's a sad case," Rhiow said. "One of many. The *ehhif* would say that he fell through the safety net." She stopped washing, sighed again: Rosie's sadness was sometimes contagious. "When we're not minding the gates . . . we try to spread our own net to cushion the fall for a few of those who fall through. People . . . *ehhif* . . . whoever. We take care of this place, and since they're part of it for a while . . . we take care of them too."

"Why bother?" Arhu burst out. "It won't make a difference! It won't stop the way things are!"

"It will," Rhiow said. "Someday . . . though no one knows when. This *is* the Fight, the battle under the Tree: don't you see that? The Old Tom fought it once, and died fighting, and came back with the Queen's help and won it after he'd already lost. *All* these fights are the Fight. Stand back, do nothing, and you *are* the Old Serpent. And it's easy to do that here." She looked around at the place full of hurrying people, most of them studiously ignoring one another. "Here especially. *Ehhif* kill each other in the street every day for money, or food, or just for fun, and others of them don't lift a paw to help, just keep walking when it happens. People do it, too. *Hauissh* goes deadly, toms murder kittens for fun rather than just because their bodies tell them to. . . . The habit of doing nothing, or of cruelty, believing the worst about ourselves, gets hard to break. You meet People like that every day. It's in the Meditation: ask the Whisperer. But you don't have to be the way *they* are. Wizards are for the purpose of breaking the habit . . . or not having it in the first place. It's disgusting, sometimes, yes. You should have tasted *yourself* when we found you."

Arhu turned away from Rhiow. "It's sick to be so worried about everybody else," he said, refusing to look at her. "People should care about themselves first. That's the way we're built."

"You've bought into the myth too, have you," Rhiow said, rather dryly. "Sometimes I wonder if the *houiff* started that one, but I'm not sure they're that subtle. I suspect the concept's older, and goes back further, to our own people's version of the Choice." She looked at him, though, saw the set, angry look of his face, and flirted her tail sideways, a *why-am-I-bothering?* gesture. "I think your stomach is making you cranky," she said. "Let's go down and see about a bite more of that cheese— Oh. Wait a moment—"

An *ehhif* in a suit, and carrying a briefcase, was coming along the colonnade. Arhu stared at him with alarm, for the *ehhif* plainly saw them and was making directly for them. He got ready to jump—

"Not that way!" Rhiow said three hurried words in the Speech, and hardened the air behind Arhu just before he launched himself straight out into the main concourse. "It's all right, sit *still!"*

Arhu sat back down, shocked, digging his claws into the marble. The approaching *ehhif* paused, glanced around him casually, put the briefcase down, then turned around and leaned on his elbows on the railing, and stared out across the concourse himself.

"Nice to see you, Har'lh," Rhiow said. "Thanks for the backup yesterday."

"Don't mention it. I would have come myself, but I was otherwise occupied." He glanced sideways, only very briefly. "Good to meet you, Arhu," he said. "Go well. An excellent job you folks did. Nice going with that, Rhiow."

"Thanks, Har'lh. I could have done without the last part of it, but at least we brought our skins home whole. Going down to inspect the catenary?"

"I doubt I'll need to go down that far . . . I just want a look at the main matrices up top."

"All right. But Saash thinks the whole thing needs to be rewoven."

"So she said. When she makes her full report, I'll look into it in more detail and have a word with the Supervisory Wizard for the North American region," Har'lh said. "It's not a job I'd care for, though. Logistically it would be something of a nightmare. Not to mention unsafe for Saash if the job started to get more complicated than she thought."

"Don't things usually?" Rhiow said. Then, a little mischievously, she added, "I'm curious, though, Har'lh. You don't seem much bothered by these inspection runs. What happens to *your* physicality, Downside?"

"Well now, I would think some people might consider that a personal question," Har'lh said, giving her an amused look. "But let's just say I won't be able to stop going to the gym any time soon. My looks don't change down there the way People's do. Pity."

Rhiow put her whiskers forward at him. "Is Tom back from Geneva yet?"

"Later tonight. I'm glad he'll be getting back. . . . Between work and Work, I've been getting short of sleep."

Rhiow had figured that out already: Har'lh's rugged good looks had acquired a rather brittle edge over the past few days. "The way you keep pouring cappucino down yourself, are you surprised?" she said, and whisked her tail back and forth in a *tsk, tsk* gesture. "Your body isn't going to thank you, Har'lh."

"All right, now, you wait just a minute, Miss Cream Junkie," Har'lh said, smiling slightly. "You're lecturing *me* about *my* body?"

Rhiow put one ear back in the mildest annoyance. Hhuha had discovered that Rhiow was very partial to whipping cream . . . and Rhiow had not exactly talked her out of it. It was a couple of weeks after that time that Rhiow had first heard the bizarre adjective "plumptious." Shortly thereafter Hhuha had stopped bringing cream home and had subjected Rhiow to a very annoying withdrawal ("Is it smart to just do this 'cold turkey'?" Iaehh had asked, and Rhiow had practically shouted, "Cold turkey would be very nice in these circumstances, yes, *give me some!*"—to no avail). There had followed a course of what purported to be diet cat food, but which Rhiow firmly believed to be textured, compressed sawdust in a shiny gravy consisting mostly of lacquer. Next to it, the foul disgusting tuna of recent days could actually have been considered an improvement, though that was not something that Rhiow was ever going to let Hhuha know. "Life around *ehhif* can be a little too fat-free sometimes," she said. "I'm just grateful she didn't try to turn me vegetarian." She shuddered, knowing cats whose well-meaning but very confused *ehhif* had tried this tack. Mostly the People involved had found themselves short a life very quickly, unless they managed to get away and start over elsewhere.

"Completely the wrong lifestyle for you guys," Har'lh said, and glanced down. "I wish my kind wouldn't keep trying that crap. —Hey, Urruah, how they shakin'?"

"In all directions, as usual," Urruah said, and jumped up on the railing next to Rhiow. "'Luck, you two." He leaned over toward Arhu, breathed breaths with him. "Is that mozzarella I taste? Rhi, you spoil this kit."

Arhu looked at Urruah, and said, "Half a Quarter Pounder with cheese and bacon. You *ate* the *lettuce?*" He grimaced. "What a big bunny!"

"Oh yeah? So how do *you* know what lettuce tastes like?"

"I'm going Downside," Har'lh said, "before something gets out of hand here. Give Saash my best, Rhiow. I'll talk to her as soon as I get topside again."

"'Luck," Rhiow said, and Har'lh strode away toward the stairway, swinging his briefcase idly.

Urruah was looking at Arhu a little oddly. "*Half* a Quarter Pounder?" he said. "How do you know?"

"I see you eating it," Arhu said.

"Saw," Urruah said pointedly.

"No. I see you eating it *now*," Arhu said. He was looking at the blank marble wall as if there was far more there to see. "The MhHonalh's down in the subway, at Madison and Fifty-first. A tom-*ehhif* and a queen-*ehhif* are eating outside it, and talking. Then talking louder. Real loud. All of a sudden they start fighting—" Arhu's look was blank but bewildered. "He hits her, and tries to hit her again but she ducks back, and then he comes at her again, now he's feeling around in his jacket for something, but all of a sudden he trips over something he can't see and falls down, and he's getting up and feels in his jacket again—and then the transit cops come around the corner: he gets up and runs away, and the queen is standing there—'crying'"

Urruah's eyes were very round as he looked over at Rhiow. "It really *is* the Eye, isn't it?" Urruah said softly.

"The *ehhif*'s dropped his Quarter Pounder on the floor there," Arhu said, as if he hadn't heard. "I see you pick it up and take it away behind the garbage can. No one else sees, they're all looking at the *ehhif*-queen and the cops—"

Rhiow looked at Urruah, her tail twitching thoughtfully. "That was a nice move," she said.

"I might have done it only for the burger," Urruah said, looking elsewhere.

Rhiow put her whiskers right forward at the phrasing, for the one thing wizards dare not do with words is lie. "Of course it's the Eye," she said. "The symbol for it was in the spell. We worked the spell . . . and spells always work. I think he may have had this talent in latent form, before . . . but the presence of the symbol in the spell reaffirmed it, and now it's really starting to focus."

Arhu was looking at Rhiow again. "I see you now," he said, a little desperately. "But I see *that,* too. And other things. A lot of them at once . . ."

"It's the 'eternal present,'" Rhiow said. "I heard about it once from Ffairh: if you ever get stuck in a gate, in an artificially prolonged transit, you can start seeing things that way. Not a good sign, normally . . ."

"But I'm not normal," Arhu said, suddenly sounding very weary.

"No," Rhiow said wearily. "And neither are we. We are all weirdoes together . . . but the 'together' is the important part."

She sighed then. "Look, I could use a small dose of normalcy myself. Let's all go back to my neighborhood; they're starting the day's bout of *hauissh,* and we can sit and just kibitz for a while. You two skywalk over: Arhu can use the practice. *No birds,*" she said to Arhu, at the sight of that gleam starting to creep back into his eye. "I have a little something to take care of here; I'll meet you there in half an hour or so. Yafh's stoop, maybe?"

"Sounds like a plan. Come on, youngster, let's you and the Big Bunny show them how we do it uptown."

And Urruah turned and strolled straight out onto the air over the main concourse, forty feet up, heading for the front doors.

Eyes wide, suddenly delighted, Arhu scampered out across the air after him. Rhiow stood there, absolutely transfixed with horror lest they be seen. But no one looked up. No one in the city ever looks up.

She watched them go, unnoticed; then let out a long breath at the lunacy of toms and headed back toward the Italian deli.

When Rhiow got home, she found that her *ehhif* had been out as well, to dinner and a movie, and apparently had been back only a little while: Iaehh was going through the freezer, apparently hunting a frozen pizza. Rhiow walked over into the little kitchen and found her food bowl empty. She looked meaningfully at Iaehh, and said loudly, "I wouldn't keep *you* waiting for *your* dinner."

Iaehh shut the *ffrihh* and started going through the cupboards. "Sue?"

No answer. "Sue?"

"Oh, sorry, honey . . ." came the voice from the bedroom. "My mind was elsewhere."

"I was looking for that tuna stuff."

"Oh, there isn't any . . . the store was out of it."

"*Thank* you, Queen of us all," Rhiow said, heartfelt, waited for Iaehh to open a can and fill her bowl, and then put her face down in it. It was a nice hearty mixture, beef and something else: rabbit? Turkey? *Who cares? Delightful.*

"I'll pick up some of the tuna tomorrow."

"I'll enjoy this while it lasts," Rhiow muttered.

"She seems to like this all right, though."

"Good . . ." Hhuha said, as she came back into the living room.

"You sound tired."

"I *am* tired. Another day of fighting with the damn system, and the damn network, and the damn air conditioner . . ."

He came over to her and held her. "I wish you could find a way to get out of there."

Hhuha sighed. "Yeah, well, I've been thinking about that, too. It's making you as unhappy as it's making me."

"I wouldn't put it that strongly."

"I would. So, listen . . . I've got an appointment in a couple of days."

"Oh? Who with?"

"A headhunter."

"You didn't tell me about this!"

"I'm telling you now. The guy's been on the phone to me a couple of times over the last year. At first I didn't want to do anything; you know, I thought things at the office might improve."

"Yeah, sure."

"Well, I did. But the other day I thought, 'Okay.'" She snickered. "You should have seen me sneaking out to a pay phone at lunchtime, like some kind of crook."

"Well, it wouldn't be great for you if they heard you talking about it in the early stages of the negotiations, I admit."

"In *any* stages. Someone else in the company was that dumb, last year. They were pink-slipped within minutes of the word getting out. I don't plan to have that happen, believe me."

"So who's he headhunting for?"

"A couple of different companies, apparently. He's willing to arrange interviews with both if my resumé holds up. We'll be talking about that day after next. Lunchtime appointment."

"Hey, wow. Good luck!"

A brief silence while they nuzzled each other. "It's a little scary," Hhuha said after a little while. "Jumping before I'm pushed . . ."

"You were always the brave one."

"No. I just hate being taken advantage of . . . and I've been starting to get that feeling . . ."

Another small silence. "Want to be taken advantage of *now?*"

"I thought you'd never ask."

They went into the bedroom, chuckling. Rhiow lifted her head to watch them go, then put her whiskers forward and went out her little door, softly, so that they would not think they had scared the cat.

On the rooftop, she lay comfortably sprawled in the still warmth. Air conditioners thundered around her, a basso rumble and rattle through the night, the fans of the cooling towers showing as gleaming disks in the light of the nearly full Moon that was sliding, golden, up the eastern sky.

Rhiow looked up at it thoughtfully. Rhoua's Eye, its glory hidden behind the world, glanced past it (as legend had it) into the Great Tom's eye; this reflected the other's light, growing from slit to eye half-open to eye round and staring, and then shrinking down to slitted eye and full-dark invisibility again, as the month went round. There were People who believed, in the face of ubiquitous evidence to the contrary, that the feline eye mirrored the Moon's phase. Rhiow had been amazed, and very amused, to find that some *ehhif* had the same story.

There were wizardly connections as well. Apparently the *ehhif* version of *The Gaze of Rhoua's Eye,* the defining document that contained descriptions of all beings and all wizardry in this particular part of the universe, originally took the form of an actual book that could be read only by moonlight: hence its *ehhif* name, *The Book of Night with Moon.* Supposedly the *Book* had to be read from, at intervals, to keep all existence in place, and everything correctly defined. *I wouldn't care to be the one who does the reading,* Rhiow thought, looking out over the city as the Moon went quietly up the sky. *Too much exposure to such power, such knowledge, and you could lose yourself as surely as you might lose yourself Downside if you stayed too long . . .*

But that was the danger all over wizardry: there were so many different kinds of existence, alien and fascinating, to lose your nature in. . . . Though was this perhaps some kind of obscure hint from the Powers, Rhiow wondered, that you might be *expected* to lose your nature eventually? . . . A hint of the way things would be, someday, when the world was finally set right, and all the kinds of existence were united in timelessness, perfected and made whole, as the Oath intimated they would be?

. . . Maybe. But *she* wasn't ready.

The question of the danger was always there, though, for a practicing wizard. When you were on the universe's business all the time, with a wizard's multifarious worries on your mind, were you likely to start losing your felinity? *I wonder,* she thought, *if the* ehhif *wizards have this problem . . . if they fear losing their "humanity" as a result of having to cope with the larger worldview, the bigger mindset, in which no language or way of life is superior to any other, and each must be valued on its own terms? I can understand why it must look crazy to Arhu that I spend so much time worrying about* houiff *and* ehhif *and whatnot. . . .*

But then, she thought, *I have* ehhif *of my own to think about, after all. The habit's hard to break. . . .*

All the same . . . the worry niggled at her, occasionally, and was doing so again. It was something she had occasionally felt she should talk to Ehef about. But then she would get busy with some assignment. . . .

Maybe that's not good, Rhiow thought after a while. *How many years have I been at this, now? And when did I last have a vacation from the Art? A real one, when I wouldn't be on call, and could stay home, and eat that terrible cat food, and lie in the sun, and purr at Hhuha . . . and just be People . . .*

The problem was, of course, that she knew perfectly well how much time and energy the Powers That Be had invested in her. Go on vacation . . . and that invested energy would be lost, even for that little while: as in *hauissh,* any move that is not an attack means lost ground. The heat death of the universe doesn't speed up . . . but it doesn't slow down as much as it might have. Lie basking in the sun . . . and know that the power that *runs* the sun is running out at its usual speed, trickling away like blood from a wound . . . and you're not doing anything to make sure the world keeps going that little bit longer to enjoy that warmth and light.

She sighed. *I will know doubt,* she thought, slipping into the Meditation, *and fear: I will suspect myself of folly and impracticality in this seemingly hard-edged world, where things clouded or obscure are so often discounted as unimportant, and mystery is derided, and uncertainty is seen as a sign of an inability to cope. But my commission comes from Those Who move in the shadows, indistinct and unseen for Their own purpose: Those Whom we never see face to face except in the faces of those we meet from day to day. In Them is my trust, until I am relieved of Their trust in me. I will learn to live with uncertainty, for it is the earnest of Their promise that all things may yet be well; and when, in the shadows, the doubts arise, I will close my eyes and say, This is no shade to Them; for my part, I will bide here, and wait for the dawn. . . .*

She closed her eyes and dozed.

Rhi, Saash's voice came suddenly.

Rhiow opened her eyes, surprised. The Moon was much farther across the sky, westering now. "What is it?" she said. "Are you all right?"

I'm fine. But Rhiow, have you heard anything from Har'lh?

"He said he was going to talk to you after he came back from Downside," Rhiow said.

Well, he hasn't.

"Maybe something else came up," Rhiow said. "He's an Advisory, for Iau's sake. It's not like he hasn't got ten million people to keep an eye on."

Rhi, you're not listening. He hasn't come back from Downside. *The gate logs show his access . . . but not his egress.*

Rhiow sat up, shaking her head. "He could have come back by another gate. And he did say he might take a look at the catenary if he had to—"

He's not there. I called him. There's no answer and no trace of any other gating. Rhi, he's gone!

Nine

◆

She headed for Grand Central at her best speed, which (this time of night) meant skywalking; but her concerns over this were fewer than usual. There were not that many people likely to spot a black cat in the dim predawn air, fifty stories up, and all the birds of prey were asleep.

Rhiow came down to ground level again at Forty-second and Lexington, and got herself sidled. She trotted past the Grand Hyatt, past a few drunks sitting against the walls, waiting for the station (or the nearby liquor store) to open; passed through the locked front doors, and hurried up past the waiting room . . .

. . . and stopped, looking around her suspiciously. There was something different . . .

The lights in the display area were mostly out, of course, with the station in closed-down mode.

No . . . that's not it.

Rhiow walked past the biggest of the mounted skeletons, strolling toward the back of the room. *No one hiding here . . .* That had been the first impression: something concealing itself, hugging the shadows, waiting . . . *Nothing. You're nervous. Let's get on with business.*

Rhiow started to walk out again . . . and then paused, looked up at the biggest skeleton.

Its position was different.

Impossible. The thing weighs tons; it's wired together much too se-curely to sag out of shape.

An illusion, then . . . born of the darkness, her nerves. The way the head hung down, the empty eyes looking at her, was creepy in this subdued lighting, seeming somehow more concentrated and immediate than they had yesterday. The nasty little front claws were held out in what might almost have been a gesture of surprise—in an *ehhif*, at least. Iau only knew what such a gesture might once have meant in a saurian. If there was threat in these poor dead bones, it was in the huge jaws, the serried ranks of fangs . . .

Rhiow thought suddenly of the back of the cavern that led into the deep Downside: the spikes of stone, the jaws ready to close . . .

She flirted her tail in annoyance at herself—there were much more important things to think about at the moment. She turned and galloped up into the brighter lighting of the main concourse, down to the platform for Track 30 and the gate. . . .

Saash was there. So was another figure, an *ehhif*, sidled as well: Tom Swale, Har'lh's partner-Advisory. He was a little shorter than Har'lh, a little broader in the shoulder, higher-cheekboned, and with silver-shot hair: if anything he looked more like an Area Advisory than his partner did, though he wore the same kind of informal clothes this time of day, shirt and jeans and sneakers. His easygoing face, though, was wearing an unusual expression of strain and concern.

"It's nice to see you, Rhiow," Tom said, hunkering down to talk to her, "but I wish to the Powers that it was under other circumstances. Saash has filled you in?"

"Yes." Rhiow looked over at Saash, who said, "I've checked all the logs of all the gates here, and the Penn team has fed me all their gates' logs as well. No sign of any access by Har'lh except to this gate: no sign of his egress from any other gate in New York, and no sign of any private gating, either."

Almost behind her, Urruah came trotting down the platform, and greeted Tom. "You still here? There's no sign of him yet?—"

"None. Wizards all over are looking for him. But no one's found him . . . which is pretty unusual. Wizards almost always find what they're looking for, especially when this many of them are concentrated on the task."

"They're looking offplanet as well?" Rhiow said.

Tom nodded. "An Area Advisory going missing is usually a fairly serious sign," Tom said. "There's concern at fairly high levels."

"He wouldn't be—dead—would he?" Saash said, with the greatest reluctance.

"I don't think so," Tom said. "I'm pretty sure I would know."

"Oh, come on, Saash," Urruah said, "you're nuts. Have you ever heard of a Advisory dying in the line of duty?"

Tom looked at Urruah fairly gently. "Urruah," he said, "*all* Advisories die in the line of duty. Any exceptions are accidents or misperceptions on the part of the living. It's within the job description: we accept it."

"That said," Rhiow said, "Advisories are also tough and smart. Maybe not as powerful as they would be if they were younger; but who is? Could it be that Har'lh's still Downside, but held somehow in a pocket of influence of some other Power"—she was not going to name names at this point—"that is making it seem that he's *not* there?"

"It's a possibility. But I'm surprised you're eager to suggest it, since you know what it would mean."

"I'm not eager, believe me," Rhiow said; and a glance at the others confirmed to her that they were in agreement.

"Well." Tom breathed out, a harassed sound. "The only good thing about all this is that it's been a slow night; there haven't been any other accesses down here. We don't know for sure that this particular occurrence was aimed specifically at Carl . . . but we also can't take the chance that other wizards on errantry might fall foul of it. Were these other gates, I might be less concerned; but this is the master system—all the world's gates are sourced out of the 'tree' structure that arises in the roots of the Mountain. That being the case, I think I'm going to have to get a little drastic, and insist that the gating system worldwide be shut down until we find Carl and get all this sorted out. It may be nothing serious at all . . ."

"But you doubt it," Rhiow said.

"I doubt it. The shutdown obviously isn't going to apply to accredited repair teams: naturally that's going to mean you. I'm sorry to put you through this again, Rhi . . . but you did the most recent intervention, and the way the Powers work, that suggests you're going to be the ones who can produce the result. How soon can you go down again?"

Rhiow looked at Saash and Urruah. Urruah was carefully studying a crack in the concrete: Saash was scratching.

Come on, you two.

This does not *work for me,* Urruah growled silently.

I hate *this,* Saash hissed. *You heard what I told you before.*

Yes, I did. Well?

They both looked up at her.

She turned to look up at Tom. "Dawn would be the soonest," Rhiow said. "I would prefer noon, though, since that way we can bring our newest member along. He's likely to be extremely useful, but not unless he's rested."

Tom too examined the concrete for a few breaths. "I hate to let the trail get cold."

"If there is a trail," Urruah said. "I'd sooner take a little extra time in preparation, and get the job right, if we have to go down there again."

"You're right, of course," Tom said. He stood up. "Let's say noon, then. I'll mind your upper gate for you this time: Carl and I have been working together long enough now that I may be able to help you somehow. Otherwise I'll be in a position to get you backup in a hurry should you need it."

Rhiow flirted her tail "yes," though privately she was unsure how fast any backup was going to be able to reach them, if they were going to have to go as far down the "tree" structure as she feared they would. "I want an override," she said, "on the number and power of wizardries we can bring down with us. I feel we're going to need to be unusually well armed this time, and while I know the Powers are chary of letting people throw spells around like water, I think our workload the last few days, and the resistance we met last time, are going to justify it."

Tom looked at her thoughtfully, then nodded. "All right," he said, "I'll take it up with the North American Supervisor."

"Don't just take it up, T'hom. *I want it done.* Otherwise—"

She didn't finish the sentence, but she was somewhat fluffed up, and didn't try to disguise it.

"You're willing to pay the price?" Tom said.

Rhiow licked her nose. Such exceptions did not come cheap. Of course, not even the smallest wizardry was without its price: usually you paid in your own stamina, in the work and pains you took over the construction of the spell, the personal energy required to perform it, and the energy you spent in dealing with the consequences. But for extra services, you paid extra . . . and the currency was usually time off your lifespan. Days, months: a dangerous equation, when you didn't know for sure how much time you might have left . . . but sometimes necessary.

She licked her nose again. "Yes," she said.

Tom looked at her, and sighed. "I'll talk to you at noontime," he said. "Saash, the catenaries will go down in half an hour—that'll give everyone worldwide who might be transiting plenty of time to finish their transits or change their plans."

"Fine," Saash said. "We'll use the Thirty gate again for the access: having just worked on it, I'm happiest with its function. If you'll see to it that power is running to that one gate for noon—"

"Consider it done." Tom stood up again. "Listen, you three . . . I'm sorry this is going to be so rough on you. I appreciate what you're doing."

Do you, I wonder, Rhiow thought, but then she felt guilty, for the thought was unworthy. *Of course he does. It's his job. All we can do is do ours.*

"Let's go, you two," she said. "We've got a lot of preparation to do. T'hom—go well."

"So may we all," he said, and vanished.

The three of them repaired to Rhiow's rooftop and spent the next few hours discussing what spells they might possibly bring with them that would do any good against a force much bigger and more dangerous than the saurians they had met the other day. It was certain that they would meet such force, since they had defeated the saurians so bloodily last time, and (worse) because Har'lh's disappearance was almost certainly a provocation to draw them, or others like them, down again.

"My guess is that they're going to try something more spectacular than the last time," Urruah said. "If you're right, and they managed to sabotage the catenary...then worse is coming. We've got to get down there and have enough power to stop whatever we find."

"If T'hom gets us that override," Saash said, looking out over the rooftops as the sun came up, "it's going to make our jobs a lot easier."

"Plan for it," Rhiow said, "but also plan without it. I for one am going to be prepared to survive this intervention: I'm not going to plan to get stuck in circle again, either. I know the Oath says we have to let these creatures survive if at all possible—but not at the cost of our own lives or our mission. I'm going to use that neural degenerator as liberally as I need."

"So will I," Urruah said, "but Rhi...even an override may not be enough to save us, if the kind of numbers turn up that you're expecting."

"What are you suggesting we do about it?"

"Conjunct coupling," Urruah said, and licked his nose.

So did Rhiow. Saash just stared at him, round-eyed, then turned around and started to wash her back.

"I've been thinking about what Arhu was saying," Urruah said. "'He's coming. The father...the son.' Something bigger than the rest of the lizards. Something much more dangerous...that was the impression I got, anyway."

Rhiow switched her tail in reluctant agreement. "You're saying you think conjunct is the only way we're going to be able to maintain power levels high enough to handle something like...that." Whatever *that* was: she was becoming afraid to follow that line of reasoning to its rational conclusion, even here in the burgeoning light of day.

"It means," Urruah said, "that no matter whether one or another of us has a lapse, the others' combined power will be able to feed the wizardry they're doing, and keep it going."

Saash sat up and glared at him. "It also means that if we go down there hooked up in conjunct, we *all* have to come back that way . . . or *none* of us can come back up again at all! If any of us die down there, the others will be stranded—!"

There was a pause. "Yes," Urruah said, "it would mean that. But think about the alternative, even with the override that T'hom may or may not be able to get us. You're doing a wizardry. Your concentration, or your power flow, fails. You blow the wizardry . . . and you die . . . and then the others are put at risk trying to keep you from dying, and *their* wizardries fail." He would not look away from Saash. She stared back at him; the tension stretched itself across the air between them. "Everyone dies. The whole job goes straight to sa'Rráhh. And not just *our* lives . . . whatever happens to them when you die down there. A whole lot of other lives. All those that depend on the gates working. Har'lh's, too, for all we know. —At least this way we would have a better chance of supporting one another's wizardries. I'm no hero . . . but it's all about getting the job done, isn't it? Rhi?" He turned to her.

Rhiow looked down at the gravel where she sat, her tail twitching. Finally she glanced up again. "If it were just me," she said at last, "I would sanction it. But it's *not* just me. There are two other team members who must agree to be bound in this manner . . . and this isn't something I can decide for the others involved."

Saash would not look at her. "I'm not going to ask for a decision now," Rhiow said. "Noon will be soon enough. Between now and then I'm going to have to go explain it all to Arhu anyway, which should be interesting." She looked east, at Rhoua's Eye, rising nonchalantly in the sky as if this were just another day; and from the streets came the early hoots and tire-screeches of the beginning of rush-hour traffic, reinforcing the feeling of normalcy, spurious though it was.

"It's all in the Queen's womb anyway," she said. "All we can do is wait and see how the litter comes out . . . and meantime, make sure our claws are sharp. Saash, wait awhile before you head back to the garage."

She walked off to her usual stairway in the air, leaving Saash and Urruah pointedly not looking at each other. *Please, Iau, let them sort it out,* she thought.

But she couldn't help but wonder how effective prayer was likely to be today, of all days. . . .

The garage was deep in its morning business, cars going in and out at a great rate, and Rhiow questioned whether the *ehhif* working there would have seen her whether she had been sidled or not. As it was, she was, and she walked up the air again to the high ledge in the back, where Arhu was sleeping.

She sat down on the concrete and simply looked at him for a moment. He was sleeping a little more easily, if nothing else: stretched out long and leggy, rather than hunched up in the little ball of previous days. *He's beginning to fill out a little,* Rhiow thought, *even after just a few days. A few months of this and he's going to start looking like a proper young tom.*

If we survive that long . . .

She was aware, suddenly, of eyes half-open and looking at her.

"I heard you," Arhu said, not moving, just watching her with a sleepy look, but one that was nonetheless unusually knowing.

Rhiow stuck out a leg and began to wash it in a casual manner.

"Something bad's happening, isn't it?" Arhu said.

"Much worse than usual," Rhiow said. "Har'lh is missing."

"I know," Arhu said, rolling over to lie upright. "I see that. Or, at least, I know it's happened . . . but I don't know how or why."

He paused, as if looking at something else; then said, "You can't go after him now. Something's coming . . . trying to break through."

"What?" Rhiow said.

"The one who chooses," Arhu said, gazing out into the fumy air of the garage. "And the one who didn't choose. There's a darkness pushing against the gate; I see it bending outward, and there are eyes, they're staring, they want—" Suddenly Arhu scrabbled to his feet and pushed himself right back against the concrete wall, as if he had forgotten how to melt through it, and he started to pant as if he had been running. "It's coming," he gasped, "*they're* coming, all the choices, all the eyes . . . coming upward . . ."

"Sit down, Arhu," Rhiow said, and went over to him, leaning to wash behind his ear briefly. He sat, but he was still staring out into the dimness, his eyes flickering wildly from side to side as he watched what Rhiow couldn't see.

"This one's scary," Arhu said softly, his breathing beginning to slow a little; but his eyes were still wide, fixed on some spot out of Rhiow's vision, or anyone else's. "This one really wants to be real, this choice. It's going to do it soon." He quieted a little more, but a few seconds later, he said, "They can't use the gates."

"I know," Rhiow said. "Tom has had them shut down."

"That's not the problem," Arhu said. He looked at her, with some confusion, Rhiow thought, and said, "All these choices . . . .How did *we* choose?"

Her first temptation was to tell him to look himself at the ancient memories the Whisperer would show him; but then it occurred to Rhiow that he was already seeing enough at the moment—he seemed to be caught in some kind of visionary fugue—and adding more imagery on top of it might make him even more confused or cloud some perception that might be of more importance.

Rhiow nudged Arhu down into the "sphinx" position he had been lying in earlier, and hunched next to him, tucking her forepaws in. "I suppose all the Choices are odd," she said, "but ours, well, it had its own quirks. We were made before the *ehhif,* supposedly, but well after the cetaceans and the saurians, of course. The saurians had passed by then; their failed Choice had killed all of them. There were a very few saurians, you know," she said, settling her front paws more comfortably, "who had rejected that image of world-ruling power that the Lone Power offered them. They took the vegetarian option to use less life, more sparingly—but there were not enough of them in the Choice to turn it aside, and they died under the fangs of the others. The Lone One's long black winter killed the rest.

"Then, much later, after the winter was gone and the world was warm and green again, our foremothers came. There wasn't any differentiation among the various kinds of feline families yet: just one kind, who didn't look so much different from us, although they were bigger, more *houff*-sized. They all ran in prides, and so when they grew into mind, the First Queens made the Choice for them, as queens decide what their prides will do today."

"What did It—what did she say?"

"Well, sa'Rráhh came and said to them that the way of life that Iau had held out to them—to kill responsibly, to take only what they needed—was just Her plot to keep them small and weak, living on subsistence, on sufferance, and eventually to make slaves of them. The Destroyer held out to them the promise of rule over the world, the kind the saurians had wielded: power and terror, domination, all other life fleeing before them. And the Queen-mothers of the First Prides, wizards and nonwizards both—because there are always wizards in a Choice, at least a few—considered the Choice; but, being People after all, they disagreed on what to do, just as the saurians had."

"So some took sa'Rráhh's offer—"

Arhu had that faraway look again: Rhiow had no idea what he might be seeing, and continued as she had been doing. "Most did, and their Choice ruled the others. The Hungry, those who made that Choice, grew great and terrible in body, killing for power and success, but like the carnivorous saurians, they hadn't paid enough attention to the wording and intention of the Lone One's offer. They had their time to rule, but it was short—soon enough the ice crept down from the poles and buried the forests where they hunted, killing their game, and then most of them as well. There was a second group of the Eldest Kindred who rejected power and rule over the Earth, and elected to kill what they needed, only. They were the Mindful. They stayed small, for the most part, but grew wise, enough so to survive the ice when it came."

She fell silent for a moment, wondering what to make of the look on Arhu's face. "But there were more—" he said.

Rhiow switched her tail "yes." "They weren't very many, that last group: the Failed. They recognized as potentially deadly the Choice the Lone Power was offering, and they attacked her and died. But they're reborn, again and again, in one or another of our sundered Kindreds."

"They're wizards," Arhu said suddenly, and looked up at Rhiow.

"Yes," she said. "Still we die: there's no escaping the fate of the rest of our kind. But we're set apart; and we alone of all felinity may come again to that time and place where cats' bodies are once again the size

232 of their souls. . . . Other confusions between size and Kindred have

of their souls. . . . Other confusions between size and Kindred have come about over time. The Hungry are born among the smaller kindreds, and the Mindful among the great; the savage and the kindly mingle. You never know which sort you'll find yourself dealing with. Yet every feline, great or small, carries all of them within herself; we all have to make the Choice again and again, a hundred times in a life, or a thousand. Sum up all the choices, over nine lives, and your fate's decided, they say. If you fail, then there's nothing at the end of it all but silence, and the night. Pass through that last summing-up, though, under Iau's eye, and there's the last life, which doesn't end—"

"—the Tenth Life and the truest," Arhu said slowly, "of those whose spirits outwear and overmaster their bodies, untiring of the chase, the Choice, the battle, and go on in the world and beyond it; immortal, dangerous and fair, cats-become- Powers, who move in and out of physicality on the One's business—"

He looked at Rhiow, his eyes clearing. "They can't help us," Arhu said. "Something is breaking through: everything is bending, changing . . . so that there's nowhere solid for them to step. There isn't any help but what we already have."

Wonderful, Rhiow thought. "If you see anything that can be of use to us in what we're going to have to do," she said, "this would be a good time to let me know."

He looked at her with a kind of helpless expression. "You're carrying all the wrong spells," he said. "You don't want to open the gates. You need to shut them."

That perplexed her. "But they're shut already."

"Not for long," Arhu said, and very suddenly squeezed his eyes shut as if seeing something that frightened him badly.

"What?" Rhiow said.

"No . . ." He wouldn't look at her.

I wish I could push him. But I don't dare. "All right," she said. "Arhu, we have another problem. Whatever you may say about opening or shutting gates, we *are* going to have to go Downside again, very soon, to look for Har'lh. It's going to be much more dangerous than last time, and if our spells are to protect us so that we can do the job, we're going to have to link ourselves together in a particular way.

It means we'll be stronger: each of us will have all our strengths to draw on. But it also means that, if one of us dies down there, all the others will be trapped; there'll be no return."

"I know," Arhu said, painfully. "I see that."

Rhiow shuddered. "I'm not going to tell you that you have to do that. You have to decide."

He didn't say anything for a long time. And then, abruptly, he looked up at Rhiow again. ". . . What does Saash say?"

Rhiow looked curiously at him. Arhu looked at the floor. "Well," he said, "she washed me. I must have tasted horrible. And she held me, even when I kicked, and called her names."

So it's going to come down to her, Rhiow thought. *Why am I not surprised?* "She's angry," Rhiow said. "She doesn't want to go down there again, and she hasn't made her mind up."

He switched his tail indecisively. "She'll be here in a little while," Rhiow said. "You can ask her then. When you've decided, speak to me in your head, or ask Saash to. We can't wait very long to go."

"All right." He turned his face to the wall.

Rhiow sighed, and stepped out onto the air, sidled again. "But you do have mostly the wrong spells," Arhu said.

This is so reassuring. "Which ones *should* we have, then?" Rhiow said.

"The ones the Whisperer's still working on . . ."

That made Rhiow blink.

"I'll be at my den," she said. "Go well."

When she got in, Rhiow was surprised to find Hhuha still at home so far into the day. She was stalking around the apartment restlessly, dressed for work, but plainly not going there: paperwork was still lying scattered here and there, her briefcase sat open on the table. Something unusual was happening, and Hhuha was tense about it. *Possibly that meeting she was planning has been rescheduled?* Rhiow thought. In any case, she knew better than to interfere with Hhuha when she was in such a mood, though at the moment Rhiow's stomach was growling nearly as loud as her purr could get under better conditions. She went and jumped on the sofa, and curled up there.

Hhuha stopped by the window, looked out, sighed, then went over to Rhiow and picked her up. "I hate calling in sick when I'm not," Hhuha muttered into her fur. "It makes me feel duplicitous and foul. Come here, puss, and tell me I'm not duplicitous and foul."

"You're no more duplicitous than most cats are," Rhiow said, purring as loudly as she could and bumping her head against Hhuha's ear, "so why should you complain? As *ehhif* go, you're a model of good behavior. And you're not foul. The *tuna* is foul. —Oh, come on, my Hhuha, calm down." She put her nose against Hhuha's neck. "This is no good. You're not calm, Iau knows *I'm* not calm, neither of us can do anything for each other."

"My kitty," Hhuha said, rubbing her behind the ears. "I wish I knew where you were half the time. You make me worry."

"I wish I could just *tell* you! It would be so much easier. I swear, I'm going to start teaching you Ailurin when all this quiets down. If Rosie can learn it, so can you."

"At least I know you're not out getting knocked up."

Rhiow had to laugh. "With the example of the Himalayans down the street before my eyes? I'd sooner pull out my own ovaries with my teeth. Fortunately, that's not a requirement."

"Boy, you're talky today. You hungry? Want some tuna? Sure."

"I don't want the gods'-damned tuna!" Rhiow practically shouted as Hhuha put her down and went to the *ffrihh*. "I want to lie on the rug and be a *house pet!* I want to sit on the sofa and have you rub my fur backward so I can grab you and pretend to bite! I want to sit on Iaehh's chest and make him feed me pepperoni! I want . . . *oh*. You didn't say you had *sushi* last night!"

"Here, it's maguro. You like maguro. Come on. Would you stand up for it?"

Rhiow stood right up on her hind legs and snatched at the sushi with both paws. "You'd be surprised what I'd do for it, except I'm not allowed. Did you take the horseradish off it? I hate that stuff, it makes my nose run. Oh, *good* . . ."

Hhuha sat down, and together they ate tuna sushi, very companionably, on the sofa. "*He* made a big fuss about not liking maguro last night," Hhuha said, "so *he* doesn't get any. You and I will eat it all. No, you don't want this one, it's sea urchin."

"Try me!"

"Hey, get your face out of there. You had three pieces, that's enough."

"There is no such thing as too much sushi."

"Oh, gosh, it *is* awful the day after. Here, you have it."

"I thought you'd see sense eventually. —Oh, gods, it's *disgusting!*"

"Hey, don't drop that on my rug! I thought you wanted it!"

"I changed my mind."

The phone rang. Hhuha leapt up off the couch like a Person going up a tree with a *houff* after her, and answered the phone before the machine could pick up. "Hello—yes, this is she—yes, I'll hold— Yes, good morning, Mr. Levenson. —Certainly. —No problem—when? That's fine. I'll see you there. Yes. Goodbye—"

She hung up and threw away the rejected piece of sushi, then dashed across the room to pick up the jacket that went with the business skirt she was wearing, shut the briefcase and snatched it from the table, and looked scornfully at the pile of papers near it. "May be the last day I have to mess with that stuff," Hhuha said. "Wish me luck, puss!"

"Hunt's luck, Hhuha mine," Rhiow said. Hhuha headed out the door and closed it, starting to lock locks on the outside.

Rhiow sat there when the noise had finished, and listened to Hhuha's steps going off down the hallway, then had a brief wash. She was in the middle of it when she heard the voice in her head.

Rhiow?

T'hom—

You're needed. Hurry up: get the team together and get them all down here. We've got big trouble.

She had never heard such a tone from him before. She went out the door at a run.

It took about twenty minutes to get everyone together at the garage; after that it was a minute's worth of work to do a small-scale "personal" transit of the kind that Rhiow and the team had first used to bring Arhu in. The garage staff mistook the slam of air into the space where they had been for something mechanical, as Rhiow had suspected they would; when they popped out into existence on the platform for Track 30, the *bang!* of hot, displaced air was drowned out there too by the diesel thunder of trains arriving on one track and leaving on another.

There were a lot of people waiting on the empty platform. They looked like commuters . . . those of them who were visible, anyway. But visible or not, they had business in the station other than catching trains. In a city the size of New York, with a population of as many as ten million, there may be (depending on local conditions) as many as a hundred thousand wizards in the area; and New York, packed as full as it is with insistent minds and lives, populated as it is by an extravagant number of worldgates, tends to run higher than that. Obviously many wizards would be based in boroughs other than Manhattan, or would be engaged in other errantry that wouldn't leave them free to drop what they were doing. But many would be ready and able to answer an emergency call, and these were arriving and being briefed, either by other wizards or by their Manuals, on what was going to be required of them.

Tom saw Rhiow and the team immediately, and headed over to them through a crowd of other *ehhif* wizards. "I got you your override," he said to Rhiow when they had moved a little over to one side, where they could talk. "I'm afraid it wasn't cheap."

She knew it wasn't. The Whisperer had breathed a word in Rhiow's ear while they were setting up the circle for their short transit—confirmation that her demand had been accepted, and the price set—and the news had made her lick her nose several times in rapid succession. *A whole life—* She could have backed out, of course. But Rhiow had put her tongue back in where it belonged, taken a deep breath, and agreed. Now it was done. If everything worked out for them, of course, the price would be more than fair. It was simply something of a shock to have spent the last four or five years thinking of yourself as still only a four-lifer, not yet in middle age—and suddenly, between one breath and the next, to realize that you were already into your fifth life, and now on the downhill side.

"We do what we have to," Rhiow said. "Har'lh has been doing so, and the Queen only knows where he is at the moment. Should I do less? But never mind that. What's going on?" She glanced over by Track 30, where she could see the weft of the gate showing as usual. "I thought you shut the catenaries down."

"They were shut down at the source." Rhiow looked up at him, slightly awestruck, for the source of the gates was the Powers That Be: Aaurh herself, in fact. "However . . . something has brought them up again."

"The gates are active," Urruah said carefully, "but not under your—under 'our'—control?"

"Yes," Tom said. Rhiow thought she had never heard anything quite so grim. "We've tried to shut the gates down again. They don't answer."

Saash's tail was lashing. "Once it's shut down, an emplaced wizardry shouldn't be able to be reactivated except by the one who emplaced it."

"Shouldn't. But we've seen the rules changing around us, all week. Apparently the earlier malfunctions were a symptom of this one—or else this one is just the biggest symptom yet. Someone has reactivated the gates *from the other side.*"

"That would take—"

"Wizardry? Yes. And of a very high order."

Rhiow remembered the gate "saying" to her, *"Someone" interfered . . .* She licked her nose. *And my light went out,* Rhiow thought, and started feeling extremely grim herself.

"It couldn't be Har'lh, could it?" Urruah said. "Trying to get out?"

"His spells have their own signature, like any wizard's," Tom said. "Whoever or whatever is producing this effect . . . it's not Carl. But more to the point, if it *were* him, the gates wouldn't be resisting what's happening on the other side: it's a kind of power that's alien to them. Something wizardly, but not in the usual sense, appears to be trying to push through."

"I see it," Arhu said. "I told Rhiow that I was seeing it, just a little while ago."

Tom looked at him thoughtfully. "What exactly do you see?"

Arhu's tail was lashing. "It's dark . . . but I can hear something: it's scratching."

"Could be Saash," Urruah muttered.

Rhiow hit him right on the ear, hard. Urruah ducked down a little, but not nearly far enough to please her. "It's carrying the darkness with it on purpose," Arhu said, looking down into the darkness where the silver glint of the tracks under the fluorescents faded away, "and it wants to let it out into the sun . . . but until now the way has always been too small. Now, though, the opening can be made large enough; and there's reason to make it so. The darkness will run out across the ground under the sun and stain it forever."

Tom hunkered down by Arhu. "Arhu . . . *who is it?*"

Arhu squinted into the dark. "The father," he said. "The son . . ."

"He said that before," Rhiow said. "I couldn't make much of it then."

"The problem with this kind of vision," Tom said, looking over at her, "is that sometimes it makes most sense in retrospect. It's hardest on the visionary, though, who usually can't make any sense of it at all." He ruffled the fur on top of Arhu's head, which Arhu was too distracted to take much notice of. "One last thing. If we cannot prevent this breakthrough, by whatever force it is which is pushing against the gates from the other side . . . what else should we do to keep the world as it should be?"

Arhu looked up, but it was not on Tom that his eyes rested at last. The fur fluffed all up and down Rhiow's back as Arhu's eyes met hers; there was someone else behind those eyes. "You must claw your way to the heart," he said, "to the root. I hear the gnawing; too long have I heard it, and the Tree totters . . ."

In his eyes was the cool look of the stone statue of Iau in the Met. Rhiow wanted to look away, but could not: she bent her head down before Arhu, before the One Who looked through him, until the look was gone again, and Arhu was glancing up and around him in mild confusion at everyone's shocked expressions—for Urruah had his ears flat back in unmistakable fear, and Saash was visibly trembling.

Tom let out a long and unnerved breath. "Okay," Tom said, getting up. He looked around him at the ever-increasing crowd of wizards. "You four have other business," he said: "so you should hold yourselves in reserve. There should be enough of us to hold these gates closed . . . I hope. When the pressure eases up on the other side or drops off entirely, that'll be your time to run through. Meantime . . . we'll do what we can."

The hours that followed were given over to weary waiting for something that might not happen . . . if everyone was lucky. Urruah slept through it all. Arhu dozed or stared down at the *ehhif* down in the main concourse from the vantage point they had chosen, up on the gallery level. Saash sat nearby and scratched, and washed, and scratched again, until Rhiow was amazed that she had any skin left at all. But she could hardly blame her if Saash felt what she felt, the sensation of intolerable and increasing pressure below: something straining, straining to give, like a tire intent on blowing out; and something else leaning hard and steadily against it, trying to prevent the "blowout"—the many wizards who kept coming and going, new ones always arriving to relieve those who had come earlier and used up all their energy pushing back against the dark force at the other side of the gates. The ones who left looked as worn as if they had been out all night courting, or fighting, or both; and there was no look of satisfaction on any face—everyone looked as if the job itself wasn't done, even though individual *parts* of the job might be.

Rush hour started, and astonishing numbers of *ehhif* poured into the terminal and out of it again; the floor went dark with them, an incessant mindless-looking stir of motion, like bugs overrunning a picnic. There were minor flows and eddies in it—periods when the floor was almost empty, then when it filled almost too full for anyone to move; the patterns had a slightly hypnotic fascination. Rhiow wished they were a lot more than just slightly hypnotic; not for the first time, she envied Urruah's ability to sleep through anything that didn't require his personal intervention. She could never manage such a performance herself—her own imagination was far too active.

Though I wonder, she thought at one point, a good while later, *whether Urruah's simply decided that this is going to be the easiest way to deal with his disappointment.* For now there was no way he would be able to make it to his *ehhif-o'hra* concert in the Sheep Meadow. Even if the situation down at the track level relaxed, and the gates went back to something approaching normal, they would have to head down in search of Har'lh as quickly as possible. *Poor 'Ruah,* she thought, glancing up at the Accurist clock: it read one minute to eight.

T'hom? she said silently. *Any news?*

There was a pause. Tom had been spending most of his time in "link" with the wizards who were holding the gates shut—an *ehhif* version of the conjoint linkage that Urruah had insisted they would need. As a result, when you called him, the answer you got was likely to have anywhere from five to fifty other sets of thoughts, of other internal voices, wound around it as he directed the *ehhif*-wizards to apply their pressure to one area of the multiple gate matrix or another. It made private conversation impossible and required you to shout nearly at the top of your mind to get his attention.

Sorry, I missed that.

How are you doing? Rhiow said.

The pressure from the other side's been steadily increasing . . . but not by nearly as much, minute to minute, as it was earlier. We may be winning.

All right. Call if we're needed.

You've done a lot today already, Rhi.

Maybe. But don't hesitate.

She felt his tired breath as if it were her own as Tom went back to coordinating the other wizards. Rhiow breathed out, too, glanced over at Arhu: he was tucked down by Urruah, staring at the *ehhif* walking in the concourse. Deep-voiced, the clock began to speak eight o'clock; neither Arhu or Urruah moved. Rhiow turned and saw that Saash had moved over toward the escalators, where she was simply sitting still now, looking down into the concourse as well, but not washing: this by itself was unusual enough that Rhiow got up quietly, so as not to bother either Urruah or Arhu, and went to where Saash sat.

Saash didn't say anything as Rhiow came over. Rhiow sat, and the two of them just spent a while looking at the comings and goings of

ehhif who had no idea of what was going on down the train platforms.

"Tired?" Rhiow said after a while.

"Well, it wears on you . . ." Saash said, flicking an ear back toward
the tracks. "They're working so hard down there. . . . I feel guilty, not
helping."

Rhiow twitched her tail in agreement. "We've got specialist work to
do, though," she said. "We wear ourselves out on what they're up
to . . . we won't be any good at what we have to do."

"I suppose." They watched as a mother with several small noisy
children in tow made her way across the nearly empty concourse.
The children were all pulling shiny helium-filled balloons along behind them, tugging on the strings and laughing at the way the balloons bobbed up and down. They paused by the Italian deli, where
their mother leaned across the counter and apparently started chatting
with the deli guy about the construction of a sandwich.

"It's not that, though," Rhiow said after a moment, "is it? We've
known each other long enough now . . . you know my moods, I
know yours. What's on your mind?"

Saash watched the mother with her children vanish into the Graybar passage. "It's just . . . this job . . ."

Rhiow waited.

"Well, you know," Saash said, turning her golden eyes on Rhiow at
last, "I'm a lot of lives along."

Rhiow looked at her with some surprise and misgiving. "No, I didn't
know." She paused, and then when Saash kept silent, "Well, you brought
it up, so: how many?"

"Almost all of them," Saash said.

Rhiow stared at her, astounded. "Eighth?" she whispered. "Ninth?"

"Ninth."

Rhiow was struck silent for some moments. "Oh, gods," she said finally, "why didn't you tell me this earlier?"

"We've never really had to do anything that dangerous, until the
last couple of times. Besides, would it have made a difference? To
what we have to do, I mean?"

"Well, no, but . . . yes, of course it would!"

"Oh, sure, Rhi. Come on. Would you really have done anything differently the past few days? Just for *my* sake? You know you couldn't have. We have our job to do; that's why we're still wizards—why we didn't give up the power as soon as we realized it *cost* something." Saash looked down at the concourse again: more *ehhif* were filtering in. "Rhi, we've just got to cope with it. If even *Arhu* is doing that, who am I to turn aside from this just because I'm on my last life?"

"But—" Rhiow started to say something, then shut herself up.

"I had to tell you, though," Saash said. "It seemed to me—when we finally get down there again, if something happens to me there, or later, and I fall over all of a sudden and it's plain that that's the end of everything for me—I didn't want you to think it was somehow your fault."

Rhiow was quiet for a few breaths. "Saash," she said, briefly leaning close to rub her cheek against her friend's, "it's just like you to think of me first, of the others in the team. But look, you." She pulled back a little, stared Saash in the eye. "Haven't you forgotten something? We're going down in conjunct. If you don't come back up with us, *none* of us will come back up."

"Don't think that hasn't occurred to me."

"So don't consider not coming back, that's all. I won't hear of it."

"Yes, Queen Iau," Saash said, dryly, "whatever you say, Queen Iau. I'll tell Aaurh and Hrau'f the Silent that you said so."

"You do that," Rhiow said, and tucked herself down with a sigh—

Something screamed nearby. Rhiow leapt to her feet, and so did Saash; both of them looked around wildly. Arhu was running to them: Urruah was staggering to his feet, shaking his head as if he had been struck a blow.

"What was that?" Saash hissed.

"I don't—" Rhiow started to say. But then she did, for the screaming was not in the air: it was in her mind. *Ehhif* voices, shocked, in pain; and in the back of her mind, that sense of pressure, suddenly gone. Something blown out. Something running in through the blown place: something dark—

"Come on!" she said, and headed for the stairs.

The others followed. Rhiow nearly fell once or twice as she ran; the images of what wizards were seeing, down at the track level, kept over-laying themselves on her own vision of the terminal: The gate hyper-extending, its curvature bending inward toward the wizards watching at the platform, but also seeming bizarrely to curve away; the hyper-string structure warping out of shape, twisting into a configuration Rhiow had never seen before, unnatural, damaged-looking . . . and in the darkness, roaring shapes that poured seemingly more from *around* the gate rather than through it.

They're all going, came Tom's thought, *all the gates—look out!*

Rhiow and Saash hit the bottom of the stairs first and were about to run leftward toward the gates to the tracks—but a screaming, roar-ing wave of green and blue and pale cream-colored shapes came plunging through the gates first, spilling out into the main concourse. *Ehhif* screamed and ran in all directions—out into the Graybar and Hyatt passages, out onto Forty-second Street, up the stairs to the Van-derbilt Avenue exit—as the saurians charged across the marble floor, and their shrieks of rage and hunger echoed under the high blue sky. The chilly scent of dinosaur flesh was suddenly everywhere. *The cold things,* Rosie had said. *They went by. I heard them roaring . . .*

Panic was spreading in the terminal; *ehhif* were struck still with shock and disbelief, staring at the impossible invasion from their dis-tant past. Rhiow caught sight of one saurian racing across the con-course toward the Italian deli, and toward the mother, half-turned in the act of accepting her sandwich from the guy behind the counter; and toward the children, frozen, mouths open, staring, their bright balloons forgotten at the sight of the sharp claws stretched out toward them—

She thought about her Oath, to preserve life whenever possible—

Rhiow said the last word of the spell . . . a relief, for carrying a spell almost completely executed is an increasing strain that gets worse the longer you hold it in check. The unleashed power practi-cally clawed its way up out of her, leaping away toward its targets and leaving Rhiow weak and staggery for the space of a breath or so.

All over the concourse, in a circle with Rhiow at its center, saurians crashed to the floor and lay immobile. But the range of the spell was limited; and more would be coming soon. Urruah came down behind her and Saash; to him Rhiow said, "You have that spell loaded?"

"You better believe it!"

"Get back there to the gates and keep them from getting up here! And pass it to as many of the other wizards as you can. If you push the saurians back fast enough and get close enough to the gates, you can knock them down almost as they come out. Saash, go down a level; do the same. I heard Tom say something about 'all the gates.' It may not just be the one at Thirty that's popped. Arhu, come on, some of them went up toward the main doors—"

Saash and Urruah tore off through the doorways that led to the tracks. Rhiow ran toward the Forty-second Street doors, up the ramp, with Arhu galloping behind her. *Ehhif* screams were coming from near the brass doors; Rhiow saw two saurians, a pair of deinonychi, kicking at something low. Rhiow gulped as she ran, half certain there was a *ehhif* body under those deadly hind claws; but as they got closer, she saw that they were kicking actually the glass and brass of the doors in frustration, possibly unable to understand the glass—and on the other side of the door was no slashed-up body, but a furious *houff* with its leash dangling, barking its head off and scrabbling wildly at the glass to get through, while shouting in its own language, "Lemme at 'em! Lemme at 'em! I can take 'em!"

"Good dog," Rhiow muttered, a rare sentiment for her, and once again spoke the last word of the neural-inhibitor spell. The power leapt out of her, and the deinonychi fell, clutching at the glass as they went down, their claws making a ghastly screeching against the metal and glass as they collapsed.

Rhiow stopped and looked back toward the concourse. "I don't think any of them got any farther than this," she said to Arhu, looking around the waiting room. "If we—"

Any further words got stuck in Rhiow's throat for the moment as her glance fell on the mounted tyrannosaur in the waiting room. The few *ehhif* who had stopped on their way through the Terminal to look at the skeleton were now all clustered together in the farthest corner, holding on to one another with an intensity not usually seen in New Yorkers who until a moment or so ago had been perfect strangers. The air was filled with a peculiar groaning sound, like metal being twisted out of shape. . . .

Which it was, for Rhiow saw that slowly, with deadly deliberation, the skeleton was moving. Its front claws reached out and grasped at the air, clutching at nothing; its head lifted from the position of low menace in which it had been fixed, stretching upward, the jaws working—then twisted around to look, hungry, at the *ehhif* in the corner.

Rhiow's mind flashed back to what she had done to the metal track a couple of nights before. But you needed physical contact for that spell, and she wasn't very sanguine about her chances of maintaining contact for long enough to do the job without herself being ripped to shreds or bitten in two.

The tyrannosaurus skeleton leaned down to scratch and pull at the pedestal, then straightened and began trying to pull its hind legs free, first one leg, then the other. There was a *crack!* like a gunshot as one of the weaker bolts holding the bones of its left foot to the pedestal came free, ricocheting off the travertine wall and peppering the poor *ehhif* crowded in the corner with stone splinters. The tyrannosaurus skeleton writhed and struggled to get free; it threw its head up in rage. An echo of a roar . . . Then it started working on the second leg more scientifically, not just thrashing around, and it was bent over so that the clever little front claws could help, too. Pull—pull—*pull,* and another bolt popped—

Rhiow shook her head at the sight of something beginning to cloud about the bones, building on them like shadowy cord, layer on reddish layer, strung with white: muscle, ligament . . . flesh. *Damnation,* Rhiow thought, *whatever's going on downstairs is calling to its dead cousin here . . . and pretty soon we're going to have one of these loose in the Terminal?* —She shuddered. The deinonychi and smaller breeds of the present-day saurians—if it really *was* the present day, under the Mountain—were bad enough, but nothing like their terrible forefathers, like this desiccated old relic. The relic, however, was becoming less desiccated by the second; the muscle was almost all there now, organs curdling slick and wet into being, skin starting to sheet and stretch over everything, but only slowly: it was, after all, the biggest organ. For a horrible moment the skull was almost bare of everything but the red cording of the jaw muscles; then one abruptly coagulating eye, small, piggy, and entirely too intelligent, was looking down out of the wet red socket at Rhiow. The tyrannosaur stretched its head up as gaudy crimson-and-blue-striped skin wrapped itself around skull and shoulders, and heaved mightily, one last time; the second leg came free. It whirled on its pedestal, graceful and quick as a dancer, leapt down, and went for the *ehhif*—

You're lizard enough to die now, Rhiow thought, and opened her mouth to speak the last word of her spell—

Arhu, however, took a step forward and yowled a single word in the Speech.

The tyrannosaurus blew up. Flesh, ligament, all those organs and whatever had been inside them, blood and bone: one moment they were there, the next they were gone to splatters and splinters, flying through the air. The *ehhif* fell to the floor and covered their heads, certain that a bomb had gone off. The cream travertine walls were now a most unhealthy color of patchy, seeping pink; and the ceiling, just newly painted, appeared to have been redone in an entirely more pointillist style, and rained scraps and shards of flesh and other tissue down on the empty pedestal.

Rhiow looked at Arhu in amazement.

He grinned at her. "I saw it in Saash's head," he said. "She did it to the rats."

"Yes, but how did you adapt that spell to—"

"Adapt it? I just *did* it."

And to think I was complaining that he wasn't doing enough of his own wizardry, Rhiow thought. But this was more like a young wizard's behavior, more like her own when she was new, just after Ordeal, and didn't know what you couldn't pull off. "You're getting the hang of it, Arhu," she said. "Come on—"

He paused first, and ran back to the other skeleton, reared up against it.

Its metal went molten and ran out from inside the bones like water. The bones rained down in a mighty clattering and shattering on the floor.

"Where did you get *that?*" she demanded as he ran back toward her.

"I saw it in *your* head."

Why, you little peeping tom— "You didn't need to do that! It wasn't doing anything!"

"It might have been about to."

Rhiow looked at the stegosaurus skeleton and found herself willing to admit that under the present circumstances, she wasn't too sure what its dietary habits or temperament might be should it wake up just now . . . and they both had other things to think about. "All right, come on," she said. "You want to blow things up? Plenty of opportunity downstairs."

They ran back through the main concourse. For once Rhiow wasn't concerned about whether she was sidled or not: the *ehhif* would have a lot of other things to pay attention to for the next few minutes, anyway, besides a couple of cats. "Wow," Arhu said, "look at all these dead lizards. What're the *ehhif* going to do with them?"

"Nothing, because if we survive this, Tom will get authorization from the Powers That Be for a 'static' timeslide, and we'll patch this whole area over with a congruent piece of nonincidental time from an equivalent universe. The physical damage will simply never have happened . . . and if we get the patch in place fast enough, none of the *ehhif* here will remember a thing."

"Might be fun if they did . . ."

Rhiow snorted as they headed for the doorways to the gates, from which the roars and snarls and cries of battle were drifting toward them. *Saash?*

Downstairs.

How're you holding up?

Killing lizards like it's going out of style. I don't like this, Rhi.

You didn't like the rats either.

I like this a lot less. Rats aren't self-aware. These creatures are . . . not that much of the awareness has a chance to get out past the hate.

They're trying to kill the ehhif, *and the* ehhif *are defenseless; that defines the situation clearly enough for the moment. 'Ruah?*

With T'hom and his people. It's a good fight, Rhi!

Tell me you're winning.

More than I could say. We're killing lots of dinosaurs, though. The trains are helping.

The trains *are—*

Only one derailed so far, Urruah said cheerfully.

Oh, sweet Dam of everything—! Rhiow ran through the doorway for Track 30—then stopped, realizing that she had lost Arhu. She turned, saw him lingering to stare at one of the fallen saurians.

"Arhu," she said, "come on, can't you hear them down there? They need us!"

"I was seeing this before," he said, looking down at the saurian so oddly that Rhiow ran back to him, wondering if he was about to have some kind of fugue-fit along the lines of the one he had when they were coming back from Downside.

"What?" she said, coming up beside him. "What's the matter?"

"It changes everything," he said. "The sixth claw . . ."

Rhiow blinked, for that had been one of the phrases he had repeated several times as they returned from the caverns. At the time, it had puzzled her, and it did again now, for in Ailurin a "sixth claw" was an extra dewclaw, which polydactyl cats might have; or simply a slang idiom for something useless. Now, though, she looked down at the saurian, another of the splashy-pelted ones done in green and canary yellow, and at the claws that Arhu had been examining.

There were indeed six of them. This by itself was unusual, but not incredibly so. *They've always come in fives before, but maybe some mutation—* Then Rhiow looked more closely at the sixth one.

It looked very much like a thumb.

She licked her nose. "What does it mean?" Rhiow said.

Arhu stared at her, very briefly at a loss. "I don't know," he said. "But it's really important. I couldn't hear much else in my head almost all the time we came back. It was like someone kept shouting it . . . or like it was a song—"

His tail was lashing. "Later," Rhiow said finally. "They're fighting, down there: they need us. Come on!"

They ran through the door, down the platform for Track 30. The upper track level was hardly recognizable as the familiar, fairly tidy place where Rhiow walked every day. Saurians' bodies were scattered everywhere. Fortunately there seemed to be few casualties among the wizards, or else they had been taken away already for treatment. There seemed to be no station staff around: Rhiow guessed they were staying locked safely in the towers and workrooms, probably having called the cops . . . though what they would have told the cops they *wanted* them for, Rhiow would have given a great deal to hear. At least they seemed to have stopped any further trains from coming in.

Tom and a group of other wizards were gathered nearest the Track 30 worldgate, which seemed to be spewing out saurians like a fire-hose; as fast as they came out, they died of the neural-inhibitor spell being repeatedly used so that the bodies lay heaped high before the gate, and the new saurians had to clamber over the bodies of their dead or push them aside to leap, screaming, at the wizards. On Tracks 25 and 18, trains were stopped halfway down into the platforms, with saurians caught under their bogies or draped over the fronts of the locomotives; Track 32 had the derailed train, its sideways-skewed front splashed with lizard blood, a heap of dead saurians trapped underneath it, and the faint cries of *ehhif* coming from inside.

"What kept you?" Tom said as Rhiow arrived, with Arhu in tow.

"A pretty serious reanimation," Rhiow said. "Some kind of congruency to what's been trying to push up through here, I suspect. We may find that it resists being patched afterward."

"We'll worry about that later. Some of us are busy pulling people out of that wreck, but we've got other problems. You're the gate specialists—what can we do about *this?* There seem to be thousands more of these creatures waiting to come through, and if we just hang around here doing this all night, people's memory tracks are going to engrave themselves too deeply to be successfully patched."

Saash, Rhiow said, *can you get some relief? We need you up here. I've got some help already. On my way up.*

Urruah—

Heard it. Be right with you.

Saash appeared a few seconds later. "Any ideas how to stop this?" Rhiow said.

Saash shook herself all over and had only the briefest scratch before standing up again, staring at the gate, through which still more saurians were clambering. "How chaotic," she said to Tom, "are you willing to get?"

"Things are pretty chaotic already at the moment," he said. "But *anything* that would put an end to this would be welcome. We've got to start patching very soon. If you need to get a little destructive—"

"Not physically." Saash was getting that same gleam in her eye that Rhiow had seen the other night when she had turned the catenary loose, and Rhiow started to feel wary. "Just think of it this way. The gate might be more like a plant than a tree, though we tend out of habit to refer to a gate's 'tree structure.' A gate has a 'root'—the anchor-structure of its catenary, way down in the bottom of the Mountain, which fuels itself from whatever power supply Aaurh originally hooked it to: pulsar, white hole, whatever; theoretical distinctions don't matter just now. A gate has a 'stalk'—the catenary itself. And then it has a 'flower' at the top—the portal locus, where the energy is manipulated through the hyperstring structure, and actual transport takes place."

"I hadn't thought of you as having such a horticultural turn of mind," Tom said, watching with a tight, unhappy look as yet more shrieking saurians climbed through the gate and were snuffed out.

"Yes. Well . . . what happens if you pull the portal locus *off* the gate?"

Tom stared at her. "Like pulling the head off a daisy. —What *does* happen?"

"It should shut the gate right down, no matter who or what reactivated the other end."

"Should—!" Rhiow said.

"Until a new portal locus can be woven and installed, nothing can use it for transport."

Tom was silent for a moment. Then he said, "These gates are very old . . . and were put in place by, well . . ."

"Gods," Saash said, twitching her tail in agreement. "Fortunately, they are gods who left us, in the Whispering, and *The Book of Night with Moon,* very complete instructions on how these gates were constructed in the first place . . . on the grounds that someday they might need serious repair or reconstruction."

"Which they will," Rhiow said, "if you go pulling the portal loci off them! Do you know what kind of *energy* you're talking about releasing here? And if you don't do it in exact synchronization, every one of them at just the same time, one or more of the gates could pull free of its anchors to this universe and just go rolling off across the landscape wherever it liked, and only Iau knows where it would wind up, and in what condition! For all you know it would invert function and start eating anything that the portal locus came in contact with—"

"So we'll be careful about the synchronization," Saash said.

Rhiow just stared at her.

"How long would it take to get the gates going again after this?" Tom said.

"With all the available gating experts working together to do the reweave? A day or so."

"If it's so easy, why hasn't it ever been done before?" Rhiow said.

"Because no one ever needed to, since nothing has ever made the gates malfunction this way before," Saash said, sweetly, "and because there's never been a problem quite like *this!*" She gestured with her tail at the fresh wave of dinosaurs clambering over the heap of already-dead ones.

Tom looked at this, and also at the image of the plan that Saash held in her mind. Rhiow was examining that same image with great disquiet. Theoretically it was sound. Practically, it could be done. But—

"All right," Tom said. "I'll sanction it. I know you have misgivings, Rhi—so do I—but we've tried every other way to shut these gates down again, and nothing has worked. And the clock is ticking—we've got to start patching right away."

He looked at her expectantly. Rhiow sat down, trying to put her composure in place for whatever spell was going to be required of her. The thought, though, of simply—well, not destroying the gates—

but *maiming* them: it rattled her. They were not entirely just spells. They were not sentient beings, either . . . but there was still something akin to life about them. . . .

Rhi, Saash said. *I hear you. But there's a lot of life here, too. And our fellow wizards can't just stand around down here, killing lizards forever: aside from the cost to them in energy,* ehhif *life is going to be seriously disrupted by the reality of what's happening if it's allowed to persist and set in too permanently to be erased. Worse: while this is going on, we can't go find Har'lh or get any closer to the bottom of what's been going on. . . .*

You're right, Rhiow said finally. "So what do we need to do?"

"Four gates," Saash said. "Four of us. We don't need physical contact; what we're going to do is brutal enough. Rhi, you know Thirty best. Here's the portal locus's pattern." Rhiow's mind filled with it, not merely a spell-circle but a filigree sphere of light with several more dimensions implied in the diagram, all made of interwoven words in the Speech, intricate and delicate. "Just hang on to that. See that loose thread there?"

Rhiow did, and she swallowed. She had never noticed any of the gate loci as having loose threads before. "Yes—"

"Hang on to it. Don't let go until I tell you. Urruah?"

"Ready. Got it."

"There's the thread. Bite it in your mind, don't let go. Arhu?"

"Uh, yeah."

"See that?"

"Sure."

"Bite it."

He held very still, his eyes shifting back and forth, but in his mind he did as he was told.

Saash was quiet for a moment. *I've got the fourth one,* she said at last. *I'm going to count backward from four in my head. When I say zero—pull those threads. Not a second before or after.*

Right, they all said.

The wizards around them got quiet, watching, except for those still occupied with killing whatever saurians came through the gate.

Four, Saash said.

Three.

Two.

One.

Z—

There was a tremendous rumble that seemed to come from the bowels of the building, working its way upward toward them, shaking. Dust sifted down from the ceiling, light fixtures swung, and fluorescent light tubes snapped and went dark—

And sudden silence fell: the shaking stopped as if a switch had been thrown.

The gate by Track 30 vanished—simply went away like a blown bubble that pops when a breeze touches it.

Everyone held very still, waiting. But no more saurians came out of the air.

There was a restrained cheer from the wizards standing around, and Tom came over to look at the space where the gate had been. "I don't feel the catenary," he said, sounding concerned.

"You wouldn't be able to," Saash said, coming over to stand by him. "But I can see it; the hyperstrings leave a traceable pattern in the space they occupy, even without energy flowing. It's just that the sensory component usually expresses itself through—" She stopped.

"Through what? What's the matter?"

Saash stood there, gazing into the dark with an expression of increasing horror . . . then began a low, horribly expressive yowling. To Rhiow it sounded like her tail was caught in a door . . . except there was no door, and she could feel her friend's sudden fear and anger.

"What?" Rhiow said. *"What—"*

Then she felt it, too.

Oh, Iau, no—

Arhu crouched down, looking scared—a more emphatic response than he had revealed even in the face of a ten-ton tyrannosaurus. Urruah stared at him, then at Saash.

"Oh, no," Rhiow said. "Saash—*where's the Number Three gate?"*

Arhu was sinking straight into the concrete.

"It's come loose before its locus was pulled off," Saash hissed. "It's popped out of the matrix—"

There was nothing showing of Arhu now except the tips of his ears, which were rapidly submerging into the floor.

"It's not *your* fault," Saash yowled, "come out of there, you little idiot! Somebody *boobytrapped* it!"

Saash glared at Tom as Arhu clambered up out of the floor again. "Somebody *knew* we were going to do that intervention," Saash said. "One of the gates was left with a minuscule timing inbalance, hardwired in and left waiting to go off as soon as the portal locus was tampered with. *It* hasn't been deactivated . . . and now everything that was coming out of all the gates before is going to come out of just *that* one . . . !"

"My God," Tom whispered. "Where's the other gate *gone?*"

Rhiow looked at him in shock. "A loose transit gate," she said, "normally inheres to the area of the greatest density of thought and anchors there. The place where the most minds are packed the most closely together—"

"Dear Iau up a tree," Urruah whispered. They all stared at him.

He looked at them, open-eyed with horror.

"Tonight? The biggest concentration of minds?" Urruah said. *"It's in the Sheep Meadow . . . !"*

Urruah ran out. "Hurry up and start patching," Tom said to several of the wizards who had been working with him; and he, and Rhiow, and Saash, and Arhu, and half the rest of the wizards in the place ran after him.

Urruah was making for the sidewalk, which was well enough away from any of the gates inside to prevent adverse effects. Maybe he didn't really need to, under the circumstances, but Rhiow, at the moment, thought it was probably better to be safe than sorry. There were enough people sorry already.

Sabotage . . . Rhiow thought again, as she and Arhu raced, along with the others, past the waiting room. *As if from inside . . .*

Arhu glanced over at the mess that still lay all about in the waiting room as they passed. *"That was it,"* Arhu said to her, fierce, his panic of a few moments ago now replaced with a rush of angry satisfaction and aliveness the like of which Rhiow had never yet sensed in him.

"That was what I saw . . . the first night. *That* came out. Even the rats ran away from it. And I—" He winced as they ran out the front doors with the others, and then said, "We're even now. It wasn't going to do that to me twice."

"Arhu," Rhiow said, while Urruah and Tom paced out a large transit circle—it glowed in the sidewalk behind them as they paced, causing interested looks from the passing pedestrians—"when you work with words the way wizards do, precision is important. Something *like* that was what you saw? Or, *that* was what you saw? Which is it?"

He looked at her with utter astonishment. "You mean—you think there's *another?*"

"How would *I* know? I want to know what you meant."

"Ready," Tom said. "Everybody in here—hurry up!"

They jumped into the circle with Tom and Urruah and the other wizards. "You sure of these coordinates?" Tom was saying to Urruah.

"They're 'backstage,'" Urruah said. "The spot was empty yesterday. No guarantees for tonight—but it's got better odds of being empty than anywhere else in the meadow tonight. You've got a 'bumper' on this, to keep us from accidentally coexisting with anybody—"

"Yeah, but who knows what it's going to do in such a densely populated area? We've got to take the chance. Whatever our spell will do if it malfunctions, it won't be as bad as what's already happening—"

There was no arguing with *that*. Tom said three words and the circle flamed up into life, then a fourth.

Wham!

A huge displacement of air as all their masses were subtracted from the space outside Grand Central; and *Slam!* an explosion of air outward as they all appeared—

—and heard a blast of sound that staggered them all—partly from the amplification, partly from how close they all were to the stage. The orchestra was playing a massive, deliberate accompaniment to three voices—two lower, one high—that wound forcefully and delicately about one another, scaling continually upward through slow changes of key. Rhiow found herself briefly impinging on the outskirts of Urruah's mind as on those of all the others in the transit circle there—had been no time to install the usual filters—and was drowned in his instant recognition and delight, even in these horrible circumstances, at the perfection of the sound coming from two of the three *tehn'hhirs,* and a third invited guest, the new young *ssoh'pra-oh* from the Met, in the great finale of a work called *Ffauwst.* Two of the voices argued—the Lone One and a wizard, in the throes of a struggle for the wizard's soul—but the third and highest, the voice of a young and invincibly innocent queen, called on the bright Powers for aid: and (said Urruah's memory) the aid came—

Let it be an omen! Rhiow thought desperately as they broke the circle and looked around them. A few security people and police noticed them, started coming toward them—

The human wizards, prepared, all went sidled in a whisker's twitch. Rhiow and her team did, too, and they all hurried past the extremely confused policemen and security people to get around to one side of the stage and get a clearer view—

It was hard, but they managed to clamber up among some sound gear, and from that viewpoint stared out into the night. The Sheep Meadow was full, absolutely full of *ehhif,* only dimly seen in the light from the stage. They sat on blankets and in portable chairs; the smell of food and drink was everywhere, and Rhiow threw a concerned look at Arhu—but for once he had his mind on other things. His ears were twitching; he stared toward one side of the meadow—

"*Where's the gate?*" Tom was whispering.

"Not here yet," Saash said. "The locus is still moving—"

A faint sound could be heard now, something different from the susurrus of more than a hundred thousand bodies in one place. It was hard to tell just what it was with this mighty blast of focused sound, both real and amplified, coming from the orchestra. Rhiow glanced at the little round *ehhif* whom she had seen leading them earlier; now he was in the kind of black-and-white clothes that *ehhif* males wore for ceremonial these days, and conducting the orchestra as if he heard nothing whatever but his music. Perhaps he didn't. But there was more sound than music coming from the edges of the meadow. A rustling, a sound like the distant rush of wind—

The three on the stage—a tall, pale, dark-haired tom-*ehhif,* a shorter tom, more tan but also dark-haired, both in the black-and-white clothes, and a tall, beautiful, dark-skinned queen-*ehhif* in a dress glittering like starlit night—were no more aware of anything amiss than the conductor. The toms, singing the Lone Power and the doomed wizard, cursed one another melodiously; the queen, ignoring them both, relentlessly declared her own salvation, requiring the aid of the Powers That Be. In a final blast of pure sound, a chord in three perfect notes, all three took up their fates, to the accompaniment of a final, mighty orchestral crash.

The *ehhif* in the audience roared approval and applauded, a sound like the sea on the shore, rolling from one side of the great space to the other: the *tehn'hhirs* and the *ssoh'pra-oh* took their bows and walked off the stage, almost close enough for Rhiow to have reached out with a claw and snagged the *ssoh'pra-oh*'s gown. But out at the edge of that sound, over toward the east side of the park, something was going wrong. The sound leaned up and up in pitch as the queen's voice had. Rhiow, Urruah, Arhu, Tom, all the wizards looked that way, straining to see what was happening—

"It's coming," Arhu said.

"What?" Rhiow hissed, as the third *tehn'hhir,* the big furry one Urruah had shown her the other day, went up the stairs to the stage past her, and more applause rolled across the meadow at the sight of him. He too was resplendent in the ceremonial black and white now, with a long white scarf around his neck, and he once again held the scrap of cloth he had used to wipe his face in the heat. This he waved at the conductor: once more the music began. There was a further rush of applause just at the sound of it—

He smiled. *"Tu pure, o Principessa,"* he began to sing—

"It can't be coming," Arhu said, furious and afraid. "It's not fair . . . it *can't* be coming! *I killed it!*—"

—The *tehn'hhir* looked alarmed as now, above even the amplified music, he could hear the strange sound coming from the east side of the meadow . . . the sound, getting louder by the second, of screaming.

He stopped and looked up, and saw the dinosaurs coming.

The screaming got worse: thousands of voices now, rather than just hundreds, as the dark shapes plunged through into the humanity in the Sheep Meadow, confused, enraged, hungry, and in many cases half blind—for many of the Children of the Serpent do not see well by night, and hunt by scent. Scent there was, in plenty, and possibly all the picnic food bought some of the *ehhif* precious time to pick themselves up and run away while furious and hungry saurians threw themselves on whole roast chickens and a great deal of Chinese take-out. But the biggest of the saurians, those with well-developed eyesight, had more than enough light to make do with, and many of them, particularly the biggest, homed in on the brightest source of light they could find—the stage. A great herd of them, maybe twenty or thirty big ones, went wading through the crowds, loping along at terrific speed, trampling anyone not quick enough to get away; and the screams became more intense and drowned out the orchestra's last efforts.

Some of the saurians were beginning to drop now as various of the *ehhif* wizards who had come with Rhiow's team in the circle did their own short-distance transports, out into the empty areas beginning to open in the tightly packed crowd. Actinic-bright sources of wizardly light began to appear here and there, drawing the light-sensitive saurians away from the surrounding *ehhif*; once they got within range, the neural-inhibitor spell finished them. But, as before, they just never seemed to stop coming. . . .

Near Rhiow, Saash hissed softly. "I've got to get over there and pull the locus off that last gate," Saash said. "Someone come and run interference for me—"

"I'm with you," Urruah said.

"Good. That spot over there—"

They vanished together. Around them, backstage, *ehhif* were running in all directions: Rhiow wished fervently that she could do the same.

The big tom-*ehhif* stared out into the darkness, much more bemused than afraid, if Rhiow was any good at reading *ehhif* expressions. More of the big saurians waded toward the stage; seeing them perhaps more clearly than the tom-*ehhif* could, the orchestra fled to right and left in a frantic double wave; though Rhiow noticed, with grim amusement, that very few of them left their instruments behind.

Next to her, Arhu was crouched down, hissing in rage. "See what I meant," Rhiow said, "when I asked you which one you saw—"

"It was one of these," Arhu said, furious. "They're all the same one."

"What? Do you mean they're clones?"

"No. *They're the same one—*"

"If that's the case," Rhiow said, watching the vanguard of the saurians coming toward the stage more—tyrannosaurs, indeed, all identical to the one in the waiting room—"then you can kill them the same way."

Arhu's expression became an entirely feral grin. He turned his attention toward the approaching saurians, started getting his spell ready again.

Another sound started to mix with the screams out in the meadow: the bright sharp sound of gunfire, stitching through the night. *This is New York, after all . . . and entirely too many of the crowd will be armed, legally or not.* Roars followed, and some unnatural bleats and bellows of rage and pain as bullets went home. Still more screams came as some of the fallen saurians fell on nearby *ehhif. Iau grant these* ehhif *don't get so confused, they start shooting each other—*

But there were worse things to think about. Tom reappeared nearby, glanced around to see how they were doing, was gone again in a breath. Almost in the same breath, a saurian came out from the farther backstage area, where the trailers had been parked: it had leapt over or dodged around the security barriers—

The saurian loomed over Rhiow, snatched at her with jaws and claws. Rhiow leapt sideways out of the claws' grasp, said the last word of the neural-inhibitor spell; the saurian, along with a companion behind it, came crashing to the ground. *Too close,* Rhiow thought, jumping out of the way. She was starting to get tired; and "burn-in" was setting in, the wizardly problem that came of doing the same spell too often. The spell's range decreased, and its effectiveness dwindled, until you could get some rest and recharge yourself—

Arhu was hissing, hissing again; outside, well beyond the stage, there were horrific noises. "It's—it's not working so great any more—" he gasped. "I don't think I can get all of them—"

Big spell, big burn-in, Rhiow thought, *and worse than usual for a young wizard, who doesn't know how to pace himself yet.* "Stop it for a moment," she said, "and use something else. Try the neural inhibitor—"

Rhiow felt Arhu rummaging briefly in her head for the complete spell, as he had taken the explosive spell from Saash: a most unnerving sensation. Then he said the last word of the spell—

Another large saurian that had invaded the backstage area died. This was followed by a small clap of air exploding outward, almost lost in the massive sound of a hundred thousand people panicking, and Urruah was there again. "Saash took the gate out," he said. "They've stopped coming—"

Arhu opened his mouth to hiss at the next of the huge shapes loping toward the stage.

Nothing happened.

The big tom-*ehhif* had been standing and staring in utter astonishment, probably simply unable to believe what he was seeing. Now fear finally won out over disbelief. He turned to flee, heading for the side exit from the stage . . .

. . . but he was not nearly fast enough on his feet. A huge scarlet-and-blue-striped head reached down into the blinding stage lights, the little fierce eye holding a horrible humor trapped in it; the jaws opened and swiftly bit.

It took the saurian two bites to get the *tehn'hhir* down.

Urruah, turning around from dropping a couple more of the saurians, saw this, and swore bitterly. "Oh, great," he said, "we're gonna have fun patching *that!*"

Across the Sheep Meadow, the last cries of the remaining saurians were fading away. Urruah hissed out the last word of the neural inhibitor, and the saurian now leaping off the stage was hit by it in midair; it crashed into the right-hand speaker tower as it fell, and the tower tottered, sparks jumping and arcing from its broken connections. After a moment the speaker tower steadied again and sat there, sizzling and snapping, the noise fighting with the dwindling seacrash roar of angry and frightened *ehhif* voices as, en masse, the audience fled the Sheep Meadow.

Rhiow and Urruah and Arhu found Saash after a little while and went in search of Tom. He was out in the center of the meadow, helping many more wizards who had followed them from Grand Central to try to stabilize the situation and get the "patch" of congruent time in place.

". . . It's not so much a problem of power as of logistics," Tom said wearily, rubbing his face as he looked around at hundreds, maybe thousands, of saurian bodies left scattered across the great open space, and many hurt or dead humans. "We just need to keep enough wizards in the area to make sure the patch takes. Grand Central's already patched, in fact: the derailments never happened, the tracks are clean. But the price . . . " He sighed. "A lot of people volunteered a lot of time off their lives tonight. We have a fair number of sick and injured: they're outside the patch because they intervened as wizards . . . so they're stuck with the results of that timeline."

"Casualties?" Rhiow said, very softly.

"Four of us," Tom said. "We were very lucky it wasn't a whole lot more. As it is, we're going to have to find ways to cover their deaths in the line of duty . . ." Rhiow twitched her tail at the sight of the lines of pain deepening in his face. "Fortunately, there's nothing forensics can do about wizardry. There will be no trace of the cause in which they died. But their families . . ." He shook his head.

"What about the park?" Saash said.

"The patch is being arranged now," Tom said, looking with a sigh at the half-demolished stage, the bodies of saurians festooned all over the skewed and crumpled speaker towers, the orchestra chairs scattered, the heaviest instruments lying overturned. Overhead, police helicopters were starting to circle, directing their bright spotlights down at what must have looked like a most peculiar riot. The streets all around the park on both sides were full of people: not the usual leisurely walk home from a mass concert, but people hurrying to get away from something they couldn't understand and were very much afraid to. That susurrus of their voices, frightened, bemused, echoed

in the stone canyons, mingling with the ratchet of the helicopter ro-
tors overhead.

"Can we really heal all of this?" Urruah said, sounding rather desperate. "Even *that?*" He looked over toward where the last saurian
lay, the one who had made a rather high-calorie meal of the third
tehn'hhir.

Tom nodded again, with a tired smile. "We're starting work more
quickly than we could with Grand Central: the time-graft should take
perfectly. The gate will never have come rolling down here; *he'll*
never have become an hors d'oeuvre; all these other people who
were hurt or died, won't have been hurt or died . . . except for our
own people, of course." It was the practicing wizard's one weakness
where time paradox was involved. If you knew that such patching
was possible, you yourself (should you die) could not be included in
it; the unconscious mind, refusing to accept the violation of the paradox, would dissolve the reconnection with its former body as often as
such reconnection was attempted.

"You're not going to be able to do much more patching like that,
though," Saash said softly. "The Powers won't permit so much of it."

"No," Tom said. "We've got to get busy reweaving the gates so that
we can discover the source of all this trouble: it's Downside . . . far
Downside, I'm afraid. Whatever engineered this attack won't take its
defeat kindly. A worse breakthrough will already be in the planning
stages; it's got to be stopped by more conventional methods . . . for if
you patch time too aggressively in a given area, the presence of so
many grafts will start denaturing normal time, so that things that really
did happen will start excising themselves. Not good . . ."

Rhiow shuddered at the thought. "I'll speak to the Penn team," she
said. "We've got to get at least a little rest tonight, a few hours' worth.
After that we'll get at least one access gate up immediately." She
looked around at her team. "And we'll get ourselves down there and
see what the Queen may show us as regards Har'lh's whereabouts."

Tom nodded.

"He's not dead," Arhu said.

Tom's head snapped around. Everyone stared at Arhu.

"What?"

"He's not dead. But they have him."

"Where is he?"

"In the claws of the Eldest," said Arhu.

Rhiow shuddered again, harder this time. Should you meet the Lone Power in battle, the Whispering prescribed the correct form of address: *Eldest, Fairest and Fallen . . . greeting and defiance.* It was felt that you, like the Gods, might be about to try to defeat that Power, but there was no need to be rude about it.

"How will we find him?" Tom said.

"By going Downside," said Arhu, with unusual clarity but also a tremulousness in his voice that Rhiow found odd, "and crossing the River of Fire . . ."

Rhiow blinked at the phrase . . . then resolutely set that issue aside for later consideration. "Let's all go home and get some sleep," she said. "I'll be along for you all before dawn."

It was about an hour later when Rhiow slipped through the cat door into a dark apartment.

They're in bed . . . good.

But they weren't. The bedroom door was open: no one was in there. Still, Rhiow heard breathing—

—Iaehh, sitting in a chair, in the dark.

This is odd, Rhiow thought. *Can't he sleep? When he can't sleep, he sits up and reads till all hours. And where's Hhuha? Did she have to go away on this business thing?*

She went to him, wove around his legs briefly. He didn't move.

Rhiow reared up, patted his leg with a paw.

Very slowly, Iaehh looked at her. . . .

There was something about the set of his face that frightened Rhiow: it had stopped moving, seeming almost frozen into a mask. For someone whose face was normally so mobile, the effect was bizarre. Rhiow crouched back a little, then jumped up into Iaehh's lap, the better to be in contact with him.

It was not something she would normally do, but her fear spurred Rhiow on, and very carefully, she slipped her consciousness into the upper levels of Iaehh's mind. It wasn't hard; it never was with *ehhif*—

their thoughts tended to be all on the surface, though the imagery was sometimes strange, and the colors could hurt your eyes.

—not much color in the imagery here, though. White tile, on the walls and the floor, and—

—cold, on a cold steel table, Hhuha. And her *face*—

"*No!!*" Rhiow yowled, and leapt out of Iaehh's lap so violently that she scratched him.

He didn't even bother swearing at her, as he usually did when she forgot her claws. He just sat there, staring down at the floor, and then put his face down in his hands, and started to cry.

"No," he moaned, "no, no, no, no . . ."

Rhiow stood there in the dimness, staring at him, starting to go numb.

Hhuha. Dead . . .

It didn't matter how. *Gone.* Arhu's artless question started ringing in her head: *You mean die* dead? *Like a bug, or an* ehhif?

Of course you never think of it happening to one of your ehhif, something in the back of her mind said heartlessly. *They're young yet, they're in their prime; they've got years ahead of them. Until something unexpected comes along—a heart attack, or a stroke, or just a taxi that turns a corner too fast because someone in the backseat is trying to stick up the driver—*

But, you think, *there'll be plenty of time with them, plenty of time to sort out the possible answers to the question: where do* ehhif *go when they die? For there has to be* somewhere, *even though they've got only one life.*

Doesn't there? . . .

Iaehh was crying bitterly now, one long tearing sob after another. Rhiow looked up at him, simply shocked numb, unable to accept the reality of what had happened . . . but the image was real, it *had* happened. Iaehh had now known the truth for too long to avoid accepting what had happened. It was too soon yet for Rhiow to feel that way . . . but that would soon change.

Very slowly she crept toward him again; silently, carefully, jumped up beside him on the chair; inched her way into his lap. "Ohh . . ." he moaned, and put his arms around Rhiow and hugged her close, and began crying into her fur. The image in his mind was pitifully plain, and the thought perfectly audible. *All I have left of her. All I have left . . . Oh,* Susan! *Oh,* Sue . . . !

Rhiow huddled down in his arms and didn't move, though her fur was getting wetter by the second, and the pressure of his grip hurt her. Inside, she moaned, too.

Oh, if only I could tell you how sorry I am! If only I were allowed to speak *to you, just this once! But not even now. Not even now . . .*

Sinking into an abyss of dumb grief, Rhiow crouched in Iaehh's arms, and wished to the Powers That Be that she too could cry. . . .

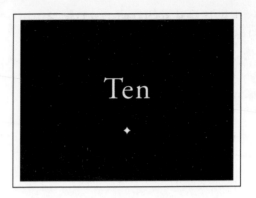

Ten

✦

Much later, very early in the morning, some of Iaehh's friends showed up at the apartment, as red-eyed and upset as he was, and took him away to "see to the arrangements." They made sure that Rhiow had plenty of food and water, and petted her, and spoke banalities about "look at her, she knows there's something wrong . . ." She was as polite to them as she could bring herself to be; she said goodbye to Iaehh as best she could, though even looking at him was painful at the moment, and she felt guilty because of that. The inevitable thought had already come up several times: *why her and not* you?!—and when it did, Rhiow fairly turned around in her own skin with self-loathing.

When he was gone, the pain got worse, not better. The silence, the empty apartment . . . which would never again have Hhuha in it . . . it all lay on her like lead. The empty place inside Rhiow that would never again resonate to that other, internal purr . . . it echoed now.

She sat hunched up in the early-morning light and stared at the floor, as Iaehh had.

This is not an accident, she thought finally.

Impossible for it to be a coincidence. The Lone Power knew all too well when a blow was about to be struck against It. This time, It had struck the first blow: a preemptive strike, meant to make Rhiow useless for what now had to be done. *And who would say a word?* she thought.

The great love of my life is gone, my ehhif *'s dead. Of course they can't ex-pect me to perform under these circumstances. Saash is the real expert anyway. They'll do fine without me. The Penn team will take up the slack.*

The predictable excuses paraded themselves through her mind. She examined them, dispassionately, to see which one would be best suited to the job.

Ridiculous.

It was almost old Ffairh's tone of voice, except that now it was hers. *You trained me too well, you mangy old creature,* Rhiow thought bitterly. *I don't even run my own mind anymore: I keep hearing you, chiding, growling, telling me what I ought to do.*

The problem was . . . dead or alive, his advice, Rhiow's thought, was right. She could not back away from her work, no matter how much she wanted to. And, thinking about it more, she *didn't* want to. If she sat here and did nothing, all she would see in her mind would be the cold tile, the cold metal table, and Hhuha. . . .

She flinched, moaned a little. *Oh, Powers That Be, haven't I served you well? Couldn't you do me this one favor? Just make it that this didn't happen, and I'll do anything you like, forever . . . !*

Rhiow—!

Saash, she said after a moment.

Rhi, where are you? Are you still at home? We need you down here—

Saash fell silent, catching something of the tone of Rhiow's mind.

Rhi—what in the Powers' names has happened *to you?*

My ehhif *is dead,* she said.

Saash was too stunned to reply for a few moments. Finally she said, *Oh, Rhiow—how did this happen?*

Yesterday evening, early. A traffic accident. A cab hit her when she was crossing a street.

Saash was silent again. *Rhiow, I'm so sorry,* she said.

Yes. I know.

A long silence. *Very sorry. But, Rhi, we* do *need you. T'hom has been asking for you.*

I'll come, Rhiow said after a moment . . . though it seemed to take about an hour to force the words out. *Give me a little time.*

All right.

Saash's presence withdrew from her mind, carefully, almost on tip-toe. Rhiow wanted to spit. *This is what you have ahead of you,* she thought to herself. *Days and months when your friends will treat you like an open wound . . . assuming you don't all die first.*

Maybe dying would be better.

She winced at that thought too.

Rhiow got up, made herself stretch, made herself wash, even very briefly, then went over to the food bowl.

Iaehh had left her the tuna cat food that Hhuha had thought so highly of.

Rhiow turned and ran out her door.

They all met in Grand Central, upstairs at the coffee bar where Rhiow had watched Har'lh drink his cappucino, about a hundred years ago, it seemed. Tom was there, with several of his more Senior wizards, two young queens and a tom a little older than they; all of them had coffee so that the staff wouldn't bother them. All of them looked as if they had had far too *much* coffee over the past several hours. Rhiow and her team, sidled, sat up on the railing near them.

"The patches aren't taking," Tom was saying. "We've been able to hold them in place only by main force, by sheer weight of will, all night and all morning . . . and we can*not* keep doing this. It's as if the *nature* of wizardry is being changed, from underneath."

"We had our first hint of this earlier in the week, didn't we?" Ur-ruah said. "That timeslide that didn't take, out in the Pacific. That seemed weird enough. But now we're seeing the failure of something as simple and straightforward as a patch with congruent time. If it *does* fail . . . then we're going to have real trouble. This is going to be-come a New York where two or three thousand people were hurt or killed in the Sheep Meadow and Grand Central, and where Luciano Pavarotti has been eaten by a dinosaur!"

"We can't have *that,*" Saash said, under her breath.

"Except it wasn't a dinosaur," said Arhu.

Everyone looked at him. "Oh, sure," Urruah said, hearing the un-certain tone in Arhu's voice. But Rhiow turned, the dullness broken for just that moment, and said, "No—let him explain. You were saying something about this yesterday. Something about all these big ones, these tyrannosaurs, being all the same one—"

"They are," Arhu insisted. "Their heads feel exactly the same inside. These big ones aren't the same as the saurians, who're all different. These big ones are all someone else . . . who doesn't mind getting killed. Getting killed doesn't *take* for him."

They all sat silent, thinking about that.

"Immune to death," Saash muttered. "A nice trick."

"It's going to be interesting to look into," Tom said, "but it's a symptom, not the main problem. Wizardry in this world is being changed. The change has to be at least arrested . . . preferably reversed. For anything that can change the nature of wizardry can also change various other basic natures . . . like science. That is *not* something the modern world would survive; and from our own planet, the change could spread . . . to other parts of the galaxy, to other galaxies, possibly even into other universes."

That was obviously not something that could be permitted . . . though to Rhiow, it all seemed faraway and somewhat unimportant, next to the pain inside her. "We will, then, be doing another reconnaissance," Rhiow said. "Much deeper, I would think. All the way down . . ."

Tom nodded. "We'll be assembling a force to come down after you. But we must know exactly what the danger is and equip ourselves properly . . . because the odds of being able to send a second expeditionary force down, should the first one fail, seem nonexistent. Once you get word back to us how to intervene successfully, we'll follow immediately."

"Very well," Rhiow said. "We'll advise you when we're ready."

She and her team left, Arhu bringing up the rear. Rhiow walked on up to the waiting room, which was quiet now: no *ehhif* walked among the bones, which stood as they had stood the day before, dry and seemingly dead.

Off in one corner, Rhiow sat down and looked at the skeletons. The others sat down with her, Arhu again a little off to one side, watching the older wizards.

"Now what?" Saash said.

"We wait till the gate's ready. Then we go down again. How are you about that?" Rhiow said.

A long silence. "Scared," Saash said simply. "You know why. But I don't see what else we can do. I'm with you."

Rhiow switched her tail "yes." "'Ruah?"

"You know I'm ready to go where you lead."

She gave him the slightest smile. He might be unduly hormonal and odd in the head about *ehhif* singing, but Urruah could always be relied upon.

"Arhu—"

He looked up at her. "I don't know about this—" he said.

"You're too damn uncertain about most things," Urruah said. "Your particular talent, especially. *I* for one want you to start doing your share of the hunting in this pride—pushing this gift of yours a little more aggressively. If you'd been actively using it for what it's *for*— looking ahead to see what's going to affect us in our work—you might have seen what happened to Rhiow's *ehhif*, and she might have been able to stop it—"

"Oh, yeah?" Arhu was bristling. "*You're* not running this team. And what're you going to do if I *don't* roll right over and do what you say?"

Urruah leaned at him, reared up, shoulders high, beginning to fluff. "Some of this, maybe," he said, lifting a paw slowly, putting his ears down. "Come to think of it, maybe I should have done this a while ago—"

Arhu's growl answered his: they began to scale up together.

"Stop it!" Rhiow said. "Urruah, *cut it out*. You can't force vision." But her anger wasn't directed so much at him as at herself. It was embarrassing enough for Rhiow to hear Urruah say, out loud, something *she* had been thinking . . . another of those loathsome selfish thoughts that made her so furious with herself. The thought of begging Tom for a scrap of congruent time, just a little of what had been used to patch Grand Central and the Sheep Meadow, to keep a cab from turning a particular corner at a particular moment . . . *The Powers will never notice. . . .* She had actually caught herself thinking that. Leaving aside the thought that all patches were an iffy proposition at the moment—and what point was there in patching that bit of time, then having it come undone, so that Hhuha would have to die *twice*—thoughts like that were a poor kind of memorial for her *ehhif,* who had always had a short temper for other people's selfishness.

How long have I been a wizard now, and not learned? Use your gifts for things for yourself . . . and they'll shut down. They're not designed for it. But Rhiow *did* have one thing that was lawful for her to use . . . her anger. *Lone One, sa'Rráhh, Tearer and Destroyer, Devastatrix—we are going to have words, you and I.*

"He sees what he has to," Rhiow said. "That's the nature of his gift. He's already doing better at that than he has previously. He'll learn to see more completely as time goes on."

Arhu had been crouched down on the floor, ears flat, through all this. But now he looked up, and he was as angry at Rhiow, who thought she had been defending him, as at any of the others. "Why *should* I?" he growled. "I didn't ask for this gift, as you call it. And I hate it! It never shows me anything good! All I see is fighting in the past, and dying in the present, and in the future—" He licked his nose, shook his head hard. "This seeing doesn't do anything for me but hurt me, make me feel bad. If I ever run across one of these Powers That Be, I'm going to shove it down Their throats—"

He hunched himself up again.

"I'd give a meal on a hungry day to see *that,*" Saash said mildly. "But right now we have other troubles." She sat up, sighed, and started scratching. "We're going to have to go down again, as soon as the other gate teams have finished work. I am going. Urruah is going. Rhiow—"

They looked at her. "I have to go," Rhiow said. "I don't feel like moving or speaking or doing anything but crawling into a hole . . . but I've blown one life of nine on the spelling dispensation we're going to need: damned if I'm going to waste that. And I have a grudge against the Lone One. I intend to take it out on It any way I can. All of this is plainly sa'Rráhh's work . . . and I'm going to take a few bloody strips out of her hide, and pull out a few pawfuls of fur, before all this is over."

Saash, in particular, was staring at her, possibly unused to hearing such bitterness, such sheer hate. Rhiow didn't care; the emotion was a tool, and she would use it while it lasted. It was better than the dullness that kept threatening to descend.

Arhu was staring, too. Finally, he said, "I have to go do *hiouh,* excuse me. . . ." He got up and hurried out.

Rhiow breathed down her nose, scornfully amused at his discomfiture. Urruah looked at her, and said, "Not your usual line, Rhi."

"But this hasn't exactly been a usual week, 'Ruah. We are being pushed into something . . . some big change. The Powers That Be are on our cases, directly. And it's all Arhu's fault."

"I'll buy that," Urruah said immediately. But he sounded less certain than usual and gave Rhiow an uneasy look.

"What kind of 'something,' Rhi?" Saash said.

"I don't know. But it's plain we are a weapon at the moment . . . and I can't get rid of the idea that Arhu is meant to be the claw in the paw that strikes. We're just his reinforcement, the bone to which the claw is attached: his bodyguards, as an *ehhif* would put it. I think he is going to be subjected to an Ordeal so extreme that he wouldn't be likely to survive it . . . and so important that he mustn't be allowed to fall. Which is why we're being sent along."

"Wonderful," Urruah said, looking slit-eyed at the door through which Arhu had left. "I just love being expendable."

"I don't think we are," Rhiow said slowly. "I think something severe is intended for us too. And the Lone Power is stepping up Its resistance." She looked over at Saash. "Better keep an eye on your *ehhif,*" she said. "Though yours is probably safe: I don't think you two were as . . . emotionally attached . . . as, as Hhuha . . ."

She had to stop. Just the mention of her name brought the whole complex of scents and sensations that had been associated with her *ehhif:* the warmth, the silent purr . . .

The others watched Rhiow, silent, as she crouched there and did her best to master herself. It was hard. Finally she lifted her head again and said, "When will one of the gates be ready?"

"This evening. It'll be our friend beside Thirty."

"All right. Load yourselves up with every spell you think you can possibly use . . . I've bought us the right to overcarry." She licked her nose, swallowed. "Ffairh went right down into the Roots, once upon a time. Not all the way down: there wasn't need. But he knew at least part of the way and left me directions. At the time, I just thought he was being obsessional about cleaning his mind out before he died. Now I'm not so sure."

The time when they would have to leave for Downside was approaching. Rhiow had returned to the apartment, hoping to see Iaehh before she left, but he seemed not to have come back, and Rhiow could understand entirely why not. The emptiness of the place without Hhuha, the silence, must have been as unbearable for him as for her. But it was all Rhiow had left of her. She sat on the sofa, in Hhuha's spot, staring at the pile of papers she had left there, saying, "Maybe never again . . ."

The memory hurt. Nearly all memories hurt, for Rhiow had been with Hhuha since kittenhood, and not until she was offered wizardry, went on her Ordeal, and achieved the power to have more autonomy did she ever begin to contemplate a life without her *ehhif*. She had started to be very active then, in the way of young wizards everywhere: going out on errantry, sometimes even offplanet; meeting and socializing with other wizards; doing research on gating in general, and specifically on the spell that had come with her Ordeal.

Well, not precisely *with* it, as if in a package. But not too long before she had gone on the errand that made a wizard of her, there she had found it, like something left on the bottom of her brain, in rags and tatters: bits and pieces of a spell, half-assembled or badly assembled, like someone's leftovers. She had gone straight into the difficult part of her Ordeal then and had forgotten about this spell until much later: when she found she was fully confirmed in her power as a wizard, still alive after the challenges that had faced her, and not yet on assignment—left with a little time of her own to recover, and look at the world through new eyes. Little by little, she had started piecing the thing together, or trying to, anyway, the way Hhuha would piece together a quilt—

Rhiow flinched from her pain. But the simile was apt, and it was too late now to get rid of the image of Hhuha sitting on the couch, completely surrounded by little strange-shaped pieces of cloth with paper pinned to them: hunting among them for one in particular, turning it around and around to find the place where it properly fit, and then slowly stitching it in place, while Rhiow rolled among the fragments and cuttings and threw them in the air, scuffling and scrabbling among the papers and the fabric scraps. The work on the spell had been very like that, except for the scuffling part.

Most wizards learned to keep a workspace in their minds, a place where a piece of information or a spell could be left to gestate, to be worked on or added to slowly over time. Words in the Speech would lie scattered on the floor of her mind, glowing with attention or dim with disuse; long graceful graphic arabesques, hisses or spits of sound, fragments of thought or imagery. You would come and sit in the dimness sometimes, or stroll through the untidy farrago of scents and sensations, peering at a word shattered to syllables, poking them with your paw to see if they could be coaxed or coerced into some more functional shape: pick them up and carry them around, squint at them to see what they did when conjoined—how the joint shape fulfilled or foiled the separated ones, when a phrase suddenly became part of a sentence, or tried to declare its independence and secede from a paragraph or sequence already fitted together. The tattered spell had been in this kind of shape for ever so long, for Rhiow had no idea what it was trying to be. Part of the problem was that it kept falling into impossible shapes, configurations that seemed to lead nowhere, dead-end reasonings.

Its power requirements when she found it were strange—seeming to come to almost nothing: its power output estimates were weird, too, for they seemed to indicate the kind of result that you would expect from, say, a gate's catenary—big, dangerous power, likely to burst out without warning. Rhiow wondered if the spell had gotten its signs reversed somehow when she inherited it, for this indication went right against the rules for wizardry. Every spell had its price, and the bigger the spell, the higher the price: magic was as liable to the laws of thermodynamics and conservation of matter and energy as anything else. She could feel those laws, particularly the last one, in her bones at the moment: there was an empty place where her fifth life had been. . . .

When a spell makes no sense, you normally leave it alone and come back to it later. This Rhiow had been doing for two years, idly, with no significant result; now as she looked again at the spell, lying there in its bits and pieces—though they were larger ones than two years ago—it still said nothing to her, except that you could get almost everything for almost nothing, just by saying that you wanted it. It was a spell for the kitten-minded, for those who would chase a reflected sunbeam across the floor and think they had caught it.

She sighed. *I've done enough of that in my time,* Rhiow thought. *Here with my* ehhif, *I thought I'd caught the sunshine under my paw. Peace, and a happy, busy, exciting life: what could go wrong? . . .*

Now I know.

Rhiow sighed again: she didn't seem able to stop. Slowly she wandered across the broad dark plain of her workspace, making her way to the place where Ffairh's instructions for the route down into the Mountain lay.

He had always been of a surprisingly visual turn of mind, even for one of the People, precise and careful: the diagram he had left her, of the twisting and turnings through the labyrinthine caverns, looked more like it had been designed using some *ehhif*'s CAD/CAM program than anything else. Through it all stretched the paths of the catenaries that fed power to the world's gates: those lines of power were shadowy now, reflecting the nonfunctional status of the catenaries. All of the catenary structures branched out in the upper levels of the Mountain, each feeding one complex of gates. Farther down, in the great depths, they began to come together; and in the greatest depth, which Ffairh knew about but to which even he had never gone, all the "stems" of the catenaries fused together into one mighty trunk, the base of the "tree structure" rooted (as far as Rhiow could tell) in the deepest regions of the Earth's crust layer, and in a master gateway or portal to their energy source, whatever that was. *White hole,* Saash had said casually, *or black hole, or quasar, or whatever . . .*

Rhiow suspected that it was more than something so merely physical; or there might indeed be such a physical linkage, but coupled to energy sources of very different kinds, in other continua right outside the local sheaf of universes. That had been Ffairh's suspicion, anyway. *Too far out for me,* Rhiow had said when he'd told her about that; Ffairh had looked at her, slightly cockeyed as he often did, and had said, *You never can tell.*

She studied the map again. The way down to the root catenary, the trunk of the "tree," was a long sequence of more caverns like the ones they had traversed earlier. But Ffairh had mentioned that the caverns were densely populated with the saurians. *That I believe,* Rhiow thought, seeing again in mind the thousands of them pouring out into the upper track level of Grand Central, and then into the Sheep Meadow. He had not said much more about what he had found, except to report continued attacks by more and more of the creatures, who howled at him that they would have their revenge on him, and the "sun-world," and anything that dared to come down to them from there: that someday they would come up into the sun themselves, and then all the creatures that lived in the sun, and squandered it, would pay . . .

He had come away, barely, and lived to tell the tale. At the time Rhiow had wondered whether Ffairh was exaggerating, just a little, to make sure that she didn't indulge herself in casual runs to the Downside for the pleasure of owning a big cat's body. Now, though, she knew much better. . . .

Rhiow looked over the map, marking with one claw the paths that seemed the most straightforward so that Urruah and Saash and Arhu could look at them. *The Powers only know what we'll find, of course,* she thought, *and we don't even know what we're looking for. A wizard of some kind, gone rogue . . . and intent on the destruction of wizardry as a whole.*

The thought chilled her, for it spoke of tremendous power in their adversary. *Worse,* she thought, *the Powers may* not *know what we'll find . . . or it may very well be one of Them. One in particular . . .*

Rhiow looked Ffairh's map over a last time, then turned her back on it and started back across the plain of her workspace, toward her usual egress point. She would consult with the others, show them the map, and attend to whatever final organization needed to be done; then they'd go find out what was in store for them. . . .

Urruah's question was still echoing in Rhiow's mind: *what kind of "something"?* She had been reluctant to answer him. It was he who had mentioned the "second Ordeal" that some very few wizards went through. The Whisperer would say only that such Ordeals were not true second ones: only first ordeals that had been somehow arrested or had a component that had not been completely resolved. *Could this really be what's happening? And which of us? Or is it all of us? . . .*

She twitched her tail in frustration. *It may simply be that we are all, together, a weapon crafted specifically to deal with whatever is going on in the deepest Downside. Now all we have to find out is whether we are a weapon that will be destroyed along with the threat we're meant to combat. . . .*

Rhiow paused and stood gazing across the bright plain littered with words. Some part of her very much wanted to simply turn around and say, *I refuse to take part. I was not consulted.* And she heard Arhu's voice again: *I didn't ask for this.*

But he consented to it when he took the Oath. And so did we. Now Urruah says he's willing. So does poor Saash, frightened as she is. If they're willing . . .

She growled, briefly angry at her own intense desire to back down from this job. *It's you, isn't it,* she said to the Lone One. *You live at the bottom of all hearts, anyway, part and parcel of the little "gift" you sold our people. Well, it won't work with me, today. I've seen your "gift" and what it did to my poor Hhuha. Maybe I'm about to claim my own version of it, and "die dead, like a bug or an* ehhif," *all my lives snuffed out together if I die Downside or if the others do. But you will not get me to walk away from the fight.*

The Claw may break. Let it. It'll be in your *throat that it breaks.*

I'm coming.

They met again in Grand Central, down by Track 30. Urruah and Saash greeted her with restraint: Arhu wouldn't say much of anything to Rhiow, but just looked at her as if she had some rare disease and he were afraid to go near her. She couldn't bring herself to care very much, just let him stare, and spent the next ten minutes briefing her partners on the route they would take once Downside.

Tom was there to meet them, looking even more exhausted than he had earlier. First of all, the Track 30 gate was up again, but it looked paler than usual, the light of the usual warp- and weft-strings of the locus duller and fuzzy-seeming. Indeed, to a wizard's trained vision, the whole station had an odd fuzzy look about it—edges and corners not as sharp as they should have been, somehow. The "patched" reality was fretting against the events of the last twenty-four hours, trying to come loose. So far it was holding—but only with constant supervision, Rhiow could see.

"How much longer can you keep all this in place?" Rhiow said.

Tom shook his head. "Your guess is as good as mine. The sooner you get started, the better."

Rhiow looked over at Saash. "This gate doesn't look any too healthy. Is it stable?"

"Oh, it's stable enough. But I wouldn't want to hazard any estimates on how long it will stay that way. Wizardry in general is starting to behave badly around here. If we don't find out what's causing the problem Downside, we may not be able to get back up again before the natural laws governing gating have been completely degraded and replaced with new ones . . . if they're replaced at all."

"All right," Rhiow said, glancing over at Urruah: he nodded and hopped down beside the gate, sitting up on his haunches to feed power into it if necessary. "Saash, when you're ready."

"Two minutes," Saash said.

Rhiow sat down to wait.

"Rhiow—"

She turned. Arhu was standing beside her. He said, "I can see—" and stopped.

"Well?"

"Your *ehhif*—I mean—"

"If you're going to say that I brought this pain on myself by living with an *ehhif* at all," Rhiow said, "don't bother. There are enough others who'll say it."

"No, I wasn't—I—" He stopped, then simply put his head down by hers, bumped her clumsily, and hurriedly went away to sit beside Urruah.

Rhiow looked up to find Saash standing next to her, looking after Arhu. "You've been coaching him, I see," Rhiow said to Saash.

She looked at Rhiow, slightly wide-eyed. "No, I have not. He's *looking,* Rhiow. Isn't that what you told him he had to do?" And Saash stalked away toward the gate, leaping down beside Urruah, and getting up on her haunches to sink her claws into the control weft.

Rhiow stood up as the usual quick sheen of light, though again duller than normal, ran down the weft. It abruptly blanked out then, showing her the rock ledge at the edge of the Downside gate cavern; the slow sunset of that world was fading away in the west.

She rose and went over to the edge of the platform, pausing there by Tom to glance up at him.

"Go well," he said. "And be careful."

She laughed, a brittle sound. "For what good it's likely to do, we all will."

Rhiow leapt through, felt herself go heavy as she passed through the weft, and landed on the stone. She shook herself, feeling almost relieved to be out of the small powerless body. Behind her, Urruah came through, then Arhu, finally Saash. As she came down, the gate winked closed.

Rhiow looked at that with some concern. So did Saash, but she simply switched her tail and said, "Power conservation measure. If we didn't shut it now, it might collapse between now and the time we get back up."

Whenever that may be, Rhiow thought. *If ever at all.*

And do I really care?

"Come on," she said. "Let's get on with it; and Iau walk with us . . . for we need Her now, if we ever did."

They wound their way back into the caverns of the Downside by the same route they originally had taken to service the catenary. The sounds around them were different this time, even to the dripping of water, and all of them walked more quietly. The Downside had a listening quality about it that it had not had before . . . but not the kind of listening that can be described as "brooding." It was charged: a silence following action . . . or before action begins again.

Their order of march was reversed this time. It was Arhu who led the way, having learned from "looking" inside Urruah how to make the tiny dim light that helped them find their way. Rhiow had shown him how to tie this small wizardry into the map in her mind so that the light led them through the turns and twists of the caverns, and left them free to keep alert and watch for any sign of the saurians. Behind Arhu, Saash was walking, and behind her, Urruah; Rhiow brought up the rear.

Their vigilance might have been for nothing: they heard no one, saw no one, and caught not a whiff of lizard except for what was stale, left over from the previous time . . . or so Rhiow thought. It was almost an hour later when they came to the catenary cavern and were almost surprised by it, for they had expected to smell it from some distance. When they came to the catenary cavern, though, it was empty, and almost perfectly clean. Even the bloodstains appeared to have been washed off the rock. *Or rather, licked,* Rhiow thought, her whiskers quirking with disgust.

Of the catenary nothing could be seen but a faint wavering in the air, like weed in water: only the barest maintenance-trickle of power was running up it, not nearly enough to produce any light. Saash went to it and looked it over while Arhu gazed around him in confusion. "Who cleaned everything up in here?"

"Who do you think?" Rhiow said.

Arhu stared at her, completely bemused.

"They eat each other," said Urruah.

Arhu's jaw actually dropped. Then he laid his ears flat back and scratched the floor several times with one huge paw, the gesture of revulsion that many People make when presented with something too foul to ingest, either a meal or a concept. "They deserve what we did to them, then!" Arhu said. "They would have done that to *us*—"

"Almost certainly," Saash said. "But as to whether they deserve to be killed, I wouldn't care to judge: the Oath doesn't encourage us to make such assessments."

"Why not? They're just animals! They come running and screaming out in big herds, and try to kill you—"

"We have responsibilities to animals too," Saash said, "the lower ones as well as the higher ones who can think, or even just have emotional lives. But leaving that aside, you haven't been in their minds enough to make that assessment." Saash wrinkled her nose. "It's not an enjoyable experience, listening to them think and feel. But they're sentient, Arhu, never doubt it. They have a language, but not much culture, I think—not since their people were tricked by the Lone One. There are memories." She looked thoughtful. "Anyone can be delusional, or believe lies that are told. But almost all the minds of theirs you might touch will have heard stories of how things were before the Lone One came—how their people really had a right to be called what we still call them as a courtesy-name, the Wise Ones; how they were great thinkers, though the thoughts would seem strange to us now . . . maybe even then. All very long ago, of course . . . but nonetheless, the Whispering seems to confirm the rumors. Now they have nothing left but a life in the dark . . . nothing to eat except each other, except at times when so many of them die off that they're forced to go up into the sun to try to hunt; and not being adapted to the present conditions here, those who try *that* mostly die, too. If the saurians hate us, they may have reason."

"I don't want to know about that," Arhu said. "We're going to have to kill a lot more of them if we're supposed to do whatever it is you have in mind. Knowing stuff like that will only make it harder." He stalked ahead of them, the epitome of the hunter: head down for the scent, padding slowly and heavily, eyes up, wide and dark in the darkness.

The other three went silently along behind him as they continued downward through the caverns, now slipping through unfamiliar territory and moving a little more slowly. Rhiow was still thinking of how she had seen the saurians eating one another, down there in the dark, with a ready appetite that suggested this kind of diet was nothing new at all. They would be seeing much more of that kind of thing, she was sure. *I should be grateful, maybe,* she thought, *that my emotions are so dulled at the moment, that everything seems so remote. . . .*

"So where are all the lizards that came out of the gates the other day?" Urruah said softly, behind Rhiow now.

"Maybe they all came out," Saash said, in an oh-yes-I-believe-this voice, "and they all died."

"I doubt that very much," Rhiow said. "Never mind. How was the catenary itself?"

"Structurally sound. But something is starving it of power, from underneath."

"Could it be reactivated later?"

"Probably," Saash said, "but I've got no idea whether the rules for reactivating it will be the same as they were yesterday."

Arhu had gone down and around a corner, ahead of them, out of sight, and Urruah paused for a moment, looking up. "Interesting," he said, coming over to Rhiow. "Look at the ceiling here."

Rhiow and Saash gazed up. "Very round, isn't it?" Saash said.

"One of those bubble structures you get down here," Rhiow said. "The water comes in through a little aperture and then rolls loose stones around and around inside the larger one. It hollows the chamber right out, as if someone blew a bubble in the stone. There are a few chains of them down here; they show on old Ffairh's map. He seemed to be interested in them."

They walked on down through the spherical chamber, up and out the other side, and went after Arhu. There was indeed another such chamber on the far side, and they went through it as well, down into the depression at the center and up again to the exit. Past this was a long, high-ceilinged corridor devoid of the usual stalactites and stalagmites, trending very steeply downward so that they all had to slow and pick their way as if they were coming down one side of a peaked roof.

At the bottom of the corridor, the tiny point of greenish light that they had been following vanished; then their vision caught its glow, diminished, coming from off to the left, and reflecting on the shadowy shape of Arhu heading around the corner and leftward as well. The sound of water could be heard again, soft at first, then getting somewhat louder: an insistent *tink, tink, tink* sound, almost metallic in the silence. "Are we still going to be following that catenary down the tree," Urruah said, "or is it another one?"

"Another. We pick it up"—Saash looked at her own mental "copy" of Rhiow's map—"another five or six caverns down, and a little to the east. Maybe a hundred feet below where we are now."

"I hate this," Urruah muttered, as ahead of them the light got dimmer, and they followed it doggedly. "All this stone on top of us—"

"Please," Rhiow said. She had been trying not to think about that. Now, abruptly, she could feel all the weight of it pressing on her head again. *As if I need this now! This isn't* fair—

Urruah looked up and suddenly stopped. Rhiow plowed into him and hissed; Saash ran into her but held very still, following Urruah's glance. Rhiow looked up, too.

"Is it just me," Urruah said, ". . . or does that look like a perfectly straight line, carved from the top of this tunnel all the way down?"

Rhiow stared at it—

The light ahead of them went out.

They all stood stock still, not daring to move, hardly daring to breathe.

No sound came from above but the steady *tink, tink, tink, tink . . .*

And there were stumps of the stalagmites and stalactites back there, Saash said suddenly, *but where were the leftover pieces? They should have been all over the place. And what about your stone bubbles? Where were the little stones that should have been left lying around? . . .*

Rhiow licked her nose, licked it again. They stood there blind in the dark; even People must have some light to see, and the darkness was now absolute.

Arhu! Rhiow said inwardly.

No answer.

Arhu!!

I'm trying to sidle, he said silently, *and I can't.*

But what for? Rhiow said.

It's going to cause you tremendous trouble to try to sidle down here; there's too much interference from the catenaries, even when they're down, Saash said. *Stay still. What is it?*

There was a silence, and then Arhu said, *They're down here. I put the light out. They didn't see me.*

In absolute silence, Rhiow and the others inched their way forward, going by memory of what the corridor had been like before the light failed. Rhiow's heart was hammering, but at least this time the light had gone out for a reason she didn't mind.

"They?"

I hear five of them breathing, Arhu said. *They're not far away.*

Rhiow and Saash and Urruah crept forward. Then something tickled Rhiow's nose, and she almost sneezed. It was Arhu's tail, whipping from side to side.

Which way? Rhiow said, as soon as she got control of her nose again.

Straight forward. Then right. See that? It's faint—

It was: Rhiow could hardly see it at all. From ahead and to the right, and sharply downward, came the reflection of a diffuse light, reddish, seeming as faint as their own had. It leached the color out of everything: there was nothing to be seen by it but furry contours in dull red and black. In utter silence, they crept closer; and in her mind, Rhiow felt the familiar contours of the neural-inhibitor spell, felt for its trigger, that last word. She licked her nose.

Tink. Tink. Tink. Tink . . .

A pause, then a peculiar hissing sound, followed by the sound of stone falling on stone, breaking. And then the hissing voice, like another version of the sound they had heard first.

"Done . . ."

"Done. We have finished what we were told we must do in this work time."

"I'm hungry."

"There will be no food now."

"But we will eat later."

"How much later . . ."

"The Master will give us something in time. He gave us food not-long-ago."

"That was good."

"It was. And there'll be much more."

"There will be. When the work is done, there will be as much to eat as anyone wants."

There was a kind of sigh from all of the speakers after this. Arhu moved a little forward, during it, and Rhiow cautiously went after him, slinking low, knowing that behind her the others were doing the same. The source of the light was getting stronger, rightward and downward: Rhiow could now clearly see Arhu silhouetted against it. He was bristling.

"How much farther must we drive this tunnel?"

A silence, then *sss, sss, sss,* as if someone was counting. "Three lengths. Perhaps as many as four: there's another chamber to meet, upward, and another baffle to put in place. Then the power-guide that supplies that gate will be cut off, and the guide can be redirected to meet the others, below."

"Good, good," the others breathed.

"That will be the last one for a little while. All the others have been damaged by the sundwellers. The Master must restore them. Then we may begin work again, and finish the new tunnels, and wall up the old ones. It's for this we were given the Claw. The sundwellers will not come *here* again."

There was much nasty hissing laughter at that. Arhu took the opportunity to move forward, very quickly, so quickly that Rhiow was afraid he was slipping on the steep downward slope. But he was well braced, so that when Rhiow came up against him, he didn't move, and made no sound. Behind her, Saash and Urruah came up against Rhiow as well: she braced herself so as to put no further pressure on Arhu. The four of them looked around the corner, into the red light.

Another of the spherical chambers lay around the corner of the passage. Or at least it had been spherical to start with. One side of it had been carved out into a perfectly smooth rectangular doorway, breaking through into another chamber off to Rhiow's left as she looked through the opening. In that chamber, lying curled, or sitting hunched, were five saurians: two deinonychi and three smaller ones that looked like some kind of miniature tyrannosaur. Their hides were patterned, though with what colors it was impossible to tell in this lighting. On the floor in front of them lay . . . Rhiow stared at them, wondering just *what* they were. They were made of metal: three of them looked like long bundles of rods, some of the rods polished, some of them brushed to a matte finish. A fourth device was a small box that was the source of the red light, without it being apparent in any way exactly how the light was getting out of it—the surface of the box was dark, but brightness lay around it.

The mini-tyrannosaurus nearest the carven door had been looking through the doorway into the darkness. Now it turned away and picked up one of the bundles of rods in its claws. As it did, the bundle came alive with a stuttering, glittering light, dull red like that which came from the box, though in a sharper mode: sparks of it ran up and down the metal rods. The saurian clutched the rods in one claw, ran its other claw down one of the sills of the door. More of that red light followed the stroke, as if it had flowed unseen through the body of the tyrannosaur and up to the stone; from the stone, a fine powder sifted down, remnants of some slight polishing of the surface. The other saurians watched, keeping very still but looking intent. From the rods came a soft, tiny sound: *Tink. Tink. Tink. Tink . . .*

The sixth claw . . . Arhu said silently. Rhiow looked where he did, and saw that other claw, the "thumb," bracing the bundle of rods exactly as a human's thumb would have. Her tail twitched at the sight of a saurian using a tool, something half-mechanical and, from the look of it, possibly half-wizardly. *If an* ehhif *came in and found his* houff *using the computer,* she thought, *I bet he would feel like this. . . .* At the same time, she found herself thinking of many a pothole crew she had seen on the New York streets in her time—one *ehhif* working, four of them standing around and watching him work—and suspected that she might have stumbled upon a very minor way in which her home universe echoed this one. . . .

"There is nothing more to do here," said one of the saurians who sat and watched.

"Yes. Let's go back to where the others are and wait for them," said another.

The mini-tyrannosaur, though, kept polishing the doorsill for a few more strokes. "This work gives me joy," it said. "When it is done, the gates will all be ours and will be turned to the Master's plan. When all is ready, he will lead us up out of the chill and wet and darkness, as he has done with others in the not-long-ago, up into the warmth and the light, and we will take back what was taken from us. The sundwellers may take our places down here, if they like. But none of them will; the Great One says they will all die, and there will be such a feasting for our people as has not been seen since the ancient days. I do not want to wait for that. I want it to come soon."

The others sighed. "The Leader, the Great One, he will know the way, he will show us . . ." they hissed, agreeing, but none of them got up to do anything further. Finally the mini-tyrannosaur lowered the bundle of rods, and the light of them went out.

"Let us go back, then," it said. "We will come back after sleep and begin the next work."

The saurians who had been relaxing on the floor got up, and picked up the other bundles of rods and the light box. The deinony-chus with the box went first, and the others followed behind, hissing softly as they went. Slowly the light faded away.

What do we do? Arhu said.

Follow! Rhiow said. *But be careful. It's very hard to sidle down here, as Saash said: better not to waste your energy trying.*

Should I make the light again? They didn't see it before.

Rhiow thought about that. *Not if we have their light ahead of us. But otherwise, yes, as long as we can't be seen from any side passages,* she said. *Normally they shouldn't be able to see in our little light's frequency . . . but things aren't normal around here, as you've noticed.*

Arhu twitched his tail in agreement, then waited a few breaths before following the way the saurians had gone, out the opening in the far side of the spherical chamber, and farther down into the dark. Close behind, silent, using the warm lizard-scent to make sure they didn't stray from the proper trail, Rhiow and Saash and Urruah followed.

Far ahead of them, over the next hour or so, they would occasionally catch a glimpse of that red light, bobbing through long colonnades and tunnels, always trending down and down. At such times Arhu would stop, waiting for the direct sight of the light to vanish, before starting forward and downward again. At one point, near the end of that hour, he took a step—and fell out of sight.

Arhu!

No, it's all right, he said after a moment, sounding pained but not hurt. *It's what we went down the other day, in the Terminal—*

?? Rhiow said silently, not sure what he meant.

When we went to see Rosie.

Stairs. Stairs? Here??

They're bigger, Arhu said. Indeed they were: built for bipedal creatures, yes, but those with legs far longer than an *ehhif*'s. From the bottom of the tread to the top, each step measured some three feet. A long, long line of them reached far downward, past their little light's ability to illumine.

Where are we in terms of the map? Saash said to Rhiow. *I'm trying to keep track of where the catenaries are going to start bunching together.*

Rhiow consulted the map and stood there lashing her tail for a few moments. *My sense of direction normally isn't so bad,* she said, *but all these new diggings are confusing me. These creatures have completely changed the layout of the caverns in this area. I think we're just going to have to try to sense the catenaries directly, or do a wizardry to find them.*

As to the latter, I'd rather not, Saash said. *I have a feeling something like that might be sensed pretty quick down here. You saw those tools. Someone down here is basing a technology around wizardly energy sources. . . .*

Yes, I saw that. Rhiow hissed very softly to herself.

So what do we do? Arhu said.

Go downward.

They went: there was not much option. The stairs reached downward for the better part of half a mile before bottoming out in a platform before a doorway. Cautiously they crept to the doorway, peered through it. The saurians had passed this way not too long before; their scent was fresh, and down the long high hall on the other side of the door, the faint red light glowed.

Arhu stepped through it—then stopped.

What?

It's not the same light, he said.

What is it, then?

I don't know.

Slowly he paced forward, through the doorway, turning left again. Another hallway, again trending down, but this one was of grander proportions than the corridors higher up in the delving, and it went down in a curve, not a straight line. Rhiow went behind Arhu, once more feeling the neural-inhibitor spell in her mind, ready for use. Its readiness was wearing at her, but she was not going to give it up for anything, not under these circumstances.

They softly walked down the corridor, in single file. Ahead of them, the red light grew, reflecting against the left wall from a source on the right. This light was not caused by any box carried by a saurian: Arhu had been right about that. It glowed through a doorway some hundred yards ahead of them, a bloom of light in which they could now detect occasional faint shifts and flickerings. The box-light had produced none such.

About twenty yards from the doorway, Saash stopped. Rhiow heard her footfalls cease, and turned to look at her. The faintest gleam of red was caught in her eyes—a tiger's eyes, in this universe, set in a skull with jaws big enough to bite off an *ehhif*'s head; but the eyes had Saash's nervousness in them, and the tortoiseshell tiger sat down and had a good hard scratch before saying, *I am* not *going through that door unsidled; I don't care* what *it takes.*

Rhiow looked at her, and at Urruah behind her.

Not a bad idea, he said. *If I have to go out there visible, I can't guarantee the behavior of my bladder.*

Let's do it, then, said Rhiow.

It was surprising how hard it was. Normally sidling was a simple matter of slipping yourself among the bunched and bundled hyperstrings, where visible light could not get at you. But here something had the hyperstrings in an iron grip, and they twanged and tried to cut you as you attempted to slide yourself between. It was an unfriendly experience. *I think the hardboiled eggs in the slicer at the deli around the corner must feel like this,* Urruah grunted, after a minute or so.

Trust you to think of this in terms of food, Rhiow said, having just managed to finish sidling. Arhu had done it a little more quickly than she had, though not with his usual ease: he was already padding his way up to the door through which the brighter reddish radiance came, and Saash was following him. *I suppose,* Rhiow added for Urruah's benefit as she came up between Arhu and Saash, and peered through the space between them, *we should think ourselves lucky there's not a MhHonalh's down here. . . .*

And she caught sight of the view out the doorway, and the breath went right out of her. She took a few steps forward, staring. Behind her, Urruah came up and looked past her shoulder, and gulped. Then he grinned, an unusually grim look for him, and said, *Are you* sure *there's not?*

A long time before, when she had first become enough of a wizard to get down to street level from the apartment Hhuha had before she and Iaehh became a pride, Rhiow had done the "tourist thing" and had gone up the Empire State Building. Not up the elevator, as an *ehhif* would, of course: she had walked up the side of it, briefly annoying (if not actively defying) gravity and frightening the pigeons. Once there, Rhiow had sat herself down on the parapet, inside the chain-link fence meant to dissuade *ehhif* from throwing themselves off, and had simply reveled in the sense of height, but more, of *depth,* as one looked down into the narrow canyons where *ehhif* and *houiff* walked, progressing stolidly in two dimensions and robustly ignoring the third. It was wonderful to sit there with the relentless wind of the heights stirring the fur and let one's perceptions flip: to see the city, not as something that had been built up, but to imagine it as something that had been dug *down,* blocks and pinnacles mined out of air and stone: not a promontory, but a canyon, with the river of *ehhif* life still running swift at the bottom of it, digging it deeper while she watched.

Now Rhiow looked down into the heart of the Mountain and realized that, even so young and relatively untutored, she had been seeing a truth she would not understand for years: yet another way in which the Downside cast Manhattan as its shadow. The Mountain was hollow.

But not just with caverns, with the caves and dripping galleries that Ffairh had charted. Something else had been going on in these greater depths for—*how* long? She and her team looked over the parapet where they stood, and gazed down into a city—not built up, but delved through and tunneled into and cantilevered out over an immense depth of open space as wide as the Hudson River, as deep as Manhattan Island itself: a flipped perception indeed, but one based on someone else's vision, executed on a splendid and terrible scale. The black basalt of the Mountain had been carved out of its heart as if with knives, straight down and sheer, for at least two miles—and very likely more: Rhiow was not much good at judging distances by eye, and (like many other New Yorkers) was one of those people for whom a mile is simply twenty blocks. Reaching away below them, built into those prodigious cliffs of dark stone, were level below level and depth below depth of arcades and galleries and huge halls; "streets" appeared as bridges flung across the abyss, "avenues" as giddy stairways cut down the faces of those cliffs. Hung from the cliffsides, like the hives of wild bees hung from the sides of some wild steep rocks in Central Park that Rhiow knew, were precipitous shapes that Rhiow suspected were skyscrapers turned inside out: possibly dwellings of some kind. There had to be dwellings, for the place was alive with saurians—they choked the bridges and the stairs the way Fifth Avenue was choked at lunch hour, and the whole volume of air beneath Rhiow and her team hummed and hissed with the saurians' voices, remote as traffic noise for the moment, but just as eloquent to the listening ear. All that sound below them had to do with hurry, and strife—and hunger.

Far down below in that mighty pit, almost at its vanishing point, a point of light burned, eye-hurting despite its distance: the source of the reddish light they stood in now, caught and reflected many times up and up the whole great structure in mirrors of polished obsidian and dark marble. Rhiow stared down at it and shuddered: for in her heart, something saw that light and said, very quietly, without any possibility of error, *Death.*

They stood there, the four of them, gazing down, for a long time. *Look at the carvings down there,* Urruah said finally. *Someone's been to Rockefeller Center.*

Rhiow lashed her tail in agreement. The walls of the cliffs were not without decoration. Massive-jawed saurian shapes leaned out into the abyss in heroic poses, corded with muscle; others stood erect on mighty hind legs, stately, dark, their tails coiled about their bodies or feet, as pillars or the supports of arches or architraves: scaled caryatids bent uncomplaining under the loads that pillars should have borne. Many of the carvings did have that blunt, clean, oversimplified look of the Art Deco carvings around Rockefeller Center—blank eyes, set jaws, nobility suggested rather than detailed. But they were all dinosaurs . . . except, here and there, where a mammal—feline, or *ehhif*, or cetacean, or canid—was used as pedestal or footstool, crushed or otherwise thoroughly dominated. No birds were represented; perhaps a kinship was being acknowledged . . . or perhaps there was some other reason. But, on every statue, every saurian had the sixth claw.

All right, Rhi, Saash said finally. *How many years has this been going on, would you say?*

I wouldn't dare guess. Saash—'Ruah—whoever even heard of saurians using tools?

It's news to me, Saash said. *But I wasn't thinking developmentally. How are we supposed to find the catenary "trunks" down in that? And you heard what's-his-face back there: they've been moving the catenaries around. Our map is no good anymore.*

And what about Har'lh? Urruah said. *If he's down here somewhere—how in the Queen's name are we supposed to find him?*

The sixth claw . . . Arhu said.

Yes, Rhiow said, *I'd say this is what that's for. And he said they were given it.*

She stood silent for a moment, looking into the depths. *We're going to have to try to feel for the trunk of the "tree,"* Rhiow said at last. *I know the feel of Har'lh's mind probably better than any of us: I'll do the best I can to pick up any trace of him. But range is going to be a problem.* Especially with her mind growing wearier by the moment of carrying the neural-inhibitor spell . . .

Behind her, Arhu was gazing down into the abyss, toward the spark of fire at its bottom. Rhiow looked at him, wondering what was going on in that edgy young mind. Perhaps he caught the thought: he turned to her, eyes that had been slitted down now dilating again in the dimmer light of the level where they stood. And then, very suddenly, dilating farther. Arhu's face wrinkled into a silent snarl: he lifted a huge black-and-white-patched paw and slapped at Rhiow, every claw out—

Completely astounded, Rhiow ducked aside—and so missed, and was missed by, the far longer claws that went hissing past her ear, and the bulk that blurred by her. Arhu did not make a sound, but he leapt and hit the shape that had leapt at Rhiow, and together they went down in a tangle, furred and scaled limbs kicking.

Urruah was the first to react, though Rhiow heard rather than saw the reaction: six words in the Speech, and a seventh one that always reminded her of the sound of someone's stomach growling. But at the seventh word, one of the shapes kicking at each other on the stone froze still; the other one got up, and picked his way away from the first, shaking each paw as he stepped aside. *I could have taken him!* Arhu said.

Bets? Urruah said. Perhaps the comment was fair, for the saurian was twice Arhu's size and possibly two and a half times his weight: lithe, heavily muscled, and with a long, narrow, many-toothed muzzle that could probably have bitten him in two, given opportunity. Rhiow stood there thinking that the opportunity might have fallen to her instead. She leaned over to Arhu, breathed breaths with him, caught the taste of fear but also a sharp flavor of satisfaction.

Thank you, she said. *I owe you one.*

No, Arhu said, *I've paid you back the one I owe you. Now we're even.*

Rhiow was taken aback—but also pleased: by so much this wayward kitten had grown in just a few days. *Whether he'll live much longer to enjoy the threshold of his adulthood,* she thought, *is another question.* But then there was no telling whether there was much left of *hers.*

She turned, as he did, to have a look at the saurian, lying there struck stiff as a branch of wood on the stones. *It's a variant of the neural inhibitor,* Urruah said. *Lower energy requirement, easier to carry: it's not instantly fatal. Say the word, and I'll make it so.*

No, Rhiow said. *I'll thank you for a copy of your variant, though. You always were the lazy creature.*

Urruah made a slow smile at her. Rhiow stood over the saurian, studied it. Compared to many they'd seen recently, it was of a slightly soberer mode: dark reds and oranges, melded together as if lizards were trying to evolve the tortoiseshell coloration.

We've got places to be, Rhi, Urruah said, *and we don't know where they are yet. Kill it and let's move on.*

No, Arhu said suddenly.

Urruah stared at him. So did Saash. *Are you* nuts? she hissed. *Leave it alive and it'll run to all its friends, tell them right where we are . . . and so much for—* She declined to say more.

Arhu stared at the saurian; Rhiow saw the look and got a chill that raised her fur. *Let his lungs go,* Arhu said to Urruah. *He's choking.*

Urruah threw a glance at Rhiow. She looked down at the saurian, then up at Arhu. His expression was, in its way, as fixed as that of the lizard—but it was one she had never seen on him before: not quite in this combination, anyway. Loathing was there. So was something else. *Longing . . . ?*

Who is *he?* she said to Arhu.

He switched his tail "I don't know." *The father,* he said. *My son. — He's got to come along. Urruah, let him go—!*

Rhiow had heard all kinds of tones in Arhu's voice before now, but never before this one: authority. It astonished her. She glanced over at Urruah. *Go on—*

He blinked: the wizardry came undone. Immediately the saurian began to roll around, choking and wheezing for air; Arhu backed away from him, watched him. So did all the others.

After a few moments he lay still, then slowly gathered his long hind legs under him and got back up on his feet. He was another of the mini-tyrannosaur breed, bigger than the last one they had seen. He turned slowly now in a circle, looking at each of them from his small, chilly eyes. His claws clenched, unclenched, clenched again. Each forelimb had six.

"Why am I still alive?" he said. It was a hissing, breathy voice, harsh in its upper register.

"*That's* the question of the week," Urruah said, throwing an annoyed glance at Arhu.

"Why did you attack us?" Rhiow said.

"I smelled you," it said, and glared at her. "You should not be here."

"Well, we are," Rhiow said. "Now, what will you do?"

"Why have you come down out of the sunlight into the dark?" said the saurian.

Glances were exchanged. *Tell him? Certainly not—* Then, suddenly, Arhu spoke.

"We are on errantry," he said, "and we greet you."

The saurian stared at him.

"You are not," he said, "the one who was foretold."

"No," Arhu said, in a tone of absolute certainty.

Rhiow looked at Urruah, then at Saash. *What* is *this?*

"What, then, will you do?" said the saurian, looking around at them.

Be extremely confused? Saash said. *I'll start chasing my tail right now if it'll help.*

Lacking any other obvious course of action, Rhiow decided to assert herself. "We have business below," she said: that at least was true as far as she knew. "We can't leave you here, now that you've seen us. You must come with us, at least part of the way. If you agree, we'll do you no harm, and we'll free you when we're done. If you disagree, or try to trick or elude us, we'll bring you by force; if you try to betray us, we'll kill you. Do you understand that?"

The saurian gave Rhiow a cool look. "We may be slow, trapped down in this cold place," it said, "but we are not stupid."

Rhiow licked her nose.

"Lead us down, then," Urruah said. "We don't wish any of your people to see us. But we must make our way well down there." He gestured with his tail over the parapet.

The saurian looked in the direction of the gesture. Rhiow wished desperately that there was some way to read expression in these creatures' faces, but even if there was, it was not a subject she had ever studied.

"Very well," the saurian said, and turned toward another passage-way that led from the parapet, the one from which it had leapt at Rhiow.

"Wait a minute," Arhu said. The saurian paused, looked over its shoulder at him: an oddly graceful position, tail poised in midair be-hind it, strong lithe neck supporting the long toothy head as it glanced around at Arhu.

"What's your name?" he said.

"*Sehhff'hhihhnei'ithhhssshweihh,*" it said: a long breath, a hiss, a breath again.

Urruah screwed his eyes shut in annoyance. Rhiow almost smiled: here was a creature who could sing *o'hra* in six different *ehhif* di-alects but who also claimed to hate languages. *Only new ones, and not for long,* Rhiow thought. "Well?" she said.

"Ith," Urruah said. "We'll call you Ith. Come on, Ith, walk in front of me."

Ith stepped forward and through the doorway, making his way downward on the path that led from it. Urruah went close behind him; after him went Arhu. Rhiow looked closely at Arhu's expression as he passed her. It was peculiar. There was scorn there, distaste, but also an intent look, an expression of near-relief, as if something that was supposed to happen was now happening. *And almost some kind of longing*— She would have given a great deal to slip into Arhu's mind and see more closely what was going on. The thought of sabo-tage, of wizardries being undone as if from the inside, was still on Rhiow's mind. But in the back of her thoughts, a voice whispered, *Don't disturb him now. Let what happens happen. It may make no dif-ference—or all the difference in the worlds.*

Saash gave Rhiow a glance as she passed her. Rhiow stood still for a moment, licking her nose nervously; the Whisperer was rarely so uncertain. *But ignoring her advice is rarely wise.*

Rhiow slipped through the doorway after Saash and followed her down into the darkness.

Eleven

♦

The way led along more dark stairs and corridors, all winding downward. Deep narrow openings pierced some of the walls: they might have been windows, except that no face could ever be seen looking through any of them. Others resembled doors, but they led nowhere except into small rooms that held only more darkness. "Why isn't anybody up here?" Urruah muttered, as they passed yet another of those deep windows and looked at it nervously. "There are enough of your people down that way."

"This is not a place where we are allowed to go," Ith said, and gave Urruah a look that to Rhiow seemed slightly peculiar.

"Oh, really?" Urruah said. "Then what were *you* doing up there?"

Ith paced along, his tail lashing, and made no answer.

Waiting for us, Saash said. *A spy, probably.*

"I was told to come," Ith said then.

"Why aren't you allowed to go up there?" Saash said.

A few more paces, toward the end of a colonnade, where Saash paused and looked through an empty doorway. "The upper levels are only for those on the Great One's errands to the world above," Ith said. "Others must stay in the depths until the time is right. It will not be long, we are told."

Saash threw Rhiow a look on hearing that: Rhiow twitched her tail to one side, a feline shrug. She was noticing that there was always a pause between a question to Ith and its answer. Rhiow found herself wondering whether this was because the creature was having comprehension problems—unlikely, they were working in the Speech— or whether it was simply deciding how it would best tell them as little as possible before it led them to where others of its kind, in greater numbers, could deal with them.

The situation was uncomfortable enough as it was. Rhiow now knew that Saash was right; Ffairh's map was useless in the present situation. The temptation to withdraw to safer territory above, and try to make another plan, with better intelligence, was very strong—but at the same time Rhiow was sure there was no time for this, that they would probably not make it back up, and even if they did, the only way to get better intelligence would be to keep on going downward, into the heart of this terror. *Either Ffairh never got down quite this far,* Rhiow thought, *or else this whole delving was still completely sealed off from the tunnels and passages he was exploring.* Which suggested another nasty possibility: that the saurians had been completely aware of where Ffairh had been *doing* his exploring, and had purposely avoided breaking through into any area where he might have discovered what was going on down here. Then, during some period when everything was running smoothly and there was no reason to expect an intrusion, the catenaries were relocated. . . .

Wizardry again, Rhiow thought. *There's no other way to do it. Some other wizard, or wizards . . .*

Her head was still going around and around regarding that problem. There were no saurian wizards. Which meant that either a renegade wizard of some other species was involved, maybe more than one; or (horrible concept) even one of the Powers That Be . . . with strong odds that Rhiow knew *which* one. The Lone Power did not often reveal Itself openly or work directly: that way It risked failure. But there had been exceptions to the rule, and doubtless would be again. . . .

The idea of renegades itself was controversial enough. Accepted wisdom was that the Lone Power could not "take over" a wizard, or influence him or her directly. But It could certainly try to turn the wizard's deeds dark in other ways: by trickery, propaganda . . . or sheer pain. And there were always whispers of wizards who had gone entropic, slowly but willingly going over to the broad, easy, downward path. . . . Rhiow remembered Har'lh's uneasy look as they discussed it. No one liked to think of the Oath abused—of that power, once given, turned against the Powers bestowing it.

The team walked on, passing down another long stair leading to yet another dimly lit doorway. The way they went, the way they *had* to go, unsidled, seemed all too exposed to Rhiow, but they had little other option now. At least they had remedied their oversight of scent. Rhiow was still cursing herself inwardly for missing this detail: it could have been fatal to them all.

Except it wasn't, Saash said to her privately. *Something has preserved us this far. You know what Ehef would say about it: this meeting was meant to happen this way. . . .*

Ehef's not here, Rhiow said as they made their way down a long deserted stair. *I wish to Iau he were.*

Any scent or touch of Har'lh?

Nothing. I just hope this spell's not interfering . . .

The spell that Urruah had quickly cobbled together to mask all their scents seemed to be working well enough. Saash had thought it might be worthwhile trying to smell like saurians rather than felines, and working a full shapechange to go with it, but Rhiow had disliked the idea. Besides the possibility of getting the saurian scent wrong and attracting attention that way, it seemed like too much expenditure of energy at a time when they were very likely to need it for something else much more important. So they went in their own shapes, as silently as they knew how, though there was some inward muttering. *I can't* smell *myself,* Saash said, pausing to scratch. *It's like being sidled, but worse. . . .*

Please. We've got other problems. We're running blind here: we have no real idea where our little friend is taking us.

I'm not sure we have any alternative but to keep working our way downward and seeing what we feel, Saash said. *It's almost impossible to sense the lesser catenary branches directly, with all this stone between us and them; you have to get close first. And even when you sense them, there's no way to tell how to get at them. There's no wall-walking down here, with the interference from the catenaries scattered all around; it's so fierce you might not even be able to initiate the state, let alone finish a wall-walk once you'd started.* One *of them, though, I can sense with no trouble.* Saash paused to scratch and wash again briefly, then indicated the point of light far down in the chasm. *The "River of Fire" down there . . . that's the trunk catenary, the main conduit.*

Rhiow stared at it. "It can't be. It was erect, and so were the branches, according to Ffairh's map! They would have run straight up through the Mountain. And as for it being the River of Fire, the *real* River—"

"I wouldn't know about that . . . except for what Arhu was saying. He said we'd have to cross it . . . and that certainly looks like one, down there, doesn't it? . . . even from way up here you can see the structure, it looks a little wavy . . ."

Rhiow lashed her tail. The true River of Fire, in the tales of the Fight between Iau and her litter and the Old Serpent, was formed by the Serpent's poured-out blood: it was the border between life and death, or rather between life and life. The pains and unneeded memories of a cat's last life were burned away in its crossing. . . "There's no way *that* can be the River," Rhiow said.

"Rhi, the ceiling of Grand Central—" Saash said.

"It's backwards," Rhiow snapped, "thank you very much, I know all about it."

"*Is* it?" Saash said. "Which direction are you coming at it from?"

Rhiow closed her mouth and thought about that.

Saash gave her a look. "If the 'Song of the Passing Through the Fire' *does* speak of the River, it doesn't say anything about which angle you come at it from! In space *or* time! A legend can just as well be founded in the future as in the past."

"It's called a 'prophecy,'" Urruah said, with a sideways glance at Arhu. "You may have heard of the concept."

"I'm going to hit you so hard . . ." Rhiow said to Urruah. "But you're in line behind sa'Rráhh, right now, and you'll just have to wait your turn. . . ."

But is this problem just with me? she thought. *Is it just that I find offensive the idea that the Last River is actually down at the bottom of a hole in the ground full of lizards?*

She sighed at herself then. The Old Downside *was* a more central reality than her "home" one . . . and there was no reason, really, why the physical reality of the gates' main catenary trunk could not itself be a mirror or reflection of the true River elsewhere. Though her own voice, speaking to Arhu, suddenly reminded her: *Don't start getting tangled up in arguments about which reality is more real than the next. . . .* And another thought occurred. Often enough, as you worked your way closer to the heart of things, other realities' myths started to become real around you. This otherworld might be more central than even Ffairh had suspected.

In any case, Saash said, *that's the main catenary trunk: no doubt whatsoever.*

With about a million lizards between it and us, Urruah said. *Wonderful.*

If we're supposed to be down here to find out what's the matter with the gates, Saash said, *and what's going wrong with wizardry, I'd say that's as likely to be a good place to start as any. If we head straight down there and start tracing the branchings outward—sideways, wherever they're going now—we can start troubleshooting.*

Rhiow sighed. Saash had a single-minded practical streak about repair work that sometimes ignored larger issues, like a whole inverted city full of nasty saurians between her and her proposed work area. Or maybe it was just a way to keep from thinking about issues closer to home. *Like being on your ninth life . . . How many of us put off thinking about it until it's right on top of us? And how do you know if, when you walk through the River the last time, whether you've done enough good over the course of your lives to come out on the far bank at all? . . .*

And Rhiow knew perfectly well that the crossing of the River was itself an idiom. She wondered—as Saash had to be wondering—was there time to bid farewell to one's mortality, one's felinity? Or did you simply find with your last death that you were now marooned in immortality forever, parted from the friends and the world you loved? The Tenth Life, always in the stories a thing yearned-for like the warm-milk-land of which queens sang to their kittens, suddenly now seemed less than desirable—high ground, yes, but barren and cold. . . .

She sighed. "Ith," she said, turning to him, "we need to get all the way down to the bottom . . . to where that great fire shines. Do you know a way?"

"Yes," he said after a moment. But he looked at Arhu when he said it, not at Rhiow.

"Is it a safe way?" Saash said.

"Yes."

"Is it safe for *us?*" Urruah said. "Or are your people going to come piling out at us from one of these doorways all of a sudden?"

"In that way," Ith said, looking from one of them to another, "there *are* no safe ways into the depths. The deeper you go, the more of my people will begin to fill every hall and stair. There are ways that are less frequented . . . for a little distance farther."

Every one of the team had his or her whiskers out, feeling for the sense of a lie; but it was harder to tell with a saurian than it would be with a Person. *If not impossible . . .* Rhiow thought, for the "feel" of a lizard's mind was nothing like a Person's. *We could spellbind him to tell the truth . . . but it might not help: who knows how truth looks to a saurian? And who wants to waste the energy at the moment? If we fritter away what we've brought, and find there's not enough to do the job we came to do . . .*

She lashed her tail. "Lead on, then," Rhiow said. She was about to add, "Arhu, watch him," when she realized that for the past while this had been quite unnecessary. Arhu had been watching Ith very closely indeed, with an expression of which Rhiow could make nothing whatever.

Ith stepped out, with Arhu behind, and the others following: downward they went again, down through long dark galleries, and down still longer stairs.

Ith stopped at the bottom of one stairway, near where it gave out onto yet another balcony. He peered out into the light, then stepped forward boldly. "Nothing funny, now," Urruah hissed, coming up behind him hurriedly, "or I'll unzip you, snake."

Ith looked cooly at Urruah. "What is 'funny,'" he said, "about looking at the Fire? Little enough good we get of it." He gazed down into the chasm.

"And little enough warmth you get out of it, either," Saash muttered, putting her head just far enough above the parapet to look down into the dim, buzzing, hissing chasm. "Why is it so *cold* down here? It's not normal. You usually get a steady rise in temperature as you head into the deeper crustal regions."

"My guess?" Urruah said. "It's being suppressed, somehow . . . to a purpose. You heard those guys before. If people are comfortable the way they are, you expect them to be good for much inflaming, much striving against another species?" He turned to Ith. "Am I right?"

A pause. "The near sight of the Fire is for the chosen of the Great One, of his Sixth Claw," Ith said, "as a reward, and a promise of what is to come, when we all stride under the sun again. The cold is a test and makes us stronger to bear what our forefathers could not have borne, and died trying to."

Arhu was leaning past Saash to gaze down into the teeming depths, toward the terraces and balconies far below them, where life went on, seemingly tiny, unendingly busy. "There's so many of you," he said. "What do you— What do you *eat?*"

Ith looked at him. "The flesh of the sacrificed," he said, his voice quite flat. "Many are hatched, and caused to be hatched, more and more each year, as the time of the Climacteric draws near. The old words speak of the time when the Promised One shall come and lead us forth; but there can be no going until we first hatch out uncounted numbers to fall in the last battle that will bring us out free, under the sky. The best and the strongest, the Great One's warriors in their hundreds of thousands, are fed well against that day that is soon to come. The rest of us live to serve them, to bring the day closer; and when our work is done . . . we find our rest within the warriors, who will carry our flesh to battle within their own, and our spirits with them. So the Great One says."

Rhiow shuddered. *An accelerated breeding program, half a species being raised as food for the other half . . .* It was worse, in its way, than the poor creature she had seen once before, being devoured by its starving comrades. Getting a little extra ration, the same way she might beg Hhuha for some of that smoked salmon . . .

Hhuha. The pain of her loss hit Rhiow again, hard, so that she had to crouch down and just deal with it for a few seconds. When she felt well enough to stand up once more, she found the others staring at her, and Ith as well.

"What exactly do you want here?" Ith said at last.

Saash threw a look at Rhiow that suggested she didn't think Rhiow needed to be quizzed by lizards at the moment. "There are other worlds besides this one," Saash said.

A pause. "That much we know," Ith said. "The Great One has spoken of it. And others," he added, a little thoughtfully; there was not quite the dogmatic sound to the addition that there had been to other such statements.

Urruah opened his mouth. Rhiow quietly lifted one massive paw and put a razory claw right into the part of his tail that was twitching above the stone. Urruah turned, snarling, and Rhiow made a sorry-it-was-an-accident face at him, which was excuse enough for the moment and caused Urruah to subside for now.

"What others?" Saash said.

"You mean other worlds?" Urruah said.

"Yes, others," said Ith, and Rhiow sighed, wishing she had put the claw in harder. "A hundred others, a thousand . . . all ours for the taking."

"By the gates," Saash said softly. "Using them not only for transit . . . but to change the nature of the species itself. Genetic manipulation . . . wizardly changes to the body and the spirit. Permanent shapechange."

Rhiow shuddered again. Such changes, from the wizardly point of view anyway, were both unethical and illegal; by and large, any given species had good reason to be the way it was, and there was no telling what chaos and destruction could be wrought in it by permanently shifting its mind-body structure.

"We must become strong and hard, the Great One has told us," Ith said. "We must not allow ourselves to succumb to the same forces that struck down our ancient mothers and fathers. When we are strong beyond any strength known by our kind before, when we no longer need air to breathe, or warmth to live, or even flesh to eat, then we will take everything that is for our own."

"But I thought what you *wanted* was the warmth," Arhu said then, sounding (correctly, Rhiow thought) confused. "And enough to eat . . ."

Ith stopped and blinked, as if coming up against this contradiction for the first time. Rhiow watched with covert satisfaction, for what she had heard Ith describing, without comprehension, was a favorite tactic of the Lone One—promise a species something better than what it had, then (after It has Its way) strip away whatever It had promised, leaving them with nothing at all. Finally Ith said, "That desire is only for this while: a remnant of the ancient way of life. Afterward . . . when we have come to our full strength, when we are no longer children, we will put aside the things of childhood and take our place as rulers of otherwhere—striding from reality to reality, making ours the misused territories of others, taking again what should have been ours from the start, had history gone as it should have. Warmer stars than this one will look down on us, strange skies and faraway nights; we will leave our people's cradle and never find a grave. No cold will be cold enough to freeze the spirit in us again; no night will be dark enough. We will survive."

More dogma, Rhiow thought, *but does he know it is? I doubt it.*

"Just who is this 'Great One'?" Urruah said after a moment.

"The lord of our people," said Ith, "who came to us in ancient days. The greatest of us all, the strongest and wisest, who is never cold and never hungry: the One who can never die . . ."

Arhu's head snapped right around at that. "And he has sent us the sixth claw," Ith said, "with which to build and make the mighty works he envisions. And more than that: he has sent us his own Claw, *his* Sixth Claw, Haath the warrior, who does the Great One's will and teaches us his meaning. It is Haath who will be our savior, the Great One's champion; he will lead us in the Climacteric, up into the sun, into the battle across the warm worlds that await us. It will be glorious to die in his company: those who do will never lose the warmth, they will bask forever."

"How nice for you," Saash murmured. Rhiow glanced at her with slight amusement, but then turned back to Ith and said something that had suddenly occurred to her.

"Why don't you sound very *happy* about all this?"

Ith looked at her and for the first time produced an expression that Rhiow was sure she was reading correctly: surprise and fear. "I am . . . happy," he said, and Rhiow simply wanted to laugh out loud at the transparency of the lie. "Who of our people would not be, at the great fate that awaits us?"

His voice started to rise. "We will take back what was once ours. Haath the valiant will lead us; and before him in fire and terror will go the Great One, the deathless Lord. We will come out into the sun and walk in the warmth, and all other life will flee before us—"

Arhu, though, was slipping up behind him, watching Ith's tail lash. For a moment Rhiow thought Arhu was having a flashback to kittenhood (not that he was that far out of it) and was going to jump on the saurian's tail; she held her breath briefly—Ith was, after all, formidably clawed and about ten feet high at the shoulder. . . . But at the same time Arhu's eyes met Rhiow's and indicated something behind her, in the shadows. . . .

The first saurian that leapt out at them met, not a spell, but half a ton of Urruah, claws out, snarling; right for its throat he went, and down they went together in a kicking, squalling heap. The others hesitated a second at the sight of the monster that had gone for their leader; the hesitation killed them, for Saash opened her mouth and hissed.

Bang!—

—gore everywhere, chill-smelling and foul, from the second of the saurians. Saash staggered with the backlash from the spell as the third saurian came at her: Rhiow aimed the same spell at it, let it go. The problem with the limited version was that you had to be careful where you aimed—and indeed, at the moment there was reason: Ith was still there, now crowded away against a wall. The other saurians were ignoring him, going for Rhiow and her team, but they would have little chance as long as the spell lasted. *That's the problem, of course,* she thought as she used it for the second time, and the third, and the fourth, and as Urruah got up, his jaws running with the pinkish-tinged saurian blood, and launched himself at another saurian, a deinonychus that was in the act of jumping at Saash from behind. Rhiow turned away from that one, which she had targeted, spun—

—something hit her: she went down. A horrible image of jaws twice as long as her head, of the perfectly candy-pink flesh inside that mouth, and set in it, about a hundred teeth of an absolutely snowy white, three times the size of any of hers, and all of those teeth snapping at her face— Rhiow yowled, as much in fury as fear; then ducked under the lower jaw, found the tender throat muscles, and bit, bit hard, to choke rather than to pierce for blood, while lower down she snuggled herself right in between the scrabbling clawed forelimbs—*not a deinonychus, thank you, Iau*—put her hind legs where they would do the most good, right against the creature's belly, and began to kick. It was armored there but not enough to do it any good; the plating began to come away, she felt the wetness spill out and heard the scream try to push its way out past her jaws. She wouldn't let it go and wouldn't let the air in: she let the rage bubble up in her, just this once, at the world that had been so cruel to her of late, and to which, just this once, she could justifiably be cruel back.

The struggling and jerking against her body began to grow feeble. It took a long time; *it would, with lizard meat,* Rhiow thought, but all the same she wouldn't let go. This body's instincts were in control for the moment and knew better than to let go of prey just because it seemed to have stopped moving. She flopped down over her kill and lay there, biting, biting hard, like a tom "biting for the tenth life" in a fight with another Person; and finally, when there had been no movement for a while, Rhiow opened her eyes, panting through her nose, but still hanging on.

Nothing else moved except with the sporadic twitching of saurian tissue too recently dead to know it yet. She mistrusted it; she hung on a little bit longer. Around Rhiow, the others were getting up, shaking themselves off, and grooming . . . though mostly for composure, at the moment.

"Come on, Rhi," Urruah said from behind her. "It's gone."

She let go, stood up, and shook herself. She was a mess, but so were all the others. It was like the catenary cavern all over again. She and Saash and Arhu and Urruah stood there, panting, recovering. Off to one side, wearing what looked like an expression of slow shock, Ith stood and gazed at the carnage. He looked hungry . . . but he did not move.

Very slowly, limping a little—Rhiow had strained one of her forelegs a little, hanging on to the saurian she killed—she went over to him, looked up at him. "Ith," she said, "why didn't you run away when you had the chance?"

He simply looked at her. "I have not yet done what I came for," he said.

"And just what might *that* be?" Urruah said, slowly making his way over to join Rhiow.

Ith looked at Urruah and said nothing. But from behind them both, Arhu said, "He warned me they were coming."

Urruah turned to look at him. "He has to be with us," Arhu said. "I've seen him here before, and farther down too. He knows the way: he's going to take us." He turned to look at Ith.

Ith leaned down a little and turned his head sideways to look at Arhu: a strange birdlike gesture, a Central Park robin eyeing a particularly juicy worm. But the "worm" was eyeing him back, and the look held for a good little while.

"Yes," Ith said finally. Rhiow and Urruah glanced at each other.

"Are you hungry?" Arhu said at last.

Ith looked at the bodies . . . then looked at Arhu.

"Yes," he said, but he did not move.

Urruah, watching all this, breathed a heavy snort of amusement and disgust down his nose, and turned to Rhiow. "We'd better clean this up and dispose of the scent, as far as possible," he said. "I'd sooner not leave any hints that we're down here; once they suspect us . . ."

Rhiow waved her tail "yes." "Your preferred method . . ."

"Right," Urruah said. "You four get ready to go on ahead." He started pacing around the space, laying down a circle to contain whatever spell he had in mind. Off to one side, Ith threw one last look at the remains of the battle . . . then turned away.

"Why didn't you help your people attack us?" Saash said to him, looking up from a few moments' worth of furious washing.

"I did," Ith said.

Rhiow stared at him. "How do you mean?"

"They heard me. That was why they attacked you."

Rhiow threw a glance over at Saash. *Does this make any sense to you?*

Rhi, it's a saurian. *Do I look like a specialist in their psychology? I can understand his words, but even the Speech can't always guarantee full comprehension when the mind-maps are so different. In any case, I'm not sure this boy isn't a few whiskers short of the full set. Why else would he be hanging around us, instead of joining in when the fight started or running off?*

Rhiow breathed out; she had no answers to that. "A few moments more for grooming," she said. "Then we'd better move out quickly. Urruah?"

"Almost set."

A few more moments was all it took. Then the team headed off as quickly as they could down the next long sloping corridor that Arhu indicated; downward again, around a bend and through a long tunnel, with Arhu in the lead for the moment, and Ith behind him. Faint echoes of the distant buzzing of the saurian city could be heard here; they raised Rhiow's hackles. *All those voices . . . all those teeth . . .*

"All right," Urruah said then, and paused, looking over his shoulder. "This should be far enough—"

Rhiow felt him complete his spell in his head. Immediately from behind them came a brilliant flare of white light. It held for two seconds, three . . . then went out. A faint smell of scorching drifted down to them.

"Let me go check it," Urruah said, and padded back up the way they had come, out of sight.

They waited, tense. Within a few minutes he was padding softly back down to them. "Clean," he said.

"What did you do?" said Rhiow.

"Heated the whole area to about seven hundred degrees Kelvin,"

he said. "Stone, air, everything. Sterile and clean." He wrinkled his
nose a little. "At the moment it smells a little like that toasted smoked-
sea-eel thing they do at the sushi restaurant on Seventy-sixth, but
that'll pass."

Saash screwed her eyes closed, and Rhiow made a little "huh" of
exasperation. "Only *you* could find a way to bring food into this," she
muttered. "Come on."

They all fell in behind Arhu and continued down the long dark
corridor. "Where are we going now?" Rhiow said to Arhu.

"Down toward the 'River' . . . I saw some of the way in his head."
He flirted his tail at Ith, who was now pacing nearby, a little off to
one side.

Rhiow twitched her tail slowly. "You've been through some
changes lately," she said.

I heard Her, Arhu said silently, looking up at Rhiow as they
walked, so intently that she almost had to look away: for the expression was entirely too close to that of the stone Iau in the museum. But
this expression was living and filled with certainty, though a sheen of
plain old mortal, feline doubt remained on the surface. *I was Her,*
Arhu said, and he shivered all over. *Now She's gone, but we need
Her . . . and if anyone's going to be Her, it has to be me. . . .*

"Playing God," Rhiow had heard her *ehhif* call it.

And the Oath? she said to him.

He twitched his tail "yes," a subdued gesture. *I took it. I think I understand it now. I have to keep it, though I'm not sure how. The Whisperer . . . has been giving me hints, but I don't know what to make of
them all. I'm afraid. I'm afraid I might screw up. I'm not an "old soul"
or anything.*

It's not "old souls" we need right now, Saash said. *Half of them keep
making the same mistakes over and over: why do you think they keep
coming back?* Rhiow shot a look at her: Saash ignored it. *We need
any soul that'll get the job done, whether its teeth are worn down or
not. Stop being self-conscious and just do what's there for you to do.*

He twitched his tail "all right," and slowly walked off.

We could let him go his own way now, I suppose, Saash said after a moment, watching him go. *He's accepted his Oath. He'll hold by it . . . poor kitten.*

Poor us, Rhiow said, *considering where our association with him has led us.*

True . . . Saash paced on a little way, and then said, *We're going to start having some trouble with defense shortly, if the number of these things attacking us increases significantly . . . and I think it will. The "explosion lite" spell is useful enough . . . but if we keep using it, it's going to "burn in" in short order. And we can't use the neural inhibitor in its full-strength version while our little friend's with us. I almost wish we could lose him . . . but Arhu says we can't . . .*

Rhiow glanced ahead of her, to where Arhu and Ith were now walking together. *Yes,* Rhiow said, *and that is* very *odd. . . .* It was peculiar to watch them: it was as if each very much wanted the other's company, though their bodies clearly loathed one another—tails were lashing, teeth were bared on both sides. The saurian was clearly shortening his pace to make it easier for Arhu to keep up with him as he paced along. Arhu, for his own part, was favoring Ith once more with that expression of recognition, unwilling but still fascinated.

". . . You said you were told to come," Arhu was saying to Ith. His voice was unusually soft, so much so that Rhiow almost couldn't hear it. "*Who* told you? Who else spoke?"

"I don't know," said Ith, after a very long pause indeed. ". . . I heard a voice."

"What did she say to you?"

Rhiow's ears twitched at that, and then at the slow certainty that started to come into Ith's voice, replacing the half-sullen, half-angry tone that had been there even while talking about his people's coming triumphs. "She said, 'The Fire is at the heart, and the Fire *is* the heart; for its sake, all fires whatever are sacred to me. I shall kindle them small and safe where there are none, for the wayfinding of those who come after: I will breathe on those fires about to die in dark places, and in passing, feed those that burn without harm to any; the fire that burns and warms those who gather about it, in no wise shall I meddle with it save that it seems about to consume its confocals, or to die. To these ends, as the Kindling requireth, I shall ever thrust my claw into the flames to shift the darkening ember or feed the failing coal, looking always toward that inmost Hearth from which all flames rise together, and all fires burn undevouring, in and of That Which first set light to the world, and burns in it ever more . . .'"

Saash, still walking along nearby, was watching Rhiow sidelong, obviously so stunned that she hardly dared to think out loud. Rhiow had hesitated only once over what she'd heard, the word "confocal," but the Speech made sense of it: *those who sit about the same Hearth, the same fire.* Rhiow licked her nose and swallowed, for all the rest of it she had understood perfectly. The words resonated in her chest and itched in her bones, as if she had known them forever, though she had only now heard them for the first time, in another species' idiom. The Oath, there was never any mistaking the Oath.

Yet at the same time she heard in her mind the words of the Ailurin verse: *Iau Hauhai'h was the Fire at the Heart.* . . .

Why is this coming in our *idiom?*

"She said, 'If you desire the fate that awaits you, then go to the heights, go to the forbidden places, the halls of the doors. Through those doors your fate will find you, and lead you to its heart. . . .'"

"She"? Which Power is he talking about? Which Powers deal with saurians, for pity's sake, except for the Lone One, way back when? Rhiow listened . . . but no answer came.

She licked her nose. *But, oh dear Iau . . . another wizard. A* saurian *wizard.*

The first *saurian wizard?*

And carrying his species' version of the Oath: an Oath in force. On Ordeal. Another wizard on Ordeal—

Great Queen of Everything, we're all *going to die down here!*

Twelve

The walk went on, and on, and on, always downward, and the air got slowly more chill. Memory of past minutes started to dull for Rhiow in the wake of the repetition of stair after long stair, endless tunnels and dark galleries. The adrenaline jangle of the earlier hours had passed now, leaving only a kind of worn feeling, a state in which moving cost much more energy than usual. Light was at a premium down here, everywhere but near the central chasm: and Ith kept leading them farther and farther into tunnels in the living rock, away from the central delving.

Maybe "living" was a bad choice of words, Rhiow found herself thinking, for once again she was starting to get that feeling that the stone was leaning in and listening to her, or as if she were trapped in some huge dark lung, the walls pressing in on the exhalation, out as the Mountain breathed.

Every now and then their path would take them out again toward the edge of the abyss. All of them went with great caution then: Ith himself began to creep along like a cat, taking a step, pausing, listening, taking another step . . . sometimes crouching hurriedly back into the dark with the rest of them as, some ways ahead, a muttering party of other saurians would pass. The occasional narrow window would give them a brief glimpse down into the abyss, but as they went deeper, Rhiow was finding these looks out into the open less of a relief from the claustrophobic "breathing" feeling than they had been at first. The buildings, the terrible dark sculptures, the scale of the place itself were beginning to weigh on her spirit. Rhiow had heard that there had been *ehhif* in times not too long past who had meant to build in this idiom: vast belittling architectures, meant to make the creatures using them feel small and impotent, minuscule parts of some mighty scheme instead of free creatures all walking in the air under Rhoua's Eye together. *The Sun,* Rhiow thought, *wouldn't I give a great deal for a sight of Her now? Real Sun, through real air . . . even New York air as brown as one of Urruah's hamburgers and full of ozone . . .*

But there was no hope of that now . . . and maybe never again. All Rhiow's life, it seemed, was being gradually drowned out in this darkness, with the occasional punctuation of glimpses of that faraway fire down at the bottom of the abyss. The city streets, sunrises and moonsets, the sound of honking horns, wind in the trees of the park, all of it was being slowly dissolved in still, black air, humming sometimes loudly, sometimes softly, with the buzz and hiss of saurian voices in their hundreds of thousands. *Maybe their millions. It seems likely enough. . . .* And as they crept very slowly closer to the fire at the bottom of things, paradoxically the cold increased: they couldn't yet see their breaths, but that would come soon, Rhiow thought. She shuddered. She hated the cold, but she hated more, at the moment, what it stood for—the One Who doubtless awaited them down at the bottom.

"These long walks," Saash said somewhat wearily, coming up beside Rhiow, "they really take it out of you. Remember that time on Mars?"

"Oh, please," Rhiow muttered. Early in their work together, she and Saash had been involved in the rescue of an Andorrin climbing expedition that had come hundreds of thousands of lightyears to scale Olympus Mons . . . not in present time, but while it was erupting, in a previous geological era. The rescue had involved a timeslide that Rhiow and Saash had had to pay for, long walks through endless caves looking for the lost climbing party, much hot lava, and a lot of screeching from the expedition leader when the climbers were spirited out of the mountain just before it blew its top in the final eruption that made it the biggest shield volcano in this or any other known solar system. After days of trekking through those caves, hunting the lost ones by scent and lifesigns, and not a word of thanks for their rescue out of any of the Andorrins' multiple mouths, Rhiow had come away from the experience certain that wizardry and its affiliated technologies should be confined to the Art's certified practitioners. But there were large areas in this universe where (in the words of a talented and perceptive *ehhif*) science had become truly indistinguishable from magic, mostly because they were recognized as merely being different regions of the same spectrum of power, both routinely manipulated side by side by species among whom wizardry was no more covert than electricity or nuclear fusion.

Rhiow glanced ahead at Arhu, half-expecting some reaction along the lines of "You've been to *Mars?*"—but he was paying no attention. He and Ith were still walking together, talking quietly. The temptation to eavesdrop was almost irresistible. Two wizards on Ordeal, one of them almost certainly the first of his species . . . *what was going on?* Impossible to tell, but their body language had not warmed in the slightest. The brains holding this discussion might belong to wizards, both part of the same kinship—but the bodies were those of cat and serpent, distrusting one another profoundly. Arhu was stiff-legged and bristling, and looked like he wished he were anywhere else. As for Ith—Rhiow was uncertain what his kinesics indicated, except that his body was leaning away from Arhu while his head and neck curved toward him as they talked. At the very least, the message looked mixed.

Saash was watching them, too. After a while she glanced over at Rhiow and said silently, *We're* all *going to die down here, aren't we? It's not just me.*

No, Rhiow said, *I'd say not.* Odd, how when it could have been just her, she would almost have welcomed it. *But no,* Rhiow thought to herself, *that's never really been an opportunity. We're in conjunct power at this point, "roped together" as the* ehhif *idiom would have it: what happens to one of us on this job, we've always known would happen to all of us. . . .* She wanted to laugh a little at herself, except that she felt so dead inside. *And here I was so worried about being shy an extra life. It's going to be a lot more than that, soon.*

Urruah, pacing along with them, looked ahead at Arhu and Ith, and lashed his tail in a meditative sort of way. *He wouldn't eat,* he said.

No. That was interesting. He didn't sound very happy, either . . . not like that other saurian we heard talking about their "Great One."

Saash looked thoughtful. *Neither did the saurians who were watching that one work,* she said. *They* are *individuals, Rhi . . . not everyone has to be completely enthusiastic about whatever's going on down here.*

All right, I know what you mean. It's just . . . it's hard to think of him as one of us. But he is . . . he wouldn't have been given the Oath, otherwise. And he definitely has a troubled sound.

They walked a little way more. Rhiow was still worrying in mind at the tone of Ith's voice. *Sweet Iau,* she thought, *I'm so tired.*

"Ith," she said suddenly.

He looked at her, as if surprised anyone besides Arhu would speak to him: and Arhu looked, too. "This way," he said. "A long way yet."

"No, that's not what I meant." Rhiow glanced at the others. "Let's stop and rest a little. I'd like to get the rest of this mess off me; the scent is potentially dangerous. And we can all use a breather. . . ."

I was wondering when you were going to suggest it, Urruah said, somewhat caustically, as he glanced around them, and then flopped down right where he was. *We don't all have your iron constitution.*

We don't all constantly load ourselves up with stuff from Mh-Honalh's, either. You should try cat food sometime. I know a good dietetic one. . . .

Urruah made an emphatic suggestion as to what Rhiow could do with diet cat food. Rhiow thought his idea unlikely to be of any lasting nutritive value. But she grinned slightly, and then turned back to Ith, who had hunkered down next to Arhu, by the wall of the long corridor where they sat. Arhu looked once up and down the corridor with a listening expression, then started washing.

"Arhu?" Rhiow said. "Anything coming?"

"Not for a while yet," he said, not looking up from washing his white shirtfront, now mostly pink.

"All right." Rhiow looked over at Ith. "You *are* hungry, aren't you?" Rhiow said.

Pause. "Yes."

"Then why didn't you eat, back there?"

A much longer pause. Arhu, in the middle of a moment's worth of washing, glanced up, watching thoughtfully.

"Because there was no one to force me," Ith said. "Workers are not given food often . . . but when it is given them, they must eat; if they are reluctant, they are forced . . . or killed. Warriors, also, are forced . . . or killed. If one will not eat and do one's work, whatever that might be . . . one becomes food."

"And you were about to . . ."

A very long pause, this time. "I looked about me," Ith said, very softly, "and realized I did not wish to be food." He stopped, and actually suited action to words, glancing around him guiltily as if afraid someone would hear; the sentiment was apparently heretical. "It seemed to me that there should be another way for us to survive. But if ever one spoke of such possibilities, one was found mad . . . and immediately sacrificed. People would say, 'The flesh tastes better when the mind is strange . . .' And they would laugh while they ate."

Rhiow looked at Saash, who shuddered, and Urruah, who simply made a face. "But I wanted to live my own life," said Ith, "not merely exist as meat in some warrior's belly." Another look around him, guilty and afraid. Rhiow found herself forced to look away in embarrassment. "A long time I kept my silence . . . and looked for ways to come away from the depths, some way that would not be forbidden. There were no such ways; all roads are guarded now, or sealed. . . . Finally I thought I would even try to go to the Fire and end myself there, rather than be food. I was going to go . . . I knew the ways; like many others I have gone out to gaze at the Fire, never daring to creep close. . . . Then the voice spoke to me."

"'All roads are guarded,'" Urruah said. "How did you get out, then?"

"I—" Ith hesitated. "I stepped—between things, I went—"

"You *sidled*," Arhu said. "Like this." And did it where he sat, though with difficulty.

Ith's jaw dropped. Then he said, "Even here, it is hard."

A second's look of concentration, and he had done it, too: though, as with many beginners, his eyes were last to vanish, and lingered only half-seen in the air, a creepy effect for anyone who didn't know what was causing it. Then he came back, breathing harder, and folded his claws together, possibly a gesture of satisfaction.

"Down here, yes, it's tough," Rhiow said. "It's the presence of the Fire down below us, and of other lesser ones like it. They interfere. It will become impossible, as we go deeper."

"But I *did* it there," Ith said, looking at her suspiciously. "My work is down deep; I fetch and carry for the warriors who are housed in the delvings some levels above that Fire. To come away I had to come by the guards who watch the ways up out of the greatest depths. It . . . was hard, it hurt . . ."

"The cheesewire effect," Urruah muttered. "Too well we know. But you got out anyway."

"I passed many guards," Ith said, looking sidewise at Urruah. "None of them saw me. Finally I came up here, where no one comes except workers who are sent under guard; they all passed me by. And I went where the voice told me to wait . . . and you came."

"Great," Urruah muttered. "He can sidle where *we* won't be able to. This is *so* useful to us."

"It might be," Rhiow said softly. "Don't laugh." But she looked at Ith uneasily. *If we needed proof, we've got it now. A saurian wizard . . .*

Saash looked at Ith, then glanced at Rhiow. *You're thinking he's responsible for what's been going on with the gates? It's crazy, Rhi. Ith hardly knows anything. He barely seems to know as much about wizardry at this point as* Arhu *did when we found him.*

If that's possible, Urruah muttered.

No, Rhiow said. *The problem's not just Ith. I want to find out more about this "Great One."*

I don't, Saash said. *I'm sure I know* exactly *Who it is.*

Me too, said Urruah, growling softly.

I wouldn't be too sure, Rhiow said. *Our own certainties may trip us up, down here. . . . After all, how certain were we that there were no such things as saurian wizards? And* now *look . . .*

"What will you do with me now?" Ith said.

Rhiow sighed, wishing she had the slightest idea. She could feel the weariness coming down on her more swiftly every second. "Look," she said to the team, "if we stay still too much longer, we're going to need to sleep, I think. I could certainly use some. Arhu, you're sure nothing's coming for a while?"

He got a faraway look. "A couple of hours."

"We'll sleep a little, then," Rhiow said to Ith, "and try to work out what to do later."

"Who'll sit guard?" Saash said, lying down with a look of unutterable relief, and not even bothering to scratch. Rhiow felt extremely sorry for her; she was not really built for this kind of stress.

"I'll take it," Urruah said. "I'm in pretty good shape at the moment . . . and I'm not hungry. Unlike some." He looked thoughtfully at Ith and settled himself upright against the wall, leaning a little on one shoulder, gazing down the long dark gallery.

Rhiow lay down and tried to relax. *At least a rest, if not sleep,* she thought; but neither seemed terribly likely. Her thoughts were going around in small tight circles, trying to avoid the image of Hhuha. . . . From off to one side, already, came the sound of Saash's tiny snore. *She never has trouble sleeping,* Rhiow thought with a touch of envy. *She confines her anxieties and neuroses strictly to her waking hours. I wish I could manage that.*

Over Saash's little snore came the sound of Arhu and Ith talking. It got loud sometimes.

"I was hungry, too," Arhu said. "All the time. Until I met them. Then things got better. They gave me *fh'astrramhi.*"

This is all we're going to need, Urruah said. *A dinosaur with a pastrami craving . . .*

Don't think I don't hear your stomach growling. You'd go for it just as fast as he would, and five minutes later you'd be telling him where to find the best pastrami on the Upper West Side.

"Come on, you two," Urruah said, "half the lizards in the place are going to come down on us if you don't shut up. Sorry, Ith, no offense."

They paid no particular attention. Urruah had to shush them several more times, and finally Arhu started staring at Ith in the fixed way that suggested he was trying to teach the saurian to speak silently. Rhiow wished him luck and put her head down on the stone, in the dark, and courted sleep. . . .

It declined to be courted. She kept hearing, in her head, one part or another of the saurian version of the Oath. *The Fire is at the heart: and the Fire* is *the heart: for its sake, all fires whatever are sacred to me. . . . I shall ever thrust my claw into the flames.*

Rhiow sighed and rolled over. *It really* is *our idiom . . . and the language is very like what's in the "Hymn to Iau," and the "First Song." All* the references to fire and flame used the Ailurin "power" words, the *auw*-stems and compounds, which had passed into the Speech as specialist terminology.

But why should this child be using our words? . . . For any species' Oath always has to do with the form of it originally taken by the wizards among the Mothers and Fathers of a species, after Choice. Its form is set in their bones and blood, so that wizards of that species find it impossible to forget, and it is most specific to their own kind and mode of existence, as it should be. Even nonwizards of many species know parts of their own species' Oath in one form or another, often restated in religious or philosophical idiom.

Rhiow smiled a little at herself then. *What do I mean, "this child"?* Who knew just *how* old Ith was? Rhiow got a general feeling that he wasn't out of latency yet; but who knew how long these saurians' latency period was? *Though there were supposedly some dinosaurs who mothered their hatchlings for years at a time. Long latency-to-lifespan ratio makes for the best wizards, Ffairh would always say.*

But I still don't get it. Why Ailurin?

She rolled over again, disturbed by the puzzle. The connection between the feline world and the reptilian world was an ancient one, easily summed up in a single word: enmity—the Great Cat with the sword in his paw, sa'Rráhh the Tearer with her fangs in the Serpent's neck. Now Rhiow found herself thinking: *Is there something* else *to this connection? Something that got lost? Do we have some old history together?*

And how could that be? The saurians passed away long before felinity evolved into even its most archaic forms or became sentient.

Time, though, was a dangerously inconstant medium . . . and it was always unwise for a wizard to automatically assume that any two events were unconnected. The structure of time was as full of holes and slides and unexpected infracausal linkages as the structure of space was full of strings and hyperstrings and wormholes—

"But why not?" Arhu suddenly said aloud.

"I can see you looking at me," Ith said.

"Of course I'm looking at you—"

"Not that way. With the *other* eye."

Rhiow flicked an ear in mild surprise.

"What's wrong with that?"

"It sees too much. It makes me see . . . you." No question about it: Ith's voice sounded actively afraid. "Your kind."

"You scared?" Arhu's voice was louder.

"I do not wish to see this," Ith said. "The things—the pain my kind have, that I have, it is enough. *Your* pain as well—"

"I told you, *do it in your heads,*" Urruah said, "or I'm going to come over there and bang those heads together. You two understand me?"

Arhu and Ith—half a ton of moon-and-midnight panther, a ton and a half of patterned hide—glared at Urruah together, and then turned away with an identical eye-rolling teenagers' look, and locked eyes again.

Rhiow sighed and lay back again, thinking with slight amusement of Arhu saying, just the other day, *I don't want to know this about them; it'll only make it harder to kill them when the time comes.*

So now you hear it from the other side. Well, probably do you good to see things from his point of view. Do us all good, I suppose, if there were more of that . . .

She sought back along the interrupted train of thought. The nature of the old saurian Choice . . . she wondered if it was less simple than the Whisperer might initially have indicated. Not just a straightforward choice between good and evil, or obedience to the Powers and disobedience . . . but something more difficult: perhaps multipartite. And prophecy and the serpentine kind had long been associated in various species' myths. *Did they look ahead then,* Rhiow thought, *during the Choice, and see their possible futures?* The meteoric winter would have been part of what they saw; the Powers would have looked ahead in time and known it to be an inevitable consequence of the Lone One's involvement with this species. And at least a couple of the fates springing from it were easy enough to imagine. One would be the fate of the saurians in Rhiow's universe—almost all their species killed, except for a few of the most rugged survivors, who would forget their former greatness and dwindle into the modern reptilia; mere animals, shadows of what was . . . Another would have been this scenario: the saurians retreating down here into the darkness to save themselves, remembering what they once were, but also longing eternally for what once had been, and hating what they had become, and the Choice they had been forced to make . . . *I wonder,* Rhiow thought, *whether the saurians in our universe got the better of the deal. Better to be animal than to live like this.*

But it wasn't my Choice. It's theirs *. . . they're stuck with it.*

It's a shame you can't trade in a Choice after a test run, though, and say to the Powers That Be, "Sorry, the Lone One fooled us, this Choice is defective, we want another chance."

The silence that fell in Rhiow's mind in the wake of the idle thought was so profound that it practically rang. It was familiar, that silence: the Whisperer suggesting that you might just have stumbled onto something. . . .

Rhiow's eyes widened as she reexamined the thought.

The Choice offered to the forefathers and foremothers of the Wise Ones . . . could it be that it was defective? Flawed, somehow? *Incomplete?*

Ridiculous. Whoever heard of an incomplete Choice before? There's a pattern. The Lone One turns up . . . says, "Would you like to live as the Powers have told you you must, or take a gamble on another way that might work out better?" And you gamble, and fall: or refuse . . .

And then Rhiow stopped.

But the saurian Choice *had* to be incomplete. *There had been no wizards there.* And there *had* to be wizards: the whole spectrum of a species' life, both natural and supranatural, had to be represented for the Choice to be valid.

Or . . . She stared at the stone between her paws. *No. A species' Choice is its own.*

Or was it? *If the species was linked to another . . .*

. . . did the other have to be there, taking part, as well?

Taken together with Ith's Oath, with the Ailurin words in it . . .

. . . the thought shook Rhiow. The People were their *own.* They were utterly independent. That some other species would have been involved in *their* Choice was unthinkable . . . a challenge to their sovereignty over themselves. That they should be *ancillary* to some other species' Choice . . .

That was simply intolerable.

But Rhiow got the cold, no-nonsense feeling in her gut, when she turned to the Whisperer, which suggested that this might indeed be the case.

If this Choice was incomplete . . . it can be completed now. By a saurian wizard . . . and those intended to help him complete it, to judge by the language in it. His assistants: his people's supplanters . . .

Us!

She writhed a little, then cursed, and went over the Whisperer's head.

Iau, why are you dumping this on me?

You were there, came the answer, definite and instantaneous, its Source unmistakable. *Or rather: You were* not *there. You are there now.*

Choose.

And the choice was plain. Choose one way, refuse your species' help, and drive the serpents out into the cold and the dark, and damn them all. Let life be as it is, unchanged and stable, to be relied upon.

Choose another way and lose your species' autonomy forever, or whatever illusion of it you have had until now. The People's whole proud history becomes merely a footnote, a preliminary to the advent of these newborns, unable to make their own way without help; midwives to a race that had its chance and lost it, a million years ago. Nature killed them. Let nature be the arbiter: their time is over for good.

Yet nature is not innocent when the Lone One drives it. Or, rather: it remains innocent, not knowing who holds the wheel and uses it as a weapon. Is the storm to blame, or the Lone Power, when the lightning strikes and kills some noble soul about the business of saving life? Do you blame nature or sa'Rráhh when a cab comes too fast around the corner and—

Rhiow's tail lashed. *Devastatrix,* Rhiow said inside her, *I know your work. You will not fool me twice.*

Yet it was not a question of anyone being fooled, anymore. Here was a Choice that had not been completed at the beginning of things. The Lone One—*illegally??* Rhiow thought, shuddering at the concept—had convinced another species that its Choice had been made. They had suffered, had died in their millions (billions?) for the Lone Power's amusement, for the sake of a technicality, an injustice done that the victim-species was incapable of perceiving.

Now someone had come along and perceived the injustice, the incomplete Choice. *What do you do?*

Pass by on the other side? Rhiow was a New Yorker; she had seen her share of this. *Make a stink? Get yourself killed as a result?* She had seen this too.

And getting yourself killed would be the least of it. You were interfering in the business of gods and demigods, here. What happens, in the human idiom, when you take the Lone Power to court and try to convict It of malfeasance? A slippery business, at best. But the destruction of much more than your body would be fair to expect if you failed.

Oh well, Rhiow thought, *what do I need all these lives for, anyway?* The thought was bitter. Memories of Hhuha, unbidden, definitely unwanted at the moment, kept shocking through her like static on a rug in winter every minute or so, and the pain they caused Rhiow was beginning to tell. Anything that would stop that pain was beginning to look welcome.

Your hands on the wheel, though, she said inwardly to sa'Rráhh, fluffing up slightly. *Not an accident. There are no such things.*

Unfair, that at the time when I would most like to die, I must now fight hardest to live longest. And for the sake of these miserable, bad-smelling, cold-skinned snakes. She hissed in fury, causing Urruah to open his eyes a little wider and stare at her. *Iau, you rag-eared kitten-eater, I hate this, I hate You,* why me?

No answer, but then, when someone was yowling abuse at you, a dignified silence was the preferred response. Rhiow thought of the two Himalayans down the block and growled at herself, at her own bad manners, at life in general. *Unfair . . .*

You found it. You fix it.

The universe's eternal principle. Repair yourself if you can. Spend the least possible energy doing it. If you can't manage it . . . tough. And Ehef's succinct comment on Rhiow's observation long ago that this seemed mean-spirited of the Powers, and hard on Their creation: *What do you think this is, a charity?*

She sighed. *I was right,* Rhiow thought, *we are certainly all going to die.* For during Choice, some of the participants always die: no Choice is valid without that most final commitment. And if even one of the team died, all would be trapped below: all would die together.

The only thing we can do, I suppose, is make sure we make it work . . . make it all worthwhile.

Yet the other side of the paradox was that, for the Choice to take, some must also survive; otherwise there will be no one to implement it.

That'll be Ith, I suppose.

But who even knows if Ith will cooperate? For everything would turn on him, at last. It was all very well to think about him taking the part of the saurian wizard who should have been present at his People's choice, and remaking it, or rather making it for the first time— becoming, as it were, his People's Father. But his ambivalences were likely enough to destroy any such chance: he was as angry and uncertain in his own way as Arhu had been.

But if we don't get him to cooperate somehow . . . Those empty doorways in the upper corridors . . . they would not be empty for long. Rhiow thought of places like the great Crossroads worldgating facility on the sixth planet of Rirhath B: many permanently emplaced gates, leading into thousands of otherwheres, and used freely for travel by species accustomed to such technologies, part science and part wizardry. The Old Downside would become such a place if the Lone One had its way with the saurians. Those doors would be filled with vistas of other worlds, forced open in places previously innocent of such travel—and out through them would pour armies of warrior lizards, intent on killing whatever they found. "Misused territories": that had been the line from the catechism taught to Ith by the Great One. Ith fortunately seemed to have renounced it, but millions of others of his kind, it seemed, would not. They would take other worlds gladly: the lost race would become masters of an interstellar empire—even an intercontinual one.

Still . . . Arhu had said it when asked who Ith was: *The father. My son. You've got to bring him along. . . .*

She glanced up at them and found them nearly nose to nose now, against the wall and glaring at each other again.

You can't just sit around when this is what happened to your people, Arhu was saying loudly to Ith. *You* have *to do something. You saw. You were tricked!* His tone was just a touch uncertain; he was new to this kind of advocacy . . . but he was doing his best.

Then Rhiow blinked. "Why, you little monster," she muttered, "you were in my head *again!!* Urruah, did you know that he—"

"Rhi, you're *loud* sometimes when you muse," Urruah said, with slightly malicious amusement. "Sorry, I know it's probably to do with—Sorry," he said abruptly, and sat down and started to wash.

Rhiow felt the pain bite her again. She swallowed, licked her nose a couple of times, tried to put it out of her mind.

The Great One would have His reasons, Ith said, very slowly.

Yeah! Killing the whole bunch of you, and everything else It can get Its hands on! Can't you see?

I see too much. You see too much. There is blood everywhere; it runs across the world's face, and nothing we do will stop it.

Arhu licked his nose. *That's not right. It's to stop that kind of thing that we've come.*

You cannot stop it, or even change it. Much less can I change it. Ith bowed his head down to Arhu again, locked eyes with him. *This is typical mammal-thought: quick questions, quick answers, the hope that everything will be all right with action taken now and done in a moment. Perhaps matters would improve for a year, or two, or ten. But in fifty? Two hundred? Five hundred? All will be again as it was. More will have died. The pain will go on, the blood will run.*

You're wrong, Arhu said. *You have to help us with what we've come to do. It's not just for us. It's for everything!*

Everything, Ith said, *is foul.*

Arhu couldn't find anything much to say for a second.

All there is here is death, Ith said. *Those who will kill eat those who must die so that others can kill. When we come up into the sun, we will kill again. How many lives must pass before it all ends? Here, under this so-warm sun, and on other worlds, and in places where there are not even stars to shine, places completely strange to us: how many more of every kind will die? Each of those places has its own life: we will come into each one and destroy it.* The image, which had run vaguely through Rhiow's mind, ran clear through his own—his gift, or Arhu's Eye, could see it all: endless planes and planets, devastated. The immense distances between galaxies, between continua, would not be enough to stop a race of saurians made immortal by combined technology and wizardry. *And finally, That Which has used us to destroy everything will destroy us as well . . . laughing that we were fools enough to be Its instruments. I hear Its laughter even now, for the process is well begun.*

. . . And you know all this to be true, Ith said, leaning down more closely to Arhu; and suddenly the air itched with wizardry, spelling done without diagrams, but in the mind . . . if it *was* spelling, and not some saurian congener to the Whispering. *I see it in you, as* you *have seen it, though you have denied the sight. I see you too have heard the laughter. Forward in time: and back.*

Arhu looked up into Ith's eyes, an expression of horror growing on his face, his eyes going wide, slowly going almost totally to dark. He crouched down, still gazing up into Ith's eyes, his claws starting to dig into the stone, scrabbling at it. Arhu seemed unaware of what he was doing.

"They were crying, first," he said softly. "Not laughing. *Ehhif* have such weird sounds, you can't tell them apart half the time . . . But it was warm. Our dam was there, so we weren't afraid of the noises they made. The little ones, the *ehhif*-kits, they were crying, but they did that a lot if you scratched them, or when they scratched each other. I didn't know the words then. Now I know them. 'Daddy, please, Daddy, let us keep them, let us keep just one, just one, Daddy . . . '"

Rhiow rolled quietly upright, glanced over at Urruah. He was still sitting, leaning against the wall, his eyes closed down to slits, but he was awake, watching and listening. Saash had her back to Rhiow, but Rhiow saw an ear flick, just once.

Arhu lay still gazing up into Ith's eyes, his claws working, working on the stone. "He said, 'We can't keep them, the landlord won't let us have more than one, I *told* your mother not to let her out until we got her spayed, well, it's *her* fault, you take it up with her. . . .' He picked us up. He wasn't bad about it, he was always careful when he picked us up. He put us in a dark place. It rustled. He closed it up. We couldn't smell our mother anymore. We heard her crying then, we tried to get to her, but we couldn't see, it was dark, we were all jammed together in the dark, and then the noise started."

Rhiow swallowed, watching the convulsive, obsessive movement of Arhu's claws on the stone. "It was loud. We didn't know what it was. A bus, I think now. We couldn't smell anything but each other, and some of us got scared and made *hiouh* or *siss* in the bag, it got all over us and smelled terrible, we could hardly smell each other anymore. The noise stopped; we were crying, but no one would let us out, we didn't know where our dam was— Then something pushed us hard against one side of the bag. It felt strange, we were falling, we tried to come down on our feet. Then there was another big noise, we came down hard, it hurt. . . ."

Arhu swallowed. The fear in his voice was growing. "It was cold. We were crying and trying to get out, but the black stuff wouldn't give no matter how we clawed at it, our claws weren't any good. And then we hit something, and after that it started to get wet inside, not just from our *siss*. Wetter and wetter. A lot of water. The bag was getting full. There wasn't air. We kept falling in the water, and it got in our faces, we couldn't breathe. We tried to stay up . . . but the only way we could stay up was by climbing on each, climbing on each other . . ."

Saash had slowly come to her feet now and was slipping close to Arhu, but he paid her no attention, only gazing up at Ith. It was as if he saw, in those reptilian eyes, the one vision he had been steadfastly denying himself, or saw it mirrored, as the other saw . . .

"They bubbled," Arhu said, his voice dropping to a whisper. "They bubbled when they breathed the water. They stopped moving. Their smells went away. They died. And the rest of us had to climb on them, on their bodies, and put our heads up and try to breathe, and there was less and less room, less and less air, and it was so cold."

Barely even a whisper, now; even that faded. "So cold. Nowhere to breathe. Sif died last. She was my twin almost, she had my same spots. She bubbled underneath me. I felt the breath go out, I smelled her scent go away. . . ." *I was the last one. I was the strongest. I climbed best. Then the last air went away. I started to bubble. It was cold inside me. It got black. I said, Good, I want to be with my littermates. But I couldn't. Something grabbed the thing, the bag we were in, and pulled us out, and broke the bag open. It was an* ehhif. *It saved me, it dumped me out on the ground.* Incredible bitterness at that. *It dried me off, it took me to a bright place, they fed me, they put me in a warm room. Later another* ehhif *came and took me away. She fed me, she kept me in her den. She gave me a* hiouh *box, but every time I made* siss *or* hiouh *in it, it would smell of them, and I would re-member my brothers and sisters, how* they *smelled finally, and how they started to bubble, and I couldn't go back to the box. I had to make the* hiouh *somewhere else in the* ehhif*'s den. And then she took me out of her den and put me in a shoulder-bag and took me in another loud thing, a bus, and she put me down in the street, and she went away fast, in another bus. I couldn't find her den again. I went to live be-hind the Gristede's.*

His claws were starting to splinter. Saash, behind him, began slowly to wash his ear. Arhu was still looking up at Ith, into the saurian's eyes.

I heard the laughing, Arhu said, over the soft grating of his claws on the stone. *When the* ehhif *threw us in the water. And while we were drowning:* that *laughing. It knows nothing can stop It, or what It does. It can do it whenever It wants. It was the Lone One at the bottom of the* ehhif*'s heart that made it do that. It's always at the bottom. I see It now. And It's at the bottom* here. *I see . . .*

You also see, Ith said, *how there is nothing but the pain, no matter what we do against It.*

There was a long, long pause: almost one of Ith's own.

I don't know, Arhu said.

He said nothing more. Saash washed him, her purr of pain and compassion rumbling and echoing loud in the long dark hallway. The flexing of Arhu's claws was slowly stopping; his head dropped so that he was no longer staring at Ith. Arhu lay there gazing down at the barren black stone of the floor, and did not move or think, at least for any of them to hear.

Rhiow slowly got up and paced over to where Urruah leaned against the wall. *What now?* Urruah said to her.

Let him alone for a while, Rhiow said. *He needs time to recover, after that. And frankly, after hearing it, so do I.* Arhu's pain had shaken Rhiow, in some ways, worse than her own had been doing.

They went away and sat down together, leaving Saash with Arhu, while Ith leaned down over them both as Saash washed, a peculiar kind of company.

So, Urruah said. *The Lone One tried with you, and failed . . . I think. Now It's tried with* him *. . . and there's no way to tell how It's done. Who's next?*

I think, Rhiow said, *It may have tried with him once already. And it failed then. I'm not sure . . . but It* may *have tried one time too many.*

But It's getting desperate, Urruah said. *If these attempts on our effectiveness fail, It's just going to try brute force, a hundred thousand saurians or more, the way it dumped them out into Central Park. It'll wear us down, and kill us without us doing anything useful.*

Let's not give It the chance, then, Rhiow said. *We'll go straight down.*

But how, *Rhi? You heard him: the lower halls are full of these things.*

I don't propose to go the way It *wants us to go,* Rhiow said. *Look. I'll watch now: I couldn't sleep now no matter what. You try at least to get some rest . . . an hour's worth, even. Ffairh always said that a rest was better than no sleep.*

I'd give a lot to have Ffairh here.

You're not the only one. Go on, 'Ruah, take a nap.

He lay down, and shortly afterward, he was snoring, too.

Rhiow sat in the darkness and watched over them. Saash had nodded off again, a little while after Arhu did, so that only Rhiow and Ith
were awake. Ith was looking down at Arhu. For a while she gazed at
him, wondering what went on inside that mind. His face was hard to
read. Even *ehhif* had been easier, at first; and there was always the
one who had become easiest to read after their association. . . .

The thought of Hhuha, of the cold white tiles and the metal table,
bit her in the throat again. Rhiow shook her head till her ears rattled,
looked away, tried to find her composure again. *Oh, to be able to howl
like a* houff *or weep like an* ehhif, she thought; *why can't we somehow
let the pain issue forth, by some outward sign? Dignity is worth a great
deal, Queen of us all, but is it worth the way this pain stays stuck inside?*

She looked up and saw Ith looking at her, silent and thoughtful.

You too know the pain, he said inwardly. Rhiow shivered a little,
for there was warm blood about his thought, but no fur, not even as
much as an *ehhif* wore: the effect was strange.

Yes, she said.

*But still you will do this. And die. I saw that in him, and in my own
vision as well.*

Rhiow licked her nose.

Yes.

He says . . . this fight has happened before.

Rhiow wondered just how to put this. *Our kind,* she said, *or
rather, the Great Ones of our kind, have fought—this deadly power,
the Lone Power—before.*

And lost.

*They defeated the Old Serpent, as we call that avatar of the Lone
One,* Rhiow said.

*But it made no difference. It lives on, though your gods themselves
died killing It.*

"Evil," said a small and very tired voice, "just keeps on going."
Arhu was sitting up again, but hunched and huddled. He glanced at

Ith. "He's seen it. So have I. And it'll still just keep happening, no matter what we do here. Even if we win. Which we can't . . ."

Rhiow swallowed. "It's not that simple," she said. "Evil isn't something the One made, Arhu. It's a broken image—a perversion of the way things should work, purposely skewed toward pain and failure. Sa'Rráhh, our own image of the Lone One, and of the evil inside us, it's the same way with her. She invented death, yes, and now tries to impose it on the worlds. But her ambivalence is a recent development, as the Gods reckon time . . . and They think the evil is something she can be weaned of. For when the Three went to war against the Serpent, didn't she go to the Fight with Them, and fall with Them, at the dawn of time? That's a way of saying how divided her loyalties are, for she *is* the Old Serpent as well."

"It's confusing," Arhu said. Ith merely looked thoughtful.

"It's mystery," Rhiow said, and had to smile slightly despite her pain, for old Ffairh had said the same thing to her, when she said the same thing to him. "Sometimes mystery is confusing. Don't fear that; just let it be. . . . But what time is *about,* they say, is slowly winning the Lone One back to the right side. When that happens, the Whisperer says—when a billion years' worth of wizards' victories finally wear sa'Rráhh down enough to show her what possibilities can lie beyond her own furious blindness and fixity—then death and entropy will begin to work backward, undoing themselves; evil will transform its own nature and will have no defense against that final transformation, coming as it will from within. The universe will be remade, as if it had been made right from the beginning." And she had to gulp a little herself then, at the sudden memory of the words the Whisperer had sent her to find, the fragment of the old spell: *he inflicteth with the knife wounds upon Aapep, whose place is in heaven—*

The look on Arhu's face was strange. "So," he said after a long pause, "the Lone Power isn't Itself completely evil."

"No. Profoundly destructive, yes, and filled with hate for life. But even the evils It tries hardest to do sometimes backfire because of Its own nature, which is 'flawed' with the memory of Its earliest history, the time before It went dark. That flaw can be a weapon against It . . . and has been, in many battles between the First Time and now.

But we have to be guided by Iau's own actions in our actions against the Lone One. For even She never tried to destroy the Lone Power, though She could have. She merely drove sa'Rráhh out, 'until she should learn better,' the song says. If the Queen Herself believes that the Lone One can be redeemed, who are we to argue the point?"

Arhu looked off into the distance, that million-mile stare again. It was a long, long look . . . and when he turned back to Rhiow, his expression was incredulous. "It's started to happen already. Hasn't it?"

"That's what the Whisperer says," Rhiow said. "When you look around the world, it's impossible to believe. All the death, all the cruelty and pain . . ." She went silent, thinking of white tile, a steel table, and a shattered body, and Iaehh's inward cry of grief. "But mere belief doesn't matter. Every time one of us stands up knowingly to the Devastatrix, she loses a little ground. Every time one of us wins, she loses a little more. And the Whisperer says that the effect is cumulative. No wizard knows whether his or her act today, this minute or the next, might not be the one that will finally make the Lone Power say, 'I give up: joy is easier.' And then the long fall upward into the light, and the rebirth of the worlds, will start . . . "

She sighed, looked over at Arhu wearily. "Is it worth fighting for, do you think?"

He didn't answer.

"You have said the word I waited to hear," Ith said. "The feline Lone Power—sa'Rráhh?—*is* the Old Serpent. Our peoples are one at the Root . . ."

Rhiow blinked.

"You're right," Arhu said, getting up. Suddenly he looked excited, and the transformation in him was a little bizarre, so that Rhiow sat back, concerned, wondering whether the shock of his traumatic memory had unsettled him, kicked him into euphoria. "And we can fix everything."

"I thought you said we were all going to die," Urruah said abruptly.

Couldn't sleep either, huh? Rhiow said.

There was a sardonic taste to Urruah's thought. *I'll sleep tomorrow . . . if ever.*

"Oh, die, *well,*" Arhu said, and actually shrugged his tail. Urruah looked incredulously at Rhiow. "Okay, yeah, die. But we can fix it."

"Fix *what?*"

"The battle. The Fight!"

"Now, *wait* a minute!" Urruah said. "Are you seriously talking about some kind of, I don't know, some reconfiguration of saurian mythology? Let alone *feline* mythology? What makes you think you have the right to tell the Gods how things ought to be done?"

"What made Them think *They* had the right?" Arhu said.

Rhiow stared at him. Arhu turned to her. "Look, Rhiow, the Gods were making it up as they went along," Arhu said. "Why shouldn't *we?*"

All she could do was open her mouth and shut it again.

"It's only legend because it happened so *long* ago!" Arhu said. "But once upon a time, it was *now!* They did the best they could, once upon a time. And *this* is now, too! Why shouldn't we change the myths for ones that work better? What kind of gods would make you keep making the same mistakes that They made, just because *They* did it that way once? They'd be crazy! Or cruel! If things have changed, and new problems need new solutions, why shouldn't we enact them? If They're good gods, wouldn't *They?*"

Urruah, and Saash, well awake now, both stared.

"I mean, if They're any *good* as gods," Arhu said, with the old street-kitten scorn. "If They aren't, They should be *fired.*"

Rhiow blinked and suddenly heard Ehef saying, in memory, *It's not like the old times anymore, no more "jobs for life"* . . . The thought occurred to her sudden as a tourist's flashbulb popping in front of the library: *can times change even for the gods? Could the process of* entropy itself *be sped up? Can old solutions no longer be sufficient to the present simply because of a shift in natural law* . . .

. . . such as the Lone One may be trying to provoke, by using the power tied up in the master Gate catenary . . .

"And if they won't do the job—" Arhu took a big breath, as if this scared even him. "Then we can fight *Their* way. She was me, for a little while. Why can't it go both ways? Why can't we be *Them?*"

"That's real easy to say," Urruah drawled. "How are you suggesting we manage this?"

Arhu turned and looked at Rhiow.

Her eyes went wide.

"You're crazy," she said.

"The spell," said Arhu.

"You're out of your tiny mind. It's in a hundred pieces—" She had a quick look into her workspace, and then added hurriedly, "I don't understand the theory; it's never been constructed enough even to *test. . . .*"

But that was all she could say about it . . . for there was no denying, having looked, that the spell appeared . . . more *whole.* Big pieces of it had come together that had never been associated before. Its circle was closing, its gaps filling in.

As a result of the extra power I demanded? She wondered. *Or as a result of being so far Downside?*

Was this assembly something she could have done long ago and had been distracted from—

—Or simply had chosen not to do . . . ?

Spells did not lie, any more than wizards did. If one implied it might work now, when before it had refused to . . . then it might work. No question of it. *If it completed itself, then . . .*

"I have to go think for a moment," she said to the others. "And then I think we have to leave, isn't that right, Arhu?"

"A guard party will stumble on us soon if we don't," he said, and looked over at Ith.

Ith lashed his tail in what might have been "yes."

"Get yourselves ready, then," she said, and walked off down the hallway, toward the distant light at its lower end.

Her tail lashed slowly as Rhiow went padding along, looking down at the dark smooth stone and trying to pull her thoughts together. She was still very tired . . . but now, maybe more than ever before in her life, she had to think clearly.

The spell . . .

She had long assumed that the old tales of the Flyting under the Tree and the Battle of the Claw were symbolic at root: simplistic story-pictures of the interrelationships among the Powers That Be, mere concrete representations of the abstract truth, of the continuing battle against entropy in general, and its author and personification, the Lone Power. It had never occurred to her that as you ventured farther from the fringe-worlds of mere physical reality into the more central and senior kinds of existence, the legends could become not less true, but *more*. This universe would plainly support that theory, however, to judge by the status of the spell.

Worse—it had not occurred to Rhiow in her moments of wildest reverie that a living Person might find herself *playing* one of those parts, enacting the Tearer, or the Destroyer-by-Fire. But that was what this spell now seemed to be pointing toward. And would it feel like "playing" to the unfortunate cat cast in the part? Did the part, ancient and powerful as it was—and moreover, closer to the Heart of things—play *you?* What if you were left with no choice?

Rhiow shook herself. There was always choice: that much she knew. *Those who deny the Powers nonetheless serve the Powers,* the Whisperer had often enough breathed in her ear. *Those who serve the Powers themselves* become *the Powers. Beware the Choice! Beware refusing it!*

How much plainer could the hint be? she wondered. But in either case, the common thread was *Beware.* Whatever happened . . . *you* were no longer the same. And fear stalked that idea, for the stories also told often enough of cats who had dared to be more than they were, had climbed too high, fell, and did not come down on their feet—or came down on them much too hard for it to matter. *How could you tell which you were?*

Yet at the same time, there might be a hint of hope lurking under this idea. If People could successfully ascend to the gods' level, even for short periods, they could possibly interact with them on equal terms. Rhiow thought about the Devastatrix. There were *ehhif* legends about her, how sa'Rráhh once misread her mandate—to eradicate the wickedness in the world—and almost destroyed the whole world and all life by fire, so mercilessly that (in the *ehhif* story) the other gods had to get her falling-down drunk on blood-beer before she would stop. Rhiow had always thought this was more symbolism for something: some meteoric bombardment or solar flare. Now, though,

Drunkenness? Rhiow thought. *A complete change of perceptions artificially imposed on one of the Powers That Be? But a temporary one . . . and to a purpose.*

Tamper with the perceptions of sa'Rráhh herself, of the Old Serpent? Fool the Lone One?

Grief-worn and weary as she was, Rhiow was tempted to snicker. There would be a choice irony to that, for the Lone Power had certainly fooled the saurians. *A certain poetic justice, there. Well, the Powers don't mind justice being poetic, as long as the structure's otherwise sound.*

But if we screw this up . . . forget death *being a problem. Forget our souls just passing out into nowhere, with no rebirth. I don't think we'd be so* lucky.

. . . Arhu's right, though. The rules are being changed. That's what all this is about, from the malfunctioning of the Grand Central gates on down. A major reconfiguration is happening. The structure of space is being changed so that the structure of wizardry, maybe of science, maybe of life itself, can be changed.

And if the Lone One can change the rules . . . so can we.

She stood there in the silence for a few moments more, her tail still twitching; and her whiskers went forward in a slow smile. There was nothing particularly merry about it . . . but she saw her chance. All she could do now was take it and go forward in the best possible heart.

Rhiow turned and walked back to the others.

"All right," she said as they looked at her. "I'll need some time, yet, to work on the spell . . . but we can't wait here: those guards will be along. Let's get out into the open and give them something to think about. Ready?"

Urruah snarled softly; Saash made a sound half-growl, half-purr in her throat; Arhu simply looked at Rhiow, silent. Behind him, Ith towered up as silently, watching Rhiow, as Arhu did: with eyes that saw . . . she couldn't tell what.

"Let's go," she said, and led them down toward the faint light that indicated the next balcony.

Thirteen

◆

"There they come," Urruah said quietly, as they walked out on the balcony and looked down into the abyss.

Rhiow looked across to the nearest visible corridor, off to their right and down one level. Under a mighty carving of rampant saurians, their six-clawed forelimbs stretched out into the emptiness, a wider-than-usual balcony reared out. It was full of mini-tyrannosauruses, and some of them that were much bigger than usual—twins to the scarlet-and-blue-striped dinosaur that Arhu had exploded in Grand Central.

"He keeps being reborn," Arhu hissed. "You kill him and he keeps coming back. It's not *fair!*"

"It's not *life*," Rhiow muttered; what defined life, after all, was that sooner or later it ended. "Never mind . . . we'll deal with him soon enough, I think."

As the team looked from their own balcony, the saurians looked up, saw them, and let out a mighty hiss of rage; the saurians dashed out of sight, making for a rampway upward.

"Well, Rhi?" Urruah said. "Which spell do you like better? The short version of the neural inhibitor—"

"We can't take a chance that it might go askew and hit Ith," she said. "Here's the one I like at the moment."

She leapt up onto the parapet, and then straight out onto the empty air.

For a horrible moment she missed her footing and was afraid the spell wouldn't take—that gravitic and intra-atomic forces were being interfered with, as well as string structure. But the difference was due only to a slight difference in the gravitic constant here: she could feel it, after a second, and amended her spell to reflect it. The air went hard. She stood on it and looked down in genial scorn at the few remaining saurians, who stared at her and pointed every claw they had available and hissed in amazement.

"Come on, everybody," she said. "Let's not be more of a target than necessary." She stared down into the abyss. Perhaps only three-quarters of a mile down now, that point of light shone up through the cold dark air. Amazing, despite how bright it seemed, how little light it gave to their surroundings.

"I'll switch the stairs back for every hundred vertical feet or so," Rhiow said, throwing a glance behind her at the balcony where Ith and Arhu still stood, and on the parapet of which Saash and Urruah now teetered. "Ith, can you see the stairs I've made?"

A long pause. "No."

"Then stay between Saash and Arhu, and step where Arhu steps. Come on, hurry up, they're coming!"

She headed down the stairway in the air, defining it as she went. She was sorry that she couldn't make the steps deeper, for Ith's sake, but he was just going to have to cope. Hard enough to be stepping down on the air, keeping the air solid before her, solid behind her, holding her concentration, while at the same time trying to poke at bright fragments of words on the floor of the workspace in her mind, trying to chivvy that spell into getting finished. *It would help if the power parameters made more sense. It would help if I didn't think the stairstep spell was likely to "burn in" halfway down. It would help if . . .*

Urruah jumped down behind her and began to make his way down the air. Arhu came next. Gingerly, Ith followed, tiptoeing delicately in Arhu's wake and looking now rather nervous, with all twelve of his front claws clenched tight. Saash came down after—

—and right up on the balcony behind her jumped the first of the saurians, reaching for her.

She turned, hissed.

Nothing happened.

The saurian lashed out at her sidewise with its tail, trying to knock her off whatever she was standing on. Saash skipped hurriedly down a step or two, knocking into Ith, who half-turned to see what was happening, lost his balance, knocked into Arhu—

Arhu leaned so hard against him that Rhiow, looking over her shoulder, was sure they were both going to fall. Then she realized that Arhu had anticipated the fall, had perhaps seen it with the Eye, and had started reacting to it almost before it happened. *His vision is clear now,* Rhiow thought, almost with pity. *The one thing he didn't dare see was what was clouding it.*

The two of them steadied each other, recovered, and headed on down the steps. Saash recovered her own balance and stopped, looked over her shoulder, and said sweetly to the saurian who was balancing precariously on the parapet, "Scared?"

The saurian leapt at her, at the air where it had seen the others step—

—and fell through it, and down: a long, long way down. It was out of sight a long time before it would have hit bottom.

Other saurians that had been climbing up on the parapet as their leader took his first step now paused there, looking down and down into the dark air through which he had fallen. None of them looked particularly eager to try to follow him, though there were hisses and screams of rage enough from them. Saash sat down on the air, lifted a hind leg, and began ostentatiously to wash behind it.

—until a line of red-hot light went by her ear. Her head snapped up as she saw one of the saurians leveling something like the bundle-of-rods-and-box at her again, for a better shot: an energy weapon of some kind. "Oh well," she said, "hygiene can wait . . ." She stood up, pausing just long enough for one quick scratch before the saurian managed to fire again. It hit her, squarely—

—and the bolt splashed off like water: she had had a shield-spell ready. Saash flirted her tail, grinned at the saurians, and then loped down the invisible stairs after the others.

Back up on the parapet, the frustrated saurians were dancing and screaming with fury behind them. "Nice idea, Rhi," Urruah said, as they made their way downward past balconies and platforms that were beginning to fill with staring, astonished saurians of all kinds and sizes. "And a lot easier than working our way through all those corridors full of, uh, spectators . . ." He glanced at the filling balconies. "Looks like Shea Stadium during a 'subway series.'"

"Now, I didn't think you were that much of a sports fan," Rhiow said, padding steadily downward. "With you so crazy for *o'hra* and all . . ."

"Oh, well, I don't follow it . . . but if a New York team is doing *well* . . ."

Rhiow smiled slightly and kept on walking. She was alert for those energy weapons, now. *Good thought, Saash,* she said, *to tempt them a little, see what they had on hand. We'll all have to be ready for that. I don't know what kind of range those things have.*

Not terribly long, I think. The wizardly component of them can't be very large, with the people handling the technology not being wizards themselves.

All right. Who's covering Ith, though?

"I'll take care of him for the moment," Urruah said.

"Right." Rhiow turned in midair to "switch back" her stairway, and started on another downward leg.

"Only one thing, Rhi. Don't you think we've, uh, lost the element of surprise?" Urruah was looking at the next course of balconies as they passed them. They were so full of saurians that some of them were in danger of pushing others who watched off into the abyss.

Rhiow had to laugh just slightly. "Did we ever *have* it, 'Ruah? We've been driven into coming down here in the first place. But in the short term, we haven't had it since Arhu told us those guards were going to be coming. I don't have any trouble with sacrificing it at this point. Let's just have a nice stroll down to where the Fire is . . . because if we can pull any surprises out down there, that's where we're really going to need them."

They walked down and down the middle of the air, and more and more saurians came crowding to see them. Most of them, Rhiow felt strongly, were not happy about seeing People down there; the buzz of their business, which had been little more than background noise before, now started to scale up into an angry roar. Cries of "Mammals! Kill the mammals!" and "Throw them in the Fire, cleanse our home!" and "Haath, where is Haath?" went up on all sides. Rhiow strolled through it all with as much equanimity as she could manage; but her main concern was for the others, and especially for Ith, as the cries of "Traitor! Traitor! Kill him!" went up from the teeming balconies. Urruah was as unmoved as if he were sashaying up some East Side avenue on a weekend. Saash glanced around her nervously once or twice, but as they moved out into the center of the great space, and out of the range of the energy weapons that were fired at them once or twice, she grew less concerned, at least to Rhiow's eye. Arhu was looking more nervous as he went; he seemed to be licking his nose about once a minute. Rhiow had no idea whether this was just general nervousness or due to something the Eye had shown him, and she was unwilling at the moment to make the situation worse by asking. Ith was more of a concern for her, as the cries of rage and betrayal went up all around them; but he stalked along between Arhu and Urruah with his face immobile and his claws at ease—at least Rhiow thought they were at ease. *It was going to be a while before she could tell his moods,* she thought . . . if she ever had that much leisure at all.

The cold was now increasing, and the River of Fire was now looking appreciably closer. *Once past it,* Rhiow thought, *once we've dealt with the catenary—assuming it* can *be dealt with in some way that will return it to its proper functioning—we're going to have to try to get Ith to do something with whatever power we can make available to him . . . through the spell, or in whatever other way. If Ith does accept the power to call on the Powers That Be to enforce his Choice, to enact his desire . . .* The chances were good, then, that the new Choice would redeem all these saurians retroactively, enabling them to find some other way of life: the Lone One would be cast out again. The trick after that would be to keep It from destroying the whole Mountain, and all the saurians in it, in a fit of pique.

The other trick will be getting Ith to do this in the first place. For Rhiow was by no means convinced that he was as yet committed. She remembered when she had thought that all this was going to hinge on Arhu, one way or another. *How simple it all looked then.*

Urruah approached her as she was making her way down in the lead, and paced alongside her. "How're you holding up?"

Rhiow sighed. "As well as might be expected, with about a million snakes yelling for my blood."

"Yeah," Urruah said. "Charming."

"How's our problem child?"

"Which one? The one with the fur or the one with the scales?"

Rhiow had to chuckle. "Both."

"Arhu's covering for Ith at the moment . . . taking good care of him, I'd say."

"Have they been talking?"

"More like, have they ever *stopped?* I don't think Hrau'f the Silent herself could shut them up if she came down and showed them a diagram of what quiet looked like." He chuckled a little. "Makes you wonder if they're related somehow."

"Oh, I'm sure." Rhiow made a slightly sardonic face.

Urruah echoed it as they walked down what was now an invisible spiral staircase into the final depths: Rhiow had gotten tired of the switchback pattern. "Still," he said. "Heard a funny story from Ehef, once. Those two could almost make me believe it. Would you believe, Ehef told me that *ehhif* have a legend that cats were actually *made out of* snakes—"

And the pain hit Rhiow worse than ever, so that for a moment she had to simply stop and try to get hold of herself again. It was an old, old memory: Hhuha reaching down and pressing Rhiow's ears right down against her head, not so it hurt, though, and pulling the corners of her eyes back a little so they looked slanty, and saying, "Snake!"

Surprised at the sudden strange handling, Rhiow had hissed. Iaehh had looked over at them and said, "See that, you're right. Better be glad she's not a *poisonous* snake."

Rhiow had privately decided to go use the *hiouh* box, come back and coax Iaehh into picking her up—and then jump down, giving him a good scratch or so with the hind legs to let him find out firsthand *how* nonpoisonous she was. Within minutes she had forgotten, of course: normally Rhiow was too good-natured for that kind of thing.

But now she remembered—and felt the pain again—and thought, *Ridiculous idea. People made out of snakes.*

Except . . .

She licked her nose as she walked downward, into the cold and the reflected fire.

Except that there is something to it. Somewhere in the dim past, on the strictly evolutionary path, we must have a common ancestor. No one made cats out of snakes, any more than they made humans out of monkeys. But we're related.

We're all related.

"We're close," Urruah said quietly.

Rhiow blinked, looking down: she had been running mostly on autopilot. They were indeed very near the bottom of the chasm now, the place where it all came to a point at last. The cold was growing bitter. Maybe a few hundred yards below, all the black basalt walls around them began to lose the ornate carving that had characterized them farther up: the last of the balconies, crowded with the mini-tyrannosauruses screaming abuse, were now perhaps fifty yards above. Below was not so much a river as a pool of blazing light that filled the whole bottom of the chasm to unknown depth. It gave almost no heat and burned the eyes to look at it. But only by looking steadily, tearing and squinting, could Rhiow see the energy-flow, the current of it, like streams of paler lightning in the main body of a river of lightning. The terrible energy was still bound as it would have been in a normally functioning catenary, and to Rhiow's trained eye, it looked more *tightly* bound than it would have been—as if something perhaps was a little afraid of it? . . .

Very tight indeed, Saash said to Rhiow silently, from behind. *Something's pegged it down in this configuration on purpose and is afraid the cinctures holding the energy in catenary configuration will come completely loose if it's interfered with.* There was a certain grim humor in her thought.

And would it?

Almost certainly. In fact, I'm counting on it.

What??

I believe that if I have to, I can release the bonds that hold the cate-

nary together as a controlled flow . . . and bust the entire energy of the thing loose. Despite the extra safeguards that Someone has tried to put up around it . . .

The thought of even one of the minor catenaries getting loose in that fashion had been enough to raise the fur on Rhiow's back. But the thought of the *master* going—you might as well drop a star into the heart of the Mountain.

Exactly, Saash said, and smiled that grim grin again. *Can you imagine even the Lone Power being able to hang on to a physical shape under such circumstances? For to interact with us at all, it has to be at least* somewhat *physical. If we let the trunk catenary loose, especially in its present deformed state, the combined release and backlash would destroy everything here.* And *destroy Earth's worldgating system. Now, that would be a nuisance—*

You have a talent for understatement! Urruah said from behind them.

But it will stop all this, Saash said, quite cool, *if there's nothing else we can do. If the Lone One pulls off what It's planning down here, there's a lot more than just Earth's well-being at stake. Thousands, maybe millions of planets, planes, and continua—you want to take responsibility for letting them be overrun by trillions of crazed warrior lizards? If it looks like we're all going to be taken out of commission before what Rhiow has in mind for Ith happens, I'm going to let the catenary loose . . . and watch the fireworks. For about a millisecond,* she added, wryly.

They stood only a few yards above the flow now, and Rhiow looked at it, squinting down until her vision was almost all one afterimage, trying to see which way the flow went. *It seems to lead out through the stone,* Rhiow said.

It may do exactly that, said Saash, *but it seems more likely to me that the stone on that side is an illusion. It's going to be tough for matter to coexist with this energy in the same space. Side by side, yes. But intermingling? Highly unlikely.*

Rhiow tended to agree.

"So what do we do?" Urruah said.

Rhiow threw a look over her shoulder at Arhu, who was standing by Ith again, as if caught in mid-conversation. Arhu looked at the stone wall.

Rhiow shrugged her tail. "We follow it," she said, and headed along in the direction in which the flow through the catenary was going, very close above the surface.

"You don't want us to get down *in* it—" Saash said, now sounding actively nervous.

"Unless it's unavoidable, no," Rhiow said, making her way slowly toward the black stone wall. "We'll just walk on it." She glanced at Arhu.

He shrugged his tail back. "All I know is that we have to cross it," he said. "Nobody told me we had to go *through*. I think that's later."

"Oh, wonderful," Urruah said.

Rhiow stepped down, and down, those last few steps . . . and hesitatingly put one paw down on the surface of the bound catenary, with her skywalk spell laid just over the surface. The sensation was most unpleasant. The spell, applied to the surface of the catenary, felt not solid, but full of holes, like chicken wire; through it, the dreadful forces of the catenary sizzled and prickled under Rhiow's paws, leaving her with the sense that it would simply love to dissolve her, like sugar in coffee. All her fur stood on end, though that was no surprise: the ionization of the air around the catenary was fierce, and the ozone smell reminded her of the Grand Central upper level, some days . . . almost a homely smell, after the last few hours. She looked over her shoulder at Saash and the others. "It works," she said, "but you won't like it. Let's get it over with."

Rhiow led the way toward the wall; the others followed, Arhu making the path for himself and Ith. As Ith stepped down onto the fire, he teetered in surprise, and Arhu braced him. "How does this feel to you?" Arhu said.

He stood quite still for a moment. "This is not as it should be," he said flatly. "There should be true Fire here." And he looked down at the catenary. "This is so bound and changed from how it was once." He looked up. "As are my people. I suppose I should not be surprised."

Rhiow looked at him, then turned again. "Come on," she said, and went up to the black stone wall. She paused, put up a paw.

The paw went through it. Rhiow glanced over her shoulder at Saash. "You were right," she said. "It's tampered with everything else It can get Its paws on, but It hasn't been able to change science that much . . . not yet."

"Not until It makes some other, more basic changes first," Saash said, looking down into the catenary.

Rhiow lashed her tail. "Let's see that It doesn't get the chance."

They passed through the wall. It didn't feel the way wall-walking usually did. The structure of the wall seemed to buzz and hum around them with the violent energy of the catenary so nearby. It was a long walk through it, though; it felt to Rhiow like a long slog through a thick bank of black smoke that was trying to resist her as she came—smoke that hummed like bees. She found herself trying to hold her breath, trying not to breathe the stuff, lest that humming should get inside her, drown her thoughts. *Don't worry about it. One step at a time, one paw in front of the next . . .*

Slowly the air before her began to clear. She came out into another open space, looked up and around it . . . and her jaw dropped in surprise. Behind her, Saash came out of the cloud-wall, paused.

It was the main concourse from Grand Central. But *huge* . . . ten times its normal size; so that, despite the fact that all their bodies were those of People of the ancient world, once again Rhiow and her team were reduced to the scale of People in New York. Four cats and a toy dinosaur came slowly out into the great dark space, illuminated only by the bound-down catenary that ran through it, flowing down a chasm carved straight through the floor, from the Forty-second Street doors to where the escalators to the MetLife building would normally have headed upward. The architecture of the genuine Terminal was perfectly mimicked, but all in black—matte black or black that gleamed. In the center of the concourse, the round information booth with its spherical clock was duplicated, but all in blind black stone: no bell tolled, no voice spoke. Above, over blind windows that admitted no light, the great arched ceiling rose all dark, and never a star gleamed in it. Rhiow, looking at it, got the feeling that stars might *once* have gleamed there . . . until something ate them. It was more a tomb than a terminal.

Rhiow looked down at the catenary's flow through the concourse. There were no escalators at the far side: only a great double stairway reaching downward, and the catenary flowed down between them, cascading out of sight. In Rhiow's world, stairs that led in this direction would have taken you to the Metro-North commissary and the lower-level workshops. She doubted that here they went anywhere so mundane.

"Down?" Saash said, her voice falling small in that great silence.

Rhiow glanced at Arhu. He said, "Follow the Fire."

They went to the stairways, stood at the top of them, and Rhiow realized that these were the originals of many stairs copied farther up in the structure of this dark Manhattan. The steps were tall, suited to saurians, but to no other life-forms. "Looks like a long way down," Saash said.

"I'm sure it's meant to be. Let's go."

They went down the stairs, taking them as quickly as was comfortable . . . which wasn't very. A long way, they went. On their left, since they had taken the right-hand stairs, the River of Fire flowed down in cascade after cascade, its power seeming to burn more deadly and more bright the farther down they went: there was no point in looking toward it for consolation in the darkness—it hurt. And the cold grew and grew. There were no other landmarks to judge by—only, when they turned around to look, the stairs seeming to go up to vanishing point behind them, and down to vanishing point ahead. For Rhiow this became another of those periods that seemed to go on forever . . . *and it's meant to,* she thought. "This is meant to disorient us," she said to the others. "Don't let it. Do what you have to do to stay alert. Sing, tell stories—" She wished then that she hadn't said "sing," for Urruah started.

Saash promptly hit him.

"Thank you," Rhiow said softly, and kept walking.

"Oh. Well, can I tell the one about the—"

"No," Rhiow said.

Arhu watched this with some bemusement; so did Ith. "Don't get him started," Saash said. "He makes *puns.* Terrible ones."

"Oh, no," Arhu said. "I wish we were down . . ."

"But we *are*," Ith said, sounding a little bemused.

Arhu stared. "He's right."

And so it was. All of them blinked as Arhu ran on down past them and to what seemed, mercifully, a flat area.

Did you see that? Saash said. *He wished . . . and it was* so. *This place may be a* lot *more malleable than we thought. But it makes sense. If the laws of wizardry are being changed, if things are in flux down here . . .*

Rhiow swallowed at that thought, and as she came down the last of the steps into the flat area, looked quickly into the workspace in the back of her mind.

A great circle lay there, almost complete—dark patches filling themselves in almost as she watched.

The spell the Whisperer's still working on, she thought. *That's what Arhu said.*

She stopped, breathed in and out, tried to center herself, and looked around her. They stood at the edge of a broad, dark plain, not smooth; here for the first time there was some sense of texture. Great outcroppings and stanchions of stone, blocks upthrust from the floor, stood all about: a little stone forest. And thrusting up out of the middle of it . . .

Rhiow had to simply sit down and look from one side to the other, to try to take it all in. Roots . . . huge roots, each one of which was the size of a skyscraper, an Empire State Building . . . spreading practically from one side of vision to the other: gnarled, tremendous, brown-barked, reaching up into a single mighty column that towered up and up out of sight. *This is what it's like when you try to perceive an archetype,* Rhiow thought, looking left toward what would have been a horizon in the real world, and right . . . and seeing nothing but the massive union of roots, reaching upward, lost in the vast darkness.

It was the Tree: the roots of the Tree, sunk deep in the Mountain . . . the stone of the Mountain's inmost cavern now rearing up, thrusting up around the separate roots as if trying somehow to bind them. From older trees in the park, Rhiow knew that in any such contest between tree and stone, the tree always won eventually. But here it seemed to have been fought to a draw: the stone seemed to be closing in.

Before it, between them and the Tree, the River of Fire spilled down the last of its steps and out into a broad channel . . . the final barrier. It looked more like the archetypal River now: inimical, a fire that would burn cold rather than hot, one in which nothing could survive—certainly not memory, maybe not even the passing soul. By the light of that River, Rhiow could make out that something else was wound about the Tree, among the stones, resting on them in some places: a long shining form, dark as everything else was here—but the light of the River caught its scales coldly, glinted black fire back. That form lapped the Tree in coil upon immense coil; the mind wanted to refuse the sight of it. Taking it all in, the trunk of the Tree, the roots of the Tree, the coiled shape, was like trying to take in a whole mountain in a glimpse from up close, as well as the River of Fire that wound about its feet, and the other river of darkly glittering light, which wound about it higher up: a river with eyes.

And near the spot where eyes lay brooding in a gigantic skull, where the massive jaw rested, at the top of one mighty root, Rhiow saw a great deep jagged gouge, gnawed into the Tree. The gouge bled pale light, too pale to illumine much. The gouge was deep—perhaps a third of the way through the whole trunk, on that side. And the old, dark, wise, amused eyes looked at them, and smiled.

Rhiow threw an almost panicked glance at Arhu, for it was in his voice that she had first heard the warning. *Claw your way to the Root. The Tree totters* . . . And *did* the trunk have just the slightest leftward slant? As if it were thinking about falling?

What else will fall with it?

They all stood there, in that massive, archaic silence, and looked at those dark eyes. Rhiow felt those eyes on her and felt ineffably ephemeral, helpless, *small*. Beside her, Saash was staring, silent. Beside her, Arhu looked once, and looked away as if burned. Ith— Ith crouched down to the stony ground in what even to Rhiow was plainly a gesture of reverence.

It was not entirely misplaced, Rhiow knew. She took a step forward, sat down, curled her tail about her feet, looked the Old Serpent in the eye, though she trembled all over, and said as clearly as she could, "Eldest, Fairest, and Fallen . . . greeting; and defiance."

Things began to shake. A long rumble, a roar, as of many voices, fading away . . . laughter. A long soft laugh, fading, as if the earthquake laughed.

Rhiow saw Arhu shudder all over at the sound. She was not in much better state herself. She was going to have to cope, though. Off to one side she caught a movement. Urruah, heading for the River—

She opened her mouth to shout at him to stop—and found herself muzzled: those dark eyes were concentrating particularly on her, and the pressure made speech impossible for the moment. But Urruah kept going. *He would probably have ignored me anyway. Urruah!!*

Straight out over the deadly River he went, as casually as if he were walking across Fifty-third Street, heading for his Dumpster. He passed the River, unhurt, though Rhiow thought she caught a scent of scorching fur. Urruah sauntered slowly over to the nearest root of the Tree where it sank among the tumbled stones, a massive gnarled pillar, and looked it over; then reared up on his hind legs, and began, thoughtfully, insolently, to sharpen his claws on it.

Rhiow stared at him open-jawed, filled with disbelief, indignation, and a kind of crooked admiration. She had leisure to indulge herself in the feelings, for Urruah didn't hurry any more than he might have rushed himself while working on some badly fenced-in sapling on a city street. Finally Urruah was done. He dropped to all fours again and strolled back over the River, back to the team: a tom finished marking just one more piece of territory.

Only you *would pull a stunt like that,* Rhiow said to him as he came.

Possibly that's why I'm here, he said, and smiled, then turned back to face their enemy. *But sometimes you can be a little too formal. If we're going to play* hauissh . . . *let's* play hauissh.

I'm surprised you didn't spray *it,* Saash said.

Hey, yeah, I forgot. He started to get up, and Rhiow put a big heavy paw down on his tail, without the claws . . . for the moment. Urruah looked over his shoulder at her, then grinned and sat down again.

Is *it the Fight?* Arhu said silently. *The one you and Yafh were showing me?*

If not the original, Urruah said, *then a bout of the regular kind. Keep your tactics in mind. Find your position and don't be moved off it. Half of a good fight is bluff, so yell as loud as you can, break your throat if you have to: it heals faster than broken claws. Don't waste your time with ears: no one breathes through their ears. Throats are the target—*

What is this, the pregame show? Rhiow said silently, annoyed, but still amused. *How am I supposed to make a mission statement with this going on? Save it for later.*

She stood up. "Well, Lone One," she said, "you've been working on something a little less obvious down here, it seems. Often enough You've tried striking directly at individual wizards, with mixed results at best. But here, now, obviously it's suited You to strike at the Gates by undermining the Tree, and enslaving the poor saurians down here, that You tricked so long ago. Well, the Queen has noticed You . . . and She and the Powers have a little surprise for You as a result. The first saurian wizard . . ."

That laughter, like the earthquake, rumbled again. And when it faded to silence, a voice spoke.

"There is *another?*" It said, amused.

From out of the shadows stepped a tall shape. Arhu looked up and growled in his throat.

It was a tyrannosaur: slate-blue, striped gaudily in red. It looked down at them all with an expression that stretched into a mocking grin, and flexed all its twelve claws.

"*You* again," Arhu said.

"You're a bit older than when I saw you last," said the tyrannosaur . . . in the Speech. "But you won't get much older than you are now, . . . never fear."

"This is the one I saw the first night," Arhu said. "After the rats."

"Haath," Rhiow said. "The Great One's 'sixth claw.'"

"Feline mammal," Haath said, and grinned at her in turn. "I will not say 'well met on the errand'; it will not be so, for you."

Rhiow's heart sank. *Surprise,* she thought, furious with herself for being so blind, for the Lone Power had been way ahead of her. Here, in the heart of this place where the structure of wizardry itself was being deranged and perverted, It had been able to cause wizardry to present itself to a saurian of Its choice, without involving any of the other Powers That Be. It had taught the wizard everything It wanted him to know, and pushed him through an Ordeal that had probably been a parody of the real thing, but real enough to produce the result: a wizard who walked the entropic side, who killed casually or for pleasure, who changed the life around him without reason, who knew nothing of preservation or slowing down the heat-death . . . who probably knew nothing but his Master's will. At the mere thought of such perversion of the Art, Rhiow hissed and spat, fluffing up.

"Now now," said Haath, much amused, "*bad* kitty," and swept a claw at her.

Rhiow said the word that would activate the shield-spell she had been carrying—and the bolt that caught her struck straight through the shield and threw her on her back, burning in her bones so that she could do little but lie on the ground and writhe in pain. "Indeed," Haath said, "you see that my Lord has taught me well. He wrested the power for me from those who would have kept it jealously for themselves and their chosen puppets. I am his chosen one, His Sixth Claw. And as for this—" He looked scornfully at Ith. "He knows his master in *me*. He has no power. I have passed my Ordeal: he barely knows what his was supposed to be. Not that he will have a chance to find out. *I* am my People's wizard. There will be no other."

The pain was wearing off enough now for Rhiow to stagger to her feet again, licking her nose. *This is why Ith was sent to us,* she thought. *And Arhu to him . . . to prepare him for this competition. This is his opposite number. There's always someone else to argue the opposite side of a Choice, for no Choice would be valid without it.*

"This is a kinship of individuals!" Rhiow shouted, putting her shield back in place. "*Not* a monopoly! Not a tyranny of power! There's *always* room for more wizards."

"Not in this world," Haath said, "and not in the new world to be, which we will bring. There will shortly be something new under the Sun."

Ith was still crouched on the black floor, head down, foreclaws clenched on the stone, as if unable to stand, even, let alone to make any Choice for his whole people. *Do something,* Rhiow whispered into his mind. *Do something! Try!*

But he could not hear her. All he could hear was Haath, that voice curling into his brain and shutting everything else out, shutting him away from his power.

"And why *should* he hear anything else?" Haath said, stepping closer, leaning over Ith and grinning dreadfully. "I am his Lord, I am his Leader! I would have brought him up into the light, into the Sun, in my good time . . . but now it is too late. Coming down here in company with you, he has enacted rebellion. It is too late for him: none of our people are allowed to do such a thing. He must suffer the fate that he has brought upon himself, and later, his name and his fate will be used to frighten hatchlings. His hide will be hung from some high spot, to show what happens to those who defy the Great One's will." He bowed to the mountainous shape coiled around the trunk of the Tree.

Rhiow, her tail lashing, looked at Haath, then turned away, turned her attention back toward the freezing cold eyes in that beautiful, gleaming-dark head. "Fairest and Fallen," she said, "Lone Power, Old Serpent, and sa'Rráhh among our People: from the Powers That Be, and from the One, I bring you this word. Leave this place and this universe, or be displaced by force."

It simply looked at her, not even bothering to laugh now. Rhiow stood her ground, and tried not to look as if she were bluffing. She knew of no wizardry sufficient to move the Lone One from a place it had invested in such power.

I *know a spell,* Saash said.

I would prefer not destroying a whole species if we can avoid it! Rhiow said.

If *we can avoid it. But there are a couple of other possibilities I want to explore.*

You do that. Meanwhile— *Ith!* Rhiow said silently. *Ith! Get off your tail and do something! This is your chance—stand up and tell him so! You have power—try to use it!*

He is the Lord of our people, Ith said with great difficulty. *Till now, I never saw him, but—now—I thought that perhaps, but—his power— it is too great, I cannot—*

Rhiow's hackles rose. *I'd hoped Arhu would have him ready for whatever he has to do,* she thought. *But he's not going to rise to the occasion. I'm just going to have to lead by example.*

She took a stride forward, opened her mouth to speak—

"All right," Arhu said, walking forward stiff-legged. "That's enough. You think I don't feel you in his head, hurting him? Taking his thoughts away? He can't stop you, but I think *I* can. *Get out of his head, Haath!* I remember when you tried to do that to *me*. I couldn't stop you myself, lizardface, not the first time; when you found you couldn't completely fry my brains, you sent in the rats to get rid of me the easy way. But it didn't work." He was stalking closer, lips wrinkled back, fangs showing. "And when the gates opened, and you showed up on my turf, I showed you a little something. I've killed you before. I'll do it again, and I'll keep *on* doing it until I get it right."

"You will *never* get it right," Haath said, backing just a little, starting to circle. "I can never die. It is my Gift from the Great One."

"Yeah, I bet it is," Arhu said. "He's just full of little presents, isn't He? Let's find out how *yours* stands up to a little wear and tear."

He launched himself at Haath.

Down they went together, kicking and rolling. Rhiow was surprised to see nothing more wizardly being used at first, but a second later she thought she knew why: there was a spell-damper all around Haath—not quite a shield, but a place where spells would not work . . . and Haath had not counted on Arhu wanting to go paw-to-claw with him. Arhu, though, had probably known: the Eye had its uses. *And he may have seen something else as well:* something Rhiow saw only now, when she turned—

—Saash crouching down by the catenary, leaning down over the "bank" . . . and dabbling one paw down into the ravening white fire.

What in Iau's name are you—!

Don't ask, It'll hear, Saash said. *Here goes nothing—*

Abruptly the white flame running in the conduit streaked up her paw and downreaching foreleg, up around her—not quite running over her hide, but a scant inch above it. Saash was shielded, but the kind of shield she was generating at the moment made Rhiow's look like wet tissue paper by comparison; to judge by the behavior of that white fire, now flowing up and around her more and more quickly, she had a second shield above it, holding it in place, holding it in. Swiftly, almost between one breath and the next, Saash became a shape completely sheathed in burning white: a statue, a library lioness with her head up, watching, with one paw hanging down into the catenary, the whiteness of the fire around her growing more intense with every breath. *A conduit,* Rhiow thought in mixed admiration and horror—and fear. *Or a storage battery . . . or both. How long can she—oh, Saash, don't—*

Saash stood up and began slowly, silently, to walk toward where Arhu and Haath were fighting; very carefully she went, like an *ehhif* carrying a full cup or bucket, intent on not spilling any of the contents. Haath and Arhu were up on their hind legs now, boxing at one another; as Saash paused, Arhu threw himself at Haath again, hard, and took him down, going for the throat, missing. Behind them, very quickly, Saash moved forward in one smooth rush—

"*Saash, no!*" Arhu screamed. Haath rolled out from underneath Arhu, scrambled to his hind legs, and made a flinging motion at Saash with one claw.

The spell he threw hit her, and her shields collapsed.

"*Saash!*" Rhiow roared. The white-burning form writhed, leapt in the air, shrieked terribly once—

—and fell. The fire went out, except for small blue tongues of it that danced over what remained for a few seconds. What remained was no longer tortoiseshell, but black, thin, twisted, charred: legs and head burnt to stumps, the head—

Urruah ran to her. Haath straightened, smiled slowly at Rhiow, and then at Arhu. "Nothing," Haath said, "literally."

At the sight of what had become of Saash, Arhu roared, a roar that was almost a scream, and threw himself at the saurian again. He was big and strong in this form, and he had the advantage of knowing what his enemy was about to do before he did it. But every time Arhu tore Haash, the tear healed: every bite sealed over. The best Arhu could achieve was a stalemate, while trying to keep his enemy's teeth out of his own flesh. He was not always succeeding.

Nearby, Urruah bent over Saash's body, touched it with a paw, then left it and began circling toward Arhu and Haath. Half-crippled with rage and a new grief, with the memory of the last look in Saash's eyes, seen through the fire as she leapt up, Rhiow joined Urruah and started to circle in from the other side. The thought of wizardry was not much with her at the moment. Blood was what she wanted to taste: that foul thin pinkish stuff that saurians used. One of them might not be enough to take Haath down, but weren't they a pride? *Three may be enough—*

Haath, though, was laughing. With one eye he was watching Arhu, keeping him at bay with those slashing claws; and he too circled, watching first Rhiow, then Urruah as they came.

"Don't you see that it won't matter?" Haath said softly, grinning. "You have killed me before, cat, and nothing has come of it except that now *I* shall kill *you* . . . and that will end it."

"It's not enough," Arhu yowled at Rhiow. "I know what I need to do this, but I can't get *at* it! Rhiow!"

She opened her mouth—

Slash. Haath straightened up, and Arhu went down, thrown fifteen feet away, staggering another ten or so with the force of the throw, with his rear right leg hanging by a string, the big groin artery pumping bright blood onto the dark stone. Rhiow started to hurry to him as Arhu fell over and tried to get up again, squalling with pain.

"No," Arhu yelled at her, "the Whisperer's telling me what to do, I can hold the blood inside me for a while, I'm wizard enough for *that*. Don't waste time with me!"

"Waste some," Urruah growled. "Haath, you and I are going to polka."

"*What* is a polka?" Haath asked, mocking.

"You may be sorry you asked," Rhiow said softly, watching to see what Urruah had in mind.

It was a slower stalk . . . less the scream-and-leap technique that Arhu had used, and all the while he stalked around Haath, Rhiow could feel Urruah weaving a spell, fastening words together in his head, one after another, in a chainlike pattern she couldn't make much of. Haath turned as Urruah circled him, his head moving slightly from one side to the other, as if somehow watching what Urruah was doing—

"Rhiow," Arhu cried from where he lay, "none of this is going to be good enough! What are you waiting for? Use the spell! *Use the spell!*"

"I can't, it's not—" But it *was*. It was ready. It lay shining, complete and deadly in her mind, and Rhiow wondered that she had never perceived the sheer unbalanced dangerousness of it, even earlier when it had first started to come together. A spell is like an equation: on either side of the equal sign, both sides must balance. This one, though, was weighted almost all one way . . . toward output. The power and parity configurations, the strange output projections, they were all complete now . . . and all of them violated natural law.

Except that the natural law Rhiow knew was *not* the one operating down here.

I don't know how natural law operates down here! It could backfire! It could—

Sometimes you can be too reasonable, Urruah had said: or something very like that. But sometimes, maybe reason wasn't enough.

Sometimes you might need to be *un*reasonable. Then miracles could happen.

It worked for the younger wizards, didn't it?

But I haven't been young for a while, Rhiow thought desperately. She was a team leader. She had to be responsible, methodical, make sure she was right: others' lives depended upon it. And even now, all that method hadn't helped her team: they were all going to "die dead," and she felt old—old, failed, and useless.

Don't listen to It, Rhiow! Arhu yelled into her mind, writhing, trying to get up. *I've got enough young for all of us!* But I can't do this for you. *You have to do it. Let go, Rhiow, just do it,* do the spell!

It could destroy everything—

Big deal, Saash was going to do that! And we all agreed *she should! Now she can't! Do—*

Urruah leapt at Haath, turning loose whatever spell he had been working on. Haath slashed at him, and Rhiow felt that spell abruptly come to pieces as Urruah went down, kicking, then froze, held pinioned on the stone, spell-still. Rhiow launched her mind against the wizardry that held him, trying to feel what it was, to pry it off Ur-ruah . . . but there was no time, she couldn't detect the structure—

Haath leaned over him, lifted his claws, and slashed Urruah open as casually as an *ehhif* would slash open a garbage bag with a razor.

Everything spilled out. . . .

Haath reached in one more time, hooked one long claw behind Urruah's heart, pulled. It came out, as if on a hook, still beating; beating out its blood, until none was left. Smiling, Haath released the spell. Urruah rolled over in Rhiow's direction, squirming; he cried out only once. His eyes started to glaze.

Just let it go, he said. *Just do the spell. Rhi—*

And then silence.

Haath looked at her and grinned.

Rhiow held very, very still, and the rage and horror grew in her . . .

. . . for it was almost exactly what she had been saying to everyone else: Arhu and Ith in particular.

Sometimes we do not hear the Whisperer even at her loudest because she speaks in our own voice, the one we most often discount.

Rhiow took a long breath . . .

. . . and started to use the spell.

It was not the kind you could hold "ready-for-release" and then turn loose with a word: within minutes you would be staggering under the weight of its frustrated desire to be let go. It had weight, this spell. You had to shoulder into it, boost it up to get at the underside where the words of activation were. The weight of it pushed down your neck and shoulders, your eyes watered with the strain of seeing the symbols, and then you had to get the words out: big hefty poly-syllabic things, heavy with meaning. Rhiow fought with the spell, pushed past and through its inertia and got out the first two words, three, five—

—when something seized her by the throat and struck her dumb.

She gagged, clawed at her face . . . but there was nothing there. *Trickery,* she thought, but her throat would still not work. *The Lone One.* And, *Aha,* she thought. *It must be worth something after all—*

She fled inward, into her workspace, where the spell lay on the floor of her mind, and hurriedly started to finish it there. Spells can be worked swiftly inside the practiced mind, even when working through the graphical construct of a spell diagram; Rhiow, terrified and intent, was too swift, this once, for even the Lone One to follow her in and stop her. Power flashed around the spell-circle. The whole thing flared up, blinding. Its status here inside her was as far along toward release as it had been when her outward voice was choked. Only a few words left to complete the activation: but here they were not words but thoughts, and took almost no time at all. One word to make all complete, knotting the circle together, setting the power free—

Rhiow said the word.

The spell went blasting out of her like a wind that swept her clean inside, threw her down on the stone, left her empty, mindless, half-dead.

There Rhiow lay, waiting for something to happen.

Silence . . . darkness.

Nothing happened.

It didn't work, Rhiow thought in complete shock, and started to stagger to her feet again. *How can it not have worked?*

A spell always *works!*

But the nature of wizardry is changed, said that thick, slow, soft, satisfied voice in her mind. *It only works if* I *want it to.*

Slowly, slowly, Rhiow sat down.

Beaten.

Beaten at last.

She hung her head . . .

. . . and then something said, *No.*

Liar, it said.

Liar! You've always *lied!*

It lied the last time. It's lying now.

She had trouble recognizing the voice.

It's live! Activate it!

Arhu?

Call them! They have *to come! Like in the park—*

She staggered, blinked, unable to think what on Earth he meant.

Wait a minute. The park. The *o'hra*—the *ehhif*-queen in the song who demanded that the Powers That Be come to her aid, on her terms—

—and They *did*—

—but to *require* the Powers to descend, to demand Their presence: it was not something that was possible, They would laugh at you—

No, Rhiow thought. That was someone else's idea, some*thing* else's idea. *Yours!* she said to the Old Serpent. *Yours! As it was your idea what happened to my Hhuha. As it was your idea what happened to Arhu's littermates and almost happened to him. No more of your ideas! You have had only one, and I've had enough of it for today.*

Reconfiguration, Rhiow thought. *To change the Lone One's perception . . . it would take this kind of power.* And others' perceptions could as easily be changed.

Rhiow staggered to her feet again, opened her mouth, looking for the right words . . . *Let it come,* she said, *let it come to me: I will command!*

Instantly the huge power blasted into her, as the activated spell had blasted out, leaving room for her to work. She tottered with the influx of wild power, staggered like someone gone distempered, unable to see or hear or speak, unable to feel anything but the fire raging inside her, striving to get out, get up, *do* something. It did not know what it wanted to do, though. *This is always the problem,* said the Voice inside her. *It must be disciplined, or it will ruin everything. Hold it still, keep it until the right words come.*

But with that power in her, she *knew* the right words.

"*What has become of My children?*" Rhiow cried. She knew the voice that shouted; it was her own—but Someone else's too: the sun burned inside her, and fire from beyond the sun readied itself to leap out. She could not believe the rage within her, the fury, but there was a core of massive calm to it, the knowledge that all could yet be well, and the two balanced one another as the sides of the spell had not. "*Where is Aaurh the warrior, and sa'Rráhh the Tearer, wayward but dear to Me? And what has become of My Consort and the light of his eye, without which My own is dark?*"

The ground shook: the Tree shook: the Mountain trembled under her. "*Old Serpent, turn You and face Us, for the fight is not done—!*"

She could not believe her own strength. It filled her, making the initial release of the spell from her seem about as worldshattering by comparison as a stomach-growl. And she could not believe that the Old Serpent, the Lone One Itself, now looked at her from the Tree with eyes suddenly full of fear. Rage, yes, and frustration . . . but fear first. *Is that* all *it takes?* she thought, astonished. *One sentence—one word, one command? "Let there be light—"*

Here and now . . . the answer seemed to be "yes."

It was "yes" before too, said Queen Iau. But the voice was Rhiow's own.

The Serpent began, very slowly, to uncoil Itself from around the Tree. As it did, the huge gouge that It had bitten in the Tree's trunk began to bleed light afresh.

Oh *no You don't,* Rhiow thought furiously, stepping forward. *Where do you think* You're *going?*

She was immediately distracted by the way the ground shook under her when she moved. Rhiow would have been frightened by it except that inside her, acting with her—part of her, as if from a long time before—was One Who was not afraid of Her own power in the slightest.

Rhiow was abashed beyond belief. Not in her wildest expectations had she anticipated the spell might have this kind of result: she would hardly have dared to think of herself and the One in the same sentence. *Oh, my Queen, I'm sorry—I mean, I—*

Don't apologize, came the thought of Iau Hauhai'h, and it was humorous, if momentarily grim. *Usually gods don't. Not in front of that One, anyway. Say what It needs to hear! We've got a lot of work to do.*

Rhiow stood there, feeling the majesty cohabiting with her . . . and then held her head up, thinking of that statue in the Met, poor cold copy that it was. *"Am I not the One,"* She cried, *"to make power against death strong, and power for life stronger still? Shall I allow the darkness to prevail against My own? Their life is in Me, and of Me: save that You destroy Me as well, never shall they be wholly gone; and Me You cannot destroy, nor My power in Them. Rise up then, Aaurh My daughter, and be healed of Your dying; the dark dream is over, and awakening is come!"*

Off to one side, where a shape lay dark and charred on the stone, there was movement—and then a flash of fire. If a form can burn backward, this one did. Flame leapt from nowhere to it, filled it, wrapped it round—not the cold white fire of the catenary, but flame with a hint of gold, the Sun's light concentrated, made personal and intense. Substance came with the fire: the shape filled out, rolled to its feet, shook itself, and stood, looking proud, and angry, and amused. It was a lioness, but one in whose pelt every hair was a line of golden fire, and the Sun rode above her like a crown—though it was not as bright as her eyes, or as fierce. "*I am here, my Dam and Queen,*" said the voice of Aaurh the Warrior, the Queen's Champion, the Mighty, the Destroyer-by-Fire; but it was Saash's voice as well, and Rhiow could have laughed out loud for joy at the sound of that voice, itself nearly shaking with laughter under the stern words.

Oh Iau, Saash— I mean, oh— And Rhiow *did* laugh then: it was amazing how your vocabulary could be lessened by realizing you suddenly had the One inside you, and that it sounded surpassingly silly to be swearing at, or by, Yourself. *Saash, are you all right?*

A snicker. *Are you kidding? I'm* dead. *Or I* was. *But live by the fire, die by the fire.* And she chuckled. *It's an occupational hazard.*

"*Rise up then, sa'Rráhh My daughter, and be healed of Your sore wounding; stand with Us against the Old Serpent that would have worked Your bane!*"

The prone form that lay clutching painfully with its foreclaws at the stone now lifted its head and slowly began to glow both dark and bright, like its fur—night-and-moonlight, the pale fire and the dark one mingling, starfire and the darkness behind the stars: the essence of conflict and ambivalence. But neither fire burned less intensely for the other's presence; and as the tigerish shape rose up to stand with its Dam, the eyes that looked out of its mighty head were terrible with knowledge of past and future, decisions well made and ill made, and action and passivity held in dangerous balance. Those awful, thoughtful eyes looked down at the body they inhabited . . . and suddenly went wide.

"*Look at me! Just* look *at me! I'm a* queen!"

Iau Kindler of Stars let out a long sigh. "Son," She said, "*shut up. It happens to the best of us.*"

Rhiow put her radiant whiskers right forward in amusement. It had not occurred to Rhiow that *Arhu* might manifest as sa'Rráhh, but the Tearer had always been as ambivalent about gender as anything else. "*Oh all right,*" said the Dark One. "*I am here, my Dam and Queen. Now let me at that ragged-eared—*"

"*In a moment. Rise up then, My consort, Urrua Lightning-Claw; be risen up, thou Old Tom, O Great Cat, O Cat Who stood under the Tree on the night the enemies of Life were destroyed. Urrua, My beloved, My Consort, rise up now, and stand with Us, to slay the One Who slew You!*"

Off on the black stone, where blood lay pooled around a torn, silver-striped shape, darkness now pooled as well. It gathered together about that shape and began to weave brilliance into itself, the tabby coloration shading pale, to moondust grays and silvers and a brilliant white like the Moon at full, a light as pitiless in its way as the Moon looking down from a clear sky on those who would wish to hide, and can find no hiding place from what stalks them silently. That shape stood up, and was a panther's shape, heavy-jowled and white-fanged, with unsheathed claws that burned and left molten spots on any stone they touched. The mighty shape shook itself, shedding silver light about it, then padded over to join the others, looking at them with one eye that was dark and terrible, knowing secrets; and the other that burned almost too bright to look upon, for battle was in it, and the joy of battle. "*I am here, My Dam and Queen, My Consort,*" he said, and then added, "'*My consort,' huh?*"

"*Don't get any ideas, you . . . the post is purely ceremonial. —Lone Power, Old Serpent, for these murders, now We pronounce your fate—*"

"*No, wait a minute, him first,*" said sa'Rráhh suddenly.

Slowly, very slowly, Haath had begun backing away as he first caught sight of his Lord and Master beginning to unwrap Itself from the Tree. By the time Queen Iau had begun to raise Her dead, Haath was already running away across that great dark expanse at the best speed a tyrannosaur could manage, which was considerable. Now, though, the Queen looked after him . . . and suddenly Haath appeared directly in front of them again, and fell on his face with the suddenness of his translocation.

"*Haath, Child of the Serpent,*" said Rhiow and the Queen as he struggled to his feet, "*you have brought your fate upon you: but still it lieth with you to save yourself, if you will. Renounce your false Master, and you may rejoin your kind, though your wizardry, not coming from the One, is confiscate.*"

Haath crouched, his head low, and looked from the blazing, terrible forms before him to the dark radiance still in the process of slowly, slowly slipping from around the Tree. "I . . ." he said. "My Master . . . perhaps I was deluded in thinking . . ."

Allow Me to save you this crisis of conscience, said a huge, soft voice, *by first renouncing* you.

Haath looked up in horror, already feeling the changes in his body. Rhiow knew, as Iau knew, that the Lone One had not told Haath the whole truth about his immortality: that even for the gods, death comes eventually, and mortals who try repeatedly to put it off may succeed for a while, but not forever. With his master's renunciation, all of Haath's deaths simply caught up with him at once. All that could be seen of the process was the look of shock and rage and betrayal on his face, those twelve claws lifted for one last wizardry . . . but there was no time for anything else, either action or reaction. Suddenly, he simply was not there; and if there was even a little dust left, the wind blowing through the darkness swept it unregarded into the River of Fire.

The Serpent's cool eyes dwelt on this, unmoved. And then another voice spoke. "Great One," it said, "Lord—"

The Four turned their attention to the source of the voice. It was Ith. He stood now, gazing at the Serpent with an odd intensity.

Ah, my son, said the Old Serpent's voice. *Now that the other is gone, we may speak freely, you and I.*

This *should be fun,* said Aaurh silently to the others.

Pay no heed to the strange violence you have seen done here, said the Old Serpent softly. *These creatures are our ancient enemies, and need have nothing further to do with our kind or our power. Our kind have different needs, different desires.*

"Lord," Ith said, "the Sun. The world above . . ."

None of our kind can live in that light without My help, said the

Old Serpent, slow, persuasive, reasonable. *It is fair, but it kills. Nor would they, would you, be able to find food enough for all. You will die there unless you are ruled by one who is wise, who knows time and the worlds. Long I have ruled you, to your advantage. It shall be so again. And* you *shall be My Sixth Claw, this time. You have won the right. You have proven Haath flawed, and that flaw would sooner or later have done your people, My people, great harm. Now you shall rule in his stead, and order all things for Me.*

Ith swayed, looking up into the great, dark, wise, forgiving eyes. The others watched him.

They will bow before you like a god, a true god . . . not like these up-starts. But you must in turn surrender yourself to Me, to be filled with the power. This you must see and do.

A pause.

". . . No."

The Lone One's eyes suddenly went much darker. "But this I *do* see," Ith said, and paced slowly over to stand straight and still beside sa'Rráhh, or Arhu in her shape, now flowing with fire both dark and bright. "Our kinship with these others is greater than You claim. He came into my heart, the one You say is my enemy, and tried to save me. And I saw into *his* heart, and his mind. He had pain like mine, loneliness like mine, and anger. But he rose up again, through them, and tried. Death and hunger came to him, but he did not give in to them, did not cast himself in the fire. His clutchmates all died, but he lived, and *kept* living, though the pain pierced like a claw. And when we met, he felt pain for me, and did not run away, but bore it. This is *his* Gift. To try again. We tried once and failed . . . and never tried again, for You told us that trying was no use. But gifts can be passed on to others who need them, even when the others are old enemies; and choices can be remade. *They can be remade!*"

It was a roar, and slowly the Mountain began to shake with it, a huge sympathetic tremor, like fear in a heart finally decided.

"I choose!" Ith said. "*I* choose for my people! We will walk with the light, in the sun, in the free sun that You cannot control; we will walk with these others who struck us down only when there was need, rather than for pleasure or for power. And if we die of the light, of our own hunger freely found, then that was still worthwhile. For we would have owned ourselves for that little time, and an hour's freedom in our own bodies, our own lives, under the sun, is worth a thousand years as slaves, even pampered slaves, in the dark under the ground, or killing other beings under strange stars!"

The Old Serpent was hissing softly to Itself now, while still slowly unwrapping Itself from around the Tree. *Fool,* it said—again that soft voice, the anger never overt—*fool of a race of fools: too true it is that you have overstayed your time in this world. You shall not overstay it much longer—*

"*Too late for that, Old Serpent,*" said Rhiow, said Iau. "*The Choice is made.*"

And already things were shifting. The landscape looked less rocky; the catenary looked less like a restlessly bound energy flow, but more than ever like a river, and one in which fire flowed like water. Rhiow, within Iau, rejoiced at the sight of it, for now she saw that this was where the River of Fire *belonged*—at the roots of the Tree: at the scene of the battle, where the souls of all felinity would at one time or another pass through the place of Choice, of the Fight, the gaming-ground that was the mother of all bouts of *hauissh*. All would see it and remember, or be reminded between lives, of the incomplete Choice, of the business still to be attended to, not in the depths of time behind them, but in the depths of time yet to come. Except that time was not as deep as it had been anymore . . .

"*The Change is upon them now,*" said Aaurh, moving slowly forward. "*You might destroy this whole race, and still they would find possibilities they would never have known otherwise because of this their Son, their Father, Who Chose them a different path. They will go their own way now.*"

They will die! the Old Serpent hissed.

"*And whose fault is* that? *They will pass,*" said sa'Rráhh, "*but to what, You will not know for aeons yet. And meantime You have a passage of Your own to deal with.*"

"*Old Serpent,*" cried Iau then, "*stand You to battle; this is Your last day . . . until we fight again!*"

The Serpent reared away from the Tree, and Rhiow realized belatedly that Its withdrawal had been strategic only. Now It threw Itself at them, Its whole terrible mass coming down at them like a falling tree, lightnings flailing about it—

What started to happen after that, Rhiow had a great deal of trouble grasping. All the Four threw themselves upon the Old Serpent; claws and fangs blazed, and blinding tracks of plasma burned and tore where Urrua's claws fell; fire spouted and gouted from Aaurh and sa'Rráhh, blasting at the Lone Power. As Haath had, It healed itself. The Four kept attacking, with energies that Rhiow was vaguely certain would have been sufficient to level whole continents, if not to devastate the surfaces of some small planets. Rhiow fought as she might have in her own body, clutching and biting, feeling fangs slash at her and find their mark: But the terrible pains she suffered still had triumph at the bottom of them, like blood welling up in a wound; and the violence she did, and sensed all around her, had a stately quality to it. They had done this many times before, and would do it again—though this time there had been minor changes in the ritual.

But then came one change that was not so minor; it particularly attracted her notice. Suddenly there was a Fifth among them; and sa'Rráhh laughed for joy and plunged anew into the battle beside that Fifth one; and the others cried out in amazement. For it was another Serpent, a bright one, as great as the Old Serpent, and its scales glittering like diamond in the light of their own fires. It thrust its mighty head forward and sank fangs like splinters of star-core into the great barrel of the Old Serpent's body, just behind the head; and the bright Serpent wrapped its coils around the Old Serpent's coils, and they began to strive together—

Rhiow suddenly thought of the twined serpents on the staff of the *ehhif* god above Grand Central. *How did they know,* she thought, *how did even the* ehhif *suspect, and we never—*

—and in their battle, the bright Serpent began to get the better of the Old Serpent, and started to crush the life out of It, so that It writhed and thrashed and made the world shake. And the Tree began, ever so slightly, to lean.

"*Quick,*" cried the bright Serpent, "*the wound, it must be healed!*"

"*Once more the Serpent's blood must flow,*" said Urrua, and Rhiow in Iau looked, and saw him rearing up on his hind legs and holding, in his huge paw, the sword. At least an *ehhif* a long time ago, seeing it or hearing it described, might have taken it for a sword. It was a hyperstring construct, blindingly bright to look at, but a hundred times narrower than a hair. *"Just hold It there, Ith,"* he said, *"this won't take long. Yeah, right there—"*

The Old Serpent shrieked as Its head was chopped from Its body and rolled down the trunk of the Tree to lie bleeding over the roots. Its blood ran down into the River of Fire, and tinged its flames, as had happened many times before . . .

. . . while above, from the thrashing, headless trunk, the blood ran flaming into the wound in the Tree. The whole Tree shuddered and moaned, and heaven and earth together seemed to cry out with it.

Then the moaning stopped. Slowly, as they watched, the wound began to close. As slowly, the body of the Old Serpent began to fade into the darkness, the last of its blood running into the River of Fire. Soon nothing was left but a scatter of glittering scales among the stones; and the Tree stood whole—

Silence fell, and the Five looked around at one another.

"Are we alone again?" Arhu said, looking around him with some bemusement, for his form had not changed back to his normal one, nor had those forms of the rest of the team.

Rhiow listened to the back of her mind and heard only herself . . . she thought. "After that," she said, "I'm not sure we can ever, any of us, be sure we're *alone* . . . but it's quieter than it was."

Saash smiled. "A lot. Ith, that was a nice job."

The bright Serpent blinked. A moment later, he was back in his true form, though there was an odd look to his eyes, a light that seemed not to want to go completely away.

"I'm told," he said, "that I have passed my Ordeal." His tail lashed. "I'm also told that it is not unusual to find the details . . . obscure."

Rhiow chuckled at that. "What happened to us all," she said, "had something to do with mine, something I'd been putting off. 'Obscure'? I'll be working on the details of this one for years. But I think we've got our job about done."

"One thing left," said Saash. "Let's get back upstairs—"

Rhiow blinked. They *were* back upstairs, near the "pool" created by the binding down of the main catenary trunk.

Urruah looked around him with his "good" eye and swore softly. "I told you this place was malleable."

"I may have done that," Ith said. "I do not yet understand the nature of space down here. This was where you wanted to be?"

"Just the spot," Saash said. She paused to look up at the balconies, which were much less crowded than they had been earlier. "I think I can keep this from jumping right out and destroying everything." She leaned down and got ready to put a paw down into the pool.

"Is that safe??" Arhu said.

She smiled at him. "This time it is. Watch—"

Saash reached down, dabbled in the cold bright flow of light— then stood up, stood back. Slowly the light in the "pool" reared up, bulging like a seedling pushing itself up out of the ground, then, more quickly, began to straighten, pulling branches and sub-branches of light up out of the depths of the stone beneath the bottom of the abyss. Still more quickly it started to reach upward, a tree of fire branching upward and branching again. Then all in one swift movement it straightened itself, shaking slightly as if a wind was in its branches. The separate branchings started to drift into their proper configurations again, the bemused saurians getting hurriedly out of the way of the slowly moving lines of energy as they passed through walls and carvings like so much cheesewire through cheese.

The saurians stared down at them.

"Well," Arhu said, staring up at the reconstructed catenary tree, "*that's* handled. Now what?"

Ith looked up at the balconies, at the many curious faces looking down. The feeling of hostility that had been there before now seemed, for the moment at least, to be gone. He looked over at Arhu then and smiled.

"Now," he said, "we bring my people home."

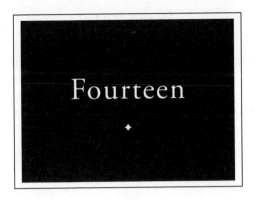

Fourteen

◆

They started the walk upward through the tunnels and balconies wondering how much explaining they would need to do . . . and found that little was needed: for every saurian who saw Ith immediately seemed to recognize him and to be willing to listen to him, if not specifically to obey him.

"Well," Rhiow said, "he's their father. Why not?"

Arhu, walking close behind Ith, found this funny, and after all the difficulties associated with getting down into the abyss, it amused him even more that the team was regarded with some suspicion, but no overt hostility. As far as the saurians were concerned, if Ith vouched for the felines, that was all right with them: and soon they were near the head of a huge parade of the creatures, all eagerly climbing upward into the heights where none but workers were normally permitted.

"They really *will* be able to live up there, won't they?" Arhu said to Rhiow, worried.

"Oh, of course. Much of what you were hearing down there was the Lone One's lies to them, to keep them enslaved. They'll spread out over the surface of this world and find plenty, once they're used to hunting in the open. The other carnivores may be a little annoyed at the competition, but they'll manage. There'll be plenty of prey for everybody."

"And meantime . . ." Urruah said to Rhiow, from behind. "What about us?"

"What *about* us?"

"Well, we've been *dead.*"

Rhiow sighed, for that had been on her mind, and it had struck her that this cheerful walk up to the surface was likely to be their last. She looked over at Saash.

She had done this several times and kept having to smile, for now she thought she knew why Saash's skin had always been giving her trouble. It was not until she saw her friend suddenly manifest after her death as Aaurh the Mighty, the One's Champion, that Rhiow realized that Saash's soul, after nine lives, had simply become too big for that body; and that her Tenth Life was not merely a possibility, but a given. It was an added source of amusement that someone who could so perfectly meld into the persona of the irresistible Huntress, the Destroyer-by-Fire, could nonetheless be so hopeless at catching something as simple as mice. But then maybe the body was just resisting the role it knew was coming.

"Not that I'm going to need to catch things to eat for much longer," Saash said, and sighed.

"That was really it, was it?" Rhiow said sadly.

"That was my ninth death, yes," Saash said. "And now . . . well, after I cross through the gate back home, we'll see what happens."

"But the rest of us . . ." Rhiow looked at Urruah, who was chatting with Arhu at the moment. "He was as dead as *you* were."

"He may be short a life when we get home. I'm not sure: he'll have to take it up with the Queen. I mean, Rhi," Saash said, "we've been gods, and some of us rose from the dead while we were gods. And if you're a *god* and you rise from the dead, I think you stay risen. For the time being, anyway . . ."

"But what about you?" Urruah said. "*Look* at you!"

"Look," Arhu said, "it's the upper caverns." He loped on ahead.

The saurians were hurrying out after him at the first glimpse of some light that was not the cool, restrained light of the catenary tree. Rhiow and Saash and Urruah hurried to keep up with Arhu and Ith, partly to keep from being trampled by the eager crowd behind them. The light ahead, pale though it was, grew: spread—

—and there was the opening. Rhiow, though, wondered what had happened to the downhanging teeth of stone, and found out; many had fallen in the shaking of the Mountain. *No surprise,* she thought, *many things almost fell today.*

But not that, she thought, as she came out of the cave, onto the wide ledge looking over the world, and turned.

The weather was cuttingly clear. It was just a little while before dawn; high up the brightest stars were still shining through the last indigo shadows of night, and to the east, the sky was peach-colored, burning more vividly orange every moment. Rhiow looked at the Mountain, which lay still in shadow: but far up, on the highest peak, a spear of light was lifted to the sky, blinding—the topmost branches of the great Tree, catching the light of the Sun before it cleared the horizon for those lower down. The saurians piled out of the cave, as many of them as could, and stared . . . stared.

Some of them were looking westward and gaped open-mouthed in wonder at the round silver Eye gazing at them from the farthest western horizon: the full Moon setting as the Sun rose. Rhiow watched their wonder, and smiled. *"Night with Moon" indeed,* she thought: the *ehhif Book* was better named than maybe even the *ehhif* wizards knew. How many other hints had been scattered through Earth's mythologies, hinting at this eventual reconfiguration?

"Is that the Sun?" one of the saurians said.

Rhiow laughed softly and looked eastward again, where the sky was swiftly brightening. "Turn around," she said, "and just wait. . . ."

They waited. The shifting and rustling of scales died to a profound silence. Only the wind breathed through the nearer trees, rising a little with the oncoming day. Rhiow looked up at the Tree again, wondering: *Are there really eyes up there, the eyes of those gone before, who look down and watch what passes in the worlds? I wonder what they make of this, if they are there indeed?*

Someday I must sit under those branches, and listen, and find out. . . .

A great breath of sound went up, a hiss, a gasp—and the sunlight broke over the edge of the world and sheened off all the saurians' hides, and caught in all their eyes. Rhiow had to look away, near-blinded by the brilliance.

She leaned over to Urruah. "Let's get out of here and leave them their world," Rhiow said. "They've suffered enough for it. Time for the joy . . ."

The team made their way over to the gates, which were all in place, warp and weft sheening with power as usual: the reconfiguration below and the release of the catenary tree had completely restored them to their default settings. Through the central gate, Track 30's platform was now visible: they could see T'hom, looking back at them and seeming extremely relieved. He was sidled, which was just as well, for the place was full of *ehhif* going about their business, and he was doing the usual shuffle to keep from being knocked off the platform.

Urruah looked at the gate with some concern and turned to Rhiow. "Well?" he said.

She looked at him, shook her head, then rubbed cheeks with him.

"Consort," he said. "I liked the sound of that."

"You would," Rhiow said. "Sex maniac. Go on . . . and good luck. Get yourself sidled when you go through. But otherwise, if worst comes to worst, look us up again, next life. It wouldn't be the same without you."

Urruah snorted, meaning to sound sardonic, but his eyes said otherwise. He leapt through the gate—

—came down on the other side, a silver tabby, back to normal size, quite alive; Rhiow could see the scars. She put her whiskers forward, well pleased.

Arhu, less worried, came over to the gate next. He looked up at Ith, who walked with him and peered through curiously. "Your world . . . Is it like this one?"

Arhu cracked up laughing. "Oh, yes, exactly. Not a whisker's difference."

Ith looked at him sidewise.

"Yeah, right. Look, Ith, come on through and have some pastrami," Arhu said.

Ith bent down toward him, gave him the bird-eyeing-the-worm look, but it was absolutely cordial, the salute of one member of the great Kinship to another . . . even though there was still a glint of appetite there.

"I believe you would say, 'You're on,'" Ith said. "I will come shortly. Meanwhile, my brother, my father . . . go well."

Arhu slipped through . . . and was small and black and white again.

Rhiow and Saash looked at each other. Then Rhiow slowly leaned forward and rubbed cheeks with her friend: first one side, then the other.

"Stay in touch," she said, "if you can."

"Hey," Saash said softly, "it's not like I'm going to be dead or anything. Just busy . . ."

Rhiow took a long breath, gazed around her, then stepped through onto the platform on Track 30—

—and came down light on her paws. She lifted one to look at it. Small again: the central pad unusually large: normal for this world . . .

Rhiow turned and looked through the gate. Saash was standing there in her Old Downside guise, a tortoiseshell tigress momentarily glancing over her shoulder at the ancient world, the dawn coming up, its glitter and sheen on the hides of the saurians watching it for the first time. Then she turned, locked eyes with Rhiow, leapt through the gate—

The Downside body stripped away as she came, and Saash was surrounded and hidden in a swirl of—not light as such, but reconfiguration, self and soul shifting into some new shape. *Not vanishing, please, Iau—*

That swirling, shifting, faded. Saash stood there . . . but not in her old body, which seemed to have declined to continue any further. This new shape was one that no nonwizardly *ehhif* could have seen, and even an *ehhif* wizard might have had to work at it if the body's owner didn't wish to be seen. To Rhiow's eyes, she was still looking at Saash . . . but something subtle had happened to her; her physicality seemed to have been refined away, leaving her standing in the familiar delicate form, but now filled with forces that made Rhiow blink to look at them steadily. They were the forces with which Saash had always worked so well . . . and it was now obvious why, for they filled her the way light fills a window.

Saash shook herself, looked down at her flanks, and dulled down the glow by an effort of will. She turned then and smiled at Rhiow. *Sorry,* she said.

"For what?" Rhiow said softly.

Well . . . yeah. Oh, Rhi, there's a lot to do, I have to get going!

"Go on, then. Go well, Tenth-lifer—and give the Powers our best when you see Them."

Saash smiled; rubbed past Urruah, trailed her tail briefly over his back; took a friendly swipe at Arhu with one shining paw as she passed; saluted T'hom and Har'lh with a flirt of her tail; and walked off down the platform, glowing more faintly as she passed on—a wizard still, but one now in possession of much enhanced equipment, now reassigned to some more central and senior catchment area. Only once she paused. Rhiow stared, wondering—

Saash sat down on the platform and had a good long scratch. Then she washed the scratched-up fur down again, flirted her tail one last time, walked off into the darkness, and was gone. . . .

T'hom came over to them then and hunkered down to greet them: Har'lh was with him. As she trotted over to them, it occurred to Rhiow that there was something odd about the track area: it looked cleaner, brighter, than usual. However, for the moment she put that aside. "Har'lh!" she said, and rubbed against him: possibly unprofessional behavior toward one's Advisory, but she was extremely glad to see him. "Where in Iau's name have you *been?*"

"About half a million lightyears away," Har'lh said with annoyance, "freezing my butt off on a planet covered a thousand miles deep with liquid methane. Somebody wanted me way out of the way while something happened here, that was plain. Met some nice people, though: they needed help with some local problems . . . I did a little troubleshooting. No point in wasting the trip." He looked at them all. "Now what's been going *on* here??"

"That'll take some telling," Rhiow said.

"Let's walk, then," T'hom said.

They headed out of the track areas, up into the main concourse. Arhu and Urruah looked up and around them as they went, and Urruah's tail was lashing in surprise. The Terminal looked satisfyingly solid and hard-edged again, much improved over the last time they had seen it, with multiple time-patches threatening to slide off the fabric of reality like a wet Band-Aid. *Ehhif* were going about their business as usual.

"Have they cleaned this place again in the last day or so?" Urruah said. "It looks so . . . bright, it's . . . no. It's not just the sun. I know this place always looks good in the morning, with the sun coming in the windows like that, but . . ."

T'hom smiled a little as they walked up past the waiting room and toward the Forty-second Street doors. "It won't often look this good, I think," he said. "This is how we knew you'd succeeded, down there, in some big way. All the manuals went crazy for a while, and all they would say was RECONFIGURATION, RECONFIGURATION, all over them. But then everything steadied down, and all the time-patching we'd been holding in place by force just hauled off and *took,* hard. Something of a relief."

They stepped out into the street, and Rhiow saw in more detail what T'hom meant, for the brilliance in the streets was more than sunlight. This was a city in unusual splendor: skyscrapers all around seemed consciously clothed in the fire of day, their glass molten or jeweled in the early sun; and down at the end of the block, the silver spear of the Chrysler Building upheld itself in the dawn like an emblem of victory, blinding. Everything hummed with the usual city sounds—traffic noise, oddly content with its lot for once, very little horn-honking going on. There was a peculiar sense of *ehhif* all about them being abruptly, and rather bemusedly, at peace with one another . . . for a little while. "The city's risen," Rhiow said, "as some of us rose. But it won't last."

"No. It's understandable that you would get some resonances from more central realities," Har'lh said, "some spillover . . . possibly even from Timeheart itself. You can't do that big a reconfiguration without some reflection in neighboring worlds: any of them directly connected by the catenary structure, anyway."

"It'll fade back to normal after a while," Arhu said. "It can't stay like this for long: you can conquer entropy only temporarily, on a local scale, She says . . . It never lasts. But while it lasts, enjoy it."

They walked down Forty-second Street, heading toward the river and the view of the Delacorte Fountain, a great silver plume of water rising up from the southernmost tip of Roosevelt Island in the morning sun. Rhiow started her debrief, knowing it was going to take a good while and might as well start now when everything was fresh in her mind. The only thing she knew she would have trouble explaining was how it had felt to have the One inside you. That knowledge, that power, had started to fade almost as soon as the experience proper was over. *Just as well, I suppose,* she thought. *You can't pour the whole ocean into one water bowl. . . .*

The team and the two Advisories finally came up against the railing that looked down at FDR Drive and the East River. There the People sat down, and the Seniors leaned on the railing, and they went on talking for what Rhiow normally thought might have been hours: the sun didn't seem to be moving at its usual rate today . . . morning just kept lasting, shining down on a river that, more than usually, ran with light. In the middle of a technical discussion about what Saash had done to the catenary, T'hom suddenly looked up and said, "Well, they couldn't keep *you* down on the farm long, could they?"

"What is a 'farm'?" Ith said innocently, and leaned on the railing beside them, folding his claws and staring out over the shining water.

"Ahem," Rhiow said. "Har'lh, have you met our new wizard? Ith, this is Har'lh, he's the other Advisory for this area."

"I am on errantry, and I greet you," Ith said courteously, and bowed, sweeping his tail. Arhu ducked to let it go over his head.

"This is an errand?" T'hom said, with humor. "This is a *junket.*"

"It is 'research,'" Ith said cheerfully, glancing at Arhu with the conspiratorial expression of a youngster who's borrowed a friend's excuse. Arhu rolled his eyes, working to look innocent.

Rhiow wanted to snicker. It was a delightful change in Ith from the morose and somber individual they had first met; she suspected Arhu had had a lot to do with it, and would have much more.

"At any rate," Rhiow said to the two Advisories, "the worldgates are all fully functional again, and I don't think we need to fear any further interference from the Lone Power in that department. The Tree and the gate-tree, the master catenary structures, now have guardians who will never let the Lone One near them again. Some of them may not yet be plain about what It had in mind for them, but Ith will soon set them straight."

Ith turned his attention away from a passing barge and toward Rhiow and the team. "I am hearing more and more in my mind," Ith said, "of what the Powers will ask of us by way of guardianship. The requirements are not extreme. And little explanation will be needed as to why their present life is more desirable for my people than their former one. Hunger is something they are used to: until we distribute ourselves more widely, we will help one another cope with it . . . by more wholesome means than formerly. Meantime," and he glanced over at Rhiow, "I will need some help tailoring spells that will function on a large scale, with little maintenance, as sunblock." He grinned. "We have been down in the dark a long time."

They all looked out at the glowing water. "The dark . . ." Arhu said, looking down into water in which, for once, no trash bobbed. "I could never look at this before," he said to Rhiow. "But I can now. I won't mind seeing the river, even when it's back to normal. I could never stand going near it before: I was stuck on the Rock. But I don't think I have to be stuck here anymore."

"Of course not," Har'lh said. "Be plenty of demand for a hot young visionary-wizard all over the place. In other realities"—he glanced at Ith—"and offplanet as well. You're going to be busy for a while."

"I am," Arhu said. "Getting used to being in a team . . ." He glanced over at Rhiow.

Rhiow looked over at him affectionately and put her whiskers forward, smiling. "You're well met on the errand," she said.

They fell silent for a while, looking out at the light. The sense of power and potential beating around them in the air was as tangible as a pulse; for this little while, in this New York, anything was possible. Rhiow looked out into the glory of the transfigured morning—not quite that of Timeheart, but close enough—and said softly, only a little sadly, *I had to tell you. The tuna wasn't all that bad. . . .*

She did not really expect an answer. But the walls between realities were thin this morning. From elsewhere came just the slightest hint of a purr . . . and somewhere, Hhuha smiled.

Rhiow blinked, then washed a little, for composure's sake.

She would head home soon. She would have to start drawing close to Iaehh now. He would be needing her, for there was no way Rhiow could tell him about anything she had seen or experienced . . . except by being who she now was.

Whoever that is . . . And if in the doing Rhiow brought with her a little of the sense of Hhuha—not as she was, of course, but Hhuha moved on into something more—that would possibly be some help.

It was so nice to know that *ehhif* had somewhere to go when they died.

For Rhiow's own part, she had had enough dying for one day.

The talk went on for a while more. Only slowly did Rhiow notice that the interior light was seeping out of things, leaving New York looking entirely more normal: the horns began to hoot in the distance again, and a few hundred yards down FDR Drive, there was a tinkle of glass as a car changing lanes sideswiped another one and broke off one of its wing mirrors. Tires screeched, voices yelled.

"Normalcy," Har'lh said, looking with amused irony at T'hom. "What we work for, I suppose. Speaking of work . . . I'm going to have to go make some phone calls. My boss is going to be annoyed that I took this time off without warning."

"Wizard's burden," Urruah said. "I feel sorry for you poor *ehhif.* Wouldn't it just be easier to tell him you were off adjusting somebody's gas giant?"

Har'lh gave Urruah a look, then grinned. "Might make an interesting change. Come on—" He looked over at T'hom. "Let's go catch a train."

The team walked the Advisories and Ith back to Grand Central, as far as the entrance to the subway station: it was not a place Rhiow chose to plunge into during rush hour while sidled, as you were likely to become subway-station pizza in short order. "Go well," she said to T'hom and Har'lh, as they went through the turnstiles.

We will, Har'lh said silently. You *did. . . .*

Rhiow strolled back up to the main concourse level and put herself against a wall, where she could look out across the great expanse. *Working properly again,* she thought. With time, everything would. Someday, if things went right, the New York they had spent this long morning in would be the real one, and this one just a grubby, shabby memory. *But meantime you make it work the best you can.*

And meantime the scent in the air caught her attention.

Pizza . . .

The others came up out of the entrance to the subway, glanced across the concourse, and down at Rhiow. Ith in particular looked across at the Italian deli.

"Now, about that pastrami . . ." he said to Arhu.

Arhu grinned. "Let me show you a trick somebody taught me," he said, glancing over at Rhiow.

"I had a feeling you'd be sorry you showed him that one," Urruah said. "Ith, don't let him talk *you* into trying it. You'll make the papers."

"'Papers'?"

Rhiow gave Urruah a look. "Come on, 'Ruah, let's leave them to it, and go do the rounds."

Rhiow and Urruah strolled off across their territory, weaving casually among the *ehhif,* up the cream marble of the Vanderbilt Avenue stairs, and out of the sight of wizards, and People, and anyone else who could see. No one noticed them, which was just as it should have been; and life in the city went on. . . .

Afterword

◆

On Hauissh

This occupation of the People, described only briefly in the literature by *ehhif* writers (the most reliable and perceptive is Pratchett*) has occasionally been called a pastime—but such a characterization is similar to calling soccer, baseball, and American-style football "pastimes"—for which human beings have sometimes wagered and won or lost fortunes, ignored almost all the other important aspects of their lives, and occasionally died under circumstances both comic and tragic.

An exhaustive analysis of *hauissh* would be far beyond the scope of this work, but it seems useful to include at least a summary explanation.

Its Origins

Hauissh is of such antiquity that it almost certainly predates the time at which felinity became self-aware. Its most basic structure implies a conflict over hunting territory between two prides, and most authorities agree that it evolved from this strictly survival-oriented behavior to a more structured but still violent dominance game between individual members of a single pride or (later) extended pride-community, with

---

*in *The Unadulterated Cat* (Gollancz, 1989)

the loser usually being run off the pride's territory, or killed. (Even now the biggest predators tend to play *hauissh* in this mode, considering the refinements of later millennia to be oversophisticated or effete.)

It would be as difficult to determine exactly when feline self-awareness arose as it would to fix a time at which *hauissh* began to develop beyond concerns of food, territory, and power into the more intellectual and entertainment-oriented version now played by cats the world over. All the families of the People seem to have at least some knowledge of the basic concepts of the Game on an instinctive level. But the demands and challenges of the modern form of *hauissh* require a great deal more of the player than instinct alone will provide.

THE RULES

There is no mandated maximum number of players of *hauissh,* though games involving more than thirty or so players in one session are likely to be considered "inelegant." Most play involves no more than ten or twelve players, though, since some level of personal relationship is considered desirable among a majority of those playing.

Hauissh started out as a rough-and-ready, territorial-control game among the big cats, with the loser usually being run off the territory or killed.

Hauissh involves controlling a space—yard, sidewalk, field—with one's presence. This presence, called *aahfaui,* is not a constant, but is in turn affected by the space one is trying to control.

"Control" is defined by *eius'hss,* "being alone." The minute a player can see another cat, the control is diminished slightly, but not in such a way as to lower one's score. Control *is* diminished more if the other cat can in turn see the first player, and the first player's score suffers.

A successful position is one in which a cat can see several others, without himself being seen. The beginner would immediately think that this could be easily achieved by being down a hole but able to see several other cats, but such concealment is not considered game-play in the rules, and a cat retreating to such a position, having previously been in play, is then considered out of it until once again exposed.

There are many other variables that affect play. Most important of these is *eiu'heff,* a variable expressing a combination of the nature and size of the space being controlled. Nearly as important is *hruiss'aessa,* the location of the "center" of the game, the (usually invisible) spot around which the game revolves, representing (in more abstruse thought about *hauissh*) the Tree under which the Great Cat took his stance against the Serpent on the night of the Battle for the World, the battle by the River of Fire. The ultimate point of the game is not necessarily to reach or occupy this spot, but to dominate or master it, while also dominating as many of the other players as possible. Feline nature being what it is, individual People tend to resist domination, even for the best of reasons; so it can easily be seen that any given bout of the Game will be prolonged and fairly stressful. Most play in *hauissh* is individual, "team" play being considered too difficult to maintain for long periods, and likely to cause what People call, in Ailurin, *laeu'rh-sseihhah,* an unhealthy shift in one's nature toward a "foreign" style of being (*cf.* the German word *überfremdung,* "over-alienation")—"teamwork" being conceived as a distasteful kind of "pack" behavior better left to other less advanced species, such as *houiff.*

Play begins when a quorum of players are determined to have arrived and to be ready to start. It ends when one player is deemed to have successfully "dominated" the *hruiss'aessa* and a majority of other players. A single such sequence is a "passage," roughly equal to an inning in baseball. Passages are grouped together in larger groups called "sequences," but there are no fixed numbers of passages-per-sequence, or sequences-per-game. Consensus usually determines when another passage is required to fill out a sequence (and it almost always is).

A detailed or exact description of how scoring is done is beyond the scope of this work. Scoring *hauissh* fairly and to all players' satisfaction is difficult work, filled with imponderables, and much more an art than a science. It is nowhere near as clearcut as scoring in any sport with which humans are familiar (and frankly, if it were, cats would probably lose interest in the game almost immediately). There are so many rules and variables influencing score—for example, weather, local conditions such as traffic or the passage of *ehhif* or other species through play, physical condition of the players, and to- tal time of play compared against time actually spent making moves, to name just a very few—and so many of the variables and require- ments are mutually contradictory that scoring a bout at the end of a round or "passage" closely resembles a discussion among Talmudic scholars than an umpire yelling "Yer out!"

To speak of how one "wins" at *hauissh* is probably a misnomer born of looking at the pastime through the human mindset: it is nearly as erroneous as speaking of "winning" at cricket—the human game that comes closest to *hauissh* in its (unspoken) expression of the idea that gameplay for its own sake is much more important than a result, of whatever kind. Like cricket, a bout of *hauissh* can go on for days or weeks, can be called on account of bad light (i.e., atmos- pheric conditions so bad that not even cats can see each other: rare), will often stop (repeatedly) for meals, and can run up extravagant scores that sound really impressive when you talk about them after- ward, but which are actually indicative of neither group really being able to get the better of the other, no matter how long the process continues. The record duration for a single bout of *hauissh* was set in 1716 (the actual date being either in January or February, but uncer- tainty involved with the Gregorian calendar shift and its coordination with the People's timekeeping makes a definite date unavailable). Six cats located in the town of Albstadt-Ebingen, then in the duchy of Württemberg and now in southern Germany, began a bout that lasted until 1738, and was completed by five of their great-grandchildren. The bout was forced to end in a draw because of a local outbreak of the plague, which killed what was judged a "threshold" number of the competitors.

The game (to People interested in it) naturally has profound philo- sophical and even mystical meaning. One saying is that "Rhoua plays best," the indication being that the Queen, in Her aspect of "Winking" Rhoua, can by definition see all People without being seen Herself, and that the Game is therefore a metaphor for life . . . which is (come to think of it) exactly what *ehhif* say about baseball, and soccer, and nearly every other sport down to tiddledywinks.

On Other Matters

The nonwizardly aspects of the New York Public Library's CATNYP online cataloguing system can be found on the World Wide Web at

http://catnyp.nypl.org/

Please do not query the librarians about the Online "MoonBook" Project, as all but a few of the staff have no knowledge that it exists, and those staff who *do* know are required to deny its existence.

Readers interested in more information about wizardry might like to look at the following books by the same author:

So You Want to Be a Wizard
Deep Wizardry
High Wizardry
A Wizard Abroad

And for more information about new developments in the "Wizards'" universe, as well as for pictures of cats who looks suspiciously like some of the principals in this book, curious readers with Web access may wish to visit the following site:

http://www.ibmpcug.co.uk/~owls/homeward.html

A Very Partial Ailurin Glossary

✦

A

aahfaui (n) the "presence" quality in *hauissh*

Aaurh (pr n) another of the feline pantheon: the "Michael" power, the Warrior; female

aavhy (adj) used; also a proper name when upper case

ahou'ffriw (n) the Canine Word; key, or "activating," word for spells intended for use on dogs and other canids

Auhw-t (n) "the Hearth": the Ailurin/wizardly term for what humans refer to as "Timeheart"—the most senior/central reality, of which all others are mirrors or variations

Auo (pr n) I

auuh (n) stray (perjorative)

auw (n) energy (as a generic term); appears in many compounds having to do with wizardry and cats' affinity for fire, warmth, and energy flows

auwsshui'f (n) the "lower electromagnetic spectrum," involving quantum particles, faster-than-light particles and wavicles, subatomics, fission, fusion, and "submatter" relationships such as string and hyperstring function

D

D does not appear by itself as a consonant in Ailurin, only as a diphthong, *dh*.

E

efviauw (n) the electromagnetic spectrum as perceived by cats

ehhif (n) human being, (adj) human

eiuev (n) veldt: a large open space. As a proper noun, *Eiuev*, "the Veldt" means the Sheep Meadow in Central Park.

eius'hss (n) the "control" quality in *hauissh*

F

ffrihh (n) refrigerator (cat slang: approximation)

fouarhweh (n) a position in *hauissh,* described as "classic" by commentators

fvais a medium-high voice among cats; equates with "tenor"

fwau (ex) heck, hell, crap

H

Hauhai (n) the Speech

hauissh (n) the Game

he'ihh (n) composure-grooming

hhau'fih (n) group relationships in general

hhouehhu (v) desire/want

Hhu'au (pr n) the Lion-"God" of Today; nickname for *ehhif* "Patience," one of the carved stone lions outside the New York Public Library main branch

hihhhh (excl) damn, bloody (stronger than *vhai)*

hiouh (n) excreta (including both urine and feces)

hlah'feihre (adj) tortoiseshell (fur)

houff (s n) dog

houiff (pl n) dogs

Hrau'f (pr n) daughter of Iau, the member of the feline pantheon most concerned with creation and ordering it; known as "the Silent"

hruiss (n) fight, in compounds with words for "tom-fight," etc.

hu (n) day

hu-rhiw (id) "day-and-night"; idiom for a black-and-white cat

hwaa (n) drink

hwiofviauw (n) the "upper electromagnetic," meaning plasma functions, gravitic force, etc.; "upward"

I

iAh'hah (n) New York: possibly an approximation of the English name

Iau (pr n) the One; the most senior member of the feline pantheon; female

Irh (pr n) one of the feline pantheon; male (Urruah refers to his balls)

O

o'hra (n) opera (approximation)

R

ra'hio "radio"; a feline neologism

Reh-t (n, abstract) the future; also, the name for the Lion-Power guarding it, the Invisible One of the Three guarding the steps to the New York Public Library main branch

rhiw (n) night. Many compounds are derived from this favorite word, including the name *Rhiow* (the actual orthography would be *rhiw'aow,* "nightdark," but the spelling has been simplified for the purposes of this narrative).

rioh (n) horse (but in the countryside, also ox, or any other animal that works for humans by carrying or pulling things; "beast of burden"). A cat with a sense of humor might use this word as readily for a taxicab, shopping cart, or wheelbarrow.

rrai'fih (n) pride relationship implying possible blood ties

ruah (adj) flat

S

sa'Rráhh (pr n) the ambivalent feline Power; analogous (roughly) to the Lone Power

Sef (pr n) the Lion-"God" of Yesterday; nickname for "Fortitude," one of the lions outside the New York Public Library main branch

sh'heih (n) "queen," unspayed female

siss (n) urine; a "baby word" similar to ehhif English "pee pee," and other similar formations

sshai-sau (adj) crazy

sswiass a pejorative: sonofabitch, bastard, brat, etc.

sth'heih (n) "tom," unneutered male

U

uae (n) milk

ur (n) nose

Urrua (pr n) the Great Tom, son and lover of Iau the Queen (from the older word urra, "scarred")

urruah (id) "flat nose" (compound: from ur'ruah)

V

vefessh (n) water; also (adj) the term cats use to indicate the fur color humans call "blue"

vhai (adj) damn, bloody